DECEIT

DECEIT

JAMES SIEGEL

sphere

SPHERE

First published in the United States in 2006 by Warner Books,
a division of Hachette Book Group USA
First published in Great Britain in 2006 by Sphere
This paperback edition published in 2007 by Sphere

A CIP catalogue record for this book
is available from the British Library.

ISBN 978-0-7515-3826-7

Papers used by Sphere are natural recyclable products made from
wood grown in sustainable forests and certified in accordance with
the rules of the Forest Stewardship Council.

Typeset in Berkeley by M Rules
Printed and bound in Great Britain by
Clays Ltd, St Ives plc
Paper supplied by Hellefoss AS, Norway

Sphere
An imprint of
Little, Brown Book Group
Brettenham House
Lancaster Place
London WC2E 7EN

A Member of the Hachette Livre Group of Companies

www.littlebrown.co.uk

To Joelle and Alexa,
two remarkable young women
who make me proud on a daily basis.

I'd like to thank Kristen Weber and David Shelley for their wise editing; and various reporters I spoke to during the writing of this book, in an effort to get things right.

Once there were two villages.

One village where they always told the truth.

Another village where they always lied.

One day a traveler came to a fork in the road. He knew one road led to the village where they always told the truth. In this village he would find food and shelter. The other road led to the village where everyone lied. In that village he knew he'd be beaten, robbed, even killed. A man stood at the fork in this road, but the traveler didn't know which village this man came from. The one where they always told the truth, or the one where they always lied?

"You can ask me one question," the man said. "Just one."

The traveler thought and pondered and finally he knew which question to ask.

He pointed to the left road and said: "Is this the road to your village?"

"Yes," the man answered him.

The traveler nodded, said thank you, and started down the road.

He knew if he was addressing a man from the village where they always told the truth, then it was of course the road to the right village. And if he were addressing someone from the village of liars, then the man would have to lie and say yes as well.

Whether the man was the liar or the truth-teller, he would give exactly the same answer.

ONE

I am writing this as fast as I can.

I am galloping through hostile territory like the Pony Express, because I absolutely *must* deliver the mail.

I've already taken my fair share of arrows. And though I'm clearly wounded, I'm not dead.

Not yet.

I'm trying mightily to remember everything germane.

I'm a bit shaky on the timeline, on the cause and effects. On specificity.

I am freely and honestly admitting to this. Just so when all the little *editors* begin flourishing their red pencils, and they will, I'll have hopefully, if only momentarily, dulled the momentum of their onrushing venom.

I don't blame them. I truly don't.

I am, after all, the boy who cried wolf. Who shouted, screamed, and plastered it across two-inch headlines.

Mea culpa.

All I can tell you is that what I'm writing in this claustrophobic motel room is the absolute, unvarnished, 100 percent truth.

So help me God. Scout's honor. Cross my heart and hope to die.

Change hope to *expect*.

This isn't just my last story.

It's my last will and testament.

Pay attention.

You are my executor.

ONE BRIEF DIGRESSION.

Writing my last story, I can't help but remember my first.

I was 9.

It was snowing. Not the paltry dusting that generally passed for snow in Queens, New York. No, the sky was actually dumping snow, as if someone had loosened a giant salt-shaker top up there. Icicles were being blown off our sagging gutters and straight into the brick walls of the house, where they splintered with the sound of ball meeting bat.

Schools would be closed all week.

My brother Jimmy slipped on the ice and he hit his head, I wrote on neatly lined composition paper. *He is always falling down and stuff like that. He walked into a door and he got a black eye. Last week he fell down in the tub, and he burnt himself. He is really clumsy and my mom keeps telling him to watch where he's going, but he don't listen. He is only 6.*

I brought the story into the kitchen where my mother was slumped over the table, staring into an empty bottle of Johnnie Walker.

"Read it to me," she slurred.

After I finished, she said: "Okay, good. I want you to memorize it. They'll be here in an hour."

4

TWO

There were no storm warnings.

No emergency disaster center urging me to board up the windows and leave town.

I can look back to that day, borrow a cliché (I apologize to my first journalism professor, who abhorred clichés as much as he abhorred the newly instituted no-fraternization-with-coeds rule), and state that with the exception of Belinda Washington turning 100, absolutely nothing that day was out of the ordinary. Ordinary, after all, was pretty much the daily state of affairs in Littleton, California—approximately 153 miles east of L.A.

Change approximately to *exactly*.

Two years ago I'd driven every mile of it in my last certifiably owned possession—a silver-blue Miata, purchased back when Miatas were hot shit. A case could be made that back then I was, too.

Now the Miata was ignobly dented in two separate places, with a sluggish transmission that complained loudly when asked to change gears.

On the morning in question, I was summoned into

Hinch's office and told to cover Belinda Washington's centennial. Clearly a human-interest piece. You could safely state that *every* article in the *Littleton Journal* was a human-interest piece. It went to press only five times a week—sometimes less, if not enough local news had taken place since the previous issue. The only serious news stories that made it into the town's paper were picked up from the AP, stories that came from places like Baghdad and Kabul, where you could almost smell the cordite emanating off the type. I perused them longingly, as if they were dirty French postcards from a long-ago era.

Belinda Washington was from a long-ago era.

You could intuit that from the wheelchair and her nearly bald pate. When I entered the dayroom of Littleton's only senior citizen home, she was wearing a ridiculous paper tiara with the number 100 printed on it. It was obviously someone's idea of cute. Probably not Belinda's. She didn't look happy as much as bewildered. I dutifully maintained my objectivity and resisted the urge to knock it off her head.

These days, I was strictly adhering to the noble tenets of my profession.

I introduced myself to the managing director of the home, a Mr. Birdwell, who was orchestrating the august occasion with the aid of a digital camera. Good. That would save me from having to snap any pictures. On the *Littleton Journal*, we multitasked.

I kneeled down in front of Belinda and introduced myself in a louder-than-normal voice.

"Hello, Mrs. Washington. Tom Valle from the *Littleton Journal*."

"What you shouting for?" Belinda asked, grimacing. Evidently, Belinda wasn't any fonder of patronizing reporters than she was of paper tiaras.

"Take that thing off my head," she added.

"Gladly." I stood up and removed the tiara, handing it to one of the male attendants who looked personally miffed that I'd intruded on their fun.

"That's better," Belinda said.

"Sure," I said. "Well, happy birthday, Mrs. Washington. What's it like to be 100 years old?"

"What you *think* it's like?" she said.

"I don't know."

"More fun turning 18."

"That would've been . . . what, 1920 something?"

"'22."

"Right. Math was my worst subject."

"Not me. I'm good at it."

I'd expected to be interviewing a drooling apparition. So far, the only one doing any drooling was myself. One of the partygoers was kind of attractive. Auburn-haired, 30-ish, seamlessly fitted into lime green capris and precariously perched on three-inch heels. There were moments I thought my drooling days were past me—not because of my age (nudging 40) but just because *everything* was past me—all the good stuff, and didn't women constitute good?

Belinda lifted a skeletal hand.

"I miss things," she said.

For a moment, I thought she was referring to the general bane of old age, things getting past her: conversations, names, dates.

7

She wasn't. She was referring to that other bane of old age.

"People have gone and died on me," she said. And she smiled, half wistfully, but half, I think, because she was flirting with me.

The feeling was mutual. Objectivity or not, I kind of liked her.

Belinda was black, a true rarity in Littleton—Latinos yes, blacks virtually nonexistent—deep black, like ebony. This made her milky eyes pop—the palms of her hands, too, pink as cat paws.

She beckoned me with one of those gnarled, ancient hands.

I wondered what had gained me this special privilege? Probably no one ever talked to her anymore, I thought. Except to tell her to take her meds, turn out the light, or put on a stupid hat.

"People have gone and died on me," she repeated, "but one, he came back."

"Came back?"

"Sure. He said hey."

"Who was that?"

"Huh? My son."

"Your son? Really. Where did he come back *from*?"

"Huh? Told you. He passed on . . . long time ago, but he came back to say hey. He say he forgive me."

"Oh, okay. Got you." I was tempted to ask what she'd done that needed forgiveness, but really, what was the point? Belinda was feeling her age, after all. When I looked up, one of the attendants shrugged, as if to say, what else would you expect? The woman in capris, evidently there to

8

visit one of the other residents, threw me a wan smile that seemed mildly encouraging.

"Looked old as me," Belinda said.

"Your son?"

"Yeah. He looked sickly."

I almost made the kind of wiseass comment I was given to uttering in the old days, when I hung with the kind of crowd that conversed mostly in cynicisms. Back before I became a national punch line. I almost said: considering he's dead, *sickly's a step up.*

I didn't.

I said: "That's too bad."

Belinda laughed, a soft knowing laugh, that made me feel a little embarrassed, and something else.

Nervous.

"I ain't fooling wit' you," Belinda said. "And I ain't crazy."

"I didn't say you were crazy, Mrs. Washington."

"Nah. But you nice."

I changed the subject. I asked her how long she'd been a guest of the home. Where was she born? What was her secret to longevity? All the harmless questions you learn in high school journalism. I avoided asking her what family she had left, since, with the possible exception of her dead son, none had bothered to show.

After a while, I became cognizant of the smell permeating the room—stale and medicinal, like a cellar filled with moldering files. It became impossible to ignore the ugly stains in the linoleum floor, the melanoma-like cigarette burns in the lopsided card table. Mrs. Washington was wearing a polka dot dress that smelled faintly of camphor, but the rest of them were dressed in yolk-stained robes and discolored T-shirts. A man had only one sock on.

I felt like leaving.

Mr. Birdwell snapped a picture of Belinda enclosed in a gleaming thicket of wheelchairs and walkers. I stuck my hand in and said bye.

"One more," Mr. Birdwell said. "And this time I want to see a *smile* on our birthday girl."

The birthday girl ignored him—evidently she wasn't in a smiling mood. Instead, she grabbed my hand and squeezed tight.

"Yeah, you a nice fellow," she said.

Her skin felt ice cold.

THREE

We had a terrible accident just outside town.

That's what Hinch's secretary said—scratch that—his *assistant*, political correctness having intruded 150 miles into the California desert. Stewardesses were *attendants* now, secretaries were *assistants*, and occupying armies in the Middle East were *defenders of freedom*.

It's a measure of fast approaching my second anniversary there that when Norma *said* we—I *thought* we. It was official: Tom Valle, one-time denizen of SoHo, NoHo, and assorted other fashionably abbreviated New York City neighborhoods, had become a true Littletonian.

"What kind of accident?" I asked her.

"A smashup on 45," she said. "A goddamn fireball."

For a dedicated churchgoer, Norma had a strange affinity for using the Lord's name in vain. Things were either God-awful, Goddamned, God-forbidden, God help us, or God knows.

"Aww, God," Norma said. "You kind of wonder how many people were in that car."

The sheriff had just phoned in the news, assuming Hinch might be interested in a suitably gory car crash. *If it*

11

bleeds, it leads, and all that. Hinch was currently at lunch. The other feature reporter, Mary-Beth, was on ad hoc maternity leave. When she got tired of watching her unemployed husband down voluminous amounts of Lone Star beer, Mary-Beth showed up. Otherwise, no. There was an intern on summer break from Pepperdine, but he was nowhere to be seen.

"Maybe I should go cover it."

Norma, who was not the editor, but the editor's assistant, shrugged her shoulders.

This time I took a camera.

I WASN'T FOND OF ACCIDENTS. SOME ARE.

The smell of blood excites them. The aura of death. Maybe the simple relief that it happened to someone else.

The problem was I felt like that someone else.

Like the unfortunate victim of a car accident. The fact that I was the driver, that I'd soberly taken hold of the wheel and steered the car straight off a cliff, didn't do anything to alleviate the uncomfortable empathy I felt in the presence of a wreck.

Norma was right about the fireball.

The car was still smoldering. It looked like a hunk of charcoal that had somehow fallen out of the backyard grill.

One fire engine, one sheriff's car, and one ambulance were parked by the side of the two-lane highway. Another car was conspicuously present, a forest green Sable. Its front fender was completely crumpled, a man I assumed to be the driver leaning against the side door with his head in his hands. Everyone was pretty much watching.

Sheriff Swenson called me over.

"Hey, Lucas," he said.

I'll explain the Lucas.

It was for Lucas McCain, the character played by Chuck Connors in *The Rifleman*. After *The Rifleman*, Chuck moved on to a series called *Branded*, where he played a Union soldier who'd allegedly fled from the Battle of Bull Run and was forever after branded a coward. He drifted from town to town where, despite selfless acts of heroism, someone always discovered his true identity. You might imagine that'd be hard to do in the Old West.

Not in the new west.

Sheriff Swenson had Googled me.

He couldn't recall the character's name in *Branded*, so he called me Lucas.

It was better than *liar*.

"Hello, sheriff."

Sheriff Swenson didn't look like a small-town sheriff. Maybe because he'd spent twenty years on the LAPD before absconding to Littleton with full pension. He still had the requisite square jaw, bristle cut, and physique of a gym attendant, the palpable menace that must've made more than one Rodney King spill his guts without Swenson ever having to pick up a stun gun.

Today he looked kind of placid.

Maybe the dancing flames had mesmerized him. He had that look you get after staring into a fireplace for longer than you should.

There was something worth mentioning beside the burning car. Something everyone was politely declining to acknowledge, like a homeless relative who's somehow crashed the family reunion.

13

If you've never had the pleasure of smelling burnt human, it smells like a mix of honey, tar, and baked potato. One of the truly worst smells on earth.

"How many were in there?" I asked the sheriff.

"Oh, just make it up," he said after a while. I imagine he was being half funny and half not. Just like with the nickname.

"Okay. But if I wanted to be factual?"

"If you wanted to be factual, the answer would be one," he said.

I looked back at the other driver, who still had his face pressed to his hands as if he didn't wish to see. When the body shop commented on the sorry state of his car, he'd say *you should've seen the other guy.*

"How did it happen?"

"You mean, how did the accident transpire?" the sheriff said.

"Yeah."

"Quickly."

"Right. But who hit who?"

"He was going south," the sheriff said, motioning to the man covering his eyes. "*He* was going north," nodding at the smoldering wreck. "Northbound car drifted into the southbound lane. At least, according to our sole witness."

"Who's that?"

"Our sole survivor."

"Can I talk to him?"

"I don't know. Can you?"

"It'd be nice."

"Then have a nice time."

I walked over to the crumpled Sable; the man had finally

14

picked his head up out of his hands. He had that *look*—the one you see in the faces of people who've just juked death. Cursed with the awful knowledge of life's ridiculous fragility. He was moving various pieces of his body in halting slow motion, as if they were made of fine, breakable china.

"Hello. Tom Valle of the *Littleton Journal*. Could I speak to you a minute?"

"Huh?"

"I'm from the newspaper. I just wanted to ask you a few questions."

"*Newspaper?*"

I'd said nothing to dissipate that dazed look of his.

"That's right."

"I don't really feel like talking. I'm . . . you know . . ."

Yes, I knew. But there were other tenets of my profession, which were maybe less than noble. The one, for instance, that says you have to get the story. Even when that story involved the kind of personal disasters that made up most of the news these days. You know what I'm talking about: murdered wives, missing babies, beheaded hostages—there were a lot of those going around.

It's pretty simple. Even when someone doesn't feel like talking, you have to feel like asking.

"I understand he drifted into your lane," I said.

He nodded.

"And then, uh . . . what's your name, sir . . . slowly, so I don't misspell anything."

"Crannell. Edward Crannell. Two Ls."

I dutifully scribbled it down. I'd always forgone the tape recorder for the more tactile sensation of writing notes. Maybe I had an instinctual abhorrence of tape's permanence—even

15

at the beginning, long before I began taking liberties.

"Where are you from again, Mr. Crannell?" An old technique; ask a question as if they've already given you the answer.

"Cleveland," he said.

"The one in *Ohio*?"

He nodded.

"Long way from home."

"I'm in sales. Pharmaceuticals."

"Rented car then, I guess?"

He grimaced as if that fact had just occurred to him; maybe he'd rolled the dice and forgone the accident insurance.

"So he came right at you, just drifted into your lane. That's what happened?" This area of Highway 45 was devoid of a single curve—it had the unrelieved monotony of a ruler-drawn line.

Crannell nodded.

"I beeped the horn at the last second. He jammed on the brakes. . . . I guess he couldn't get out of the way." He looked down in the general vicinity of his dust-covered shoes and slowly shook his head. "Jesus . . ."

"Have they checked you out, Mr. Crannell? Are you okay?"

He nodded. "I was wearing my seat belt. They said I was lucky."

"Oh yeah."

Swenson was poking around the wreck. Fine black cinders hovered in the air like gnats. The fire had mostly burnt itself out—it looked like the fire engine had sprayed it with anti-incendiary foam.

16

"Any idea why he did that? Why he drifted into the wrong lane? Did he fall asleep, maybe?"

Crannell seemed to ponder this for a moment, then shook his head no. "Don't think so. I really can't tell you."

"Okay. Well, thank you."

I walked a few feet away and snapped some pictures. Black car, purple sky, white-shirted sheriff, green cactus. If the *Littleton Journal* published in color, it really would've been something.

On the other hand, black-and-white was probably more appropriate. When I saw it on the front page of the *Littleton Journal* the next day, it seemed to capture the immutable contrast between life and death.

FOUR

I'd joined a bowling league.

It was kind of by accident. The town's bowling alley, Muhammed Alley—it was owned by a failed middleweight named BJ who thought the name was hysterical—doubled as the town's best bar.

I don't mean it had a nice decor, had an interesting snack menu, or was frequented by hot-looking women.

I mean it was badly lit, sparsely filled, and in need of fumigation. It smelled like used bowling shoes.

When I first came to Littleton, I was in fugitive mode. I wasn't seeking company; I was consciously avoiding it.

For a while, I managed to do a fairly good job of that at Muhammed Alley.

BJ doubled as the bartender, and unlike the general image of small-town barkeeps, he was blessed with no perceptible curiosity. Other than asking me what I wanted and quoting the bill—three margaritas, no salt, came to $14.95—it took several visits before he uttered an excess word.

That word—or two words, actually—was *nice play*, spoken only in my general direction, the result of center fielder Steve Finley making a tumbling circus catch in center field.

I was perfectly content with the lack of social interaction. I drank in the loneliness like I drank in the tequila—in small, bitter sips.

After a while, company found me.

One of the two insurance men in town—Sam Weitz, a transplanted New Englander with an obese wife suffering from type 2 diabetes—started drinking more or less the same time as I did. Generally late evening, when most everyone else was headed home to their families.

Not us.

Unlike BJ, Sam *was* imbued with curiosity. Maybe you get used to asking lots of personal questions in the insurance business. He struck up a conversation and stubbornly kept it going, even when confronted with my mostly monosyllabic answers.

One thing led to another.

Being that we were drinking in a bowling alley, one night he actually suggested bowling.

I was on my third margarita, already floating in that pleasant state I call *purple haze*, in honor of Hendrix, one of my musical idols. After all—doesn't enough alcohol let you kiss the sky?

I must've mumbled okay.

I bowled a ridiculous 120 that night—making generous use of both gutters. Surprisingly, I kind of enjoyed hurling a heavy ball down a wooden alley, sending pins scattering in all directions—at least a few of them. I saw a kind of life metaphor in those flattened pins, how they reset just like that, virtually daring you to knock them down again. There

19

was a lesson there about pluck and resilience, which I thought I might make use of.

Eventually, we were joined by Seth Bishop, self-confessed *town hell-raiser*—at least back in high school, where he was voted least likely to succeed, a prophecy that turned out to be pretty much on the money, since he nowadays subsisted on welfare and occasional Sheetrock jobs.

The local Exxon owner—Marv Riskin—rounded out our foursome.

After a while, we joined a league—Tuesday nights at 8.

One night Sheriff Swenson made an appearance, noticed I was keeping score, and told the league president to check the card for accuracy.

When Seth asked me what that was about, I told him I'd run into a little ethics problem in my last newspaper job.

"Boned your secretary?" he asked, kind of hopefully.

"Something like that."

TONIGHT WE WERE PLAYING A TEAM COMPRISED OF LITTLETON'S lone chiropractor, one of its two dentists, a doctor, and an accountant. No Indian chief.

Near the end of his second Bud, the doctor started talking about the body from the car.

They'd brought him the accident victim so he could fill out the death certificate. There was no coroner in Littleton, which made him the de facto ME.

"He was charred pretty good," the doctor said. "I don't get to see a lot of burn victims. Not like that."

"Thanks for sharing, doc," Seth said.

20

"Some of his insides were intact," the doctor continued, undeterred. "Not a pretty sight."

"Can you change the subject, for fuck's sake," Seth said. "What about a nice 18-year-old girl who OD'd? Don't you have any of those?"

The doctor didn't seem to get the joke. When he began describing in great detail what a burned liver looked like— apparently like four-day-old pâté—Seth leaned in and said:

"Let me ask you something, doc. Is it true what they say about doctors? I mean do you get, what's the word . . . *immune* to naked pussy after a while? It doesn't do anything to you anymore?"

Sam, who was preparing to bowl, stopped to wait for the doctor's answer. It appeared as if he was busy conjuring up images of naked pudenda being lasciviously displayed for the doctor's enjoyment. Back home he had a 280-pound wife gorging on cream-filled Yodels.

"That's an ignorant question," the doctor said.

Calling Seth ignorant wasn't really going to offend him. "I'll take that as a no," he said.

"Have they ID'd him yet?" I asked the doctor. I was nursing a Coors Light, having figured out that tequila and getting the ball to travel down the center of the lane were mutually exclusive. The headline of my story was:

Unidentified Man Dies in Flaming Car Crash

The doctor said: "Yeah. They found his license."

"It didn't burn up?"

"He had some kind of metallic card in his wallet that

21

acted like insulation. They were able to make out his name."

"Who was he?"

"I don't know. *Dennis* something. White, 36, from Iowa."

"*Iowa?* That's funny."

The doctor squinted at me. "What's funny about it? It's a state, isn't it?"

"Yeah, it's a state. I was just ruminating on the great cosmic plan. A man from Iowa runs head-on into a salesman from Cleveland on a highway in California. It's kind of funny, don't you think?"

"Actually, no."

Sam had rolled a seven, and now was edgily eyeing a difficult two-one split. He took a deep breath, sashayed into his delivery, and sent the ball straight down the middle, missing all three pins.

"There *is* something funny, though," the doctor said.

"Other than that roll?" I'd dutifully recorded Sam's score. It was crunch time; we were twenty pins behind with only five frames to go.

"He was castrated."

"Huh? *Who?*"

"The deceased."

"You mean in the accident?"

The doctor lifted his Bud, took a long sip.

"Nope," he said. He slid out of the seat—not without some difficulty since he was a good thirty pounds overweight—and rummaged through the rack for his ball.

"What do you mean?" I had to shout a little to make myself heard over the din of the alley, but it was like trying to speak through a raging thunderstorm.

The doctor lifted a finger to me: *wait.*

He bowled a strike, then went into a victory dance that reminded me of the Freddy, a spastic-looking step from the sixties I'd caught on an old *American Bandstand* clip. After he settled back into his seat and meticulously penciled in an X, he said: "I *mean*, he was castrated."

"When?"

"How do I know? Some time ago, I guess. It was done surgically."

Seth must've overheard us.

"He had no *balls*?" Seth asked.

The doctor shook his head. "You want to say it louder. The people in the back of the alley didn't hear you."

"HE HAD NO BALLS?" Seth shouted. "That ought to do it."

"You've got a problem, son," the doctor said.

"You have no idea, *pop*."

I tried to tally up what number beer Seth was on—I guessed seven. Not to mention the Panama Red he'd toked out in the parking lot.

"Why would someone have been castrated?" I asked the doctor.

"Good question."

"Well, is there any *medical* reason?"

"Not really—testicular cancer, maybe—but both testicles would be highly unusual. Not like that."

"Poor guy."

"I'd say so. By the way, that's confidential, okay? Don't put it in the paper or anything."

"I think everyone in the bowling alley might've already come into this information."

The doctor blushed. "Me and my big mouth."

Or Seth's.

THAT NIGHT I HAD A DREAM. I WAS 9 YEARS OLD AND BEING chased down an empty road by a man trying to steal my entire marbles collection.

The clumsy symbolism wasn't lost on me.

FIVE

We interrupt this program to bring you the following message.

My motel TV gets only three channels.

Nothing I particularly want to see. I leave it on to keep me company—to ward off encroaching fear.

It's like a nightlight.

A few minutes ago, someone knocked on the door. I thought it was *them*.

I have two other friends worth mentioning with me here. *Smith* and *Wesson*.

They're new friends, but considered reliable in times of need.

I pointed them toward the door of the motel room. Sic 'em.

It was the maid.

Luiza, I believe her name is, an illegal for sure. This worries me.

They can do things to an illegal. They can make her do whatever they want her to.

Okay, I know.

I sound deranged, beyond the pale.

Bear with me.

You have to see it like I did.

You have to piece it together.

Before my dad left home, he'd take Jimmy and me to breakfast at the Acropolis Diner every Sunday morning.

The paper placemats there had connect-the-dots on them.

The pretty, smiling waitress would hand me a pencil worn to the nub, and I'd wale away at it—at least till the blueberry pancakes and maple syrup arrived.

Here's the thing.

It would take me until the last dot to figure it out. Sometimes not even then—despite the generous clues provided at the top of the page.

What four-legged creature is a noisy neigh-bor?

What mammal is always spouting something?

Horse? Whale? Platypus?

I just couldn't *see* it.

I wasn't good at connecting the dots. I couldn't connect the dots, for example, between my dad and that smiling waitress, whom he was apparently sleeping with on a regular basis. He'd leave our family for her by the time I was 9.

I'm better at connecting things now.

Not right *then*, though. Not at the very beginning—before things got truly weird.

A man died in an accident and a woman turned 100, both on the same day.

Life and death.

It happens all the time, doesn't it?

*

THE NEXT MORNING, I WENT ONLINE.

There's a little-known Web site listing every registered sex offender in the United States—NSOPR.gov.

I'd already called the sheriff's office for his name. *Dennis Flaherty*. From Ketchum City, Iowa.

The Web site is mostly visited by moms and dads who want to make sure that the neighbor who's always staring at their 5-year-old hasn't ever dabbled in pedophilia. These days, the authorities are supposed to alert you when a registered pervert moves into the neighborhood. It sometimes slips their minds.

In certain states, sexual predators can avoid jail if they agree to make themselves less dangerous. And how do they manage *that*? Not through therapy. It doesn't work with NAMBLA members.

They agree to have their testicles taken off.

That's right. Repeat offenders become like nervous batters against Roger Clemens: two strikes and no balls. It's next to impossible to rape someone when your libido has been surgically removed.

I got no hits on *Dennis Flaherty*.

I tried spelling it differently.

Still nothing.

I kept at it for a while. I got a few Dennises, but no one who lived in Iowa. After a half hour or so, I gave up.

I switched to the online phone directory for Ketchum City.

There were three Flahertys.

The first one wasn't home.

The second one said there was no Dennis in the house.

Then I tried the third one.

27

"Hello?"

"Hi, this is Tom Valle of the *Littleton Journal*."

"The Littleton *what*?" It was a woman. Older, her voice sounded weary, lived in.

"The *Littleton Journal*," I repeated, remembering when I used to be able to impress people with something more prestigious. "It's a newspaper. I'm calling about Dennis."

"Oh."

Bingo.

"May I ask what relation you are to him, ma'am?"

"*Relation*? I'm his mother."

"Has anyone spoken to you about Dennis, Mrs. Flaherty?"

"Yes."

"So you know about the accident."

"Yes."

"I'm terribly sorry for your loss." It's amazing how many times I'd uttered those words. To mothers, fathers, uncles, aunts, grandparents, fiancées, husbands, wives—often enough to have long ago achieved the utter hollowness of platitude.

"Thank you," Mrs. Flaherty said.

"This must've been a shock to you."

Silence. "Yes."

"Did Dennis live with you, Mrs. Flaherty?"

"No. I'd lost touch with him."

"For how long?"

"How *long*?"

"Since you'd last seen him?"

"I don't know. Five years."

"But you'd spoken to him?"

"No."

"What kind of business was he in?"

"Business? Why? He died in a traffic accident. That's what they *told* me. What does it matter what business he was in? I'd like to go."

She didn't. She stayed on the line—I could hear raspy, shallow breathing. A smoker, I thought. Probably widowed or divorced. *I'd lost touch with him*, she'd said in the flat consonants of the Midwest—not *we'd*. She sounded half-annoyed at the unexpected intrusion, but half-flattered at the attention. Maybe she didn't want to answer my questions, but she couldn't bring herself to hang up. Not yet.

"Was Dennis ever in trouble with the law, Mrs. Flaherty?"

"*What?*"

"Was Dennis ever arrested?"

"What are you talking about?"

I'm talking about your son's castration.

"I'd like to know if he ever did anything he shouldn't have? Something, I don't know, *sexual*?"

"What is this? What are you *asking* me? My son was a good person. Any problems he had were because of *her*."

"Her?"

"His wife." She made *wife* sound like the worst vulgarity on earth.

"What problems were those?"

"His depression. His drinking. You try living with a whore."

"So they experienced some marital difficulties."

"She *experienced* every man who looked at her. She was trash. I don't even know if my grandson . . ."

"Were they still married?"

"No."

"When were they divorced?"

"I *told* you. About five years ago."

She hadn't told me. She'd told me she'd lost touch with her son around then.

"So he began drinking."

"I'm getting off the phone. I'm not going to sit here and talk ill of the dead."

Only of the dead's ex-wife.

"One other thing . . . did Dennis ever have cancer?"

This time she meant it about getting off.

"No," she said, and hung up.

IT ALL MIGHT HAVE STOPPED RIGHT HERE.

Right that very moment.

What did I have exactly?

Nothing.

A curious observation by the attending doctor—that's all.

An accident victim missing his testicles.

It had piqued my interest, sure it had, but that wasn't hard to do. Not these days. I covered birthday parties, traveling rodeos, and used-car dealership openings, a charity case quietly doing his penance.

It *might* have all stopped here.

Except for two things.

I LIVED IN A RENTED HOUSE.

When I came home, a plumber was working on my hot-water heater.

He was banging around downstairs with some kind of tool.

I hadn't called a plumber.

When I informed him of this fact, he said, okay, then the home's owner must have.

I hadn't complained to the home's owner.

My hot water was hot. There was nothing wrong with the heater.

Okay, he said, routine maintenance.

He smiled at me throughout. As if we were indulging in small talk at a party.

It made me feel uneasy. That and the slow realization we were alone in a basement. Basements are dark subterranean places you descended into at your own risk—every kid knows that. And there were other things. His face, for instance. His features were oddly indistinct—as if he hadn't actually finished *evolving* yet. And there was his voice—squeaky high, as if he'd just sucked helium. It was decidedly creepy.

"Can I ask what company you're with?" I said.

It was impossible to ignore what happened then.

To close my eyes to his ensuing hesitation.

Believe me, I tried.

There are certain questions bound to elicit a moment's pause.

Do you love me?

Where were you tonight, honey?

Did you fabricate this story?

Yes, that one, too.

What company do you work for isn't one of those questions.

31

I must've shrunk back, the way you can increase the physical distance between yourself and someone else without really moving. What you do in the presence of a stray dog who may, or may not, intend to rip your throat out.

You're not supposed to show fear—every kid knows that, too.

We were both on to each other.

I felt the metal thing in his hand before I actually saw it.

SIX

It must've glanced off my forehead.

That's what I determined later.

That I managed to turn my head just enough to avoid a dead-on blow. Nothing really hurt *then*—my nerve endings were numbed by the natural Novocain of raw fear.

I must've touched my forehead to confirm that something had in fact *hit* me—I only know this because my forearm took the next shot. I went down.

I landed on a fluffy white cloud. The white shag remnant of the sixties I'd laboriously rolled up and carted downstairs upon moving in—this memory actually rattling around the head someone was trying to cave in.

He whispered something in that eerie falsetto, and came at me.

I instinctually covered up in expectation of two hundred or so pounds crash-landing on my bones. When I didn't feel it, I picked my head up and peeked.

He was standing stock-still, staring down at me.

He leaned down and tapped me on the shoulder, then smiled and took off up the stairs.

I lay there till I heard the screen door rattle shut.

You're it.

What he'd whispered to me.

FRANK FUTILLO, MD—MY BOWLING OPPONENT OF THE OTHER night—pronounced me more or less okay.

"A contusion on your arm, a head bruise, but that's pretty much it. What did he hit you with?"

"I don't know. Something metal."

I was sitting on that waxy paper that is used to cover every doctor's examination table in America, and trying mightily not to smell the ammonia. It was a scent I forever associated with childhood falls. Only it was my brother Jimmy who was always falling.

Never me.

"Yeah, well, all in all, I'd say you got off pretty easy," Dr. Futillo said.

"You mean compared to the average person assaulted by a stranger in their basement?"

"You talk to the sheriff about that?"

Yeah. I'd talked to the sheriff about that.

Sheriff Swenson had listened to my story of assault very much like a certain editor had listened to my increasingly outlandish exclusives during my imploding days in New York. With a tired and deflated look of disbelief. *Tap dancing at Auschwitz*—that's how I'd described it later to my court-appointed therapist. On my way to the gas chambers, but soft-shoeing all the harder.

"Now, Lucas," Sheriff Swenson said. "You looking to make the front page?"

Okay. I'd expected a little skepticism. But I was standing in the sheriff's office with a clearly tattooed forearm and a darkening bruise on the left side of my head.

"I'm looking to make a *complaint*. Aren't you supposed to do that when you've been assaulted?"

"Well, sure. You want to look through our mug book of homicidal plumbers?"

"That's funny. It is. But I'm thinking maybe he wasn't actually a plumber. Just a suspicion."

"Right. Well, what do you think he was doing? Stealing your copper wiring?"

"I don't know. I asked him what company he worked for and he slugged me. We never got to the specifics of his visit."

"Too bad. The fact is . . . Lucas . . ."

"I wish you wouldn't call me that," I said.

"You do? Tell me something, would you? *Why'd* Hinch hire you again?"

"Believe it or not, I used to be a good reporter."

"Really? I thought it was because he's related to your PO. I stand corrected."

Ordinarily, I might not have minded.

That's the thing about doing penance, as the court-appointed therapist, Dr. Payne—yeah, his real name—repeatedly drummed into me. You had to learn to accept your moral failures. That meant accepting reminders of it. It meant turning the other cheek and saying: go ahead—slug me again.

Only I'd already been hit today—*twice*, by someone who probably had a lot more to atone for than me. I was going to verbally swing back, to stand up for myself, when Swenson disarmed me.

"What I was going to say, Lucas . . . is that we've had a

number of home break-ins lately. Apparently he carries a plumber's kit in case he gets surprised, or a neighbor sees him strolling in. He uses it to stash whatever he walks out with. You're not the first complaint. I was just making sure—given your past history—that you were being on the up-and-up with me. You understand?"

Sure, I understood.

I told Dr. Futillo about the burglaries.

"Apparently we have some breaking and entering going on in the neighborhood."

"You're lucky your skull didn't get broken," he said.

It occurred to me that this was the second time in two days someone was being told they were lucky when they didn't feel that way. Ed Crannell, and me.

"Has the body been sent back?"

"*What* body?"

"Dennis Flaherty's body. Was it sent back to his mother in Iowa?"

"Oh yeah, absolutely."

"I looked up a sex offenders' Web site."

"Huh?" Dr. Futillo looked like someone who'd been told an intimate secret he'd rather not have been made privy to.

"The National Sex Offender Public Registry—a kind of Pedophile Central. I thought maybe our friend's castration was court-ordered."

"Well, was it?"

"I don't know. He wasn't listed there."

"Funny thing," Dr. Futillo said, "about our friend."

I've already mentioned that two things happened.

Two separate things that made me sit up and keep going instead of roll over and slip back into sleep. Which was

36

pretty much what I'd been doing in Littleton for the past year, and two thirds.

The first was being assaulted in my own basement.

This was the second.

"What funny thing?" I said. "His castration?"

"Oh yeah, *that*. But something else. If I didn't know any better, I'd say our deceased was black."

"Huh? I thought you said he was *Caucasian*. White."

"Yeah, I know. That's what it looked like on his license."

"So?"

"His thigh bones. Longer, and thicker at the joints. A signature of the African American race."

"You sure about that?"

"Well, I saw it on *Forensic Files*."

"*What?*"

"I saw it on *Forensic Files*. On Court TV. You never watch that show?"

If I didn't know any better, I'd say our deceased was black. Only he didn't know any better. He was a village MD playing forensic investigator, which made him only slightly more qualified than the village idiot.

"I spoke to his mother," I said. "She didn't sound very black. Besides, unless I'm crazy, Flaherty's an Irish name."

"Okay," Dr. Futillo said.

"*Okay?*"

"Bones don't lie, my friend."

"Don't take this the wrong way, but you just told me your entire expertise in this area comes from TV."

"Fine, don't believe me."

Funny. For just a second, I heard myself. Sitting in the office of a truly prestigious newspaper, the kind of newspaper

37

you sweat and bleed to merely have the *chance* to work for, and calmly and with a perfectly straight face stating this to that weary editor sitting across from me.

Fine, don't believe me.

It worked for a while.

SEVEN

The town of Littleton, California, is known for two things.

Sonny Rolph, a B-actor from the fifties, was born there.

And it's known for the Aurora Dam Flood, which, in a curious kind of colloquial contraction, the locals simply refer to as that *damn flood*.

It didn't actually happen in Littleton, but in its tiny sister town, Littleton Flats, situated some twenty-three miles down the road. In the 1950s, they erected the Aurora Dam on the nearby Aurora River, renowned for its grade three rapids and its unpleasant muddy color. The dam was built by contractors who may or may not have gotten the job through generous kickbacks to the state. What's fairly certain is that they built the dam with shoddy workmanship and egregious errors of engineering judgment. It was later termed—by an independent government commission set up to apportion blame—as an accident ready to happen.

It happened.

Three days of rain in April of 1954 swelled the river to historic heights, filled the dam to heretofore unknown levels, and caused the flawed cement walls to come tumbling down.

Littleton Flats was below sea level and directly in the water's path. It ceased to exist.

The death toll was put at 892, amended from 893 when they found a 3-year-old girl downriver and still alive.

I knew about this only because I'd scrolled through the microfilm of the *Littleton Journal* when Hinch first hired me but gave me nothing to do. The fact that the back issues were still on microfilm and not computer disks gave me a hard clue that I wasn't in the big leagues anymore.

A lot of people in town at least knew somebody who knew somebody else who'd perished in that *damn flood*. It was an understandably sore subject for them, something I discovered when I tried to interest Hinch in a retrospective piece on its fiftieth anniversary.

"We tried that before," he said. "Your predecessor, anyway."

My predecessor was named John Wren. I knew this because I'd appropriated more than his desk; he'd lived in the same rented house. He'd clearly been something of a pack rat; I'd found ancient bills from cable, phone, and Amazon.com addressed to a John Wren, hand-scrawled notes stuffed in various places—only half-decipherable and alluding to who knows what—and one of his stories, about a hard-luck and disoriented Vietnam vet who'd wandered into Littleton one day and bedded down in the town gazebo. "Who's Eddie Bronson?"—the title of the story. It had evidently been put up for some kind of local journalism prize. It lost. My first day on the job, I'd been greeted with a list Scotch-taped to the inside of my desk: *Wren's Rules*. Rule number one: *back up your notes for protection*. Rule number two: *transcribe your tape recordings for in case!*

According to Norma, Wren, a transplanted Minnesotan, had gotten a bad case of desert dementia, Santa Ana Syndrome, the small-town willies—that weird fugue that sometimes takes hold of people stuck in California desert towns in the middle of nowhere—and gone to trout fish near the Oregon border. Or pan for gold in the Yukon. Or ice fish on Lake Michigan—the details were hazy.

"You want to give the damn flood a shot, go ahead," Hinch said, "if you can get anyone to speak about it."

I couldn't.

Hinch might've spoken about it, but he wasn't really old enough to remember anything. He'd spent his entire adolescence somewhere else—Sacramento, I think. He came back to Littleton to take care of his ailing mother and somehow never felt the urge to leave. Maybe his marriage to the local beauty queen had something to do with that. He kept a picture of her—*Miss Azalea 1974*—on his desk. Miss Azalea had since contracted breast cancer and twice lost her hair to chemo. I think that picture helped Hinch keep the image of what she once was planted firmly in his heart. As far as I knew, Hinch remained true-blue to her— not my usual experience with editors, who tended to have a hard time remembering that they were married.

I was married once.

I don't feel like talking about it.

I DROVE OUTSIDE TOWN TO DO A STORY ON AN ALPACA RANCH.

Apparently alpacas are big business now, not so much

for their fleece as the alpacas themselves, able to fetch upwards of twenty thousand dollars.

The owners of the ranch, Mr. and Mrs. Childress, showed me around, insisted I feed their *babies* some food, and regaled me with stories about the trials and tribulations of alpaca breeding.

Apparently the desert heat wasn't ideal for them.

They were used to grazing thousands of feet above sea level in the Andes. Their ankles tended to swell on the worst days, causing them to lie down and play dead. Some of them were doing just that as we tramped around the property.

They looked like the inspiration for "Woolly Bully," I thought. As if some aesthetically challenged geneticist had combined the lamb with the camel, then stood back and said *whoops*. Picture walking balls of yarn, with unkempt mop-tops cascading down over mournfully sad eyes.

It got worse. Mrs. Childress led me past troughs of oats into the dark coolness of a barn. She wanted to show me something. At first I thought it was two alpacas lying side by side on a soft bed of hay.

It wasn't. There was only one alpaca in there.

It had two heads.

"We didn't have the heart to kill him," Mrs. Childress said. "One of his heads is blind. Poor thing."

I asked Mrs. Childress for something to drink; I wanted to get out of there.

We sat on their porch sipping sour lemonade, and when I ran out of questions and they ran out of stories, we still sat there and sipped our drinks in silence, just like I imagined real families do.

I finished my lemonade, stood up, said good-bye.

"Thanks for stopping by, Tom," Mrs. Childress said. "Drive carefully."

It must've been her parting words.

I started thinking about someone who *hadn't* driven carefully.

I turned left on Highway 45 instead of right. I looped around Littleton in a wide circle. I passed a decrepit sign for Littleton Flats—they'd never taken it down, leaving it as a kind of memorial, I suppose.

I kept going, and eventually got to the place I'd been to before.

The evening sky was a messy palette of roses and purples, making the desert look nearly nuclear. The distant flats were glowing red, the cacti luminous green.

The wreck had been towed away. There wasn't a single car out on the road.

I pulled off to the side of 45 and parked my Miata where the ambulance had been.

I stepped out, noticed a mud brown snake slithering off into the underbrush. Rattlesnakes were fairly common here. Every so often, someone got bit by one, didn't get to the doctor in time, and died a horrible, lonely death.

Dennis Flaherty had died a horrible, lonely death.

I walked onto the highway, to the very spot where the two cars collided.

I kneeled down on my haunches, hands firmly clasped under my chin—I don't know why—maybe as a kind of prayer, a sign of respect for the dead.

Then I noticed something.

The *absence* of something.

I tried to remember what Ed Crannell had said. His exact words.

I stood up, walked back and forth, stared at the ground. Something was rumbling down the highway like a coming storm. I stepped back to the side of the road and respectfully watched an eighteen-wheeler roar past, massive enough to make the ground actually stutter.

WHEN I GOT BACK TO THE OFFICE, NO ONE WAS THERE.

I found my notes in my desk drawer.

I beeped the horn at the last second, Ed Crannell told me when I asked him what happened. *I beeped the horn at the last second. He jammed on the brakes.*

Dennis Flaherty had jammed on the breaks to prevent himself from crashing headlong into the pharmaceutical salesman's car.

Too late to stop it, of course.

Something happens when you hit the brakes in a car doing sixty. You can safely assume that's how fast Dennis Flaherty's car was traveling on a mostly deserted highway in the early a.m.

It's simple physics.

When you jam the brakes of a car traveling that fast, the tires can't help but skid. Dry pavement, wet pavement, it doesn't really matter. Somewhere it will leave little particles of rubber adhering to the road.

That was the something I noticed was missing.

Skid marks.

There wasn't a single skid mark on the road.

EIGHT

I lie, therefore I am.

I'd discovered those words carved into my desk with a Swiss army penknife one day back in New York.

I *assumed* a Swiss army penknife had done the damage, because one of my fellow reporters had once shown it to me. It was his lucky talisman, he told me. It had gotten him through two wars and a near kidnapping in Tikrit.

Lately, he'd begun reading my copy with avid interest. He asked me for drinks one night and marveled at my sources. At my knack for being at the center of things. At my *nose for the story*.

He asked me fawning questions about my obvious alacrity at ferreting out the truth.

It was only later that I realized that he might've bought more drinks than I could count, but they were all *my* drinks. His vodka—Grey Goose, straight up—had sat untouched exactly where he'd placed it.

One of us did have a real alacrity for ferreting out the truth, but it wasn't me.

I lie, therefore I am.

Guilty as charged.

AFTER I REREAD MY NOTES, WISHING FOR ONCE I'D DEVELOPED AN affinity for tape recorders, I drove to Muhammed Alley. I ordered a margarita—no salt—from BJ's cousin, who tended bar on nights BJ stayed home and played dad. BJ apparently had four children from three different women, none of whom he'd ever married.

It was a little like the old days, I thought.

If you went back. Way back, to the *old, old* days.

When I'd first fallen in love. When I'd first bowed to the deities of Woodward and Bernstein. When I'd offered them up daily sacrifices, including my every waking hour, forswearing anything resembling a social life. When I'd pounded the pavement like I pounded the keys on my Mac—with a desperation born of true-blue obsession.

Those days.

When I believed I *did* have a nose for the story—I might've been the only one who did—that I could sniff them out like a customs dog. Someone would say something offhand—a state congressman, a mayor's aide, a police official—and alarms would go off. Only I could hear them; they were at a pitch unknown to ordinary working hacks. I'd feverishly start digging, looking for something hidden and odious, never meant to see the light of day.

Most of the time, all you found was mud. Murky and insubstantial. You couldn't sling it without two-sourced and verifiable proof.

There were exceptions, of course. Occasional investigations that actually uncovered something half-interesting. Nothing major, nothing incendiary enough to burn a hole into the public consciousness, but worthy enough to land me somewhere north of page 10.

On those mornings, when I perused my byline with awe and gratitude and even humility, I thought it was just possible I was on the side of the angels.

I was hearing alarms again.

Someone had tripped the wire, set off the circuitry, and jarring bells were going off in my head.

Seth stopped by.

"What's shaking?" he said, hopping up on the next stool.

Me, I wanted to say. *I'm shaking, rattling, and rolling.*

"Working on a story," I said.

"That's funny. It looks like you're working on a margarita. Heh-heh."

I kind of liked Seth, in the way one fuckup feels genuine empathy for another, but tonight I felt this, well . . . distance between us. Wasn't I back in the saddle, and wasn't he still stuck in the mud?

"I need ten," I said to him.

"Barking up the wrong tree, amigo," he said. "I'm tapped out. Honest."

"Ten *minutes*."

"Oh." He looked embarrassed, momentarily he did, and I suddenly felt kind of rotten for relegating a bowling team member to the ranks of the annoying and superfluous—even one with a noticeable mullet.

"Okay," he said, sliding off the stool with feigned indifference. "That's cool."

"Buy you a drink when I finish," I said.

"No problem."

The question was, finish *what*?

I asked BJ's cousin for a pen. I used my napkin to jot things down—basically everything I knew.

I was in the Acropolis Diner playing connect-the-dots again.

What has no testicles, no skid marks, and two races?

Got me.

I even threw in the assault in the basement for good measure—scribbled it there at the bottom of the napkin as a kind of addendum.

Still no clue.

Or many clues, but no answers.

Or simply random incidences.

Which would make them *co*incidences.

I doodled in the margins. I drew lines from one thing to another. I Etch A Sketched.

I drew two cars and blackened one till it disappeared.

I wrote down their names. Ed Crannell and Dennis Flaherty—who might or might not have been a black man.

I'd start with him, I decided.

The dead man.

When Seth came back and asked for his drink—7 and 7, a leftover from high school days, I imagined, when Seth was still hot shit and maybe the future even looked promising—I stared at him with what must've been a curiously blank expression.

"My *drink*, man. Did you or did you not offer me a *cocktail*?"

"Oh, sure. Just order it. I gotta run."

"Oh? Why's that?"

"Writing an obituary," I said.

That's how I began.

Stuffed in a cluttered cubicle preparing obits for still-living, breathing people—mostly famous ones, of course—

chiseling their headstones for that time when they'd be needed. The hardest part was remembering the right tense, to relegate legions of the still upright to the recent past.

Is into *was*. *Doing* into *did*. *Living* into *lived*.

My first professional lies.

NINE

My Miata didn't start.

I gave it the gas, once, twice, three times.

I must've flooded the engine.

I got out, opened up the hood, and stared at the tangle of wires, tubes, and metal as if I knew what I was doing.

I didn't. I couldn't tell a carburetor from a transmission.

It doesn't matter. That's what you do when your car doesn't start. You open up the hood and stare knowingly at the engine.

I was hoping one of the parts might speak to me. *Over here, Tom—it's me. I'm the culprit.*

No such luck.

I was agitated, pissed off, finally on a roll and suddenly no wheels.

I was wondering where my friend Marv the Exxon owner was when I really needed him. I was going to head back into Muhammed Alley and ask Seth for a lift.

Then I didn't have to.

A cherry red Beetle pulled into the parking lot. A woman got out, began walking in the general direction of the alley entrance, turned, and noticed me.

"Car problems?"

"That would account for the open hood," I said, more caustically than I'd intended.

She swiveled around and continued on her way in.

"Wait a second. Yes. Car problems. *Big* car problems."

She stopped and turned back toward me.

I recognized her.

I felt that little flutter. That unexpected bump in the bio-rhythms.

"I saw you at Belinda Washington's birthday party," I said.

"Oh, that's right." She'd stopped about five feet from me. She was wearing a skirt this time—denim, ending just above her calves. It was hard not to notice those calves were tan, toned, and gently rounded. "The reporter, right?"

"I used to be."

"*Used* to be? I thought you were doing a story?"

"I was. I'm being self-deprecating."

"You might want to leave that to someone else," she said.

Her smile accented the soft dimple on her left cheek. I used to have one, too. My mom, in one of her sentimental moments, as opposed to her terrifyingly volcanic ones—both of them alcohol-induced with no way to predict which one she'd slide into any given day—told me God had stuck his finger in my cheek when he was done molding me. After a certain age, I couldn't find it anymore. It just disappeared.

"My car won't start," I said.

"Yeah, I kind of got that." She walked over and peeked under the hood.

It was around 8 p.m. on what had been a sizzling June day, still light enough to see but growing dimmer by the second. The kind of light that softens everything, that might've sent an impressionist sprinting for the canvas and brushes. That makes a woman bent over at the waist a thing of rare and numbing beauty.

Clang. Bang. Clink.

She unscrewed something, poked inside the engine.

"Your coil wire's loose," she said after a few minutes. "Try it now."

I crawled into the front seat, gave it some gas.

Vrooooooooooooom.

"I guess this is what they call role reversal," I said, once I'd extricated myself from the car and shaken her hand. "Thanks."

"My pop was a mechanic," she said. "He basically lived under the hood. It was the only way I could spend time with him."

"You must've been paying attention." Her hand was back by her side, but I could still feel the impression of her fingers—hot flesh and cool lacquer.

"Enough to spot a loose coil wire," she said. "It's really not that hard."

At least she smiled when she said it.

"Tom Valle," I introduced myself, cognizant that the flutter hadn't gone away, that it was still flitting madly around my chest like a butterfly caught in a net.

"Anna Graham," she said.

"Were you visiting someone? At the home?"

"My pop. He's got Alzheimer's."

"I'm sorry."

52

"Me, too."

Silence. I was trying to stare and not stare at the same time. The kind of thing you do your first time at a nude beach. It's easier with sunglasses on.

"Well," she said, "I was on my way in."

For a moment, I was going to say, *what a coincidence, me, too. I was on my way in, too.* Clearly, I'd been on my way out.

"Are you . . . uhh . . . ?"

"What?" She was shading her eyes against the sun's glare, but even squinting, her eyes were wide enough to meander around in.

"Are you staying here? In Littleton?"

"Just for a few days. I live in Santa Monica."

"Santa Monica, huh."

"On Fifth, right off the promenade."

"Ever had drinks at Shutters?"

"No."

"It's got a pretty bar."

"That's what I've heard."

"Well," I said, "maybe I'll see you there someday."

Her expression said maybe not.

I DROVE HOME.

When I walked through the door, I was going to turn right and head up to the bedroom to watch Nick at Nite reruns of *I Love Lucy.* I did love Lucy, at least maintained a true-blue affection for her. After all, Lucy, Ethel, Fred, and Ricky had babysat my brother and me through numerous afternoons when my mom was present but otherwise occupied, when she'd traded Jim, Jack, and Johnnie for Tom,

Dick, and Vinny, a parade of mostly faceless men who sometimes tousled my hair on their way upstairs.

I didn't go watch *I Love Lucy*. Instead I flicked on the basement light at the top of the steps and walked down. Tentatively. Making sure to stop at each step and peek.

As far as I could tell, the basement was empty this time.

I'd given it a cursory look after the assault, when I'd finally lifted myself to a wobbly semblance of standing.

He'd been kneeling halfway between the heater and the wall.

The place I'd first seen him.

Banging around with that metal thing in his hand. You could safely assume he hadn't been fixing the boiler.

So *what* had he been doing?

If he was breaking and entering, why had he come down here?

I felt along the wall. There were two lopsided shelves nailed into the plaster. Some old paint cans, stiffened rags, a broken radio from the fifties sitting on top of a tattered board game. I wiped off the coating of dust. Milton Bradley's Life. For a brief moment, I saw myself hurrying a tiny blue car around the labyrinthine road to Millionaire's Mansion, hoarding my pile of funny money from my mother's rheumy eyes. Not that she didn't see things. Jimmy cheating, for instance. She always saw that. Swiping money from the bank like a *little thief*.

A sudden pang of dread lodged itself in the center of my chest.

I looked down where the drywall met the floor. A brown spider scurried beneath a paint can.

A jar of bottle caps.

A cracked hockey stick with the faded logo of the San Jose Sharks.

A nearly unraveled baseball.

Some old books. A biography of Edward R. Murrow. A History of the Cold War. Stanley Karnow's *Vietnam*. *Hiroshima* by John Hersey.

Wren's, I imagined.

There was plaster dust sitting on the cover photo of a mushroom cloud. When I pushed the books aside, I uncovered a large, ragged hole in the wall. You would've needed something pretty heavy to do that, I thought, trying to picture that metal thing in the plumber's hand. The thing he'd ended up whacking me over the head with.

I peeked into the hole but saw nothing but drywall and ripped edges of newspaper insulation.

When I continued my way around the basement, I stepped on something.

Small and plastic.

I kneeled down, assaulted by the strong scent of mildew, and picked it up.

A phone-jack cover. The screw was still dangling in the hole.

Where had it come from?

There. Along the base of the wall.

The phone jack was open, red and yellow wires separated from their respective screws, reaching into the air like fingers frozen in rigor mortis.

I brought the cover over to the single naked bulb dangling from the basement ceiling. The jack was obviously unused—there was no phone down here. The cover might've been lying around forever, years even.

There was no dust on it.

So, okay, it hadn't been.

TEN

This time Mrs. Flaherty was warier.

"What do you want *now*?" she asked.

"I'm investigating the accident," I told her.

"*Investigating*?"

"That's right. I'm beginning to think it didn't happen the way they said it did."

"*Who* said? I don't understand."

"The other . . .driver. I don't think it happened the way he described it."

"You think he's *lying*?"

"Maybe he's confused. Or he thinks the accident was his fault, so he made things up."

"They told me Dennis drove into the wrong lane."

"Yeah. That's what the other driver said."

No, I realized. The other driver had said Dennis *drifted* into the wrong lane.

I suddenly understood.

His depression, his drinking . . .

Mrs. Flaherty thought Dennis had done it on purpose—steered his car into oncoming traffic in a moment of suicidal clarity.

"You don't believe him? This other driver—what was his name, Earl?" she asked.

"Ed. Ed Crannell."

"You don't believe him?"

"Maybe not."

"It doesn't matter, does it?" she said softly. "My son's dead."

I heard what sounded like sobbing.

I waited. It was 8:32 a.m. Norma hadn't come in yet. The office of the *Littleton Journal* was a simple storefront sandwiched between Foo Yang Chinese takeout and Ted's Guns & Ammo, which offered Michael Moore targets with every purchased handgun.

"Mrs. Flaherty? Can you describe Dennis for me?"

"*What*?"

"Can you describe your son?"

"Why?"

"He wasn't biracial, was he?"

"Bi*what*?"

"I mean, Dennis was Caucasian. White, right?"

"What's going on?" she asked.

"Nothing. I'm just trying to . . ."

"What are you saying?"

"Just clarifying things . . ."

"The police said it was *Dennis*. I *buried* him."

"Of course. Five-foot-nine, brown hair, olive eyes. That's your son, Dennis?"

"Why'd you ask if he was *negro*?"

"Look, forget I even . . ."

"You think it wasn't him, is that it?"

"No . . ."

"That's what you're saying, isn't it? You think it might've been someone else. A *negro*. He was all *burned* up . . . black." She wasn't asking anymore; she was *stating*. Hope had infused her voice with the sudden fervor of the true believer.

I should've stopped her, of course. Right there. I should've said that wasn't my point at all, no, I was merely getting his description in the interest of journalistic accuracy.

Maybe the words *journalistic accuracy* were legally banned from my vocabulary. There was that catch in her throat to contend with. That thrilling willingness to swallow something whole. I'd heard that seductive sound before—around the table at editorial roundups, where I'd offer stories for approval amid the sweet buzzing of acolytes.

Understand and forgive. It was like blowing smoke in the face of a nicotine addict.

"Just supposing," I said to Mrs. Flaherty, "that someone *robbed* Dennis? What if someone stole his car, his wallet? The body was unrecognizable. I'm just trying to be 100 percent sure here."

"*Yes* . . . yes, of course," she said. "Dennis had brown hair, olive eyes—just like you said. He had a little scar on his right cheek. He fell off the monkey bars when he was 5. Is it *possible* . . . Mr. . . . ?"

"Valle. Tom Valle."

"Is it possible they're wrong? It is, isn't it? It's *not* him? It's *someone else*?"

She took down my address.

She told me she'd send me a picture of Dennis.

She rattled off a few particulars of Dennis's sad travesty of a marriage.

She provided me with the phone number of Dennis's ex-wife.

She told me Dennis had won five merit badges as a Boy Scout.

I had a hard time getting her off the phone.

When Hinch came in, he asked me what I was working on.

Hinch was big-boned, broad-shouldered, a largess that had lately migrated south to his stomach. Some mornings he arrived with gray stubble still clinging to his chin. I suspected Miss Azalea wasn't doing well.

"Following up on the crash."

"That crash on Highway 45? Old news, isn't it?"

"There are a few things I'm trying to clean up."

"Like?" Hinch had made his way to the coffee brewer, which I'd generously started percolating—usually Norma's job.

"Like there was no definite ID. Except for the man's wallet."

"Meaning what?"

"Meaning I don't know exactly. But the ME thought . . ."

"The *who*?"

"Dr. Futillo. He was convinced . . ."

"Dr. *Futillo*?" Hinch snorted. "He's no medical examiner. You know anything about Dr. *Futillo*?" As owner, editor in chief, and sole editorial columnist of the *Littleton Journal*, Hinch made it a point to know just about everything about everyone in town.

"He's a good bowler."

"He's also good at prescribing OxyContin to patients who don't actually need it. He relocated here under, let's say, murky circumstances. I wouldn't believe everything Dr. Futillo tells you. Especially about forensics."

I thought Hinch was making a point. That there were two people who'd relocated to Littleton under murky circumstances, and neither one of them was remotely trustworthy.

Sheriff Swenson was right; Hinch *was* related to my probation officer, who'd asked me at our last meeting what I intended to do with my life, now that no paper within 3,000 miles would hire me. The answer was simple. Find a paper within 3,001 miles. Once my PO had a word with its editor in chief—Hinch, her cousin on her mother's side. It wasn't much of a paper, of course—one step up from the penny circular—but its desert location had appealed to my desire for isolation and self-scourging.

"I won't write it unless it checks," I said.

Which was pretty much word-for-word what *Hinch* had told me the day I arrived in my beat-up Miata. That he wouldn't *publish* anything unless it checked.

Even if all we were talking about was the annual book sale down at the Littleton Library. It better be the right date, okay?

I'd promised I wouldn't let him down.

Hinch stared at me for a long moment, as if credibility was something that could be visibly gauged.

"All right," he said.

He retreated into his office and shut the door.

I'd gotten an iPod.

Norma had sold me on its myriad benefits. She'd recently begun performing lunchtime aerobics to the latest from Outkast, slipping into baggy pink Danskins and mouthing along to Andre 3000.

In a very short time, I'd fattened up my iPod with 1,032 songs. Mostly oldies-but-goodies.

The entire canon of Hendrix.

Some Jackson Browne.

Santana. Fleetwood Mac. Jethro Tull.

A few anomalies thrown in. *Side by Side by Sondheim.* Sinatra at Caesar's. Judy Collins singing "Where or When."

If you've never heard her rendition of that haunting Richard Rodgers tune, you're really missing something.

I was listening to "Where or When" on the way to my car.

I was going to cover the opening of a new department store. And maybe something else.

I was focusing on the words.

Things that happened for the first time seem to be happening again. . . .

Yes.

ELEVEN

You *always remember your first time.*

I overslept.

I was supposed to be on a plane to Shreveport, Louisiana, to interview the family of a dead National Guardsman, one of the first casualties in Afghanistan. Back when the war on terror still had the imprimatur of a just revenge.

Before we blew into Iraq after WMDs that weren't there and unleashed holy hell.

Maybe I was inherently dreading it. The knock at their door, my protestations about how sorry I was to be bothering them in their moment of grief. Their bewildered faces—because death is bewildering, a vanishing act of stunning skill; first they're here, then they're not. The lowered faces, the embarrassing tears, the snapshots brought out in dusty albums, opened for my respectful perusal. The childhood stories, the bedroom tour, the folded American flag sitting obtrusively on the living room mantelpiece. Maybe I was dreading it so much that I'd decided not to wake up.

See. I knew the routine so well that I could write it from memory.

That's exactly what occurred to me as I gazed bleary-eyed at my alarm clock, which uncomprehendingly was hours past where it was supposed to be. Hours past where I could simply hop on a later plane, still get the interview, and make it into tomorrow's Sunday edition.

I'll admit something.

I'd fibbed before. All reporters do.

Little things.

Maybe I'd reconstructed a piece of dialogue that wasn't exactly word-for-word what that political bagman had told me in that desolate downtown garage. It was close, sure, but it sounded so much better, so much more infinitely dramatic this way.

Maybe, here and there, I'd described something that I hadn't in actuality seen.

I'd talked to that crack junkie outside his burned-out tenement, and yet a few particulars of his garbage-strewn, needle-littered apartment had somehow crept into the article.

Why not? What was the harm?

His apartment was probably garbage-strewn and needle-littered. Its inclusion in the article added texture. And if I hadn't actually stepped inside and seen it with my own two eyes, who was to know? It hadn't changed anything materially, had it?

Of course, this would be different. This would be making something up in its entirety. Its very audacity glued me to the bed, caused me to keep staring at my clock as if the hour hand might miraculously crawl backward of its own volition.

I think I wrote the article as a kind of exercise. At first I did.

That's, anyway, what I told myself.

Write it for fun, I whispered, and see how it turns out.

Imagine it, I told myself. Walking down a tree-lined sidewalk on a pleasantly mild Shreveport day, then up the rickety wooden steps to their front door. Mr. and Mrs. Beaumont stepping back to let me into the suffocating darkness of their living room. Imagine how they might've answered my questions.

I had some actual info. A quick trip to Google had turned up two local articles from the Shreveport Journal. *Sergeant First Class Lowell Beaumont was a high school athlete who would've gone on scholarship to LSU if not for those torn knee ligaments suffered in his senior year at Stonewall Jackson High.*

His bedroom remains filled with the echoes of the high school gridiron, with freshly polished trophies adorning both sides of his dresser bureau.

See, it wasn't so hard.
Odds are that's exactly what his bedroom looked like.
Lowell had two younger sisters, the articles said. Mary and Louise.

Mary Beaumont clutched a picture of her fallen brother in both hands. "He was always looking out for us, making sure we were home on time, stuff like that."

What older brother wouldn't keep a sharp eye on his sisters? And wouldn't a grieving sister pick up his picture, if only to stare at the face she'd no longer see again?

Lowell Beaumont had worked on an assembly line at the local tire factory. He'd joined the National Guard one week after 9/11.

"He thought he had a duty to his country," Mr. Beaumont said, shaking a white-haired head bent in grief. "He felt it was worth even his life."

Isn't that the only reason someone would join the National Guard after the Twin Towers fell? Duty to country? Wouldn't the father be wracked with an amorphous mixture of pride and sadness? If he hadn't said those exact words to someone, he'd undoubtedly thought them.

Once I got going, it was hard to stop.

It was easier than having to refer back to my notes. Much easier. My fingers virtually flew across the keys.

Speaking of notes.

Let's suppose I actually handed the story in. Let's suppose this one time—never again of course, only this once—I saved my ass with a little creativity. If someone were to challenge something in the story, I could supply proof. Not tape—I was the traditionalist who famously abhorred the tape recorder. I would give them my notes.

What notes?

The ones I'd instantly conjure up if push came to shove.

The simple brilliance of this deception comforted me and spurred me on.

When I finished the story, I thought it read exactly like it would've if I had gotten on that plane and made it to that shuttered home in Shreveport.

Still, I admit to the slightest trembling in my hands as I walked it over to the backfield editior that evening.

As I stood and watched it make its way from copy desk to proof.

The next morning, he called me into his office.

My trembling increased geometrically. I quivered, consumed by the absolute dread you feel on your way to the principal when you've been caught red-handed with crib notes in your pocket.

I rehearsed a story on the way to his office: "I missed the plane, so I called them and did the interview on the phone. . . . It'll never happen again. . . . I should've told you. . . . I'm so sorry. . . ."

When I made it through the door, the first thing I saw was the paper folded to my article. First page, lower left.

A Soldier's Sad Return

He peered up over his old-fashioned bifocals, looking even more rumpled than usual. Ever since smoking was banned in New York City offices, he'd taken to chewing anything in arm's reach. This morning it was a red pencil nearly bitten in half, which he carefully removed from his mouth and suspended over the article with the deliberateness of a firing hammer being squeezed back into position.

"Nice writing," he said. "Moving without being mawkish. Really, really good."

"Thanks," I said.

I might've even blushed.

TWELVE

Once upon a time, Littleton had aspired to a kind of Palm Springs–hood. They'd broken ground for a Robert Trent Jones golf course and two sprawling resorts, ascribing to the build-it-and-they-will-come theory of urban development.

They didn't come.

Maybe because Palm Springs had Bob Hope and Shecky Greene and a host of other aging Friars Club members, and Littleton had Sonny Rolph.

It didn't help that Littleton's major real estate developer went belly-up in the stock collapse of the early nineties, just as Vegas turned into a cheap ticket option for Los Angelenos looking to grab a weekend getaway.

The resorts were never finished—the golf course suspended at nine holes and counting.

Now mall openings were true cause for excitement.

This one was first-rate.

Rodeo clowns handed out balloons twisted into tiny pink dachshunds. Humming machines spun out glistening spools of cotton candy. Someone who looked like Billy

Ray Cyrus sung a country song about his girlfriend leaving him red, white, and blue.

Which happened to be the color of the ceremonial ribbon deftly cut in two by Littleton's three-term mayor. Patriotism was clearly *in* these days. The voracious crowd promptly surged through the massive doorway in search of bargains and air-conditioning. Not necessarily in that order.

Nate Cohen, my intern from Pepperdine, accompanied me to cover this earthshaking event. *Nate the Skate* his frat buddies called him, he informed me the day we met.

Why?

I don't know, he said, looking puzzled at the question.

Nate tended to pepper me with journalism questions when he wasn't gabbing to his girlfriend. They had matching cell phones, he stated proudly, both of which could take camera-quality pictures. He proved it by showing me his girlfriend, Rina, reclining nude on an outdoor chaise longue.

"Isn't she cute?" he asked.

"You sure you want to be showing people that?" I asked him.

"You're not people. You're my mentor. Sort of."

"Maybe she wouldn't want your mentor seeing her naked?"

"Oh, she wouldn't care. We go to Black's Beach like all the time."

Black's Beach was a notorious clothing-optional cove just south of La Jolla.

We discharged our duties with perfunctory professionalism.

Somehow interviewing the middle-aged saleswoman

who generously splashed me with Calvin Klein's *Eau de something* failed to get my journalistic juices flowing. Same for the home-appliances manager—despite his flawless demonstration of a combination juicer-toaster, and hand vacuum with built-in computer chip.

I was preoccupied.

Belinda Washington had made it to her hundredth birthday and then suddenly passed away. I'd heard it on the radio this morning.

On a sad note, the local radio announcer had said, *our very own centenarian kicked the bucket today. Belinda Washington has moved on to that great big nursing home in the sky.*

We should all be so lucky, the show's cohost had cheerily intoned.

After I dropped Nate off, I drove back to the home.

I'm not sure why.

When I entered the lobby, Mr. Birdwell was ushering a middle-aged couple out the door.

"So let us know," he said to them. "Space is kind of limited."

He was already trying to fill her bed. Old-age homes were like *in* restaurants these days; the good ones had waiting lists that were miles long.

Mr. Birdwell had no trouble remembering me.

"What brings you back, Mr. Valle?"

"I heard about Belinda. Just following up."

He stared at me with a puzzled expression, as if he were waiting for a second part of the sentence.

"I was wondering what she died of," I said.

"She was *100*," he answered, as if that provided all the reason necessary.

"She seemed pretty okay the day I was here."

"Her heart," he said. "It just gave out."

"I see." I remembered the chill of Belinda's hand—the opposite of Anna's hot-blooded grip. Cold extremities were a sign of pure blood circulation. Her *heart*, sure.

"Can I see her room?" I asked.

"What for?"

"For the story."

There wasn't a story. Even as the words passed my lips, I knew I was lying.

"There's not a whole lot there," Mr. Birdwell said. "But okay."

He turned and motioned for me to follow him.

We passed the nurse's station, where wheelchairs were lined up like shopping carts. The nurses seemed subdued today. Maybe they'd been fond of Belinda, too.

A bathrobed man was tortuously making his way down the hall with the aid of walker and oxygen mask. He looked up and squinted at me as if trying to focus. He had been in the rec room that day, I remembered, and briefly wondered if he might be Anna's father, the one withering away from Alzheimer's.

Belinda's room was at the end of a long fluorescent-lit hall.

It was conspicuously empty.

She'd had it all to herself. Just one double bed. A TV screwed into a movable platform was tucked into the corner.

A small brown dresser supported a lone picture frame half turned to the wall.

I picked it up and peeked.

A mother and son.

It was unmistakably *her*—just sixty years younger.

The same smile she'd bestowed on me the day I interviewed her. She was sitting on a bench with a small boy nestled in her arms.

Just above her head was a sign suspended by chains: *Littleton Flats Café*.

"She grew up in Littleton Flats?" I asked Mr. Birdwell, trying to remember if she'd mentioned that to me.

"Oh yes," Mr. Birdwell said. "Belinda was our home-grown celebrity. You know that weatherguy on NBC—Willard, what's his name, Scott—who wishes happy birthday to 100-year-olds around the country? He put Belinda's picture on a few weeks ago."

I looked down at the boy sitting in her lap.

He passed on a long time ago . . .

"Her son. Did he die in the flood?"

"Uh-huh," Mr. Birdwell nodded. "A real tragedy. Belinda worked as a live-in for a family here in Littleton. Apparently she always spent the weekends home. Not *that* weekend. She was asked to babysit the family kids. The flood happened on a Sunday morning when everyone in Littleton Flats was home. Including her son."

I tried to imagine what that must've felt like—taking care of someone else's children while your own drowned. And you not being there to hold him.

He say he forgive me, she'd said.

Now I knew why.

"Did she have any other children?" I asked.

Mr. Birdwell shook his head. "She had him kind of late in life. I'm pretty positive Benjamin was it."

I miss things.

Yes. She'd missed Benjamin enough to conjure him up from time to time. A woman in the first throes of dementia, and the last throes of loneliness.

"Can I have it?" I asked Mr. Birdwell.

"The picture? What for?"

"The story," I said, lying again.

He hesitated, evidently debating the ethical parameters of releasing personal property to a journalist.

"I'll return it," I said.

"Well, okay. Don't see why not."

I'd already slipped it into my pocket.

LATER THAT NIGHT, AFTER I'D DOWNED TWO GLASSES OF TEQUILA while watching back-to-back episodes of *Forensic Files*, I lifted the phone and punched in some familiar digits.

I waited four rings until he picked up and said: *Hello, hello . . . ?*

Sometimes I form the words back.

In my head I do.

I say I'm sorry, that I've been meaning to pick up the phone and tell him just how sorry I am, and that I apologize for taking so long. I hear the words in my head, and they sound genuine and contrite. I just don't hear them coming out of my mouth. They get lost on the way from here to there.

Tonight I formed them again and they sounded slightly boozy and sad.

Hello? Hello . . . who is this?

It's me, I said wordlessly. It's me. Tom. I'm sorry, really.

He hung up.

I waited till I heard the depressing hum of an empty line.

When I leaned over to put the phone down, I painfully discovered the picture lying on my floor.

It must've fallen out of my pocket when I tried, unsuccessfully, to fling my jeans over a chair back. The glass had cracked, leaving small shards where my left foot stepped on them.

I was bleeding.

I hopped into the bathroom on one foot and managed to locate a bottle of iodine. I extricated a sliver of glass from just below my big toe, then swathed and bandaged it. I gingerly shuffled back into the bedroom, carefully scraped the remaining slivers into my right palm, and deposited them in my overflowing trash bag reeking of four-day-old food.

There was the wounded photograph to tend to. Speckles of bright blood had given the mother and son the look of accident victims. I felt as if I'd desecrated something fine and irreplaceable.

I wiped it with a tissue, but the blood had seeped into the fabric of the photo and dimpled it. I carefully removed it from the cracked frame and gently blew across its surface.

Something dropped to the floor. A folded piece of paper that had been stuck to the other side.

I placed the picture on my dresser and reached for it. My lacerated foot screamed.

It was a note.

Happy hundred birthday, it began.

I sat on the bed, spread the letter out over my knee.

Happy hundred birthday.
I wish you hundred kisses.
I wish you hundred hugs.

Love, Benjy.
P.S. Greetings from Kara Bolka.

THIRTEEN

Sam Weitz called me at work to ask if I'd like some life insurance.

"Why?" I asked him.

"Because everyone should have life insurance. Didn't you just get beat up?"

"Yeah."

"There you go."

"What does *that* have to do with anything? If I died, whom would I leave the money to?"

"You evidently aren't up on the latest advances in the insurance paradigm. It's not just about *dying*. There's protection for long-term medical absences, for example. So you can keep getting paid. Haven't you seen those commercials with the duck? What if you were laid up and couldn't be a reporter anymore?"

I was tempted to tell him my salary, so he'd understand that if I couldn't make it to my job at the *Littleton Journal*, I could always follow the path of upward mobility and go to work at McDonald's.

"That's okay," I said. "I think I'll forgo the insurance, if you don't mind."

"It's your funeral," he said, then added, "poor choice of words."

"No. It's funny."

"Really?" he said, his voice brightening. He'd probably been called a lot of things as an insurance agent. Annoying, boring, bloodsucking—*funny* might've been a first. "Well, if you change your mind . . ."

"You'll be the first to know."

"Okeydokey."

Norma asked me if I wanted anything to eat. She was making a lunch run next door; Nate had already put in his order for moo goo gai pan and fried wontons.

"No, thanks," I said. "I'm not hungry."

"You always say you're not hungry, and then I have to give you half of mine because I feel God-awful sorry for you."

"That's me," I said. "The proverbial object of sympathy."

Maybe she took her cue from Hinch on that score. After all, Hinch had felt God-awful sorry enough to hire me.

"I can't interest you in a half-pint of shrimp chow fun, huh?"

"Sure," I said. "I could use a little more fun in my life."

My attempt at a witticism flew right over Norma's head.

I'd put the phone down after Sam's call, then immediately picked it up again, only I'd forgotten whom to call. Then I realized I hadn't forgotten, but had simply run out of possibilities.

There was no Ed Crannell listed in the entire city of Cleveland.

I'd tried everything in a hundred-mile radius and come up empty.

I wanted to ask Crannell whether the face he'd glimpsed through the oncoming windshield had been black or white.

Cleveland never heard of him.

The one in Ohio? I'd asked Crannell to be sure we were talking about the right Cleveland.

He'd nodded and told me he was a pharmaceutical salesman.

I tried that next. Wrote down every major drug company I could think of, then called each one of them and asked for an Edward Crannell.

No such salesman on payroll.

Maybe he was part-time, I suggested. *Freelance?*

There was a freelance saleswoman at Pfizer named *Beth* Crannell. Couldn't be her I was looking for, could it?

No, it couldn't.

Okay. There was a clear pattern developing here. No skid marks and no Ed.

I called the sheriff's office.

He'd have all the valuable particulars from Crannell's license. Assuming those particulars were in any way, shape, or form true. Assuming the license wasn't bought mail-order or forged.

Sheriff Swenson wasn't in, a female officer informed me. He would have to get back to me.

Something else was gnawing at me, of course.

I hadn't forgotten. No. The note from Belinda Washington's room hadn't slipped my mind, been summarily dismissed, or relegated to the file of very strange things.

Happy hundred birthday.

Love, Benjy.

Could it have been another Benjamin?

Someone, for instance, *not* her dead son?

Sure. This was possible. Given the fact Benjamin Washington had died fifty years ago in the Aurora Dam Flood, even plausible.

I called Mr. Birdwell.

"Did a middle-aged black man visit Belinda before her birthday party?" I asked.

"Not that I know of," he responded.

"Well, who *would* know if someone visited someone in the home?"

"Guests would have to register at the front desk," he said. "What's all this about?"

"Trying to get hold of a relative who might've stopped by," I explained. "Could you check for me?"

He sighed and said he'd get back to me.

Twenty minutes later he called and said, "No one visited Belinda in years."

"Really? What if someone didn't want to register at the front desk? What if they decided to just waltz in? Couldn't they?"

"No," Mr. Birdwell said. But he'd hesitated before saying it, and it came out defensively enough to make me think he was lying.

I drove back to the home.

I parked two blocks away in front of an aging Rexall.

I tried to ignore the midday heat. Natives are fond of noting there's no humidity in the California desert. True. They conveniently leave out the part about the 110-degree summer temperatures, which make it feel as if you're breathing in a sauna, and the murderous Santa Ana winds. The Santa Anas *are* murderous, but not in the way you might imagine. They don't blow you away like the wolf huffing and puffing at the pigs' door; they kill you by attrition, by blowing so incessantly that people go mad. Just ask John Wren, who'd allegedly gone Littleton loco—reclusive and squirrelly enough to barricade himself in the *Littleton Journal* one night, before absconding to parts unknown. It's true. Suicide rates soar during the Santa Anas.

Speaking of suicide.

I'll admit to contemplating it once or twice back in New York. Not seriously—not like I was about to do it that very second, the way OSS agents dropped behind enemy lines must've fingered the strychnine capsules sewn into the waistbands of their pants. They knew what Gestapo interrogation entailed; there had to be true comfort in knowing peace was a simple swallow away. If it got bad enough.

During my agonizing stretch as a public piñata—for a while I was assaulted by daily articles, from sensational exposés to sober treatises on how good reporters go bad—it had now and then been comforting to consider the eighteen stories from my apartment window to the graffitied sidewalk below.

When I reached the nursing home, I ignored the front door.

I meandered around the back, where an expanse of brown lawn sloped down to a muddy pond, choked with cattails and milkweed. There was a metal gate circling the backyard, but I simply reached over and flipped the latch. Evidently, Mr. Birdwell was more concerned about residents wandering out than visitors wandering in.

80

There was no one strolling the lawn.

This wasn't surprising since the brutal heat would've been lethal for your average 80-year-old. The raucous hum of the massive air-conditioning unit sounded like an army of angry cicadas. I walked up to the back door and turned the knob.

It trickled open.

Anyone could've walked in this way. If they hadn't wanted to be noticed or have their signature dutifully added to the guest register. If they'd wanted to make a surprise visit.

I walked in and was immediately enveloped by an artificial chill.

I passed two male orderlies, one of them pushing a wheelchair-bound patient who looked comatose. Neither orderly asked me what I was doing there, demanded ID, or redirected me elsewhere.

I made it all the way to Belinda's old room.

It seemed even emptier now.

There's something pathetic about the ease with which a room gives up its owner. Especially when it was someone who'd lived over a century.

The door across the hall creaked open. A withered man with a large liver spot on his forehead peeked out at me.

"Dan?" he said.

"No."

"Dan, is that you, Dan?"

"No, my name's Tom. I'm not Dan."

"Oh." Suddenly at sea, he retreated behind a door festooned with faded children's drawings.

I walked in and sat down on Belinda's old bed.

Hello, Mom. It's Benjy. Happy birthday. I forgive you.

On the way out, I ran into Mr. Birdwell.

Literally.

I was walking with my head down, kind of mesmerized by the alternating black and white tiles in the linoleum floor, and bumped straight into him as he turned the corner of the hallway.

He didn't seem pleased.

"What are *you* doing here?"

"I needed to check something."

"Check *what*?"

"Whether I could get in without anyone knowing."

Mr. Birdwell looked even less pleased than before. He folded his arms and stared at me as if I were one of his elderly charges who'd been caught disobeying a home rule. Snatching an extra cookie at snack time, or pinching a nurse's bottom.

"Now that wasn't very smart of you."

"Why not?"

"For one thing, that's *trespassing*. I explained that you have to register at the front desk. For another thing, you *didn't* get in here without anyone knowing, did you?"

"Well, I didn't get *out* without anyone knowing. I'm not sure that's the same thing. Getting in was kind of easy."

"To what purpose? You mind telling me that?"

"I'm not doing an exposé on nursing home security, if that's what you're worried about."

"Why don't you let me decide what I'm worried about? You broke into my home and I'd like to know why."

"Isn't 'broke' a little dramatic? The back door was open."

"You entered without *permission*." Mr. Birdwell was getting flustered. His cheeks had reddened; he was rocking back and forth on his heels. "You think we can have anyone just walk into a nursing home filled with sick and frightened people?"

"Exactly."

"Exactly *what*?"

"You can have anyone walk in. I just did."

"We're talking in circles here, Mr. Valle."

"I wanted to know if Belinda Washington might've had a visitor you didn't know about. You said it wasn't possible. I wanted to see if it was. That's all."

"What visitor?"

"I don't know. But she had one."

"Great. Bravo. I'm sure you're on your way to a Pulitzer. On the other hand, the halls of journalism aren't exactly ringing with your praises these days, Mr. Valle, are they?"

He smiled. That was the worst part, really—the smile. Not that he knew, not that he'd looked me up or talked to Swenson or bumped into Hinch and *knew*, but that smugly superior smile.

I had no answer for that smile. None.

Once upon a time, my dad bought me a Hardy Boys crime-detection magnifying glass on the last birthday we celebrated as a family. After he left, I would sit outside in the searing afternoon sun and train the glass on my naked palm until blisters formed and I couldn't stand the pain.

That's what Mr. Birdwell's smile felt like on my quickly retreating back. It burned a hole in me.

FOURTEEN

Where was I?

I'm losing track here.

Maybe because I've eaten once in the last two days. Make that three days—I'm not sure. I'm all out of Nabisco crackers—that's the sad truth. No more Tostitos or Jolly Ranchers or beef jerky, provisions scored from my last foraging expedition to 7-Eleven, when I emerged from the motel room wearing Ray-Bans and a cowboy hat and scared the 7-Eleven clerk half to death. When I pulled out my loose cash, she looked relieved that it wasn't a gun.

I have to take precautions.

They're looking for me. I am a marked man.

Where *was* I?

Finding the note?

I've been through that, correct? The note from *Benjy*, complete with postscript greetings from the mysterious Kara. Kara Bolka. Who's this *Kara* anyway? Benjy's wife? His girlfriend?

Hold on. Be patient. Soon enough you'll know who Kara Bolka is. You'll know who everyone is. Soon enough you'll know about the accident, about everything. The dead will all stand up and take a bow.

Not yet.

I need to pick up the thread.

To sew things up nicely and neatly, even professionally.

My journalism professor used to say that every reporter has one great story in them.

This is mine.

I told you about the note. I distinctly remember telling you about it.

Happy hundred birthday.

Love, Benjy.

Greetings from Kara Bolka.

Like a haiku.

Haikus may read simple, but they're infused with mystery.

Wait.

Did I mention my Miata? That it broke down?

No, not the first time, at the bowling alley.

The *second* time, four blocks away from the nursing home.

FIFTEEN

I was driving, then I wasn't.

The engine went dead, and the car lurched to the side of the street like the victim of a stroke.

I was pissed off on two counts.

No car and no air-conditioning.

It was wicked hot.

On the other hand, at least I had a chance. Something about a loose coil wire, Anna had said. I had a clue.

I lifted up the sizzling hood and looked inside with a vague sense of hope. I zeroed in on the place I'd seen Anna poking around. Sure enough, there it was—a loose wire hanging out of the fuselage.

I managed to reconnect it. I was about to shut the hood when I noticed the words written on my transmission cover. I *believe* it's a transmission cover.

Someone's finger had traced the letters through the built-up grime.

It was an SN. *Screen name*, for those of you who haven't yet joined the Internet generation.

AOL: Kkraab.

Anna had left me the modern equivalent of her phone number.

I thought that was kind of cute. Okay, more than that.

I'm not going to pretend casual indifference. I hadn't had a woman I liked like *me* for a while. It had been a long time between watering holes—a Bedouin expression.

I was parched.

When I got back home, I tried it out. I signed onto AOL, where I was known as Starreport, a screen moniker I'd taken before Ken Starr spent 80 million taxpayer dollars investigating oral sex. Also before my own actions made a derivation of *star reporter* farcical in the extreme.

I'd never bothered to change it.

The profile for Kkraab read as follows:

Name: Anna Graham.
Location: The State of Confusion and occasional Kkrabbiness.
Gender: Guess.
Marital Status: Isn't that an oxymoron?
Hobbies and Interests: I play the conundrums.
Occupation: Yes.

Her personal quote was a song lyric from one Robert Zimmerman, a.k.a. Bob Dylan: *You better start swimming or you'll sink like a stone.*

It was hard to resist a profile like that—especially her homage to one of the seminal songs of the twentieth century, a personal favorite of mine already safely ensconced in my iPod.

I checked to see if Kkraab was currently online. She wasn't.

I sent her an e-mail.

At least, I attempted to. I tried to strike the right balance between casual friendliness and raging lust. To do so in a manner that seemed remotely intelligent and witty.

I was stuck on *Hello*.

Like I said, it had been awhile. I used to be able to manufacture flirtatious banter with no trouble at all. Of course, that was back when I was manufacturing news stories. Perhaps they went hand in hand, creating fiction about other people or myself. Isn't that what people do in the gloom of bars—make up personas they hope will get someone else to like them?

Now that I wasn't making things up anymore, I was finding it difficult to construct a complete sentence to Anna.

I managed.

Hello, Anna, I wrote.

Good thing my coil wire came loose again or it might've been awhile before I saw your message.

I briefly considered whether that might've occurred to Anna as well and if she might've loosened it on purpose. No—believing that for one instant was the height of hubris.

I was hoping I would run into you again. I was considering driving to Santa Monica and taking a seat on the Third Street Promenade until you passed by. Are you still in town? If so, I'd love to buy you a drink. Or an island. Whatever it takes.

After I sent it, I thought it smacked of desperation.

Too late. There might be a way to cancel a sent e-mail, but I didn't know it.

It reminded me of high school. Blabbing something into the phone and instantly regretting it.

Then again, maybe she was desperate, too.

There was a lot of desperation going around these days.

BOWLING NIGHT.

Muhammed Alley was unusually crowded. Unusually noisy, too—even for a bowling alley. For some reason the women's league had been forced to switch nights.

Sam began the evening by propositioning me about buying life insurance again. I declined again.

Seth was another matter. He was acting weirdly hyper— a 2-year-old in dire need of Ritalin. Every time he threw a strike, he gave an impromptu rendition of "Who Let the Dogs Out"—the guttural choral part. *Ooho-ooh-ooh-ooh-ooh*, accompanied by a series of Lil' Kim–like pelvic thrusts.

Some of the women bowling four lanes down froze in mid-throw to watch him, as if they couldn't quite believe what they were witnessing.

I questioned Marv about my car problems.

"Coil wire, huh? Bring it in and I'll take a look," he said. "Gratis."

"Thanks."

"No problemo."

Marv was famously low-key, the kind of person who might actually watch grass grow and get a kick out of it. A demeanor you'd want at the other end of a suicide hotline. If I ever contemplated offing myself again, I'd call Marv.

Now I was contemplating other things.

The accident investigation was going nowhere. When Sheriff Swenson returned my call—after several days—he'd greeted my news about Cleveland having no record of Ed

Crannell with a barely suppressed yawn. It was an *accident*, he reminded me. Meaning, who *cared* about finding Ed Crannell?

There was also the intriguing but ultimately unfathomable note from Benjy.

And there was Anna.

She'd actually gotten back to me.

I'll take the island, she wrote. *Palm trees and warm water preferable. While you're shopping, I'll take a Cosmo.*

It was kind of pathetic how happy I was to receive three lines. As if she'd whispered the three little *words*. I immediately e-mailed her back. We were meeting tomorrow night at Violetta's Emporium, the only decent Italian restaurant in town.

I was surprised to realize I was feeling magnanimous and even happy—at least hopeful. But then, happiness is reality divided by expectations, and expectations had clearly risen.

When I noticed Seth being confronted by two pissed-off men, I was initially ready to offer them a beer.

Something had evidently escaped my attention. I was scoring tonight; I was contemplating scoring tomorrow night. Two men were yelling at Seth for some unknown reason.

"Let's take a walk outside," one of them was saying.

Seth was resisting that suggestion.

"Go fuck yourselves," he exclaimed. He was holding his bowling ball in his right hand, swinging it loosely up and down as if considering using it as a weapon.

Sam was attempting to intercede.

"Let's all calm down, shall we?"

"Keep out of it, fatty," one of the men said. "Fuckwit here insulted our ladies."

Insulted?

Then I understood. Seth had been doing the dog thing and one of the women objected. Seth's impromptu wailings sounded like the epithets construction workers hurl at passing women in New York. Seth could've simply told them they were mistaken, that his yells of jubilation weren't directed at anyone but the universe.

This was Seth.

"Those *bow-wows*?" he asked. "You ought to put a muzzle on them."

That was all it took for one of the men to shove Seth into the ball retrieval. He came back swinging.

As I sprang up to play peacemaker, I could see BJ lumbering out from behind the bar. It appeared he had a Louisville Slugger in his hand. This had all the makings of an ugly incident—a banner headline across tomorrow's *Littleton Journal*.

"Hey fellas," I said. "This is a bowling alley."

"Thanks, asshole," the bigger one muttered without actually looking at me. "I thought it was the public library."

Seth had awkwardly swung his ball in the direction of the bigger man's head and badly missed. His momentum had carried him sideways into the scoring table. It occurred to me that five or six beers had probably taken their toll on Seth's general equilibrium. Bowling ball or no bowling ball, he was a sitting duck.

The man smashed Seth in the side of the face. Seth went down hard. A woman screamed from somewhere in the alley—probably *not* one of the women who'd sent these two idiots out to defend her honor.

I managed to grab the closer one's arm—he might've been physically less imposing than his friend, but I still felt a generous amount of muscle beneath his bowling shirt.

He jerked around to confront me, his right hand back and balled into a fist. I felt a crackling jolt of adrenaline, similar to the effect I used to get from the stepped-on coke I'd begun inhaling during my last excruciating days in New York. I ducked as his fist skittered over my left ear. Everyone seemed to be surging to our alley, mostly just to gawk, but some of them looking as if they had an old-fashioned barroom brawl in mind.

Crack!

BJ's baseball bat slammed down on the scoring table, sending one and a half Miller High Lifes flying into the air.

A generous amount landed on the seriously pissed-off man I was holding on to for dear life.

Some of it got in his eyes; he cursed, squinted, then covered his face with his free hand. I used his momentary blindness to trap him in a semblance of a bear hug—more Yogi Bear than grizzly.

Seth had made it back to an upright position, frozen in a boxing stance of dubious merit. Everyone seemed to be waiting for something.

Maybe for the man holding the baseball bat over his head.

"You don't want to be doing that here," BJ said in a remarkably calm voice.

No one ventured a counter-opinion, including the man I was hugging like a long-lost friend.

I smelled a mixture of sweat and aftershave. I slowly let go. Aside from stepping back and flashing me a halfway murderous look, he made no effort to resume hostilities.

Seth was still bobbing and weaving.

"He was woofing at my girl," Seth's attacker said, obviously feeling a need to explain. It might've been his appearance—Jerry Springer miscreant, "Why I Can't Stop Beating People Up"—a mostly shaven head with a Judas Priest tattoo garishly displayed on his right forearm.

"He was just woofing," I said. "Honestly. That's him. He gets boisterous."

Seth didn't look appreciative of my effort to defend him. It was possible he didn't know what *boisterous* meant and was wondering if I was accusing him of something embarrassing.

"There you go," BJ said, still holding the forty-ounce bat at chest level. "No harm, no foul," switching sports in an effort to reach for the appropriate idiom. "I think you tough guys should call it a night."

I believed his *tough guys* comment was sarcastic.

"Hey," Sam said, "why don't we all shake hands?"

He was trying to be civilized about it; maybe after we all made up, he was going to try to sell them some life insurance.

"C'mon," he said, seemingly undeterred that no one had taken him up on his suggestion. "What do you say?"

Not much. The guy who'd punched Seth in the face snorted derisively, turned his back, and simply strolled away.

Sam flushed and turned to the other guy, tendering his slightly wilting olive branch. Still no takers. The guy shook

93

his head as if Sam were a moron child, then followed his buddy down the lane.

It was about then that I saw him.

I was watching the two guys make their way down the alley, to collect the *ladies* Seth had grievously offended, I suppose. A few men patted them on the shoulders, whispered words of encouragement at their retreating backs.

I knew one of them.

The last time I saw this person, he was holding a plumbing tool in his hand. Or not a plumbing tool. Maybe just something to punch a hole in the wall and pry off a phone-jack cover. Staring at me with those muted features, as if he'd somehow missed his final trimester as a fetus. I could swear he was smiling.

I felt slightly nauseated.

I didn't step forward, or step back, or yell for the police.

I turned to Seth as if eliciting silent support. When I turned back, the plumber was gone.

I know. It sounds as if I were hallucinating.

I wasn't.

He was there, then he wasn't there, just long enough to smile in my direction and disappear.

I hustled over to a table where two middle-aged couples in matching bowling shirts were snacking on greasy fries and chili dogs.

"The guy who was just standing here—did you see where he went?" I asked them.

They looked wary. Also confused. *What* guy who was just *where*, their faces said.

"Who?" One of the women finally asked.

"The man who was standing by your table . . ."

94

"You mean the man you were fighting with?" the woman said. "He's over there."

"No. Not him. The guy who whispered something to him when he walked by."

"Whispered something to *who*?" one of the men asked. He looked kind of eager for me to take BJ's suggestion and leave the bowling alley. Or at least leave them alone.

"Look, I'm a reporter for the paper here. . . . I just want to know who that guy . . ."

"We don't know what guy you're talking about." The woman again, looking almost sorry for me.

I stopped, scanned the alley. Most people had resumed bowling after the night's entertainment break, something they would talk to their coworkers about over morning coffee. *And then he picked up a bowling ball and . . .*

I dashed into the men's bathroom. A high school kid was busy admiring his tongue ring in the mirror. That's it.

When I finally made it outside, the plumber wasn't there, either.

Just the remnants of my bowling team.

Seth was telling Sam and Marv how he was going to get even with the *pussy* who'd sucker-punched him in the face.

Just you wait, he promised. *It's a done deal.*

SIXTEEN

After my story about the moving homecoming of Lowell Beaumont passed muster, after it earned me a verbal hug from he-who-must-be-pleased, not to mention scattered praise from the peanut gallery of copy-desk drudges, I did it again.

I wrote a piece about an American soldier of fortune who sold his services to the highest bidder—including a Taliban warlord—leaving him in the awkward position of battling his own countrymen.

The piece was alarming, dramatic, and even sad.

It just wasn't in any way, shape, or form true.

I'd never met this soldier of fortune.

He was an amalgam of different people I'd talked to, read about, or possibly dreamed up.

No matter.

It went over like a charm.

Other pieces followed, one after another, a dizzying anthology of truly creative writing.

A group of out-of-work Hollywood actors who loaned themselves out to the Russian mob for various cons, impersonating everyone from computer-parts salespeople to temple cantors.

A Republican evangelical think tank that asked what Jesus would do on every major policy issue.

A game of Auto Tag sweeping the nation's highways—cars tapping each other's bumpers at eighty miles per hour, till the loser crashed and burned.

A secret society of pyromaniacs who traded videos of their greatest hits—forest fires, block burnings, gas station flash fires—over the Web.

There was something exhilarating about it, of course.

Creating stories out of thin air. Giving them the black-and-white imprimatur of fact. Telling bigger and bigger fibs and holding my breath till I saw if I'd gotten away with it. It was like betting the house on every turn of the wheel.

It was, in a way, addictive.

So was the resultant praise and clamor for more of them. Even the jealousy it kicked up among my peers was addictive.

After all, they were jealous of me.

Of course, one of those jealous reporters ended up taking me out to Keats and pumping me full of Patrón tequila. All the while pumping me for something far more valuable—the fascinating details concerning my series of scintillating scoops. Especially my latest one—red-hot and read all about it—the abortion-clinic–bombing pediatrician. As I remember, he spent a lot of time that night scrounging for details: how did I meet this doctor? Where? How did I figure out the doctor was feeding me anagrams—for his place of birth, his city of residence?

Okay. Maybe my drinking partner wasn't jealous—maybe he was simply being diligent, protecting his chosen profession from what he perceived as a dangerous polluter.

He tipped off a certain editor, of course.

I should've known when he requested my notes.

Not that it hadn't happened before. I'd become remarkably adept at conjuring up voluminous notes whenever they were needed.

Sometimes they were. Someone—real as opposed to made up—would complain that what I wrote never happened, that they'd never been interviewed by me, never laid eyes on me, never even heard of me. It didn't hurt that I'd portrayed the majority of these people in an unflattering light. It was fairly easy to attribute their motives to anger, to the simple desire to discredit their muck-raking accuser. *Of course he says he never heard of me*, I'd say, dismissing their accusations as if they were hardly worth the trouble. *What would you do if I'd just exposed you in the paper?*

It helped that we live in a plausible denial world.

Just pick up today's news. Everyone denies everything.

It was taken out of context. It was misguided, misheard, misunderstood, misrepresented, or just made up.

Accountability is out; ask our president if he's found any WMDs lying around Iraq lately. I was a creature of our times, someone who otherwise couldn't have existed.

Which is not in any way an excuse.

No.

I might've scored sympathy points long ago by going the Oprah route and dredging up my childhood for national TV. Sprinkling my public absolution with select anecdotes from the Valle childhood album.

One anecdote, at least.

After all, these days the only thing more popular than denying your sins is going on television and confessing them. It's okay to do bad stuff, America keeps reminding us, as long as you've got a reason.

I resisted that temptation.

I still resist it.
Speaking of temptation.
This is what it looks like.

LIKE ANNA.

We were sitting in Violetta's Emporium, the two of us.

Our table came complete with glazed netted candle that threw a soft, flickering light on the remarkable face sitting across from me. Not that it was in any particular need of mood lighting. Not with those eyes.

The table was cozy enough to make it hard to avoid touching knees. As if I wanted to avoid them, as if I didn't do everything within my power to brush against her knees again and again and again. Two years ago, on my cross-country journey into ignominy, I stopped at a resort in Arizona and blew my last remaining cash on a hot-stone massage. That's what Anna's naked knees felt like— smooth hot stones sending shivers of fire shooting down my legs. And in the opposite direction.

I know. Mush, of the most egregious kind.

I'm simply trying to paint you a picture, to sit down with my inner police sketch artist and re-create for you what hit me.

We ordered matching pastas, though I did little more than move the vermicelli around my plate.

Women who've had the misfortune of going on first dates with me generally came away with the misconception that I wasn't much of an eater.

I can eat with the best of them.

It's simply that my hunger for one thing generally takes precedence over my hunger for another. I'm perpetually famished for *love* and *approval*—this according to Dr. Payne, who tried mightily to delve into the underlying reasons for my sociopathic behavior.

You had an absent father and an alcoholic and abusive mother, he concluded, *so what else would you do but seek massive and extreme pats on the back?*

Sounded sensible to me.

After all, it would help account for why so many first dates failed to materialize into second ones. Apparently neediness wasn't an attractive quality in a man. The one woman who did find it endearing married me. She lived to regret it.

Anna and I made small talk.

She asked me about working for a newspaper.

"I took journalism classes in college," she said, with a small pout meant to convey, I think, her ineptitude at it. "What, when, where, how . . . what's the fifth one? Anyways, it wasn't me. I'm not an *observer*. I lack objectivity. I flunked."

"Okay, you're not a reporter. What do you do? It didn't say in your profile."

"Sure it did. I play the conundrums—remember?"

"Yeah. That was cute."

"Ya think?"

"Yeah, I think."

"I work for a nonprofit organization," she said. "Very Berkeley, even though it's in downtown Santa Monica."

"Oh? A nonprofit organization for *what*?"

"The usual. Clean planet, clean politics, dirty movies, the stuff near and dear to a blue stater's heart."

She ran her middle finger around the edge of the candle

100

glass, catching a small drip of hot wax, then holding it up to the light, wincing. "Ever try it?"

"Try what?"

"Hot wax." She giggled, took another sip of her Chianti.

"Try it how? You mean, like have it *dripped* on me?"

"Oh yeah."

"Does dripping it on myself count?"

"I don't know. Were you practicing self-abuse at the time?"

"I was filling bottle caps for scully. I was 7."

"Then I'd say it doesn't count. What's *scully*?"

"A New York street game. You fill bottle caps with crayon wax, draw this chalk square on the sidewalk, and try to knock the other guy out of the game—it's like bocci with soda caps."

"New York, huh?"

"Yeah, New York—you mean you didn't spot the accent?"

"I thought it was Lithuanian. Stupid me."

I wanted to tell her that she wasn't stupid at all. Even though I knew she was just being funny. I wanted to tell her that she was the most dazzling, most special, most alluring woman I'd ever seen. Of course, that's something I'd told other women at other Violetta's Emporiums. I had the unfortunate habit of falling desperately in love after two drinks. Just seeking *massive and extreme pats on the back*, Dr. Payne.

"What's a New Yorker doing *here*?" she asked.

"Working on my tan."

"No, really. Why *are* you here?"

"I needed a break." It was one of those answers that a

government commission might term deceptive, though not actual perjury.

"From *what*?" she asked, not letting go. Her cheeks glowed with matching wine-blooms, crème brûlée topped with raspberry swirl.

"I had a rough time on my last newspaper job," I said. I needed to change the subject.

"So, do you have a boyfriend?" I asked.

"Boyfriend? What's *that*?"

I felt a sudden surge of sweet, seductive hope. "Been awhile?"

"A long while. I'm married."

"Oh."

Hope said *see ya*, exploded into flames like that car on Highway 45.

"Don't look so depressed," she said. "I'm seriously thinking of dumping him."

"You are?"

"Well, he's living with a 24-year-old Pilates instructor. So, yeah, it has crossed my mind."

"So, are you going to get a divorce?" I asked.

"I don't know. Eventually. Sure. It's not that easy. We have a son."

"Really? How old?"

"He's 4."

"What's his name?"

"Cody. Can I be a boringly cliché mom and show you his picture?"

"Do I have to be boringly cliché and *ooh* and *ahh* over it?"

"Yeah."

"Okay."

She pulled out her wallet and held it open for me. "Go ahead—*ooh*."

A blond munchkin pumping away on one of those toddler pedal bikes, with Anna hovering right behind.

"What's that thing you're holding on to?" I asked her.

"You haven't seen the newest contraption for instilling self-confidence and independence in your preschooler?"

"Guess not."

"It's a push-and-pedal. Your kid pedals while you push. They think they're charging down the open road like Dennis Hopper in *Easy Rider*, but you're the one really steering. Dirty trick, huh?"

"Yeah. Can I get one?"

"The next time I hit Toys 'R' Us, it's yours," she said. "So, what about you?"

"Me what?"

"Single? Married? Divorced? Divorcing?"

"Number three."

"Ahh. What's it like? Getting a divorce?"

I hesitated just long enough for Anna to apologize for being nosy.

I answered her anyway.

"It was pretty much my fault. I kind of fucked it up."

I remembered something. I didn't want to—someone starts talking about *their* failed marriage and the toxic memory drifts over you like secondhand smoke. My sweet and stalwart bride going out for some Starbucks and never coming back. Muttering something about *vanilla frappuccino* and *needing to figure this thing out* just before she went through the front door of our apartment. This thing being

103

the very public fraud I'd perpetuated on a major American newspaper—on my marriage too, I guess, since she'd said *I do* to a bona fide investigative journalist who wasn't. My ex, an architect specializing in high-rises, tended to see life in structural terms—the blueprint for a good relationship being a foundation built on trust. I'd put too many cracks in the retaining walls, and the structure would not hold.

"Sorry it didn't work out," Anna said.

"Me too."

I asked her why she just hadn't given me her phone number that night in the parking lot.

"I did. Kinda."

"You wrote your screen name on my *transmission*. How'd you know I'd even look?"

"I didn't. But if you did look, maybe it's because you were supposed to."

"Like fate?"

"Maybe. Your engine's beat to crap—I mean, have you ever changed your oil even *once*? I thought you'd be under that hood again. By the way—I wrote it on your carburetor, not your transmission."

I laughed and she laughed back and when I reached for my wine glass, I knocked it over onto her lap.

"Shit," I said.

We both sprang up, Anna trying to shake off the excess wine, while I grabbed for a napkin, dipped it in water, and lamely wiped at the lap of her clearly ruined dress.

Which is when she did something kind of lovely. Other than *not* calling me Shrek and storming out of the restaurant.

She said: "If you wanted to sexually assault me, all you had to do was ask."

SEVENTEEN

Nate informed me that *some lady* had called.

He swirled his finger by his ear, the universal gesture for *certifiably off the wall*.

The reason Nate had answered the call from this crazy person was that I'd overslept and wasn't there.

I'd woken up with what felt like a stupid grin on my face. It was confirmed when I stared in the shower-fogged mirror and didn't see Mr. Dour staring back. Instead it was Mr. Stupid, back from enforced obscurity. I'd kind of missed him.

When I waltzed into the office, Norma took off her glasses and squinted.

"You look different," she said.

"Who was it?" I asked Nate the Skate.

He was on his cell, probably conversing with his nudist girlfriend.

"I don't know. Her number's on your desk."

I found the number—*Mrs. Flaherty*. Probably wondering what progress I'd made, which was zero. I felt a sudden pang of pity for the lonely downtrodden of this world, a social stratum I'd once called home.

I didn't call her back immediately. No.

I savored my morning coffee, blessed the poor Colombians who'd toiled in the bean fields in order to bring it to me. I suppose if you get enough love and approval, you begin spreading the excess.

To Hinch, for example.

He came out of his office with a vacant look in his eyes. His gray stubble had reached near-beard level. His wrinkled shirt was partially untucked.

"How's your wife, Hinch?"

Norma began shuffling some papers on her desk.

"What?" Hinch stared at me as if I were a Jehovah's Witness who'd shown up at his front door on his day off.

"I was just curious how your wife is doing."

Suddenly Hinch's eyes became red-rimmed. Just like that. First bland and unfocused, then harbingers of a coming maelstrom. Call it the Aurora Dam Flood Two.

He clumsily wiped at one eye, looked down at his shoes, murmured something under his breath.

"What, Hinch? I'm sorry, I didn't hear you."

"How my wife is doing . . . how my wife is doing is none of your business," he said. He didn't say it meanly. More sadly.

"I'm sorry. I hope . . . well, that everything, you know . . ." I said, letting my stab at consolation stumble into incoherence.

Hinch went back to his office.

There was an embarrassing silence. Nate, who'd held his phone call in abeyance, resumed with a whispered *got to get off, baby*. Norma peeked at me sideways and sighed.

"She's back in the hospital, Tom," she said softly. "God knows, it doesn't look good."

"Sorry. I didn't know."

My expansive mood had pretty much dissipated. I thought I might as well call Mrs. Flaherty back.

"You want to talk to him?" Mrs. Flaherty asked me after I said hello.

"Talk to whom, Mrs. Flaherty?"

"Dennis."

"*Dennis*? What are you talking about?"

I should've known what she was talking about. *My son came back to say hey*, 100-year-old Belinda had told me.

It was getting to be a trend.

WE HAD A NICE CONVERSATION.

Dennis and me.

It was a tad one-sided, since Dennis Flaherty wasn't big on conversing, and seemed to be speaking underwater. I slapped the receiver against the desk in an effort to clear the foggy reception. It wasn't the reception; it was Dennis.

"It's the drugs," Mrs. Flaherty told me after Dennis relinquished the phone to her and went to his childhood bedroom to nap. "They make him sleepy."

What drugs were those?

The ones the VA psychiatric hospital used to keep Dennis docile and happy.

"Do you know you were in a fatal car crash?" I asked him after I'd introduced myself.

"Uh-huh," he answered, in a lugubrious monotone that would never waver.

"How do you think that happened?"

"Dunno."

"Someone had your wallet."

107

"Yeah."

"Dennis, you understand what I'm telling you? You were *buried*."

"Right."

"Where did you lose your wallet?"

"Dunno. On the street."

"On the street? You mean, you were *living* on the street?"

"Yeah."

"Well, when was the last time you saw it?"

"Dunno. Didn't have it in the hospital."

"What hospital?"

"VA."

"You were in a veterans' hospital?"

"Yeah."

"What were you in the hospital for?"

"My head's not right."

"Your head's not right. What's that mean? You have . . . mental problems?"

"Yeah."

"Were you ever in Littleton, California, Dennis?"

"*Where*?"

"You weren't in California a week ago, right?"

"Huh?"

"Never mind. You understand someone died in the accident. It wasn't you—it was somebody else who, for some strange reason, had your wallet."

"Yeah."

"But you don't know how he got hold of it. How you lost it? Somewhere on the street, you think?"

Nate had strolled over to my desk as if following the

tantalizing aroma of moo goo gai pan. Even half of the conversation must've been kind of irresistible. Someone dead was alive and kicking. How often did that happen?

Dennis hadn't answered my last question. It sounded like he was snoring.

"Dennis? Dennis, are you there?"

"Huh?"

"I said, you think you lost your wallet on the street?"

"I'm tired. Oh man, I'm tired."

"Just a minute, few more questions, okay?"

"What time is it? Is it nighttime?"

"It's 1 in the afternoon, Dennis," I said, allowing for the difference in time zones. "Just a couple more questions." I didn't have any more questions. Dennis was drugged up and stupid. He'd had his wallet and then he didn't. It had eventually shown up in the pocket of an accident victim burned beyond recognition.

Dennis must've passed Mrs. Flaherty the phone; the next voice I heard was hers.

"You were right, Tom," she whispered. "After we talked, I actually went to church. First time in forever. I lit a candle. I prayed Dennis was still alive and would come walking through the door. He did."

"How long was he in the hospital?"

"Who cares? It's a *miracle*, don't you see? I have my son back."

"Yeah, it's a miracle." I took a second to motion a hovering Nate away from my desk. "Can I call you back, Mrs. Flaherty? I may have some other questions."

"Of course, Tom. You can call me anytime you'd like. Thank you."

"For what? I didn't do anything. Your son wasn't dead. Someone stole his wallet or found it. Whoever was driving that car. Dennis would've come walking back into your house whether I'd called you or not."

"Oh really?" she said. "I know better."

EIGHTEEN

I resisted the temptation to enlighten anyone.

I kept the inquisitive-looking Nate the Skate out of the loop.

I walked outside after borrowing a smoke from Norma, who chided me for revisiting a forsworn habit. *Just one*, I told her, *for old times' sake*.

I lit up under the overhang that sheltered Foo Yang Chinese takeout from the broiling sun as Mr. Yang's 13-year-old daughter stared at me listlessly through the dust-coated window.

The jolt of nicotine gave me an immediate buzz.

The accident.

Two people had collided on that road.

Dennis Flaherty and Ed Crannell.

Only they weren't Dennis Flaherty and Ed Crannell.

There was no record of an Ed Crannell. Dennis Flaherty was demonstrably alive.

Let's play editor.

Pretend the story—the story so far—has been placed on this editor's desk. You know *which* editor too, the one wearing bifocals and a world-weary expression he's justifiably earned. This particular story's been offered up for approval by a journalist who's seen better days, okay, whose reputation is less than crap, who's literally disgraced his profession.

Let's watch the editor wearily pull out his tooth-marked pencil as I tell him that Dennis Flaherty was never in that car.

Okay, he says, *so that doctor was right. The dead man was black. He stole Dennis's wallet, found it, bought it from some street hustler. Anyhow, he ended up with it. So what?*

You're forgetting about the *other* car. Nobody's heard of Ed Crannell.

So the man lied about his identity. Ed Crannell lied about who he was. People lie about their identity all the time. Maybe he was driving with a suspended license. Maybe he had a record. Maybe he owes back alimony in the state of California. Or maybe he is Ed Crannell, just not a pharmaceutical salesman. And he doesn't live in Cleveland. Maybe all he did was lie about that. It happens.

There were no skid marks.

Haven't you been listening? Ed Crannell lied. You're familiar with lying, aren't you, Tom? The accident was his fault. He was changing radio stations, chatting on his cell. He was admiring the scenery, daydreaming, glazing over. Next thing he knew, he'd caused an accident. He was the only survivor, so he concocted a story—the other car drifted into his lane, the other driver noticed him too late, jammed on the brakes. No one jammed on the brakes. He made it up.

The editor is clearly smirking at me. Worse. He has that tired, defeated look you offer in the face of a habitual liar.

Don't insult my intelligence, the look says. Enough.

It's not just the accident, I offer tentatively.

He sighs, shakes his weary head.

It's not just the accident, I repeat myself. It's Belinda.

Belinda, the editor says. *Oh boy.*

She said her dead son came back to say hello. I know, she was 100 years old. She was maybe dotty. Only there was that note from Benjy. *Happy hundred birthday.* Mr. Birdwell said no one had visited Belinda, but Benjy had. What other Benjamin would've come and written her that note?

Her son died, the editor says. *You understand what died means, right, Tom?*

Mrs. Flaherty's son died, too. Only he's alive.

Have you even checked to see if there's another Benjy in the home? It's New York all over again, isn't it? The editor has clearly had it with me. He's pointing to the door; he wants me gone. *There's no connection. You're offering me two things with no connection to each other.*

And then I say it. I don't know why I didn't say it before. I do now. I take my worn pencil and place it against the place mat in the Acropolis Diner. I draw a shaky line from Belinda's dead son to the incinerated driver—to *him*.

My father smiles, reaches across the table to tousle my hair.

Good boy.

I know what you're thinking, Dr. Payne.

My dad. My editor.

I'm not listening.

113

NINETEEN

"I suppose I'll have to call Iowa and ask them to exhume the corpse."

Sheriff Swenson sounded as if he were going over his shopping list. I'll have to pick up some milk and margarine, grab some frozen french fries and six cans of Bumble Bee tuna, and, oh yeah, call Iowa and ask them to dig up the body from whatever cemetery they'd buried the fake Dennis in. That is, if they're interested, which he himself clearly wasn't.

I was back in the sterile air-conditioned confines of the Littleton sheriff's office. Not like an urban police station at all, more like an insurance office in your typical neighborhood mall. Everything neat, tidy, and prefabricated.

No crime had been committed. That was pretty much Swenson's point of view. No crime had been committed, at least as far he could tell. Maybe stealing Dennis Flaherty's wallet was a crime, but that would be out of his jurisdiction, wouldn't it? Maybe the accident hadn't happened the way Crannell related it, but it was still an accident. Not a crime. And if Crannell had lied about his identity, okay, score one for him. It didn't warrant a task force.

"What are you so interested in?" he asked me, not as if

he wanted an answer, more as if he was dismissing me so he could get back to more important police matters like issuing parking citations.

I didn't enlighten him about the note I'd discovered in Belinda's picture frame.

"Two people are in an accident and neither one turns out to be whom they were supposed to be. That doesn't bother you?"

"Not really."

Maybe it didn't bother him because it was me who was asking him about it.

"Isn't there a car dealership opening you can go write about?" he said.

Yeah, that was probably it.

"I saw the plumber," I said.

Sheriff Swenson untangled his legs, which were propped up on his desk in a physical attitude of *I'm in charge here*. There's something belittling about staring at the soles of someone's boots—the whole point, I guess.

"Did you now?" he said. "Where?"

"At Muhammed Alley. The other night."

"Uh-huh. You sure about this?"

"Yeah. I'm sure."

"Now *that* I am interested in. Why didn't you call me?"

"He got away."

"*Got away*? What's that mean? Did you chase him or something?"

"No. He was just there, and then he wasn't. When he saw me notice him, he took off."

"He took off. Great. And he looked pretty much like the description you gave us last time?"

"Yeah—he's kind of hard to miss. Have there been any others?" I asked.

"Any other what?"

"Break-ins."

He didn't answer me. "You should've called me, Lucas. You know that?"

"Yes."

"Okay, fine. If he shows up in your bowling foursome next time, you'll let me know, okay?"

"Sure." I turned to leave, then stopped. "Do you know anything about the flood?"

"What flood?"

"The Aurora Dam Flood. Back in the fifties."

"What about it?"

"Well . . . did anyone who was supposed to have died in it . . . were they ever found later? People that were counted in the original death toll, but somehow survived?"

For a moment, I thought he was going to say yes.

Say something other than: "The Aurora flood was a little before my time. What the fuck would I know about it?"

But that's what he said.

Just before picking up the phone, an unspoken invitation for me to leave.

I ASKED NORMA IF JOHN WREN HAD LEFT ANY OF HIS NOTES behind.

When I'd asked Hinch if I could do a story on the fiftieth anniversary of the Aurora Dam Flood, he said good luck, my predecessor already tried.

"Nope," Norma said. "If he did, they would've been thrown out by now," Norma said.

"You sure?"

"Ninety-nine point nine percent." Norma was attempting to read the latest issue of *Us*, *read* admittedly being generous for a newsweekly sporting a wedding-veiled Britney Spears on its cover. *Oops, she did it again*—this week's bouncy headline.

"Well, if they weren't thrown out, where would they be?"

"*Gawwd* . . . can't you let an executive assistant read her trash in peace?"

"I'd like to, but this is an executive assistant kind of job."

Norma put Britney face down. She shuffled over to the file cabinet, which doubled as the coffee percolator table and fax bin. Norma had been married to a church choir leader who'd absconded with the church organist; she'd heard they'd ordered *Hymn* and *Hers* bath towels. She was just this side of middle age now—or sometimes that side, depending on whether she was in one of her dieting and exercise phases or not. Currently she was on the South Beach Diet and doing aerobics to Andre 3000 and friends. She opened the third drawer and began rummaging around.

"Nope," she said. "Just empty folders, like I told you." She'd withdrawn a handful of worn-looking manila folders that looked conspicuously bereft of anything.

"Can I see them?"

"There's nothing in them, Tom."

"Humor me."

She dropped them on my laptop.

"You know, that Spears kid is some kind of dopey."

The folders had various subject matters written on the tabs. Wren's handwriting, I knew, having seen enough of his leftovers stuck in various places around my house.

A litany of the mostly banal: *World's Biggest Hula Hoop Collection, July 4th Parade, Cow Punching Contest*. They could've been on my assignment list for the coming year.

There were exceptions. A folder labeled: *Veteran's story*.

This folder wasn't empty, not entirely—when I opened it, two pictures fell out.

The Vietnam memorial in Washington, D.C.

One was a wide shot: that black granite V that somehow manages to be achingly graceful and starkly imposing at the same time. The other was shot closer up—you could see the depressing roll call of the dead chiseled into the stone.

That article I'd found in my house.

Sad story.

The traumatized vet who'd wandered into Littleton one October afternoon, staying long enough to establish that he had no known residence, no family to claim him, and a name he'd appropriated from an MIA he'd served with in the deltas of Mekong. *"Who's Eddie Bronson?"* An ex-Vietnam grunt wracked with survivor's guilt—all Wren really managed to answer before the unknown soldier was hustled out of the town gazebo and institutionalized. Wren had used the sorry incident to craft a moving little piece about the debilitating neglect faced by veterans of the war America would just as soon forget.

"Norma, did Wren go visit the Vietnam memorial? When he did the story on that vet?"

"Not on Hinch's dime," she said. "Why?"

"He must've. He took some pictures."

"Uh-huh." Norma had made it back to her desk and immediately reimmersed herself in the lives of the rich and silly.

I stared at the close-up shot. *Eddie Bronson* clearly legible—the MIA name the vet had taken as his own, resting on a bed of black granite, even if his bones were rotting away in some tunnel in Chu Lai.

Wren's Vietnam vet story, while nicely written, hadn't been exactly appreciated. This, according to Norma. For one thing, Hinch believed that small-town newspaper reporters should stick to small-town news. *Mall openings*, for example. For another thing, some of the debilitating neglect the vet was experiencing had come courtesy of the good people of Littleton, who hadn't taken kindly to a disheveled and half-crazy vagrant setting up living quarters in the town gazebo and calling it home.

This all coincided with Wren going a little half-crazy himself. Maybe all that animosity got to him. Or the Santa Anas blew through town. Or the blistering ever-present heat finally baked his brain.

Whatever it was, his turn at serious and socially relevant reporting seemed to have given him delusions of grandeur. Mall openings were for hacks. He'd immediately submerged himself in a retrospective exposé on the Aurora Dam Flood. I could tell from the date carefully written on the third folder, simply labeled: *Flood*. One week after the story on Eddie Bronson.

This folder was empty.

"You think he took them with him? *Norma . . . ?*"

"Took what?" she said, peeking out from behind Britney's silicone-enhanced breast.

119

"His notes. His *files*. You think he took them with him, or did you throw them out after he left?"

"I don't remember," she said. "He wasn't exactly operating on all cylinders at that point. Know what I mean? He locked himself in here one night and howled at the moon."

"He *howled at the moon*?"

"Just an expression."

"Right. What *was* he doing in here?"

"God knows. All I know is they had to call the sheriff to get him out."

"Okay. When did he leave town, Norma?"

"The next day—I'm not kidding. He must've been embarrassed by the whole thing. God knows the man needed a change of scenery."

He'd gone somewhere north, I remember Norma telling me. The details were kind of hazy.

"He leave a number, Norma?"

"Number?"

"Yeah. The digits you dial on the phone when you want to speak to someone. A number."

She leafed through her desktop Rolodex. "Nope." Then she cocked her head and said: "Hold on."

She went into Hinch's office, where I heard the sound of drawers being opened and closed. She reappeared bearing a piece of wrinkled paper.

"Thank you, Norma," she said.

"Thank you, Norma."

John Wren's last known phone number. Judging by the area code, Northern California. I wrote it down on the back of one of the photos and stuck it in my wallet.

Wren's answering-machine message sounded like some-one who was already feeling put-upon, even though he hadn't actually been made to answer the phone.

We're out fishing, but if you'd like to leave a message, fine.

"Hi, this is Tom Valle. I took your position at the *Littleton Journal*." *I took your house as well*, I could've added. "I'd like to ask you about a story you were working on before you left. Could you please call me back?"

I left my work and cell numbers.

Then I called Anna.

She was due to leave tomorrow. Back to Santa Monica. We were supposed to go out again and I wanted to confirm the where and when like any responsible journalist should.

She picked up on the fourth ring.

"Hey," I said.

"Hey."

"So we're on for tonight?"

"Of course. Didn't we make plans?"

"Yeah, sure. Just wanted to be sure they were still on."

"I would've called you if there was a problem."

"Okay. Great. So we're still on then." Mr. Stupid, meet Mr. Needy. "*Where* are we meeting again?"

"Violetta's. Just like we said two days ago. You do have a touch of ADD." At least she sounded friendly when she said it.

"Just confirming," I said.

"Oh, one thing."

"Yes?"

"We're ordering *white* wine," she said.

"Yeah, I'm really sorry about that. Is your dress ruined?"

"It'll be fine. I use a dry cleaner that's absolutely

121

scorched earth on stains. If Monica Lewinsky had given them that blue frock, there never would've been any impeachment hearings."

I laughed, then immediately wondered if her reference to seminal stains had some kind of invitation inherent in it. *All you had to do was ask*, she'd said when I wiped at her dress.

There was a brief silence, as if her allusion to sex had consumed all available air, then I asked her how her father was doing. I'd previously skirted this issue, thinking that when she wanted to talk about it, she would. But its absence was starting to feel conspicuous.

"The same," she said. "Thank you for asking."

"Your mom still around?"

"Yeah. They'd divorced, though. So it's kind of just me."

"That's tough."

"Oh, I don't know. It's what you do for someone you love, right? He's my dad. I'd do anything for him. How about you?"

"Me?"

"Your parents? Still alive?"

"No. They're both gone."

Gone. A label my father earned while I was still playing scully on the streets of Queens. He'd come back once, before the funeral, and asked me if I'd like to take a ride on the fire truck the way I used to. We'd gone around the block and parked in the shadow of St. Anthony's church. *What happened, Tommy?* Sitting next to me in the cab but not really looking at me. Looking at a picture of the four of us tucked into the windshield. *What happened?*

"Sisters, brothers?" Anna asked me.

"No. I . . . not anymore."

"What's that mean?"

"I had a brother. He died. A long time ago."

"Oh. I'm terribly sorry. What happened?"

"Nothing. He just died. It was an accident."

"Oh God. How old was he?"

"He was 6."

"Jesus, that's terrible. I guess you don't like talking about it."

"No, it's just . . . it's been a long time. . . ."

"Sure, I understand."

No you don't, I thought.

Some things are beyond understanding.

TWENTY

Kara Bernstein.
Kara Betland.
Kara Bolinsky.
Kara Brill.

I used the half hour I had between showering and shaving and combing and recombing my hair and spritzing on some ancient Stetson for Men then washing it off because it smelt like old leather—the half hour between that and actually needing to leave the house—to look up *Kara Bolka* in the online phone directories.

No luck.

Not that there weren't a generous number of Karas in California; I pictured legions of OC girls still wearing their braces, chilling at the mall or flaunting their hard bodies at the beach and in the waiting rooms of San Fernando's porn industry. Kara Bolka sounded like a name Eastern European immigrants might give their American-born daughter. It whispered half woman and half nymph.

Of course, it might've been my libido doing the whispering.

The night hadn't actually begun, but I was wondering how it would end. I was counting down from my last intimate encounter and contemplating whether it really was like riding a bicycle, and if we were talking ten-gear or mountain bike.

I hadn't completely been a sexual hermit since my arrival in Littleton. No. I'd cohabited at the Days Inn with a certain married woman who'd ventured into Muhammed Alley pretty much for the same reason I had—as a retreat. In her case, from an unfaithful husband who tended to knock her around when his golf game was off or a business deal went sour. He was in real estate, where business deals tended to unravel on a regular basis—especially in Littleton, which still boasted two half-finished resorts.

I won't tell you her name. It doesn't matter. We went to the Days Inn instead of my rented home because I didn't want her husband showing up at my front door. We went there three times, and it was satisfying only in the most rudimentary definition of the term. Like eating cooked-to-death food when you're hungry.

When she called my cell after our third liaison, I didn't call her back. I discovered a message on my phone from her a week later.

So this is it, huh? Have a nice life.

If you were going to end an affair, those words were as good as any.

Now I was awash in Karas, which is to say pretty much at sea.

I left them there to meet Anna.

SOMEWHERE BETWEEN SALAD AND ENTRÉE, BETWEEN TALKING AND flirting, between 8 o'clock and 9 o'clock, Anna mentioned John Wren.

That she knew him.

We'd somehow ended up on the subject of journalism again. Not just talking, either. I was pretty much proselytizing, though it might've been the Chianti doing most of the self-righteous babbling. I sounded the way I used to, when I was first starting out and consumed with the fever. A divinity student discussing his faith. Hadn't I worked for the acknowledged bible of the industry?

Slowly, sin by sin, I'd managed to subvert the very reason for a newspaper's existence, to turn truth inside out. Like one of those Soviet moles from the thirties who burrowed their way into the heart of the British democracy. And just like Philby and company had spilled innocent blood—so did I.

I have skirted the particulars with you; I have played coy.

The resulting carnage from my exposure and dismissal included one brilliant, dedicated, and generally worshiped editor who did nothing much but believe in me.

He went down with the ship.

Or with the rat.

I'd be pecking away at a story and I'd feel him just behind me, like a divine presence keeping tabs. He had that kind of status, had earned a special kind of reputation, even at a newspaper where journalistic luminaries were the norm.

For some reason, he took an interest in me, saw something there worth cultivating. Maybe he simply knew a fatherless boy when he saw one. He invited me for drinks one night, and when it went okay, when I didn't bore him with a fusillade of mostly fawning questions, he invited me again. After a while we began having midnight heart-to-

126

hearts over smelly bratwurst sandwiches in his office. We took ambling walks in Bryant Park when he felt like stretching his legs. When he'd do the rounds, I'd sense him there over my shoulder and find myself flushing, trying to will the keys to conjure up something sharp, incisive, and brilliant. Sometimes they even obliged.

It didn't matter.

He had a habit of holding back enough praise to make you thirsty for more. What you wrote was mostly *not bad*, *okay*, or simply *workmanlike*. You were supposed to write for your readers—that great mass of news-hungry souls thirsting for truth.

I wrote for *him*.

I had a readership of one. I needed to turn *okay* into *great*.

It was irony itself that creating a story about a dead National Guardsman named Lowell Beaumont finally did the trick.

Of course, there's a problem with finally getting what you've been thirsting for. Once praised, you need to feel it again, to have all that love and approval poured over you like champagne in the championship-starved 2004 Red Sox clubhouse.

I kept it up for longer than should've been possible.

I kept it up until it wasn't possible.

Until I accompanied a certain reporter for drinks, and it all blew up.

During the course of one week, this editor, this *friend*, went from glorified ombudsman to vilified incompetent. It was followed weeks later by his sudden *retirement*.

He should've *known*, they claimed—*they* mostly being

all the lesser lights he'd eclipsed on the way up. He should've been *on top of things*. He should've been *doing his job*.

His public desecration was only mildly less brutal than mine, his fall ten times greater.

Of everything I managed to ruin—and I was pretty much a one-man wrecking crew, trashing my career, my marriage, my reputation—destroying *him* is the thing I'm most shamed by, the worm that continually gnaws at me, that I occasionally try to drown through serial shots of tequila.

Sometimes it makes me dial the number of a faded country house in Putnam County and recite soundless words of contrition.

Hello, I say, it's me. I'm sorry.

I can picture him there, holding that old-style black receiver in his hand, his bifocals sloped down over his prodigious nose, and I swallow the words down, ingest them whole, and they slide back into my gut and make me sick.

But not tonight.

No.

Tonight I was *Carl Woodward*, a hybrid between journalistic fervor and rampant horniness. Wine had loosened my tongue, all right; I was up on a soapbox with no intention of coming down. I was showing off.

"We may be in the democracy-exporting business—I mean that seems to be our only foreign policy these days, our *crusade*—but who protects democracy in a democracy? Those nine geriatrics on the Supreme Court? What protects the USA today is *USA Today*. Scary, huh? I'm not kidding. Like it or not, democracy's in the sweaty little hands of the working press. Even if we don't really know it. Even if we don't really *want* it. I'm using *we* loosely here. Because truth *always* gets the first bullet."

Truth—blithely using the one word in the English language I was least familiar with.

I was half-listening to myself, wondering if I sounded like a dangerous madman or, just as bad, a bore. But Anna seemed to be listening with semirapt attention. She seemed to *like* this me, this superhero of truth, justice, and the American way.

Then she said: "Why did you need a break?"

"Huh?"

"You said you came out here because you needed a break. What *from*? It sounds like you loved it—your work. Being on important stories. Why did you bury yourself out here? I don't mean *bury*—I mean . . ."

I should've been more careful.

I'd started the night talking about things *un*related to journalism, hadn't I? The New York Yankees, rattlesnakes, *Caddyshack*. Somehow, without quite realizing it, I'd navigated My Dinner with Anna back into dangerous waters.

"I had a problem at my last job."

"Oh? What kind of problem?"

"Ethics, sort of."

"Ethics, sort of," she repeated. "Something you want to talk about or something you want to pretend I didn't ask you about?"

"Something I want to pretend you didn't ask me about." It's possible to become suddenly and shockingly sober— my purple haze had disappeared like protective netting blown off by an ill wind.

"Fine. Ethics sounds kind of interesting, though. Even a little dirty."

"It was. But not in the way you mean it," I said.

"Oh. Well, whatever it was, I'm sorry. I mean, you obviously adored being a reporter—you're *still* a reporter, you know what I mean. . . ."

"I made things up."

There.

Sooner or later it was bound to come out. Sooner or later, she'd mention my name to one of her friends or acquaintances and they'd tell her how familiar that name sounded—that if they didn't know any better they'd say it sounded like that reporter guy who nearly took down a newspaper. The one who wrote about things that never happened.

The liar.

"Tom Valle," she said, as if sounding out a foreign language. "Oh *shit*."

I tried to glean what I could from her expression—those few seconds when pure shock left her unguarded. Was it simple embarrassment I saw there? Disgust? Pity?

"Wow," she said, lifting the wine glass to her lips, then placing it back down on the table with an awkward deliberateness, like someone relearning to use their extremities after a stroke. "When you said you needed a break, you weren't kidding. Do you mind me asking . . . *why you did what you did*? I won't if you don't want me to."

I didn't respond right away. I could've said yeah, I'd rather you didn't, and changed the subject. I could've trotted out something tried-and-true and meant for public consumption only. *I was wrong. I didn't mean it. I was*

130

going through a lot of stuff at the time. I could've editorial-ized.

I told the truth.

How it began. The morning I woke up late. The little exercise in creative writing.

"How many times?" she asked me softly. "After that?"

"I don't know. They ended up auditing every story I'd ever written. They said there were fifty-six of them. Where I'd either partially or totally fabricated a story. I didn't think it was that much. Maybe it was."

"*Why?* You were a good reporter, right? I mean, you had a respected career. You worked at a great newspaper. You didn't *have* to."

You didn't have to. The great mystery of Tom Valle's criminal life.

"Ever walk into a reporter bar?" I asked her. "There's a hierarchy in those places—you're either holding court or bowing down. Maybe it was nice being bowed down to for a change. Besides, when you're a mediocre student, being teacher's pet feels pretty good. Being on page 1 instead of section 2 feels even better. It was nice making the B-list of talking heads, too. I even did *Larry King Live.* Once—Ben Bradlee was on the panel. Interns from the Columbia School of Journalism sought me out for pearls of journalistic wisdom. Other reporters stuck pins into Tom Valle dolls, when they weren't falling all over themselves to buy me a drink. Which turned out to be my downfall, actual-ly—one of those reporters bought me *several* drinks. It's hard to keep your facts straight on four margaritas."

She asked me how I ended up here.

"Here's pretty much the only place that would have me,"

I said. "The week I knew the jig was up, that it was all going to come crashing down around my head—the editors were already circling the wagons, beginning to sift through the wreckage; they had forensic accountants checking my expense accounts against my bylines. I mean, if I had eggs and coffee in a diner in New York on the third, I *couldn't* have been at a DNC conference in Washington, right? Anyway, I got wicked drunk and went up there at 3 in the morning. I must've had the vague intention of stealing anything incriminating, which in retrospect means I would've needed a forklift. I don't really know what I thought I was going to do. I broke into the national editor's office and tried to find his computer files; I ended up passed out on the floor. It gave them the excuse they needed to press criminal charges, as opposed to just a nice public firing. I got probation instead of jail time—they weren't going to throw me in jail for *that*. For one year I did nothing much but hibernate. My PO is related to Hinch Edwards—he owns the *Littleton Journal*. Hinch took pity. End of story."

"Yeah, he's a nice guy."

That's when it suddenly occurred to me that Anna maybe knew things I wasn't aware she knew.

"You know Hinch?"

"I knew someone who worked for him," she said.

"Who?"

"John."

"John *who*? John Wren? You knew John Wren?"

"Uh-huh."

"Why didn't you tell me?"

"Why? We've had one dinner. I haven't told you my middle name, either. By the way, it's Alicia."

132

"So you were friends or something?"

"Kind of. What's so remarkable about that?"

"Nothing. Just kind of funny that you know two reporters who lived in the same house."

"He lived in your house, huh? Of course, it's a small town. Not that many houses."

"Right." I gulped down some wine, desperately trying to recapture a suddenly elusive high. "Do you keep in touch with him?" I asked.

"I'm not sure he keeps in touch with anyone. I came to visit my dad one time, and he was just gone. That's where we'd met. At the home. He was interviewing people about that . . . flood . . . the one back in the fifties. You know about that, right? Horrible—a whole town went under. I think he went to the retirement home to try to scare up some memories."

Scare. Good word, I thought.

"I don't think he was very successful at it," I said. "The story never ran."

"Really?" Anna said. "He seemed pretty excited about it. He e-mailed me once after he left Littleton—my impression was he'd holed himself up somewhere to work on it."

"That's strange, considering he was no longer employed," I said. "Anyway, word was he was pretty excitable in general around then. He went a little bonkers."

"*Bonkers*? Is that a psychiatric term?"

"He locked himself in the newspaper offices one night and had to be forcibly removed. I think that constitutes bonkers. I ought to know."

"Was that what they said *you* were? Bonkers?"

"Only the nice ones. Everyone else said I was the devil."

133

"You don't look like the devil."

"Thanks." I blushed, took another sip of wine. "Was your father living here? Back when the flood happened?"

"Yes. He wouldn't be able to tell you much about it, of course. Not now."

Silence.

"I just tried to call him," I said. "Wren."

"Oh? What for?"

"I want to ask him about something I'm working on."

"I thought you said he'd lost his mind?"

"Maybe he got it back."

I was tempted to tell Anna that the something I was working on was the same thing Wren had been working on. The aforementioned *nut job* Wren.

It might sound paranoid to her. It might sound like a desperate reporter trying to get his mojo back.

Not that it really mattered.

Dinner had become uncomfortably awkward. It was as if the stopper had been pulled out of the bottle labeled Anna and Tom's Dinner Conversation; the contents had poured out onto the floor, leaving nothing but a few paltry drops.

I felt less than whole in her eyes, an ethical cripple. The whole mood had soured. She made a halfhearted effort to resuscitate things, but she seemed to be going through the motions.

When I paid the bill, when we walked outside and I escorted her to her car, I didn't know whether to say good night or good-bye.

We lingered in front of her red Beetle—more maroon in the moonlight—and it was like that moment in front of a girl's apartment door when you're either going to get shot down or rescued and you don't for the life of you know which.

She leaned forward and kissed me.

On the cheek.

"I'll call you sometime," she said. "Thank you for dinner."

I wanted to say *that's it?*

I wanted to take that butterfly that had begun flitting about my chest the day she fixed my car and never really stopped—I wanted to pin it down. To display it somewhere where I could hold it up to the light and stare at it.

She'd call me sometime. *Then* what? She'd call me as a friend or an acquaintance or something more? She'd call me because she wanted to, or because she had to, or she was never going to call at all?

"Don't mention it," I said.

TWENTY-ONE

The ride back was a journey into self-pity.

I was familiar with the terrain, having visited it on a number of previous occasions—mostly in that one-year period I spent holed up in my NoHo apartment like a prisoner in isolation. I journeyed frequently to Self-Pity then, sampling the local tequila and scribbling postcards to Dr. Payne: *having no fun, wish you were here*.

I'd mostly refrained from giving Anna the psychobabble, but Dr. Payne had shown no such restraint.

Why did this liar lie?

You really want to know, Anna?

Are you sure?

Because I woke up hours late one morning, and needed to.

Because the Ward Cleaver of editors patted me on the head and said good job.

Not good enough?

You want more?

Because I lied to my 9-year-old self, lied that my dad wasn't sleeping with that waitress, that he'd be home any minute, that my mom was not a sadistic drunk, that the men trooping upstairs with her really liked me when they didn't even like *her*.

That Jimmy was clumsy.

Children of alcoholics tend to see what they want to and not see what they don't, Dr. Payne said.

You have no idea.

He slipped on the ice and he hurt his head.

He slipped.

On the ice.

Lying as defense mechanism, Dr. Payne said. *Don't knock it.*

Lying as palliative, an elixir, a quicker-fixer-upper.

Lying like a cheap rug and a thousand-dollar hooker.

Lying as my MO.

Lying to caseworkers from Children's Protective Services. To the police. To everyone.

What happened, Tommy?

He slipped.

On the ice.

He hurt his head.

When I saw a black figure sauntering up the front walk of my house, it didn't register at first.

Even when I noticed he was carrying some kind of bag in his left hand, even then it took me a few seconds to organize that thought into anything resembling coherence. *That's interesting*, I said, and took my foot off the gas pedal.

He stopped. Halfway to my front door. Where his face was momentarily lit up by the bug zapper attached to the half-dead elm on my lawn, those repulsive features illuminated in a sickly flash of purple.

You're it.

Our friendly neighborhood plumber. Back for another service call.

He knew he had company.

My Miata had stopped dead in the middle of the street, as if that finicky coil wire had popped loose again.

He ran back into his pickup truck and zoomed off, quickly accelerating past the legal speed limit, assuming you weren't allowed to do ninety on a residential street.

I gunned the engine, followed his taillights.

They dodged and darted and weaved and blew past the aluminum-sided homes on Redondo Lane, past the hacienda-style stucco ranch houses on West Road, past 7-Eleven, Shakey's, and IHOP, past San Pedro High School and the motorcycle bar out in the flats. They ignored five stop signs and two lights and a bunch of rowdy teenagers on Warrow Road, who were chug-a-lugging beer from brown paper bags in the middle of the street and had to literally dive for cover.

I'm not sure if I'd ever driven that fast before.

Maybe in a video game.

I hadn't realized how drunk I was—not until I clipped my first car on a wide turn around the high school ball field, a slight jolt accompanied by the awful sound of shearing metal, sound slightly behind sensation, as if the sound waves needed a while to catch up.

I clipped my second car somewhere by Littleton's nine-hole golf course. This time not even seeing what I hit—just knowing I hit *something*, because my Miata rocked violently to the right and its victim cried out in pain, a car alarm bursting into full-throated fury.

Then something hit me.

Smash.

I'd turned a corner, and faced empty street.

I'd looked left. I'd looked right.

I should've looked behind me.

The plumber had ducked into a driveway.

Then ducked out.

It was like one of those Looney Tunes cartoons. Elmer Fudd furiously chasing the *wabbit* until positions suddenly reverse the way they magically do in cartoons—and poor gun-toting Elmer's pumping away with Bugs hot on his tail.

Only it wasn't a rabbit chasing me, and if anyone was toting a gun, it was him.

Smash.

He jolted my back bumper again, once, twice, then hard enough to actually propel me into the dash.

My chin hit the top of the steering wheel; my head snapped back.

I felt the wine coming up, the vermicelli alfredo.

I couldn't stop.

If I stepped on the brake, he was going to end up in my front seat.

I could see that blackened shell on Highway 45. It was me.

I floored the gas, resisting checking the speedometer, thinking that the actual number might scare me, not wanting to take my eyes off an increasingly blurry road. Once or twice, we sped past other cars, but they seemed like stage props, seemingly frozen in place. I caught one face registering astonishment and outright fear.

It was mutual.

The plumber smacked me again. I felt a pain shoot up my spine as my car whiplashed right, clipping a curb.

Then again—harder this time, one hand stuttering off the wheel, as the car shimmied left.

This is what it feels like when you're about to be trampled.

This is what it feels like to have something brutish and unstoppable stepping on your heels.

There's nowhere to go.

You can't stop; you can't turn right or left.

You can only try to outrace it.

Until you can't.

I flew around a corner where the road suddenly widened out and structures disappeared.

I knew where we were.

The service road that passes two billboards: Spex in the City, the eyeglass store on Main, and Binions Casino, with three 40DDD showgirls in glittering sequins luring me to possible salvation.

The open highway.

If I could make it onto the highway, I had a chance.

I gunned the engine; I said a prayer.

I didn't see the police-car lights come on until they were suddenly flashing in my rearview mirror.

"WHAT THE FUCK YOU THINK YOU'RE DOING, LUCAS?"

The first words out of Sheriff Swenson's mouth.

I told him what I was doing, suffused with the gratitude of the suddenly rescued.

"*What* pickup?" he said.

He was standing outside the driver's-side door shining a blinding flashlight into my eyes, making me feel less grateful and more as if I were in the middle of an interrogation. All that was missing was the rubber truncheon.

"The blue pickup that was right behind me," I said. "The one with the man who broke into my house and beat me up."

"*Pickup*?" Sheriff Swenson said. "What are you talking about? I didn't see any pickup."

Which was about when I felt it. That insidious chill that travels up your legs when you're standing in a stifling-hot room in dripping-wet socks. You just know you're going to be really sick.

"How's that possible? It was five feet behind me."

"Get out of the car."

The headlights from Swenson's cruiser illuminated a reject from Demolition Derby. The front fender was smashed in; there were jagged streaks of odd color crisscrossing the passenger door. The back bumper had two formidable dents.

"I caught him trying to break into my house again. Then he tried to run me off the road," I said.

"Uh-huh," Swenson said. "You said the pickup was blue?"

Blood will tell, but so will Apple Red from Earl Scheib, clearly the color tattooed into my passenger door.

"Been playing bumper cars, Lucas?"

"Okay, yeah, I might've clipped someone."

"Looks like several someones. Care to walk a straight line for me." It wasn't a question. "Go ahead, Lucas, any direction you'd like."

"I told you, he was actually trying to rob my house again. He tried to run me off the road. He could've killed me."

141

"Take a walk for me, okay, Lucas?"

"No problem."

I was hoping that was actually true—that it *wouldn't* be a problem.

That I'd walk a straight line, and *keep* walking, back into my car and out of trouble. I could do that—navigate the shortest distance between two points—couldn't I?

Maybe not.

It's hard to execute an everyday physical action when your personal freedom depends on it. I'd never paid attention to the actual physics of placing one foot ahead of the other. Tricky business.

I teetered, wobbled, overcompensated, and listed right.

Still, I managed to make it ten whole feet without actually falling on my face. Then I turned around with rapidly dwindling assuredness and started back.

I went over.

Something had tripped me.

Or someone.

I didn't realize it was Swenson's black boot until my head smacked the ground and he placed the boot directly on the back of my neck.

TWENTY-TWO

Luiza needed to come in and clean my motel room.

So she'd proclaimed in broken English through the crack of my motel door.

This was sometime yesterday.

She'd appeared to be by her lonesome. I say *appeared to be*, since my peripheral vision was dangerously restricted by the eyehole in the door. I could see Luiza, all right. I could see her vacuum and blue pail and linen cart.

I couldn't see what was waiting on either side of her.

"Pleeeeeze . . . Meeester Vallee . . ." Luiza said. "Iz been two weeks."

Had it been that long?

Two weeks?

Maybe.

There were scattered beef jerky wrappers around the room. Empty cracker boxes. Yellowed newspapers. Several houseflies dive-bombing half-empty cans of Fresca. My clothes, what remained of them, were thrown around a threadbare carpet. My shades were drawn tight.

"Pleeeze . . . Meester Vallee . . ." Luiza again.

To open, or not to open?

She seemed genuine. On the other hand, how did I know what genuine *sounded* like coming out of Luiza's mouth? There was the whole accent thing to deal with. Genuineness could get lost in translation.

Still. If I didn't let her in to clean soon, she was liable to get the manager to intercede on her behalf.

Me and my friends, *Smith* and *Wesson*, weren't desirous of company just now.

I patted the bulge in my right pants pocket, took a deep breath, let the latch off.

I stepped back into the center of the room.

"Okay, Luiza. Come in."

The door opened as if in slow motion. A second or two later, Luiza's head peeked through the crack.

It's possible she was as apprehensive as I was. She'd probably been wondering what awaited her on the other side of the door. Or was it something else? Maybe she knew exactly what awaited her—had been prepped and primed.

He'll be standing back from the door to protect himself. He'll be armed and dangerous. But don't worry—so are we.

I whispered hello to Mr. Smith, assured Mr. Wesson that we were, in fact, locked and loaded.

Luiza's little body followed her head though the door.

She averted my eyes, turned around, and began pulling the linen cart into the room. Sunlight shot past her shoulder, illuminated the twisted bedsheets and jumbled clothing, the litter fest that had become home.

I danced a few steps to my right, in an effort to improve my sight line. The dazzling sun felt like splinters of glass.

The first rule of guerrilla warfare is what?

144

Try to catch them with their eyes to the sun.

I rushed past her, slammed the door, and relocked the latch.

Luiza turned at the sound of the chain being lifted back into position. She looked, well, nervous.

"How long do you need?" I asked her.

She shrugged without answering me. Instead she pulled a black industrial-size plastic trash bag from the cart and began filling it up with the detritus of two weeks.

I took a seat on the only chair in the room and carefully watched her.

"Where you from, Luiza?"

"Ecuador," she answered, not bothering to look in my direction. She wore plastic yellow gloves on both hands.

"How long have you been here?"

"Two year," she answered.

"Two year, huh? You have family here?"

"My husband," she said, this time taking a quick peek at me.

"Your husband. That's nice."

It might sound like we were engaging in polite small talk. You'd be wrong. I was conducting an Abu Ghraib–like interrogation. Minus the humiliating photographs and electrical wires.

"Has anyone been asking about me, Luiza?"

"I don' understand. . . ."

"I'm asking you if anyone—anyone at all—has asked you a question about me? Like, who is that man in number four? Like that?"

"No," she said.

"Good, okay. Great. So no one's said anything to you?"

"The manager."

"The manager?" I felt a sudden flush of fear. "The manager asked about me?"

Luiza nodded.

"What did he say?"

"He ask why you no let me clean the room."

"What did you tell him?"

"I tell him you no want me to clean. You sleeping. Or you working."

That had been my story when she'd knocked on the door. That I was sleeping. Or I was working. That she should please come back tomorrow. Tomorrow had become two weeks.

"I have been working," I said. "See," pointing to the laptop sitting open on top of the cluttered desk. *I am writing this as fast as I can.*

She nodded.

"I write . . . *plays*. That's why I don't answer the door. Because I don't want to be disturbed. Because I'm finishing a play. You can tell him that."

"Okay."

"Great. Almost done."

Luiza didn't really appear interested in whether I was done or not. She made a hurried visit into the bathroom, towels in hand, then quickly reappeared and commenced vacuuming.

"Other man ask me too," she said, after she'd attached the trash bag to her cart and begun rolling it back to the door.

"*What?* What did you say, Luiza?"

"Other man. He ask me who you are," she said. "I forget."

TWENTY-THREE

I turned out to be two times over legal.

Drunk enough, at least, not to have noticed Sheriff Swenson placing his size eleven black boot directly in my path. I noticed it on my neck. Lying on the ground, my cheek pressed against asphalt still warm from the desert sun, I felt its blunt weight and unmistakable message about hierarchy.

I assumed this might be it. *It* being my life. It was going to end here, on this empty road in the middle of the California desert.

The sheriff, it turned out, was simply making a point about the consequences of reckless behavior.

Point taken.

I blew into a Breathalyzer, was interrogated as to where I'd hit what, got cited for driving while intoxicated and for leaving the scene of an accident—make that *two* accidents.

Then, astonishingly, I was let go.

He could've given me a night in jail to contemplate my crimes, something he reminded me of as a way to let me know how easy he was being on me.

I said thank you.

Thank you isn't what I was thinking.

He never saw the pickup. How's that possible?

Somehow, contrary to all the laws of physics, he'd missed a blue pickup dogging my tail at ninety miles an hour.

Where *had* the pickup gone? Maybe he'd seen the police lights and eased off the pedal, drifted to a stop, taken off down a side street.

Maybe Swenson hadn't seen it.

I considered the sickening possibility that I was hallucinating.

There was that face in the bowling alley, the same one I later saw lit up by a bug zapper—it had vanished on me twice.

Was it possible I wasn't okay in the head? That, like Dennis Flaherty, I was in dire need of some industrial-strength psychotropics?

No.

It's easy to question yourself lying in bed at 1 in the morning, with a throbbing Chianti hangover and a Miata sitting in your driveway that has a date with the junkyard compactor.

Something else was going on.

I pulled Benjamin's note out of my bedside drawer.

Happy hundred birthday.

It was grammatically flawed, of course. Odd I hadn't noticed that before. Happy *hundredth* birthday was what he should've written. How old would the letter writer be if it really were her son? I reached into the drawer for the picture of the two of them—still marred by faint spots of blood.

148

It must've been winter. When the picture was taken.

Not that winters were particularly cold around here. Cold enough to don a tan wool jacket and dress your only child in a brown corduroy coat with five black buttons. She was holding him under his arms and it looked like he was maybe ticklish, had spent the previous minute while the photographer was framing the shot fidgeting in her lap and giggling out loud. He wore this charming bucktoothed grin, as if any second he was going to burst into raucous laughter. They say photographs can't steal your soul—but every so often they can hold it hostage.

Who was the photographer?

Belinda's husband? Trying to commemorate this moment for posterity? *What* moment? They were sitting under the sign for the Littleton Flats Café. Maybe they'd celebrated the day with a special lunch? Celebrated what? Benjamin's graduation from kindergarten? He looked to be about 6 then.

Jimmy's age.

The disaster must've happened soon after the picture was taken. Maybe that's why the picture was so haunting—because of what was to come.

Those three days of unrelenting rain—unusual for the desert, sure, but sometimes it happened. Mother Nature went on the rag, and all hell broke loose.

Or cement walls did.

Just another Sunday morning in Littleton Flats.

Maybe Benjamin was looking at the funny papers, just learning to read, Jane running and Dick throwing and Spot barking, and maybe wondering why all these walking and running and throwing kids were white, or maybe not—

149

maybe kids were still color-blind at that age. Maybe all he was thinking about that morning was when his mom was finally going to get home and bake some of her peach pie. I don't know if Belinda baked peach pies—she was probably too busy cleaning that white family's home in Littleton, what most black people did back then if they wanted to put food on the table. Maybe Belinda was making beds, cooking breakfast, cleaning up the kids she'd been stuck with that weekend when she heard that first rumble, like *thunder*, only it was a clear day—not a cloud in the sky. How *odd*, she must've thought—*all* of them must've thought—to be hearing thunder when there wasn't a rain cloud to be seen.

The first thing the water hit was the water tower.

This was according to what I'd read on microfilm.

Kind of ironic, water hitting its own.

When the water finally stopped, they found the tower seven miles away from where it originally stood. Not that far, in fact, from where they found the lone survivor—a 3-year-old girl who'd rode out the flood on a storm-cellar door unhinged in the maelstrom. Buoyant enough for her to ride the wave of destruction like some precocious surfer at Waimea.

The town itself was flattened. News accounts likened it to Hiroshima—most Americans' image back then of what total destruction looked like.

I'd found a few photos.

They were right.

Here and there, pieces of cement or steel structures still stood, like odd abstract sculptures. You would've been hard-pressed to identify what they once were.

The area was roped off due to the threat of disease—all those dead bodies bloating in the rancid water. It had taken them months to clean it up—to recover the bodies, salvage what was recoverable, board up, pull down, and cart the rest away. Then came the hand-wringing, soul-searching, and, eventually and inescapably, the finger-pointing. They formed an independent commission to investigate the building of the Aurora Dam, to painstakingly pore over the contractor's blueprints, the requisition orders, the . . .

Ring, ring.

The sound of the phone startled me. I was lost in Littleton Flats of fifty years ago; suddenly the here and now was demanding to be acknowledged.

I picked up.

"Tom Valle?"

"Yes. Who's this?" The ringing had restarted the pile driver in my head. *Pound . . . pound . . . pound . . .*

"John Wren. You called me?" he said, in a tone of voice that sounded vaguely accusatory.

"Yes, that's right. Thank you for getting back to me."

"No problem," Wren said.

For a moment, I wasn't sure how to proceed with the conversation.

How are you feeling these days, John? Still howling at the moon?

He continued the conversation for me. He asked about Hinch.

"He's fine," I said, then corrected myself. "Actually, no, he's not fine. His wife, she's sick again."

"That's too bad."

"Yeah."

151

Silence.

"So, what do you want?" he said.

"The Aurora Dam Flood. Hinch said you tried to do a story on it."

"The *flood*? Uh-huh, that's right."

"What happened?"

"Not much."

"I don't understand."

"It was hard to get people to talk about it. Most of the people weren't even around back then."

"So you couldn't find anyone?"

"I didn't say that. I said it was *hard*. Why are you doing a story on the Aurora Dam Flood?"

"The same reason you did—893 people died."

"It was 892. You're forgetting the little girl."

"Right. The little girl."

"I met her," he said. "She's still around."

"In Littleton?"

"San Diego. I tracked her down. She was my first interview."

"How did it go?"

"Okay. For someone who was 3 years old when it happened, she had an amazing memory." I heard a match light, the sound of Wren inhaling. "There was a little problem with what she remembered."

"What do you mean?"

"I mean she remembered some very imaginative things about that day."

"Imaginative?"

"If you think a ship of space robots rescuing her out of the water happens every day, then no, it wasn't imaginative."

152

"Space robots?"

"That's right. Space robots."

"Well, you said so yourself. She was 3 years old at the time."

"Uh-huh. Of course, *some* of the stuff she remembered was half-believable. It's the *National Enquirer* stuff I had a tough time with."

"You mean, there were things besides the space robots?"

"Right. Beside the space robots. There was a lot about that day . . ." His voice drifted off.

"Like?"

"Can I ask you something?"

"Sure."

"Tom Valle. You have the same name as that . . . *fraud* . . . you know the one I'm talking about; you must get it all the time. Tough being in the same business, isn't it?"

"Yeah, tough."

"Ever think about changing your name?"

"No."

"Good for you. Why change your name because someone else pissed on it, right?"

"Right."

"What happened to him? Didn't that guy go to jail?"

"No, he didn't."

"I could've sworn he went to jail. He deserved it."

"I'm Tom Valle," I said.

"I know."

"No, the Tom Valle you're talking about. The one who didn't go to jail."

"*I know*," he repeated. "I checked you out when I got

153

your message. I was wondering if you were going to tell me."

"Well, I've told you."

"To tell you the truth—we are *truth-telling* here, right— I'm kind of surprised you *haven't* changed your name. I'm more surprised you're back working for a newspaper. Even if it's in *Mayberry*. Hinch knows, I guess?"

"Yes."

"Good for him. Is this an experiment in rehabilitative journalism?"

"You'd have to ask him."

"Maybe I should do that. I mean, it's kind of like letting a child molester back into the classroom, isn't it?"

"It's old news. I've paid my court-ordered debt to society. Honest. Why don't we drop it? I just wanted to know if you had any information on . . ."

"It's your debt to *journalism* I'm concerned about," he interrupted me. "You can't repay *that* debt. People like you come along, it leaves a stink on all of us. It breaks the sacred bond. Makes us all look like tabloid writers," he said, his voice rising. "You were legitimate. The real deal. You got to where the rest of us all hoped we could get. Even if we couldn't. You got the average Joe thinking, maybe it's *all* bullshit. Reality TV—phony baloney, all made up. That's why I called you back. I wanted to tell you that in person."

I sat there and took it without hanging up.

Maybe because he was still a little crazy, even if he was still right. You can be crazy *and* right, can't you? Or maybe it was because it had been a while, a long while, since someone had laid it out in all its awful majesty. The day I'd attempted to slink out of the office with a carton of my meager possessions, skirting malevolent stares and blatant cold shoulders, a few self-appointed avengers managed to corner me in the hall and apply a full nelson of journalistic indignation. One of them was my drinking partner, the one who'd knifed that quaint message into my desk. *I lie, therefore I am.* I'd taken their diatribe just as I took Wren's now—I didn't duck into the elevator, make a mad dash for the stairs, or take a swing at them. I listened, as stoically as Chuck Connors when they sliced the epaulets off his Calvary uniform and kicked him out of Fort Apache at the beginning of *Branded.* Part of it was because of Dr. Payne's admonitions to own up. Part of it was because I deserved it. Part of it was because I thought if I took it from them, maybe I wouldn't have to take it from *him.* The man down the hall whom I'd personally destroyed. The one who would be thrown out of the *fort* weeks later and never let back in. The one I called up when I got filthy drunk and said not one word to.

"So, you're, what's the word—*reformed* these days?"

"I wasn't an alcoholic. I made up stories. I've stopped."

"Glad to hear it."

"I'm curious about this story. The Aurora Dam Flood."

"So you've said."

"That's why I called you. I was wondering if you knew anything about the death toll? If all the bodies were actually accounted for?"

"Accounted for *how*?"

"If anyone who supposedly died in the flood—if they ever just showed up later?"

Silence.

155

"The thing is," he said, "I don't think the laws of journalistic courtesy apply to you."

"I think someone who was supposed to have died in the flood didn't. I think he popped up recently to say hi to his 100-year-old mom. I think it may have been the same person who burned up in a car crash later with someone else's wallet in his pocket. I don't know this for sure—I think it's possible. I'm trying to connect the dots."

I heard the tap, tap, tap of a cigarette against ashtray.

"What are you asking me for—help? *How*? You want me to look for my notes? Is that what you're asking me?"

"If it wouldn't be too much trouble."

"It isn't too much trouble. If I wanted to. I don't. Not for you."

I heard the impatience in his voice now, the implicit desire to get off the phone.

"Maybe that's how I repay the debt," I said.

"*What*?"

"The debt you mentioned. The one to journalism. Maybe this is how." I don't exactly know why I came out with that—I don't—but when I did, it sounded right. It sounded, for want of a better term, *true*.

I heard him take another drag, pictured a coil of blue smoke slowly spiraling up to the ceiling.

"I'll think about it," he said after what seemed like a very long time.

"Thank you."

"Don't. I haven't said yes."

TWENTY-FOUR

The color of the ground was the first clue.

It was suddenly redder, as if the earth itself had bled.

I'd driven my Miata to Marv's Exxon station in the morning.

"It's *maybe* salvageable, if you don't mind it looking like Jed Clampett's jalopy," he said, then offered me a replacement car while he performed reconstructive surgery.

I drove down Highway 45 in an old T-bird with no backseat.

Past a weathered sign and down a road to nowhere.

It was impossible not to notice the *absence* of something.

Like standing in the remains of a Roman forum with no columns to define it. The space spoke like an open mouth.

And then, here and there, columns did appear, steel structures oxidized to rust. The humpbacked remains of cement foundations littering the moonscape. Or was it more like the plains of Mars—all that red earth?

I stopped the car and got out at the place that used to be Littleton Flats.

Have you ever stepped backward at a cemetery and inadvertently found yourself standing on a grave? You nearly blurt out *sorry*, don't you?

I wandered around, past indistinguishable lumps of stone, scattered pebbles as opaque as blown glass, rusted cans of Old Milwaukee.

I tried to imagine what stood where.

The Littleton Flats Café, for example. Its small wooden bench sitting under the overhang of a sign, where a smiling black mother had held her smiling 6-year-old son up to the camera.

I skirted the edges of a large circle.

The *water tower*? The one they'd found seven miles away after the floodwaters had finally stopped?

I tried to picture it—the moment when it hit.

I'd seen the video footage of Indonesian tsunamis.

The seawater being sucked back into the ocean, grounding the fishing skiffs like little beach toys in the sand. Minutes of eerie nothingness, until the ocean suddenly roared back, deep black and two stories high, looking like some cheap cinematic trick until you realized those beaches and boats and hotels had people in them. Flailing arms and legs, bursting lungs and crumpled bodies.

Littleton Flats was populated mostly by the families of the hydroelectric plant workers that the Aurora Dam had been built to power. The very energy the townspeople harnessed and regulated had ended up turning on them, eating its own. The plant was destroyed in the flood and, with cheaper alternatives available downstate, never rebuilt.

Neither was Littleton Flats.

I stared down at the red dirt and saw someone staring back. A Lincoln penny, half obscured by moss, turning him into a kind of swamp creature. *Creature from the Black Lagoon*—one of those movies I used to bury myself in with the volume turned way up so I wouldn't hear what was happening in the next room. Where she'd brought Jimmy. *Suffer the little children.* Like Benjamin. Except Benjamin had gotten away, somehow squirreled to the surface, and disappeared.

How?

Happy hundred birthday.

I became aware of the utter quiet.

Aside from the whispering wind, I couldn't hear a single cricket or bird. Odd. No rattlers, either—kind of comforting for someone stuck out here by his lonesome.

Except I wasn't.

I was sitting on a ledge of concrete, contemplating the penny that might have once bought Benjamin a piece of bubble gum complete with Bazooka Joe comic. I was turning it over in my hand, rubbing its green mossy surface between my forefinger and thumb, when I felt someone watching me.

It was a man.

He was half a football field away.

Standing maybe twenty yards from the battered T-bird I'd used to get here. I didn't see another car, which made me wonder how he'd made it all the way out here. I was wondering something else. What he was doing here.

At first, I worried it might've been the plumber I'd last seen sauntering up my front walk with a bag in his hand.

Him.

It wasn't.

This man was clearly older. If I saw him at the local Sears, or passed him at night strolling down Redondo Lane, I wouldn't have given him a second thought. Not here.

I shot up, taking two steps back in an effort to gain my balance, which seemed to have been altered simply by his appearance.

He turned around and began walking away.

"Hello?" I shouted in his direction.

He kept walking, maintaining the same steady pace, a man on his morning constitution, a man who clearly hadn't heard someone shouting at him to stop.

I hustled after him.

As I drew closer, he appeared even older than I'd first imagined. He had an aura of quiet dignity about him— even with his back turned. It might've been 100 degrees out here, but he was wearing a natty blue sport jacket with thin gray pinstripes. No hiking boots or tennis shoes, but polished black shoes that nearly gleamed. An old-fashioned fedora sat at a slight angle on his head.

"Excuse me," I said, a little out of breath. "Excuse me, could I talk to you a sec?"

He stopped. And turned.

Late seventies, I guessed, maybe eighties. His hair, what I could see of it, was steely gray and trimmed short, just this side of a crew.

"Yes?" he said, as calmly and politely as someone asking you for the time.

"I was just curious what you're doing out here?"

"Funny," he said. "I was wondering the same thing about you." He had what could only be referred to as *piercing* eyes—that striking shade of blue that nearly causes you to reach for your sunglasses.

"Tom Valle," I said, "from the *Littleton Journal*."

"Ah. You're a reporter?"

I had the impression he was sizing me up—the uncomfortable sensation of being inside an MRI machine, innards intimately exposed to meticulous examination.

"Doing a story on what? This *place*?" he asked.

"Yes. On the Aurora Dam Flood."

"I see." He nodded, took his hat off, and wiped his brow with a clean white handkerchief that mysteriously appeared out of his jacket pocket.

"You should wear one," he said, refixing his hat and sticking the handkerchief back in his pocket. "Sunstroke can be unforgiving."

I believed him. I was starting to feel a slight wooziness, like purple haze without the fun.

"The flood," he said. "It was a long time ago."

"Fifty years," I said; I could feel a rivulet of sweat trickling down the center of my back. "So, what brought you out here?" I was going to ask him *how* he'd got out here as well, but I'd noticed the front grille of a car parked behind one of the rusting steel structures about forty yards away.

"Curiosity," he said.

"You've read about the flood?"

"Yes."

"Are you from around here?"

"*Here*? I don't think anyone's from around here. *Now*."

"I don't mean Littleton Flats. I meant from around the area?"

"No. I'm not from this area."

"Oh. Just a flood buff, then?"

"Well," he said, "I was here once."

"Here? You mean Littleton Flats?"

"That's right."

"Before the flood?"

He nodded. "Not much left, is there?"

"No. What was it like?"

"*Like?*"

"The town?" I'd read a lot about the destruction of Littleton Flats, almost nothing about the town itself. Here was someone who'd walked its streets, who might've passed Belinda and Benjamin on their way to breakfast in the Littleton Flats Café.

"It was like any town. Entirely ordinary. Families, shops, houses, backyards. Just a town."

"What year was that?"

"Year?"

"The year you visited?"

"1954."

"That was the year it happened."

"Yes."

"And you've never come back? Till now?"

He shook his head. "No. I was passing through and I thought to myself, why not?"

"It must be kind of eerie for you."

"Eerie? I would think it would be eerie for anybody. All ghost towns are."

Yes, he was right. The soft wind whistling through the rusted steel sounded like the angry whispering of ghosts.

"A terrible thing happened here, didn't it?" the man said. "You can still feel it."

162

I reached for the pad and pen in my pocket. "Can I ask your name? You wouldn't mind being quoted, would you? For my story."

"I'm afraid I have nothing much to contribute. Just a flood buff, like you said."

"But you were there."

"Yes, I was here. So were a lot of people."

"A lot of people don't like talking about it. In Littleton, anyway. You don't seem to mind."

He looked down at his polished black shoes, both feet ramrod straight, making me wonder if he'd ever been in the military. "Okay," he said, looking up. "My name's Herman Wentworth."

I scribbled it down. "May I ask, Herman, what you used to do?"

"I'm a doctor," he said. "Of course, I don't practice anymore."

Funny, I thought. That uncomfortable feeling of being examined when I'd first said hello to him. It hadn't been an accident.

"Were you in private practice?"

He shook his head. "I was an *army* doctor."

So he had been in the military. "The army, really? Where were you stationed?"

"Oh, everywhere. At one time or another. Pretty much all over the world. I started out in Japan."

"Japan, huh? When would that have been?"

"At the end of the war. Right after the surrender."

"Tokyo?"

"No," he said. "Different part of the country. I was with the 499th medical battalion."

"Treating wounded soldiers?"

"Treating everybody. Japanese, too. The Hippocratic oath doesn't delineate between friends and enemies, just those you can save and those you can't."

"So, at some point in 1954, you ended up here?"

"For a day."

"Did you know someone in Littleton Flats?"

He shook his head. "No, I was passing through. Just like today."

I wondered where someone needed to be going in order to pass through Littleton Flats. It wasn't exactly the crossroads of the world. More like its dead end.

Then he answered for me.

"I was transferred to San Diego. I wanted to take in some desert scenery. I was born up north—Minneapolis. You don't see a lot of desert up there."

"And so you stopped here for one day?"

"That's right. Just one day."

"What time of year was it, do you remember?"

"Afraid I don't." He repeated the ritual of minutes before, pulling that handkerchief out of his pocket, removing his hat, and wiping the sweat off his brow.

The wooziness I'd felt before had worsened. A dull headache had settled in the middle of my forehead.

"Do you remember anything in particular?"

"About what?"

"The town?"

"It was a long time ago. I told you—it was just a town."

"Where were you when you heard?"

"*Heard*?"

"About the flood?"

164

"Sorry," he shrugged. "I don't remember."

"Okay," I said. "Thanks. I appreciate you answering my questions."

"I don't see how I was any particular help."

"You were there. It's nice to meet someone who saw it before it all washed away."

I put out my hand and he shook it, a surprisingly firm grip from someone eighty or so. He went to leave, then turned back around.

"I wouldn't stay too long out here." He tapped his forehead. "Sunstroke can be murder. Remember, I *am* a doctor."

"Thank you; I won't."

I watched as he made his way back to his car. I heard the engine rev, then softly idle for a while, before he finally pulled out from behind the splintered steel column.

He drove off, leaving the place deathly quiet again.

My headache had reached DEFCON 3; I felt nauseated as I walked back to my car. I opened the front door and collapsed into the front seat.

It felt better than out there in the sun, but I was dizzy enough to close my eyes.

I put the seat back and thought it might be nice to rest for a few minutes.

After a while, I was walking around Littleton Flats again.

The town was alive with people. The water tower was right there on Main Street. The men all wore old-fashioned fedoras. I could smell the aroma of blueberry pancakes and maple syrup wafting over from the Littleton Flats Café.

When I walked inside, the pretty waitress, the one my father left us for—*Lillian*, her name was—smiled at me. I blushed when she brought me a fresh place mat with connect-the-dots on it.

I began drawing lines from one dot to another, and now and then I thought I could see a picture in there, but when I held it up to show my father, it was blank.

I felt this awful frustration, an excruciating embarrassment as I kept drawing and attempting to show my father and Lillian something in the dots, but every time I tried it would vanish. *Poof.* I could sense my father's growing disappointment, Lillian's boredom, and I finally drew my own picture, just ignored the dots entirely and drew a picture of a woman and child sitting on a bench.

When I opened my eyes again, it was dark and I was covered in cold sweat.

I wondered if the army doctor had been part of the dream.

TWENTY-FIVE

Marv was right.

My Miata did look like the Beverly Hillbillies' jalopy. He'd hammered out the dents, but the metal was as wrinkled as used aluminum foil. He'd replaced my front bumper with one from another car—evidently not a Miata—that was lopsided and several inches too wide.

The engine seemed pretty much intact.

I was currently doing a respectable seventy miles an hour on the Pacific Coast Highway, on my way north to see John Wren.

He'd called me back a few days later.

He'd looked for his notes. Just as he'd alluded to, there were some interesting things in there. He'd weighed his distaste for me against his belief in the story. The story won. There was a catch: if I wanted his notes, I'd have to come get them. He didn't own a fax machine, and the nearest one was a good forty miles away, as he'd retired to a deserted fishing camp on a remote lake.

My impression was he'd holed himself up somewhere, Anna had told me. Apparently, he'd turned recluse in earnest.

I told Hinch I was taking a few days off.

I didn't tell him what I was really doing, because I was afraid he might laugh at me. Then fire me on the spot.

I suppose I could've taken a plane, but money was tight, and like Herman Wentworth, I was looking forward to a change in scenery.

When you drive the PCH North, you experience several of them.

The million-dollar beach cottages, ratty surfer motels, volleyball nets, and honky-tonk piers disappear. The coastline becomes steeper, craggier, and altogether more spectacular, as if California has been sanded down in a southerly direction. Past San Francisco, towering pines actually blot out the surf, but you can hear its steady roar even above the traffic.

I stopped only once, at a motel in Big Sur, where I was given a key to the last room available, the one closest to the road. It had its own natural stereo system—engines on one side, ocean on the other—an audio surf and turf that created a stereophonic balance capable of rocking me into a semblance of sleep. I had noisy dreams filled with vivid colors—none of which I remembered when I woke to a gray light filtering in through the loosely drawn blinds. The mattress was soaked through from the sea air.

I needed two coffees to shake the cobwebs out of my brain.

I'd never been this far north in California. States take on each other's characteristics the closer you get to their borders. I might've *technically* been in California—it felt more like Oregon. It was almost July, but I could feel a raw chill in the air. The surrounding vegetation was lush and tangled and reeked of decay.

I'd meticulously plotted out the route to Wren's front door.

I still got lost. Went past the correct exit and didn't discover my mistake till I'd gone twenty miles out of the way. One section of forest looked pretty much like another—I had the sensation of being inside one of those topiary mazes, turning left and right and back and forth but getting nowhere fast, continuously coming up against another impenetrable wall of green.

Eventually I retraced my route and got it right.

I followed the sign to Bluemount Lake.

Soon I glimpsed slivers of cool blue through the pines. Only the one-lane road seemed to circle the lake forever, offering no way in.

Then after twenty minutes or so, another sign: *Bluemount Fishing Camp—turnoff 20 yards.*

I slowed, peering ahead for the actual turnoff, which wasn't easy because the light was rapidly leaving and the thick pines put everything in shadow.

It was hardly there.

Just a bare indentation in the crawling ferns.

I stopped, finally made out the crudely drawn sign nailed to a tree—a black arrow pointing *thataway.*

My Miata wasn't meant for offroad exploring. Even when it was new, a status symbol emblematic of its riding-high owner, it wouldn't have negotiated the twisting, bumpy terrain much better than it did now.

But now its shocks were pretty much moribund.

Every yard gained was accompanied by a bone-jarring jolt. Strange sounds emanated from the undercarriage—creaks, squeals, and sick-sounding moans. It sounded like my muffler was dragging directly on the ground. At one point, I considered just leaving the car where it was and hoofing it the rest of the way. But the forest seemed less inviting outside the car than in it. Besides, the lake was getting closer; I could smell it.

I made a twisting turn around a thick ancient oak, and suddenly I was staring at a row of log cabins perched on the shore of Bluemount Lake. No longer blue exactly— more mottled purple in the evening light.

One cabin had smoke billowing out of its chimney.

I drove up to the side of the cabin, my tires spitting gravel, and stopped.

When I got out, no one came out of the door to greet me.

Odd.

My beat-up Miata must've made a terrible racket, especially out here where the loudest sounds probably came from hungry loons.

"John?" I called out, for some reason uneasy about just walking up and knocking on his door.

No response.

I called his name again. Still nothing.

I walked up to the cabin, negotiated the three steps up to the porch, and gave a good knock at the door.

No answer.

I rapped again. "Mr. Wren, it's Tom Valle. Are you in there?"

After waiting awhile, I pushed against the door—there was no doorknob, just a plank of rough wood nailed to the door.

It trickled open.

A real mess. A pack rat's lair, reminding me of the way my basement looked when I'd first taken over the house. Mounds of clutter spread over a bed, couch, table, even the floor. A cast-iron stove radiated a bare modicum of heat.

No Wren.

I turned around and peered out at the lake.

Nothing—no boats or swimmers. No fishermen, either. Just tiny skittish ripples being stirred up by a rapidly growing breeze. Which reminded me—it was certifiably cold now. I was wearing proper attire for Littleton in June. A faded New York Yankees T-shirt with *Pettitte* on the back—a testament to Steinbrenner's formidable wheeling and dealing, since Andy Pettitte, like me, was long gone from New York—but not much protection against a Bluemount Lake night. I had a windbreaker in the trunk, but I wasn't sure if it would help much.

What to do?

I felt funny about just walking in and making myself at home. It wasn't my home—it belonged to somebody else. Not a friend, either. Someone who'd called me a *fraud* and meant it. He might not like coming home and seeing this selfsame fraud sitting on his couch. It might offend him.

I went back to my car, took my windbreaker out of the trunk, and quickly pulled it on. I slid into the front seat, made sure the windows were rolled up tight, and began waiting it out.

It quickly got dark.

It was worse than desert dark. There you had the moon. Here it was blotted out by the overhanging trees, though I could see its reflection flickering on the far edges of the lake like hot licks of flame.

I put on the radio for comfort, but managed to get only the faint echo of a classical station from Sacramento. *Now for some Debussy*, the gravel-voiced host intoned. Which reminded me of a joke I couldn't quite recall, something about men being attracted to strange Debussy, something like that, trying to reconstruct it in order to have something to do.

I wondered if I'd gotten the day wrong. Had I told him *next* week? No, I clearly remembered telling him I'd be coming up today—probably late, depending on traffic, but today for sure.

So where was he?

Maybe he'd gone fishing and had an accident. The boat tipped over, he hit his head on a rock, and right this minute he was lying unconscious somewhere out on the lake. Or worse.

What then?

I couldn't sit out here in the car forever.

I could drive back.

One look at the solid wall of black that was the surrounding forest instantly dissuaded me.

You couldn't tell where the road *in* was. Not anymore. Besides, *road* was being generous. I pictured my Miata stuck in some unseen hole, myself stumbling around the tree trunks like Tom Hanks in *Cast Away*—the second half of the movie, when he'd already begun conversing with bloodstained volleyballs.

I stayed put.

I listened to Beethoven, Liszt, Chopin.

My mom had signed me up for piano lessons when I was 11, after a teacher going door-to-door selling the benefits of a musical education had caught her at the opportune time—half-coherent and full of magnanimity. I'd liked the lessons about as much as the teacher, who had to constantly hound my mom to pay her, and occasionally had to ride the right pedal in order to drown out the sounds of a furiously squeaking upstairs bed.

"And now a lovely little concerto from Schubert," the radio host whispered, like a PGA announcer during a crucial putt, classical music evidently demanding a kind of hushed reverence.

Was I sleeping by then? I don't know.

I heard the forest whispering at me. The wind through the leaves.

But it seemed to be saying something.

Listen.

The crunch of boots on dead leaves. Someone had walked up to the car. Someone was standing there.

Outside my window. Looking in at me.

He's sleeping. . . .

The person was carrying something. He raised it up over his shoulder. A long-handled ax? A mud-covered shovel? Something long, heavy, and lethal.

He was going to shatter the windshield into smithereens.

He was going to smash me to bits.

Stop. . . .

When I sputtered awake, no one was there.

I was shivering.

I left the car and walked back up the porch into the cabin.

The cast-iron stove was still going, but barely. There was a pile of chopped wood in the back of the room. I threw two logs into the stove and stood there as the fire combusted again, rubbing my arms in an attempt to wring the chill out.

I pushed some books aside to make a place to sit down. The couch smelled faintly of fish.

After a while, I began leafing through some of his stuff. Anything in arm's range. Why not—I was bored. The books reflected the same eclectic taste I'd seen in my basement—everything from a paperback of *Lolita* to a biography of Enrico Fermi. They were stuffed with ad hoc bookmarks—a grocery list, a movie ticket stub, a letter. I opened the letter and peeked, wondering if any minute Wren would come charging through the door to discover me reading his personal correspondence. From a Dearborne Labs in Flint, Michigan: *To Mr. Wren*, it said in the dry, passionless tone of official bad news. *Preliminary results of your specimens have confirmed your concerns. Please see attached lab workup.*

Was Wren sick? Was that why he'd gone off the deep end back in Littleton? Why he'd buried himself out here?

The attached workup was no longer attached.

I was looking for it when my cell phone rang.

"You there yet?" a voice said.

There *where*? I thought. It took me a second to realize it was Wren. He didn't sound particularly friendly.

"Yes. I'm in your cabin. Where are you?"

"How long you been waiting?" he asked.

"A couple of hours, I guess."

"Uh-huh. I had to go into Fishbein for supplies."

Fishbein. I thought, where's that?

"My truck broke down," he said. "Can't get it fixed till tomorrow."

"You're in Fishbein?"

"That's right. Why?"

"I thought . . ."

"What?"

"I thought someone walked up to my car before. I must've been dreaming."

"Uh-huh. So, you're sitting in my *cabin*?"

I thought there was something lurking in his tone. "Yes. Nice fishing rods," I said, attempting to deflect it.

There were three of them leaning against the wall.

I'd done a story on a trout-fishing contest in Vermont— a *legitimate* story, actually getting on a plane and traveling two hours down back roads to a roaring stream near the Canadian border. Professional fishermen were as protective of their rods as professional baseball players were of their Louisville Sluggers. The ones against the wall looked kind of expensive.

"They're okay," Wren answered.

I asked him what kind they were. *Trout rods*, he said. Then I asked him if he lived alone.

"That's right," he said. "Why?" When I didn't respond, he said: "Oh, the voice mail."

We're out fishing, but if you'd like to leave a message, fine.

"Old habit," he said. "Always pretend there's more than one of you—if someone's planning to rob you, it'll make them think twice."

I wondered who might want to rob a cabin in the middle of nowhere. A fishing-rod thief, maybe.

175

"Well," I said, "are you coming back?"

"I told you. My truck broke down. I can't get it fixed till tomorrow."

"Oh."

I'd traveled two days; Wren wasn't here.

"Well, maybe I can come to you?" I asked.

"Sure. If you want to get lost, you could. Drive into the woods now and they won't find you till next year."

"That's great. I drove a long way to see you. All the way from Littleton."

"Boo hoo," he said. "You came for my *notes*. I found them."

Judging by the look of the place, that might've been more difficult than it sounded. There was stuff everywhere—newspapers, dirty clothes, ripped magazines, scribbled-on legal pads. Not to mention dire-sounding notes from laboratories in Michigan.

I heard him light a match, then the sound of him puffing away interrupted by a cough. *Lung cancer?*

"You know," he said, "after the flood, they did a major investigation."

"I know," I said. "I read about it. They set up some kind of government commission."

"Some kind, sure. They subpoenaed the construction company. Hired their own engineering experts to review the dam blueprints, check the requisition orders, the whole nine yards. One thing. The hearings were *closed-door*. Not open to the public."

"Was that so unusual?"

"For a Public Works project, very. They said reputations were at stake. No one had been proven guilty of anything.

Not yet. They didn't want anyone's name dragged through the mud."

"That's not unreasonable, is it? I mean, you could make a case for that."

"You could make a case for anything." He coughed again. "Let me ask you something. The first time you did it . . . any pangs of guilt?"

"Did *what*?"

"*Lied*. Did it prick your conscience or not?"

"Yes," I said, "it pricked my conscience."

"But you did it again."

"Yes, I did it again."

"Why?"

It was evidently the question of the week. First Anna, now him.

"What's the difference? I did it. Pick any reason you'd like. Look, why don't we stick to . . ."

"I read them."

"*What?*"

"Your *canon* of deceit. You know, they're still online, in that internal review your paper put out there to show the world how diligent it was being. I noticed something. How your stories got progressively wackier. You had a geometrically increasing suspension of disbelief. Nothing was too hard to swallow at first—but later on? Come on. That story about the abortion-clinic–bombing pediatrician? Anagrams, secret meetings in deserted fields. It reads like a bad movie. I just wondered if accelerating the outrageousness was on purpose? Maybe you wanted to get caught."

"I needed to feed the beast." I said. "That's all."

The beast was frightening and ever-voracious, I could've

177

added. After a while, I found myself in a game of Can You Top This, only I was playing against myself. It was ultimately exhausting.

I heard him take another puff—the muted background *clink-clink* of silverware scraping plates. A diner?

"Where was I?" he said.

"The closed-door commission."

"Right, the commission. They took their testimony and made their report, and in the end they got their pound of flesh. Someone went to jail."

"I didn't know that. Who?"

"An engineer. Lloyd Steiner. Interesting guy—a borderline genius. One of those left-leaning, Lower-East-Side Communist summer camp kids—back in the thirties, when it was all the rage."

"Was he guilty?"

"Of what? Being a liberal Jew? Sure."

"Of building a dangerous dam?"

"I don't know. He was the assistant to the assistant engineer. Hard to imagine he had enough control over *anything* to be guilty."

"What are you suggesting?"

"I'm not sure." Then he lowered his voice, making him sound nearly conspiratorial; evidently he didn't want other diners to hear. "I can tell you he went to prison for ten years, and when he got out, his family had moved from a one-bedroom apartment in a government subdivision to a four-bedroom split-level adobe in La Jolla. I checked. He couldn't get a job as an engineer, of course. Not anymore. He took auto-mechanic classes in jail— that's what he ended up doing when he got out. Must've

178

been excruciating for him. The boy-wonder engineer, fixing cars for a living. He must've had the only blue collar in the neighborhood."

"You think he was paid off? That he was some kind of patsy?"

"I told you. I don't know. Unlike your method of journalism, I can't say if he was or he wasn't. I can't go put it in print. I'd need proof. It does make you wonder. Think about it—they could've hit him with all the Communist crap, summer camps where everyone wore red in color war. Remember, we're talking 1954—McCarthy, bomb shelters, all that paranoia. And if he *still* felt like not playing ball? They *entice* him. A little payoff for his loved ones. The carrot and the stick. You *do* this, because if you don't, we'll bury you. But just to show our heart's in the right place, we'll let your family realize the American dream and get their house in the suburbs. I've seen the house in La Jolla—it's *some* suburbs. I stopped there when I went to interview the girl. You remember her?"

"Space robots in the water."

"Right."

"Is he still alive? Lloyd Steiner?"

"Barely."

"Did you try to speak with him?"

"Uh-huh. Let's just say he's not talking."

"So you think Lloyd Steiner went to jail for ten years to appease the public and kept his mouth shut all that time?"

"It's plausible. More plausible than a bomb-throwing pediatrician, don't you think?"

Sticks and stones may break my bones. . . .

"Is there anything else?"

"There's *always* something else," he said. "You just have to find it."

He put the phone down; I heard him ask for the check. When he came back on, he nearly whispered: "I'm out of the game. Not you. They've let you back in. You said you want to repay the debt. Go ahead. *Repay it.* If you can."

A shutter banged against the wall of the cabin; it sounded like a gunshot. It was certifiably spooky up here.

I asked him about the girl.

"What about her?"

"Your interview with her—it's in your notes?"

"Among other things."

"And she still believes all that stuff—about the space robots rescuing her out of the water?"

"See for yourself. They're on my desk."

I looked over at his rolltop antique. Like something blown up—but I thought I could just make out a small spiral notebook peeking out from the top of the trash, like the winner of King of the Hill.

"Why bother," I said. "We can safely assume spacemen didn't make a visit to Littleton Flats."

"Not unless you believe in fairy tales," he said. "Do you?"

"What?"

"Believe in fairy tales?"

"No."

"Ever read one as an adult?"

"Can't say I have."

"Maybe you should. Even when you stop believing in goblins, they can scare the shit out of you. *Especially* when you stop believing in goblins."

I didn't know quite how to respond to that.

"I guess you're going to want to stay the night?" he asked.

"If it's not too much trouble."

"No trouble. You have six empty cabins to choose from."

I said thanks. Wished him luck with his truck in Fishbein.

"My *notes*," he said. "You can copy them or memorize them. I want them back where I left them. I'd pick a cabin with wood inside. Sweet dreams."

TWENTY-SIX

The interview with Bailey Kindlon had obviously been taped, then both sides of the conversation transcribed.

Wren's Rule number two: transcribe your tape recordings for in case!

He'd begun by jotting down his general impressions of her. The 3-year-old survivor of the Aurora Dam Flood was middle-aged by now. She was divorced and lived alone. He noted her living room was lined with books on alien abductions.

He soon found out why.

He began by thanking her for seeing him and reiterating the purpose of his visit. He was doing a story on the Aurora Dam Flood. He was hoping she could remember some things about that day, even though she was so little at the time.

Actually, I remember a lot, she told him. *You'd be surprised what a 3-year-old brain retains. Of course, doing the whole therapy thing's helped.*

Wren acknowledged that it must have been horrible for her.

You know, at the time, you're a little kid, and in a way, that helps. And in a way, it doesn't. I remember being photographed for some newspaper two days after I was rescued and cracking this big smile because I was going to be on the front page of a paper. This is two days after I was orphaned. So yeah, it helped being 3, but let me tell you, as the years went on, and all sorts of psychic shit began raining on my parade, it wasn't so cool after all. Kids bury it, that's all. And in some ways, that's worse.

Wren asked her if that meant she'd remembered things only later on.

No. She'd always remembered *some* things. Playing in her backyard that Sunday morning.

I remembered putting my Raggedy Ann in a stroller and singing a lullaby to her. I remembered my mother flying out of the screen door, yelling something to me, but not really hearing it very well because there was this roar—like a jet engine, but then not like a jet engine, like some 747 landing right on top of you. It was too close. I remembered that sort of confluence of sound and sensation. Then it was as if I'd been lifted up—my dad would do that, grab me around the waist from behind and swing me up in the air like a loop-de-loop. It was like that. I was suddenly picked up except my dad wasn't there, and my mother was gone too, and I was all wet. I was suddenly in a pool—but the pool was my whole backyard, the whole street. I remember whizzing past Mrs. Denning's house—she was our neighbor—and seeing the house itself; her entire house began moving, spinning past me like a top, and it was like I was in The Wizard of Oz, that scene where Dorothy gets picked up by the tornado and everything is swirling around in the air, only this was water. I remembered all that.

Was that it, then? Wren asked her. All she remembered before therapy?

No. She remembered being rescued. She'd grabbed onto a piece of wood—or it grabbed onto her. Who knows? That's what saved her. An old cellar door. She was on it for at least a day before they found her.

Who found her? Wren asked. The police, the firemen?

No, she said. *Not the police or firemen.*

Then who?

Aliens.

Wren managed to keep his incredulity in check. He asked her to tell him about that. The aliens.

Well, they weren't exactly aliens, she explained. *Not at first. It was their robots.*

I was on the door. I remember being hungry and thirsty and wet and feeling like I was in this dream that I just couldn't wake up from. There were all these dolls in the water, floating Raggedy Anns and Raggedy Andys. But they weren't dolls, of course. When my therapist took me back, I saw them. All the dead people in the water, hundreds and hundreds, open-eyed, but like the eyes of dead fish, you know, that white, filmy, soulless look. They kept bumping up against the storm door, bobbing up out of the water as if they were trying to climb up there with me, but of course they couldn't. They were all dead. That's when the robots came.

Wren asked her to tell him everything she remembered about the robots.

She was drifting, she said. Maybe she'd even fallen asleep. She suddenly woke up, heard this kind of *sloshing* sound. They were coming through the water for her. White robots. They had arms and heads, but no hands or faces. That's how she knew they weren't human. They moved in slow motion, like mechanical dolls.

How *many*? Wren asked.

Six or seven, she said.

And did they speak to her?

How could they? she reminded him. *They had no faces, no mouths. They just made these clicking sounds—like dolphins.*

The robots had lifted her up from the cellar door. Then they'd carried her off.

Where? Wren asked.

Their spaceship.

I was on this table. Some of this stuff I always remembered, and some of it came back later under hypnosis. I was strapped onto this metal table and they were examining me with these awful-looking instruments. As you know, or don't know, that's pretty common with alien abductions. Have you ever read Whitley Schreiber's book?

Wren said he hadn't.

She explained that it was pretty much the bible among alien abductees. Schreiber had been abducted *three* times.

Wren said he'd be sure to pick up a copy. He asked her to go on.

I was on the table, she said. *I couldn't move my arms and legs. There was this . . . light shining down on me—a kind of blue glow—it was endless, as if there were no real source to it, understand? They were staring at me.*

Wren reminded her she'd told him that the aliens didn't have eyes.

Those were the *robots*, Bailey corrected him. These were the *aliens*. She was in their spaceship now. The aliens had eyes. But no mouths. Which means they couldn't speak to her, either. But they could *communicate* with her. They could put their thoughts into her head. Like *telepathy*.

What thoughts were those? Wren asked her.

Well, she couldn't really remember exactly. That she shouldn't be afraid, mostly. That they weren't going to hurt her. Even if that didn't turn out to be entirely true.

A couple of things did hurt. They put some of the instruments inside me—my mouth, and, well . . . lower down. I remember crying and asking for my mom and dad.

Wren asked her to describe what the spaceship looked like.

She couldn't really see it. She was strapped down. There was this blue light boring into her eyes. She could only see *them*, pretty much. The aliens. There were a bunch of them. But one alien—he seemed to be their leader.

He was the one right there, examining me. The others seemed to be . . . well, kind of like his helpers.

It went on and on, she said. As if she were strapped onto that table for days. She knew it couldn't have been days, that it wasn't possible she was there that long, but that's what it felt like. Then it was just over.

Wren asked her if she could describe that. How it ended?

She couldn't.

That's the part I don't really remember. They must've put me back—that's all.

Where? Wren asked.

Somewhere dry. Somewhere people could find me. I guess they did—because I'm here, right? The lone survivor and all that? I was a big story for a day or two. Of course, if it had happened now, they'd put me on CNN. Not those days. Anyway, I was taken in by cousins in Sacramento. And I've never been back— not that there's anything to see, I guess. It all washed away.

TWENTY-SEVEN

The next morning, Wren was still absent.

I walked into his cabin to return his notes and make some coffee.

I was only half-successful.

He'd gone into Fishbein for *supplies*, he'd said. He needed them. He was out of coffee—seemingly out of everything.

A gray mist was hovering inches above the lake. It felt like fall. I half expected to see swirling leaves carpeting the ground.

On the way back to the highway, I reached over to turn up the heat just as a panicked deer flew across the dirt road. It clipped my hood with its back hooves, then tumbled off into the brush.

I lurched to the right and stopped dead, then took a good minute or two to catch my breath.

My heart wasn't the only thing racing. My mind was too, replaying Bailey Kindlon's surreal story. Floating houses spinning down the street. Hundreds of dead people bobbing around in the water. The part of her story that was real.

Do you believe in fairy tales?

If you did, you would have to believe in the rest of her story. Little blue aliens with no mouths. White robots with no faces. Medical exams in the bowels of a spaceship.

A fairy tale worthy of the Brothers Grimm. If they were on mushrooms maybe.

I drove straight down the PCH without stopping.

The forests thinned, the surf quieted, the steep cliffs turned into flat sand, the B&Bs into motels and fish fries. I found a classic rock station with a DJ named Frankie Foo and tapped the steering wheel to "Soul Sacrifice," "Layla," and "Brown Sugar."

When the sun went down, I could just make out the Ferris-wheel lights on the Santa Monica Pier. It made me think of my one and only childhood visit to an amusement park. Not really a park—one of those traveling carnivals with junky rides and shoot-water-in-the-clown's-mouth concessions. After Jimmy died. After I told the police and the caseworkers that he slipped on the ice. That he fell in the tub. That he walked into the door. *What happened, Tommy?* An accident. He was clumsy. At the carnival my mom took her lying son for a spin around the Ferris wheel, then threw up while we were suspended at the top. The resulting screams had nothing to do with the cheap thrill of being carted up to the stars. One sniff of her breath once we were back on the ground was enough to secure her a lecture on responsible child-rearing—this from an itinerant barker who looked like he did a fair amount of drinking himself. It was enough to swear me off carnivals forever—though not enough to swear her off Jim Beam. *Do you still blame her?* Dr. Payne had asked me. He meant did I blame her for being a drunk—for being verbally abusive, for fucking anything in pants. He didn't know what I really blamed her for.

How could he?

I remained the ever-dutiful son.

I didn't tell.

I'm not sure when I chose not to turn off to the 405, when I made the conscious decision to keep motoring straight into Santa Monica.

Maybe I wanted one more turn on the Ferris wheel—figuratively speaking. There's 2 percent of your brain that can believe just about anything. I should know—I made liberal use of it in other people's brains. The Children's Protective Services caseworkers, for example, who somehow believed a 6-year-old boy could have a strange affinity for hard surfaces. My editor, for another, who swallowed stories about Jesus think tanks, con-men actors, and bomb-throwing pediatricians. It's the same 2 percent that tells you that the beautiful woman who sat across from you in Violetta's found you irresistible. Or at least mildly attractive. The 2 percent, in other words, where dumb hope resides.

I didn't have a plan.

I was fairly sure I wasn't going to fulfill my e-mail threat and park myself on the Third Street Promenade till she passed by. I had a general address and her cell number—I was kind of chicken to use it. The other 98 percent of my brain remembered her expression when I told her the good news—that she was dining with a famous liar. I remembered her good-sport attempt to keep the conversation rolling; it was more painful than silence.

I parked in the municipal parking lot on Fourth and strolled around for a while.

It was prime time on the promenade. Once, in the not-so-distant past, downtown Santa Monica had been a haven for America's refuse—an army of strung-out, homeless, down-on-their-luck, just-released-from-a-mental-asylum kind of people. After all, it was warm, and there was always a place under the piers to lay your head.

The Third Street Promenade had changed all that. It had turned downtown Santa Monica into a crowded outdoor mall, replete with street jugglers, musicians, and dinosaur topiaries.

I window-shopped, wondering who that disheveled middle-aged man was staring back at me through the window of VJ Records, and was only mildly surprised to discover it was me.

I escaped the crowds by ducking through an alley onto the next street, where there were still people milling around, but not as many. Where it was at least breathable.

I knew I was slowly working my way somewhere, even if I wasn't exactly admitting it.

There was a coffee shop on Fifth called Java.

An Adidas store. A Blockbuster.

Two residential buildings connected by a single lobby, with wraparound terraces and what appeared to be an inner courtyard with a pool. I could just about sniff the chlorine.

On Fifth, she'd said, *right off the promenade.*

I stopped and took in the scenery. I admired the rhododendrons and bougainvillea fronting the buildings. I noted the new coat of black paint on the filigreed railing that lined both sides of the walkway.

The one I was strolling down toward a suddenly beckoning lobby.

It was lit by two banks of blue fluorescent lights.

There were mailboxes on either side—one per building. I casually perused them, doing a little window-shopping again, even though, okay, I might've, just possibly, you never know, been searching for one particular hard-to-find item.

The girl with Botticelli eyes. The one who'd made me tell the truth to her and then instantly made me regret it.

No Anna Graham listed.

For either building.

Fifth, she'd said, but Fifth stretched on for blocks.

I wandered out of the lobby, stopped short by the momentous decision of whether to turn left or right. I picked left, changed my mind, crossed the street, and drifted into Fatburger for something big and greasy.

No false advertising there. I walked out with half a cow.

I found myself in front of a playhouse. Or maybe I didn't just find myself there. Maybe I was guided there.

It was a play called *The Pier*.

Evidently some kind of comedy, since the actors featured in several photos seemed to be mugging for the audience, one of the actresses holding up women's lingerie in front of a man sporting an *okay, you got me* look on his bug-eyed face.

I was going to turn and keep walking. To where?

I didn't know.

I'd walk until I couldn't. Until I ran across *her*, the odds of which were slim to none.

But something caught my eye.

191

Caught is right.

Picture one of John Wren's lake trout hooked right through its gut.

It was an ensemble shot—that moment where all the actors come on stage hand in hand to take their bows.

There were maybe eight of them.

I leaned in till my breath smudged the glass and I had to step back, wipe it clean, then crouch down to stare at it again.

I stood there transfixed. I might've been meticulously reading the review from *Santa Monica Weekly*, which promised a riotous night in the theater.

You'll shake with laughter, it said.

Or with fear.

I BOUGHT A TICKET, CENTER AISLE, NINTH ROW.

I was right about it being a comedy. A sort of French bedroom farce, except most of the action took place on the Santa Monica Pier. It involved mistaken identities, mismatched lovers, lots of sexual innuendo. The funniest thing was the scenery—a painted backdrop of the pier that kept folding over. One actor or another would deviate from their marks in the middle of a scene in order to mosey over and casually push the Ferris wheel back into place.

Still, the audience seemed to like it well enough. It's hard to tell with theater audiences, since they always seem to try so hard. It must be the proximity to the actors, who are not up on some celluloid screen but *right* there in front of you. No one wants to be impolite.

By the second act, all the mistaken-identity stuff basically worked itself out. With one exception.

He made his appearance at the end of act one.

He played a gay actor pretending to be his straight roommate in order to impress a female William Morris agent, who had the hots for his roommate who she thought was him. The William Morris agent kept having conversations on one of those invisible cell-phone speakers that various bystanders took to be directed at them. That was the running gag, leading to all sorts of mistakes and would-be hilarity.

He first appeared stage right, in tank top and running shorts, seconds away from bumping into the talent agent who was telling some producer—over her cell phone, of course—about some hot project, using words certain to be construed two ways.

I leaned forward in my chair, nearly planting my chin into the person sitting in front of me.

It was meant to be dusk, that twilight hour Shakespeare was so fond of. Magical things happened at dusk; people turned into donkeys, spells were cast and lifted, lovers parted and reunited. I leaned forward because the dimmed lights made it hard to see and I couldn't be 100 percent sure.

By the time he appeared at the beginning of act two in the full, glaring sunshine of morning, all doubts were dispelled.

It was him.

THERE WASN'T A STAGE DOOR.

This was off-off-off-Broadway. The actors exited from the same door the audience did, the one in the front.

I had to wait them out, mingle with the handful of other theatergoers waiting for the actors to appear.

After ten minutes, they began straggling out, first an actress met by a middle-aged couple I imagined were her parents. They wrapped her up in a big hug and gushed on and on about how *hysterical* the play was, exhibiting the acting genes they must've passed on to their daughter.

Then one of the male actors, barging through the theater door and already yakking on his cell phone.

What d'ya mean, not right for the part . . . you tell them . . .

When he came out—his name was *Sam Savage*, according to the playbill—he was with two other members of the cast, a man and a woman. I was half-turned to the wall, undecided whether to go up and confront him or wait back for a while.

I waited.

They slipped out the door where the man waved goodbye. That left Sam with the lithe blonde actress; they sauntered down the sidewalk hand in hand.

I followed them, trying to keep a respectable distance. Maybe half a block or so.

If you've never followed anyone, it's harder than it looks.

They weren't just a moving target—they kept *stopping* too, peeking into one window or another, mostly her. He would separate from her, wander away, and sometimes turn around and stare back in my direction.

I tried to mirror them, to anticipate, to stop, turn, and hope that when I turned back, they'd still be there.

They turned right on Santa Monica and walked up to Seventh.

The whole time, as I followed and ducked and covered, I kept asking myself one question. Like a mantra. Hoping that if I mumbled it long enough, I might figure things out.

I was starting to connect the dots—here and there beginning to draw very shaky lines from one thing to another. But it was like that dream I had—every time I looked at the half-finished picture, it had disappeared like Littleton Flats itself.

They ducked into a bar on Seventh.

The Piñata.

I didn't have to walk inside to know what it looked like. Frozen margaritas with little pink umbrellas, plastic table tents with sombreros on them, wooden bowls of chips and salsa. I waited outside, listening to the strains of Los Lobos as people wandered in and out.

Finally, I pushed the door open and walked inside.

It was loud and packed.

She was sitting alone at the bar. The actress. Sipping a gargantuan frozen margarita, the kind you could only dream about at Muhammed Alley.

Where was he? Bathroom?

I walked to the end of the bar farthest away from her, managed to squeeze myself in next to a group of five very drunk women, and ordered an Excellente, the house specialty according to the drink menu, a margarita made with Cuervo Gold, peach liqueur, and a secret ingredient they refused to divulge upon pain of death.

I was halfway through my Excellente when I spotted him.

I'd been staring at him for a while before I knew who it was. There was the actress—already starting on margarita number two. There was the fashionably decked-out couple sitting next to her—he with shaven head and sunglasses, she with tan, silicone-enhanced breasts. There was the waiter taking their order. It wasn't until the waiter closed his pad, smiled, and leaned down to whisper something into her ear that I knew it was him.

Why not?

He was an actor. In an off-off-off-Broadway theater. Which meant he was also a real estate hawker, a telephone sales solicitor, a parking lot valet. Or a waiter. After the curtain went down, he simply traded one costume for another.

I was starting to feel the margarita. Good.

It was helping to dull the fear.

I was sucking the last remnants of my second one when the lights suddenly began flickering on and off, on and off, on and off.

Closing time.

The five girls disappeared.

Not the blonde actress.

He came out from the back, apron off, and whisked her off her stool.

I took the opportunity to slink out of the bar, making sure to stand several yards away from the front entrance.

They didn't make sidewalks like they used to; this one was swaying like a rope bridge in a gale.

The two of them came out the door and walked right past me without exhibiting the slightest recognition.

I was just an audience member. Someone sitting out there in the dark.

I became bolder with that realization, tailing them by mere feet. Stumbling after them like a third wheel.

They turned the corner, and five seconds later I followed.

196

Which is when an odd thing happened.

I was greeted by empty sidewalk.

Nothing.

There was a car illegally parked on Fifth, but when I peeked through the window, no one was sitting in it.

I felt the panic of walking into a dark and unfamiliar room when you have no idea where the light switch is.

When you lose something, retrace your steps.

I staggered back to the corner—looking for a doorway I might've missed. Somewhere they might've ducked inside.

I felt his forearm smashing into my lower back before I actually saw him. Then I was on my knees, staring straight into very blurry pavement.

"Okay, motherfucker, why are you following us?"

My lower back was on fire. When I tried to get to my feet, he pressed his knuckles into my shoulders and shoved me back down. I felt his hot spittle spray against my neck.

"*Answer* me, asshole!"

"I had a follow-up question," I said.

"*Huh*?"

"There was something I forgot to ask you." I could see the girl now. They must've been hiding behind the quaint, retro lamppost, waiting for me to come sauntering by.

"What the *fuck* are you talking about?" he asked.

"I'm talking about the story."

"What story? Who the hell are *you*?"

"I want to get up." I was this close to throwing up. Too many Excellentes.

He hesitated, then said: "Okay. But slowly, right, chief?"

I managed to push myself up to a standing position

197

without falling over. My left pants knee was ripped and bloody.

When I turned and looked at him, I saw someone who'd simply been taking on a role before—that of the tough, streetwise *hombre*—but who now looked pretty much like an actor uncertain of his lines. For one thing, he'd stepped back as I turned around, a physical surrender of previously hard-won territory.

Maybe he'd recognized me.

"Hey there, Ed," I said.

He didn't answer me.

"He's not *Ed*," his girlfriend said, looking wary and spooked. "He's Sam. You obviously have the wrong person. We thought you were trying to mug us. So we'll just continue on our way home, okay?"

"I know his name's not Ed," I said. "But he played someone named Ed. You remember, don't you? A pharmaceutical salesman named Edward Crannell. On a highway outside Littleton."

TWENTY-EIGHT

L.A. doesn't have a lot of after-hours clubs like New York. L.A. wrapped up earlier. Maybe it was all that healthy living—everyone needing to be pumping their legs up on Mulholland Drive at 6 a.m.

But there was at least one after-hours club in L.A.

I followed Sam's gray Mustang there.

Sam had denied and denied and denied, and then pretty much given up when I told him I'd be happy to send him the story in the *Littleton Journal* with his picture in it. I hadn't taken his picture that morning.

He didn't know that.

We pulled up at storefront with completely blackened windows, stuck between a *Live Nude Girls* strip bar and an outdoor taco stand. Both appeared long closed. So did the store, but when Sam knocked on its door, someone answered and let us in.

There seemed to be a lot of actor types in there—in that they were all various shades of beautiful and somewhat desperate-looking.

We settled into a red leather banquette that might've

come straight out of *Goodfellas*. The tables were a hodge-podge of styles, art deco to fifties luncheonette.

"The owner ran props at Paramount," Sam explained.

Sam had his request for a dirty martini countermanded by his girlfriend—Trudy, she said her name was, who instead ordered him a ginger ale with no ice.

"I don't want to be carrying you home," she said. "I saw you sneaking drinks at the Piñata."

Sam meekly acquiesced.

After his ginger ale was delivered by a waitress in a black catsuit, I asked him, "Okay, who hired you?"

"Some guy."

"Some guy. That's it? Did the guy have a name?"

"I don't remember. I'm not shitting you. He was just some guy who needed an actor."

"Okay—fine. Where did you meet him?"

"He got my name from a bulletin board. On the Web. You know, you place your headshots there and lie about all the productions you've been in, and sometimes you get a call. Mostly extra stuff."

"What did he say to you? This guy whose name you don't know?"

"That he needed an actor for one day's work. Not even a day—a morning. An out-of-town job."

"Did you ask him what the work was? A film, a commercial?"

"Sure. He said it was live theater."

"For one day? For one morning? Didn't that strike you as kind of unusual?"

"Yeah."

"But you still went?"

"He was paying me five thousand dollars."

"*That's* where you got the money?" Trudy said. "You said you sold your bar mitzvah bonds—liar."

Sam looked suddenly sheepish. I couldn't help feeling—just for a moment—the empathy that one liar feels for another. In another context, I might've bought him a drink and commiserated with him like two kindred souls.

"You know what extra work pays?" he asked me. "Two fifty a day. *If* you can get it. And that's more than they're paying me for that moronic play. This was five *thousand*, okay? I have bills to pay."

"Did you drive out to Littleton with this generous benefactor? Or just meet him there?"

"I drove out myself."

"To Highway 45?"

"Yeah."

"And what did you find there?"

He'd begun playing with a matchbook, flipping it back and forth between his middle finger and thumb—flip, flip, flip. "The car was already on fire," he said softly.

"So, what'd you do—call 9-1-1. Flag down a passing car?"

"He said it was *empty*. Just a dummy in there—part of the *show*. I swear to God, on my mother's life."

"Your mother's dead," Trudy said flatly.

"It's an *expression*. Okay, fine, I swear to God on *my* life. . . ." He was staring at me in full pleading mode, as if it was very important for me to believe him. "Nobody was *in* there. That's what he said. Nobody real. You think I would've gotten involved in any kind of . . ." His voice trailed off.

"Any kind of *what*?" his girlfriend said, looking more disgusted by the second.

"Well, you know . . . *crime* or something. The guy needed an actor and he paid me five thousand to act. That's it."

"He was there when you got out there?" I asked. "The man who paid you?"

Sam nodded.

"What did he look like?"

Sam took a sip of his ginger ale. "Weird. You know . . . like, it's hard to put into words exactly . . . he had a sort of pushed-in face. . . . No, not pushed in, just not fully pushed *out*. . . . Understand what I'm saying? He had this really high voice, too. Like a girl's . . ."

You're it.

"Okay," I said. "There's a burning car there. And him—anyone else?"

"Not yet. He said other people would be coming—just like a regular accident. You know, the police, an ambulance—I should play it like we'd collided, me and this car, even though no one was really in there. It was just for show."

"And you believed him?"

Sam nodded.

"I was there, Sam. Remember?"

Sam looked away, down at the floor, at the smoky throng by the bar, at the walls plastered with old Peter Max prints, scanning the room as if searching for the nearest exit.

"Remember the smell, Sam? Remember that odor coming from the car? You knew what that was, didn't you? You knew what it meant? Who's the dummy here, Sam?"

202

Sam had redirected his stare at his lonely glass of ginger ale, as if he wanted to dive in and drown. His eyes began tearing up. For the first time that night, I knew he wasn't acting.

"I . . ." He picked his hands up in a gesture of hopeless remorse. "Look, I tried to *believe* him, okay. The guy said it was an act. I'd driven all the way *out* there already, he tells me no one's in the car, then suddenly the police drive up, and an ambulance, and then you show up. . . ."

"The other car—your car. The smashed-in Sable. Whose was it?"

He shook his head. "I don't know. It was there when I got there. I think *he* drove it."

"Okay. What about after?"

"After what?"

"After I left? After you politely answered my questions about the accident? By the way—were you improvising, or was there some kind of script you were supposed to follow?"

"He told me what to say. More or less. The basic idea of it—how the accident happened. I just riffed on it."

"To the sheriff?"

He nodded. "And you."

"Right. That didn't bother you, making things up to a policeman? You weren't concerned you might get in trouble?"

A black girl on six-inch heels had wandered over to our banquette. She reached down and hugged Trudy.

"*Rudey* . . ." she said. "You haven't called me in a dog's age, girl. What's going on?"

"Nothing much," Trudy said.

203

"I heard you're doing *the-a-ter*."

"Yeah," Trudy said without much enthusiasm.

"With your significant other, huh?"

"He's not as significant as you think," Trudy said.

Sam turned to look at her with a hangdog expression of pure agony.

"Look," Trudy said to her, "we're engaged in something kind of private here. Promise to call you, okay?"

The girl said: "Private, huh?" giving me a glance that seemed mildly lascivious. "Okay, *see ya*."

"After I left, what happened?" I asked Sam.

"Nothing. I got paid. That's it."

"That's it. You didn't ask him what the little play was *about*? You get called to the middle of the California desert and find a car on fire with the obvious smell of burning human being in the air, and you lie to a sheriff and a local reporter and you take your money and you don't ask him, not even once, what the hell was going on?"

"I asked him," Sam said, an almost whisper.

"And what did he say?"

"He said it was a *reality show*. Have a nice life."

"That's it. You didn't ask him again?"

Sam shook his head. "Maybe I didn't want to know. Okay?"

Like someone else, I suddenly remembered. There'd been moments, when this someone else had sat there and listened to my overheated explanations, my rationalizing away one inconsistency or another, and I thought, he knows, it's right there on the tip of his tongue, but he will not say it. He won't.

"So you drove back and that's it?"

"Yeah."

"Never picked up a paper or looked on the Web to see if anybody really died out there? No curiosity at all?"

He shook his head. "I told you. I wanted to forget about it."

The first gray glimmer of morning was beginning to poke through the front window where the black paint had flecked off; it looked like a canopy of washed-out stars.

"Tell me about that place on the Web again. Where he just happened to pick you."

"What about it?"

"How did he know you wouldn't get out there and just turn around and leave?"

"I told you. It was a lot of money to me."

"Yeah, you told me. But there's a limit to what people will do, even for a lot of money. How did he know you'd go along with it?"

Trudy folded her arms and fixed him with a withering stare.

Sam shrugged.

"I don't understand what you're asking me."

"Sure you do. I'm asking you why he picked *you*. Come on, Sam. What kind of Web site are we talking about here?"

"I told you. Just an actors' bulletin board."

"What *kind* of actors?"

Sam sighed, squirmed in his chair, looked up at the ceiling for divine guidance, maybe.

"I heard about it from another actor, okay—this new Web site that helps actors, you know, who need a little extra cash. . . ."

"Yeah?"

"Actors who are willing to act in nontraditional formats."

"*Nontraditional formats*. Is that what you call it?"

"What's he talking about?" Trudy didn't get it; maybe she'd had to swallow a lot in this relationship, but she couldn't digest this. Not yet.

"Tell her, Sam. *Say* it."

"Well, you know . . ."

I said it for him. "*Cons*. For enough money you loaned yourself out for con jobs. That's the only kind of acting that would pay five thousand dollars for one morning, isn't it?"

Sam didn't answer me. He didn't have to.

A chill was slowly working its way up my spine, one vertebra at a time.

I turned to Trudy.

"I would watch your back if I were you."

When Sam looked up at me with a suddenly queasy expression, I said: "The man who paid you. He might not like the fact that you're walking around. Not anymore. Okay?"

THAT SHOCK OF RECOGNITION.

Confronted with something half-familiar and half-remembered.

A group of desperate Hollywood actors selling themselves to the Russian mob for cons.

Remember?

One of my stories.

Only it was one of *those* stories.

Currently featured on a certain online Web site courtesy

of a great American newspaper that I'd almost brought to its knees.

Fodder from Valle's prodigious canon of deceit.

Dramatically constructed. Exquisitely detailed. Rigorously recounted.

But not true.

Not true.

Not one single fucking word of it.

TWENTY-NINE

I can hear helicopters outside my motel room.

They sound military. If I had to guess, I'd say Black Hawks, buzzing low in formation, out on a search-and-destroy.

My first instinct is to hide, to dive under the bed and stay put until they pass.

I can't move. I am frozen stiff. I am stuck in quicksand.

Then I wake up.

My TV's on. It's 4 a.m. They're showing a movie about Vietnam. Bursts of napalm and the rat-a-tat of hopped-up machine gunners as thatch-hatted villagers run for their lives.

Okay, no helicopters.

Still, it reminds me.

They're looking for me.

I have a deadline.

I am writing as fast as I can.

I am.

I'll get no extensions. Either I'll make it, or I won't.

I'd say the odds are fifty-fifty. No better than that.

I've taken to peeking out the window to see if that man is there.

The one Luiza said asked about me.

When I asked her what he looked like, she shrugged and made a distasteful face.

I asked her what he wanted to know.

How long you be here, Luiza said.

Did you tell him?

She shook her head. *I say I no know*.

That's it?

He ask what you look like.

Okay, fine. Did you tell him what I look like?

Yes.

Luiza remembered he had a badge.

She didn't know if it was a policeman's badge or a dog-catcher's.

Only that she was afraid of them. Badges.

There was *Immigration*, after all.

Which is why I don't 100 percent trust her. I can't.

They *can* do things to an illegal. She'd confided in me when she understood I didn't care and couldn't hurt her. Her torturous journey up the Central American isthmus and across the Rio Grande at the mercy of a nineteen-year-old *coyote* high on mesquite. The paper mill that will supply you with a very legitimate-looking license. Not to someone from the INS, though. No. Not to them.

And I'm at a crucial part of the story—the crux of it.

You can sense it, can't you?

You're sitting there connecting the dots like I did. I need to present it to you this way, chronologically, so you can

209

follow along and see the way it unfolded, piece by piece. So in the end, you'll *believe*. As much as you distrust the messenger, you'll believe the message.

You'll know what to do.

THIRTY

When I reported back to work at the *Littleton Journal*, Hinch was at the hospital with his wife.

Norma appeared to have been crying.

"It's touch and go," she said.

Nate didn't look all that happy himself. He'd received a Dear John letter from Rina—or, more accurately, a Dear John text message, modern times being what they are—and was sulking at his desk in the back.

The overall mood was somber and restrained.

Hinch had left me the usual number of local stories that needed to be written up. I zipped through them like a driver focused solely on his end destination, following the street signs by rote. The Littleton Street Fair was kicking off next week. The Lone Star Rodeo, featuring a women's bronco-busting tournament, was coming to town. A meeting of the California Historical Society was going to be held at the Littleton Library.

I finished in record time. I patted Nate the Skate on the back and told him to hang in there. I brought Norma a cup of coffee and told her to keep the faith.

Then I disappeared into the microfilm.

I was falling down a rabbit hole and I wanted to see where I'd land.

I was going forward by going back.

To the place I'd visited before when I'd first been hired, when I perused the local history like a traveler scanning the guidebook of a forthcoming destination. When I nosed around town and asked people for their memories. No matter where I seemed to go—up and down the PCH, twenty miles outside town, or through the looking glass—I kept coming back to it.

It had been waiting for me all along.

1954.

The Aurora Dam Flood.

The death of Littleton Flats.

THIRTY-ONE

They were listening to Eddie Fisher and Rosemary Clooney on the radio.

Hey there, you with the stars in your eyes. . . .

They went to the Odeon on Sixth and Main to see Brando play an ex-boxer with a conscience.

They read dispatches from Seoul in the *Littleton Journal*. The Korean War had just ended—the full dress rehearsal for that Asian land war still to come. They perused the back pages for the baseball box scores as the New York Giants surged to the National League pennant.

Those who owned General Electric TVs chose between two major heavyweight bouts that year—Marciano versus Ezzard Charles, or Army versus McCarthy.

It hadn't been a good year for Tail-Gunner Joe.

America liked Ike, but it wasn't so sure about Joe anymore, the rabid Red-baiter who'd sworn on a stack of Bibles that there was a Red under every bed. Or at least, inside every department of the U.S. government. The incredible irony of his bellicose claims was still years from exposure—that lying-through-his-teeth Joe, this cheap

213

opportunist whose name became synonymous with un-deserved character assassination, was more or less on the money. There *were* Communists scattered throughout the U.S. government—Senator McCarthy just didn't know it.

What he did know, or was at least beginning to catch a dangerous whiff of, was his own political mortality. He'd gotten angry at the U.S. Army because they wouldn't give an exemption to his favorite hatchet man. Suddenly, the army was riddled with Communists, too. They held a public hearing on the matter—where Joe questioned the loyalty of an aide to the army's chief counsel, Joseph Welch, where Welch uttered the now-famous line asking the senator if he had *no sense of decency*, and where the relatively newfangled medium of TV caught every mesmerizing, career-dooming moment of it. By the time the hearings ended, McCarthy was a power broker in name only. His bullying and general ugliness of character had been exposed for all TV-owning Americans to see. He was political toast.

Of course, there was the man and there was the movement.

Red-fearing was still very much alive and well.

One sniff of the mushroom cloud drifting over Russia was sufficient to send Americans running and screaming into their bomb shelters. *Russia had the H-bomb!* There was a picture in the *Littleton Journal* of a state-of-the-art shelter stocked with an entire wall of Campbell's soups and two hundred boxes of Kellogg's Sugar Frosted Flakes.

The innocent fifties, they called it.

It was innocence poisoned by fear. People always knew they were going to die; now they knew how.

Still, in Littleton Flats, they cleaned homes and diapered children and flipped burgers. Three-quarters of the men in town—give or take—worked for the hydroelectric power plant attached to the Aurora Dam. They wore steel construction hats and slipped cotton into their ears to keep out the constant roar of rushing water. They held barbecues on Sundays where they listened to the Giants take the World Series 4 to 0. They danced like William Holden and Kim Novak at the local church. Teenagers spent Saturday nights hot-rodding outside town. An article mentioned several smashups, one fatal, and the subsequent efforts of the sheriff's department to channel youthful energies into more wholesome pursuits.

Like sports.

There was a little league made up of three teams. The local high school football team was known as the Littleton Flat Rattlers and went 3–7 in 1953.

The seniors put on a production of *Oklahoma!* where the lead was played by Marie Langham; the school paper called her *transcendent* and noted that the boy who played Curly was also split end and defensive back on the football team. The high school boasted five Westinghouse finalists.

The town held a May Day celebration in the town square that year. They danced around a maypole and sang "It Might as Well Be Spring."

During Christmas, they carted in a big fir and decked it in electric lights, topping it off with a gleaming star of Jesus. A toy collection was taken for down-on-their-luck families. The fourth-grade class at Franklin Pierce Elementary School wrote a letter to Eisenhower pledging their help against Godless Communism.

There was a Bing Crosby fan club in town.

The Rotary Club, staunchly Republican and a must if you were running for town office, advertised a June social.

Bingo tournaments were held every week at the Our Lady of Sorrows church.

The Littleton Flats Café served a breakfast special of three eggs—any style—home fried potatoes, orange juice, coffee, and toast for just fifty cents. Free refills on the coffee.

There were summer concerts at the gazebo—a barbershop quartet called the Flats Four was the main draw.

There would be two banner headlines in the history of the *Littleton Journal*. The day after Lee Harvey Oswald left his perch at the Texas Book Depository building was the second.

The first was the Monday after the Aurora Dam Flood.

Flood Disaster Wipes Out Littleton Flats!

The what, where, how, and when in a succinct six-word statement. The why of the matter wouldn't be determined till later—other than the fact that three straight days of rain had raised water levels to ominously high levels.

Total Loss of Life Feared!

That was the next day's headline—before 3-year-old Bailey Kindlon was discovered downriver and still alive.

There were the pictures.

A town swallowed whole, with bits and pieces peeking out of the water like dead cypress branches in a swamp.

One of the photographs appeared to have been taken from a helicopter. You could see a faint chop in the flood-water stirred up by the rotor blades, and the barest shadow like a whale hovering just below the surface.

There was a closeup of Littleton's fire chief, looking somber and bleary-eyed, the expression of a surgeon informing the family that despite his very best efforts, the patient has died.

In the days that followed, a list appeared. It grew longer and longer, as if it were a living thing voraciously fattening up on the bodies of the dead.

Benjamin Washington—6 years old appeared by the third day.

By then, the list covered six columns and two entire pages.

By then, the National Guard had been called in, with an entire battalion from Fort Hood.

By then, the governor of California had held his obliga-tory press conference at the site of the disaster, the bishop of Los Angeles had said a benediction over the watery grave in which he referenced Noah's flood, and blockades had been posted to keep the curious and grief-stricken away. There was the threat of disease—all the dead bodies in the hot sun. All that water—a natural breeding ground for dangerous microbes.

By the end of the week, fingers were already being point-ed. There was no mention of Lloyd Steiner—not yet. Just rampant curiosity about how a dam built by top engineers could've crumbled like a Toll House cookie. Local corrup-tion was suspected. *Half the state's underwater*, someone was quoted as saying, *and the other half's under indictment.*

An expert on dams, Major Samson from the Army Corps of Engineers, was quoted in the *Littleton Journal*: "Desert or not, you have to account for a rise in water levels and the increase in pressure. Any dam built to U.S. standards should've been able to withstand it. There had to have been severe structural faults to precipitate this kind of disaster."

President Eisenhower conveyed his personal condolences to the families of the dead. Of course, most of the families of the dead were dead. Not everyone. Belinda Washington had been somewhere else that morning—taking care of another family's children. There was no Mr. Washington on the list of the dead—maybe he'd gone MIA a long time ago.

The Congrave Funeral Chapel in Littleton went into overdrive, scheduling one funeral after another—sometimes three a day—in order to get everyone into the ground. The spillover went as far as San Diego, bodies outsourced to whoever had room. The Littleton Cemetery expanded by one half.

A few politicians of note attended the funerals. The vice president, Dick Nixon, came all the way from Washington and held Pat's hand as they lowered a local alderman into the earth. The lieutenant governor of California attended two burials. Billy Graham said last rites over the Littleton Flats priest.

Life magazine sent a photographer who dutifully immortalized the massive outpourings of grief. One of his photos was reprinted in the *Littleton Journal*, of an elderly man from Minnesota, head bowed, dressed in black, white handkerchief dabbing at his eyes, paying respects to no one in particular—subscribing to the quaint notion that we're all relatives in the family of man.

Flags in California drooped at half-mast for an entire week.

Bailey Kindlon's smiling picture appeared four days after the disaster. She had two full moons for eyes and a smattering of freckles on both cheeks, a female Howdy Doody.

Lone Survivor!

The article said she was found floating on a storm door that had once been attached to Littleton Flats Grocery but was discovered six and a half miles away. She was rescued by a National Guardsman named Michael Sweeney. No mention of space robots clicking away like dolphins. She was reported to be in good physical health, despite minor scratches and bruises.

By the second week, articles about Littleton Flats followed the fate of the town itself and disappeared. Newspapers are constant reminders of that banal cliché uttered by survivors everywhere, that life goes on.

Local elections had to be followed and reported on. Box scores had to be reprinted and scrutinized. Weather had to be forecast and complained about. Senators in Washington who'd offended the national sense of fair play had to be reprimanded (quietly) and nuclear blasts in far-off places dutifully chronicled. *Beetle Bailey*, *Li'l Abner*, and *Peanuts* needed to be caught up with.

The next mention of the Littleton Flats disaster concerned the government commission that was going to get to the bottom of it all. That would decide who'd be publicly flogged to satiate the national bloodlust for a villain; 853 deaths demanded it.

Lloyd Steiner would get his fifteen minutes of infamy.

There was just one picture of him.

He was exiting the courtroom after a day of what must've been useless and damning testimony. A smoking gun had been found and brandished: secret blueprints found in Steiner's possession that clearly illustrated a foreknowledge of certain structural shortcuts that had been approved and implemented.

Ostensibly by Steiner himself.

He'd evidently been caught unawares by a flashbulb, his head whiplashing back like a performer being whisked offstage by an unseen cane, his glasses lit up like Christmas bulbs. Which was metaphorically apt—the villain of the piece being snatched off the national stage to a federal prison cell, where he'd spend the next ten years.

I WANDERED BACK TO MY DESK.

I devoured a cup of Norma's awful coffee, then went back to the coffeemaker and poured another.

Nate the Skate asked me for something to do, evidently believing that hard work was just the ticket for a ruptured heart. I gave him my hastily scribbled articles to proof.

Norma was monitoring the phone for news from the hospital. A nurse in ICU was calling periodically with updates on Hinch's wife, none very promising.

I sat back in my swivel chair and played back the microfilm in my head, an endless loop flickering with stark and sobering images that nearly lulled me to sleep.

Nearly.

"Nate?" I said.

He peered up from his desk, looking suddenly older. I suppose loss will do that to you.

"How many Westinghouse finalists are there every year?" I asked him.

"What?"

"The Westinghouse Awards for high school kids. How many science finalists do you suppose there are every year?"

"I don't know. Why?"

"Take a guess."

"Not a lot."

"Yeah. I wouldn't think there are a lot either. I would guess fifty, maybe. Probably wouldn't be more than that."

"Why are you asking?"

"Let's put it another way. What would you say the odds were that there'd be five from the same high school?"

He shrugged. "I don't know. Isn't there some big science high school in New York—the Bronx High School of . . . whatever?"

"The Bronx High School of Science. Sure—there might be five finalists from that high school. What about some other high school?"

"Is this a trivia game or something? Because I don't want to play, Tom. Sorry, I really don't. I'm in pain here. I'm dying."

"I'd say the odds of there being five Westinghouse finalists from a single high school other than the Bronx High School of Science would be, to use a scientific term, astronomical."

"Okay, fine. You win."

"Now, what if it were a tiny high school? Some school literally out in the middle of nowhere? You'd be talking odds so ridiculous that Vegas would have to take it off the boards. Wouldn't you think so?"

"I guess. Why?"

"Nate, I do have something for you to do. Something to get your mind off Rina." At the mention of his ex-girl-friend's name, Nate actually winced.

"What?"

"I want you to find out everything you can on the people who lived in Littleton Flats."

"Littleton *Flats*? The town—the one that got, you know?"

"Wiped out, right. I want you to see if you can find out who those people were."

"You mean, their names?"

"I have their names. Names are easy. I want to know who they were. What they did for a living. Where they came from. That kind of thing. Some of them must have relatives that are still alive. I need anything you can find."

"Excuse me for asking, but *when* did those people die?"

"Fifty years ago."

"Right," Nate said. "*That's* going to be easy," exhibiting a sarcasm rare for him. Maybe it was his newly wounded heart—there he was skating through life, and he'd gone and taken his first tumble. He was all skinned innocence and bloodied optimism.

"Try the Internet," I said. "Aren't you the computer whiz? Didn't you discover how to get on PinkWorld.com without paying?"

That seemed to momentarily brighten his disposition.

"Okay," he said. "I'll give it a shot."

THIRTY-TWO

Hello, who *is* this? Hello?"

I'd followed the usual pattern of first getting drunk—soused enough to dial his number, but not so drunk that I couldn't remember it. It was a delicate balancing act.

"Hello, *hello* . . ."

It's me. Tom.

I was the second most surprised person on the line to realize that the words had actually been said out loud.

"*Tom?* Tom Valle?"

I reverted back into silence—for a moment I did, contemplating the enormity of finally beginning a two-way conversation with the man whose life I'd personally and irrevocably destroyed.

"Yeah."

Now it was his turn to retreat into silence, a silence so complete that I thought I could hear the second hand ticking away on the grandfather clock that sat against the east wall of his study. I'd been invited into that inner sanctum in the halcyon days of yore, when I was the rising hot shot and he the editorial conscience in residence.

"Was that you?" he finally said. "All those other times? That was you on the phone?"

"Yes, that was me."

"I see." Another moment of silence. "Mind telling me why, Tom? Did you wake up one day and decide to add phony phone calls to your oeuvre of phony journalism?"

Okay, it hurt. But the pain was accompanied by a sudden sense of relief. I once wrote a piece on a sect of self-flagellators; it had taken till now to understand the rapture on their faces as they punished themselves for sins against God.

"I *wanted* to talk to you," I said. "I didn't have the balls. Every time I called, I thought I was actually going to say something."

"Well, that's good to hear. I was beginning to think I had a female admirer."

"No. Just a male one."

Silence again.

"You had an odd way of showing it."

"What I wanted to say, what I need to tell you, is *I'm sorry*. I am so fucking sorry. I should've—look, I know it doesn't change anything, but I needed to say it. I needed you to know . . . I never intended . . ."

"To what, Tom? Get caught? What didn't you intend to do? When you sat in your little cubbyhole and practiced your creative writing, where did you think it would lead? To a Pulitzer Prize?"

"I never thought that far ahead. Just to the next deadline."

"I see." The creak of a chair, the soft shuffling of papers. "I wondered if I'd ever hear from you. It was kind of ungallant of you not to drop me a line. Or something."

"I know. I apologize. It was incredibly unfair what they did to you. It was . . ."

"*Unfair*? Not at all. I was in charge. I looked at your stuff and didn't have the brains or the God-given cynicism. Rumor has it that was my stock and trade. I lacked the editorial wisdom to see what was right in front of my nose. I failed, grandly and publicly. Unfair? Nah."

"They didn't have to take you down with me. . . ."

"No? You know, after it happened, after I took the long walk home, I had more than enough time on my hands to think things through. You were my star, Tom—every editor wants one. It's our legacy to some extent, what we leave behind. Maybe I got as caught up in that as you did. Maybe, just occasionally, that little voice in my head looked at something I was supposed to pass judgment on and said *wait a minute. Stop. It's too perfect—Mercury's too aligned with Mars here.* Maybe I told that voice to take a hike. I think here and there I did. I forgot the oldest axiom there is. Don't believe everything you read in the papers."

I felt something large and inexorable welling up in me. I put the phone down, tucked my face into my shoulder to keep him from hearing.

"Tom? You still there?"

"Yes."

"I've often wondered about you. Where you washed up. Are you still in New York?"

"California."

"California. Doing what?"

"Reporting."

A small but noticeable intake of breath. "The prodigal son, huh?"

225

"What?"

"Nothing. They must be rather forgiving in California, that's all."

"It's not much of a paper."

"Maybe so. But it's a hell of a profession. Don't look a gift horse in the mouth. Not this time, okay?"

"That's why I'm calling you."

"I thought you were calling to offer your much-belated apologies."

"Yes. And this other thing."

"What other thing?"

"Something's happening. I've fallen into a story. It's a hell of a story, the one you look for your whole life. I know it. It goes back, it goes forward, it goes places it's not that healthy to follow. But I am. I am following it. I wanted you to know."

"Be careful, Tom."

"I am. I think one person's already dead because of it. I am being careful."

"I'm not talking about your safety, Tom. I'm talking about the nauseating stink of déjà vu that just wafted in over the phone. I'm talking about being able to finish your sentences. You understand what I'm saying, Tom? I've heard this already. This is old news. This is a tired script from a tired fabulist. Rip it up."

"It's not like before. This is real. This is genuine. I'm telling you, something incredibly weird is—"

"And I'm telling you, Tom. It was always real. It was always genuine. The weirdness was all yours."

"Not this time. I'm being legitimate."

"Legitimacy isn't about *being*, Tom. You either are or you

aren't. You can't try it on like a coat. It doesn't work like that."

"When I'm done, when I put it all together, you'll see. I'm going to send it to you and you'll see."

"Don't bother. I'm not your editor anymore. And you're not my star. I really have to be getting to sleep, Tom. It's a lot later here than there."

No, I thought. *It's a lot later for both of us.*

THIRTY-THREE

I was 99 percent sure I was being followed.

This feeling manifested itself whenever I turned a corner or pulled into a parking lot, whenever I entered or exited my home, whenever I snuck outside the *Littleton Journal* for a smoke, or ducked into JP Drugs for some Tums, or grabbed a cheeseburger at the DQ, or drove to bowling night.

In other words, all the time.

Whenever I stopped and turned and looked, I felt as if I'd just missed him. Or them. Like seeing your shadow suddenly vanish when the sun darts behind a cloud.

That quick.

I walked into Ted's Guns & Ammo and walked out with a .38 Smith & Wesson handgun—I was a neophyte concerning the benefits of one gun manufacturer over another, but the plurality of the name somehow made Smith & Wesson feel more substantial. There was a little problem, of course. As someone who'd served probation, I was legally banned from owning a gun in the state of California. Luckily, Ted, who offered Michael Moore targets gratis with each purchase, had an NRA mentality when it came to state and federal gun laws.

He refused to acknowledge them.

I went two miles outside town and practiced shooting the arms off cacti. I was accurate only about 25 percent of the time.

I started locking my front door, kept all the shades in my house drawn tight. One night I ventured downstairs, gun in hand, and rechecked the basement. Looking for what, exactly? *Bugs*, maybe, remembering the open phone jack; the only one I discovered was a six-inch centipede tucked inside a drainpipe. I took another look in the hole the plumber had punched into the wall. Plaster dust and the ripped paper they used for cheapo insulation in these parts. That's it. I remembered I was going to ask Seth to fill it in—he'd done Sheetrock work on the house before. That's how I'd first met him, when he came around to check on something for the landlord.

I had the feeling that half of Littleton was playing a part, everyone in on the joke but me.

I was having a hard time telling who was playing whom. I needed a playbill.

Sam Savage in the part of Ed Crannell, sure.

Someone else in the crucial if unrewarding role of Dennis Flaherty's corpse. But who exactly?

Benjy Washington?

The second survivor of the Aurora Dam Flood? How could I prove it?

Then I did. Sort of.

I received corroboration.

I'd called the sheriff to ask if they'd dug up that body in

Iowa yet, even as I held back telling him that the man in the pickup truck had hired a desperate actor willing to take *nontraditional* parts for enough cash—that Ed wasn't Ed. I wanted to tell Swenson how I'd stumbled onto that theater in Santa Monica, how I'd followed this actor down the block and even been knocked to the sidewalk, how I'd gotten back up and wheedled the story out of him.

I kept hearing my editor's voice.

This is old news. This is a tired script from a tired fabulist. Rip it up.

He was right.

It was a tired script. Very tired. L.A. actors moonlighting as con men. You could look it up.

The sheriff told me that the body was still stuck in the fallow Iowa ground, that it took an amazing amount of *bureaucratic shit* to get someone unburied, even when the name on the gravestone was still walking around. Then I asked him about the day I came in to tell him that Dennis Flaherty was still alive.

"Remember, I wanted to know if anyone who supposedly died in the flood had ever come back. You looked like you were going to say something. Like maybe you were going to say yes. Why?"

"Huh?" he said. "Oh, that. It was just a little odd."

"A little odd, how?"

"The timing. Someone had called one of my deputies. A week before, maybe. Said he had some information we needed to know. About the Aurora Dam Flood."

"What did your deputy say?"

"He said, 'What the fuck is the Aurora Dam Flood?'"

"The information? What was it?" I asked. That feeling

230

again, like when I stared at the picture on the theater wall. Like the world was a kaleidoscope that wouldn't stop turning.

"Who knows? He made an appointment to come in, then never showed up. Of course, when my deputy discovered the Aurora Dam Flood happened fifty fucking years ago, he wasn't too surprised. Phony phone callers usually don't bother stopping by for coffee."

"Did he give his name?"

"Yeah. That's how he knew it was a prank call. It was one of the kids that died that day."

A VERY PREGNANT MARY-BETH CAME TO THE OFFICE TO HELP OUT in Hinch's absence. She waddled in like a mother duck and asked me if I'd switch chairs with her, since hers was small and uncomfortable, and mine came complete with the football seat cushion I'd dragged all the way from New York, though the New York Jets logo was pretty much worn out by now.

I chivalrously agreed.

Nate the Skate was furiously working the computer and phones, his new assignment having seemingly lifted the veil of despair that had settled over him with Rina's unexpected pronouncement.

I went back to searching for the girl of my dreams.

No, not Anna. The girl of my bad dreams, of my whirling dervish nightmares.

Kara Bolka.

To whose greetings neither Belinda Washington nor myself had been able to reply.

Considering I'd been through the entire state of

California, I tried other states, tried everywhere in the end, and still came up empty.

I rang up Mrs. Flaherty and asked her how Dennis was doing.

"Fine," she said. "He's alive. And how are *you* doing, Tom?" inquiring with the genuine concern befitting the miracle worker who'd brought back her son.

"I'm okay, Mrs. Flaherty. Could I have a word with Dennis?"

"I don't think so, Tom. He's sleeping."

I calculated that it was 3 in the afternoon there.

"Okay," I said. "I'll try him tomorrow."

There was something else I needed to do, something that was sitting on the ledge of consciousness that I couldn't quite coax back in. Something else that needed to be checked out. Only someone interrupted my reverie.

"Those science awards?" Nate said. "I know *why*."

HE LOOKED BOTH EXHILARATED AND EXHAUSTED—AS IF HE HADN'T slept much over the last few days, and maybe he hadn't.

"Okay," he said. "Ready?"

We'd walked outside so we could both light up—and so I could keep Norma and Mary-Beth from hearing.

"You wanted to know how one high school could have five Westinghouse finalists, right?" he said. "Well, it's not that hard when the parents are fucking geniuses."

"What are you talking about?"

"What am I talking about?" He took an enormous drag on his cigarette, then let the smoke seep out through a grin that resembled the Cheshire Cat's. "I took that death list you gave

232

me—you know, the list of flood victims. I Googled them one at a time—and pretty much got nothing. At first. I mean, it was fifty years ago, so why should I. They were mostly what . . . housewives, kids, and dam workers, right? Nothing was coming up, and I was going to tell you it was probably a statistical anomaly—you know what that is, right?"

"Yeah, Nate. I know what that is."

He told me anyway.

"I took a class on it—statistics and probabilities. You'd be surprised how often it happens. Cancer clusters for no discernable reason. Two tornados touching down at the very same spot. Anyway—I was thinking that having five big-time science award finalists from this same rinky-dink high school was just a statistical anomaly."

"But it wasn't."

"No," he said. "Uh-uh. No statistical anomalies here, boss. There was one name—alphabetically speaking, we're talking way down at the bottom. One name, one hit—that's it. *Franklin Timmerman*. Only I was going to ignore it, because Franklin Timmerman from Littleton Flats was a sluice operator at the Aurora Dam, and the Franklin Timmerman I Googled was something else."

"Okay. *What*?"

Nate took another drag and wiped away the sweat that had quickly beaded up on his forehead and in between the bristles on his nearly shaven head. It might've been 20 degrees cooler in the shade, but that wasn't saying much, since it was over 110 just two feet to our left.

"A height-of-burst tactician."

He let that sit there for a while, as if waiting to see if I'd know what a height-of-burst tactician was.

233

"Okay, Nate. I give up. What's a height-of-burst tactician?"

"Oh, *that*. Well, it's someone who makes sure that fission happens at the right height. Nuclear fission. In a bomb. In a *nuclear* bomb. That it explodes at the altitude that'll cause maximum damage. Franklin Timmerman, height-of-burst tactician, had worked on this little thing called the *Manhattan Project*. You've heard of that, haven't you?"

"Yes, Nate, I've heard of the Manhattan Project. You took a class in that too, I suppose."

"As a matter of fact . . . yeah. Pretty cool stuff. Robert Oppenheimer, Enrico Fermi—all these fucking geniuses out there in the desert at Los Alamos. Little Boy, Fat Man, racing Hitler for the big bang. You know what Oppenheimer said when they finally did it—when they tested the first A-bomb and it basically vaporized everything in a two-mile radius?"

"I think so. But go ahead."

"'*I am become death—the destroyer of worlds*,' a quote from Sanskrit. 'I am become death'—pretty eloquent, in a creepy sort of way, right?"

I nodded. "So the Franklin Timmerman listed as . . . ?"

"I'm getting to that."

Good reporting was all in the details, and Nate was committed to relating each and every one of them in chronological order. He was going to give me a blow-by-blow description of his triumph over ignorance.

"Franklin Timmerman was at Los Alamos—the Franklin Timmerman listed in Google, anyway. One of the people who put it all together. Everyone worked in teams there,

234

one team working on one thing, like actual fission, another on the bomb casing, another on making sure it exploded at the right altitude—that was Franklin's job."

"But you said the Littleton Flats Franklin Timmerman was a sluice operator."

"Correct. He was *listed* as a sluice operator on the Aurora Dam. Meaning what? That two people had the same name—which, if you've ever Googled someone, happens like all the fucking time. I mean, you put in *Quentin Tarantino* and you're suddenly reading about some sheep breeder in New Caledonia. So this was obviously the same deal, right? Because what would an expert on nuclear detonation be doing working a sluice on a federal dam?"

He stopped, took another puff of his cigarette.

"Was that a rhetorical question, Nate?"

"Uh-huh."

"So maybe you want to continue."

"Right. Anyway, I *was* going to ignore the whole thing; the only reason I read the whole entry on him was because I'm interested in that stuff—the birth of the bomb, Hiroshima, Nagasaki. But then I figure what the hell and I look up the Manhattan Project—I take all the names that worked out in Los Alamos, and just for the simple hell of it I cross-check them with the list from Littleton Flats."

Nate had reached that moment—when the rabbit is pulled out of the hat, the ripped twenty made whole, the vanished woman brought back onto the stage.

"And what do I get, huh?" Nate said. "Ten hits. *Ten fucking hits.*"

"Have you seen a pickup truck circling us, Nate?"

"Huh? *What* pickup truck?"

"Never mind. Go ahead," I said, even though I felt a sudden knot in my stomach. I leaned back against the *Free Delivery* sign posted in Foo Yang's window.

"What do you mean, go ahead? I just told you I got *ten hits*. You understand what I'm saying? Littleton Flats was teeming with all these little nuclear geniuses. Experimentalists, theoreticians, engineers. That's how one high school could have five kids vying for a Westinghouse. Can you imagine their science projects—*Susie Timmerman is going to split the atom today, class*. Right next to this poor kid from La Jolla who made a shortwave radio from a cigar box. It was like having this little Bronx High School of Science out in the middle of nowhere. Fuck high school— it was like having another *MIT*. Fucking unbelievable."

"Yes," I said, starting to understand something. Beginning to *see*. "Great job, Nate. Really."

"Okay," he said. "So why would ten nuclear geniuses— more than ten probably, because who knows who else didn't come up when I cross-referenced—why would all these top-notch A-bomb guys be living in a little pissant power-dam town?"

I was going to answer him, to recite what any legitimate journalist should memorize by heart—that when you assume, you make an ass out of you and me. That we'd assumed Littleton Flats was just a town of dam workers and that we were wrong. That maybe we needed to stop assuming something else.

That there was just a dam.

Except a loud sound punctured the stillness.

Nate the Skate heard it, too. He turned and instinctively hunkered down.

"What the hell was that?" he said, perfectly normally.

The pickup truck, I was going to say. *The one I just asked you about*. A flash of blue darting down the street.

But blood was all over my hands, as if I'd been finger-painting in it.

And Nate was staring at my bloody hands with a look of shocked concern, ready to say *are you all right*—I could see the words forming on his lips.

It wasn't me he needed to be worried about.

Nate crumpled to the ground and stared up at the sky with curiously dead eyes.

I heard Norma screaming from far away.

237

THIRTY-FOUR

They dug the bullet out of the drywall in Foo Yang, the bullet that had apparently passed straight through Nate's rib cage and out the other side, missing Foo Yang's 13-year-old daughter by six infinitesimal inches or so.

Nate wasn't dead after all. He'd looked a lot worse than he was.

All that blood.

He was taken to Pat Brown General Hospital, where they staunched the bleeding, sewed him back up, gave him two transfusions, and left him resting comfortably in ICU.

He was going to be *fine*, an Indian doctor named Dr. Plith informed us—Norma, Hinch, and myself.

Hinch had been maintaining his vigil up on the cancer ward when they'd wheeled Nate in. Of the three of us, he seemed the most calm—a wounded intern clearly not matching the emotional intensity of a dying wife.

Somehow I was elected to call Nate's divorced mom in Rancho Mirage and break the news; I opted to start with the cheery prognosis and progress backward to the actual shooting.

After she took the name of the hospital—she'd be on

the road as soon as I hung up—she asked me who in God's name would want to shoot her son.

"I don't know," I lied.

I spent some quality time off the main ward with Sheriff Swenson discussing that very subject.

This time he treated me as if I were a bona fide witness instead of a convicted liar. He wrote down my account of what happened: the circling blue pickup—I *had* seen it; that awful noise, like a tire blowout; Nate suddenly crumpling to the ground.

It was time to tell the sheriff about Santa Monica—about everything. Someone had been shot.

I started with Sam Savage. About the Web site and the plumber and that morning on Highway 45.

"An *actor*?" he said.

He looked appropriately incredulous.

"Yeah," I said. "The plumber isn't just breaking into homes anymore. He's hiring out-of-work actors for reality shows on Highway 45. He's incinerating people."

Then I told him whom it was I thought had been incinerated.

Benjy Washington.

Which is when his eyes glazed over. When he got that look.

"Huh?" he said.

I told him about the note in Belinda Washington's picture frame.

"The kid who died in the flood? This is who you're talking about? A dead kid?"

"He's not a kid anymore. And I don't think he's dead. He called your deputy, remember?"

"Oh *Jesus*, Lucas . . . it was a prank."

"Dr. Futillo said it was the body of a black person. The whole accident that day was choreographed."

Swenson sighed, shook his head. "I see. Okay—just out of curiosity. *Why?* Why was it choreographed?"

"I don't know yet. I think it has something to do with the town. With Littleton Flats."

"Littleton Flats. Right."

He got up, closed his notebook. "You have this actor's number, Lucas?"

I WAS STILL AT THE HOSPITAL WHEN NATE'S MOM SHOWED UP.

Dr. Plith had told us to go home—Nate would be sleeping it off for hours, but I was responsible for him being there. *You're it*, the plumber had whispered to me in the basement that day, but Nate had taken the bullet. What's the government's favorite buzzword these days? *Collateral damage.* Reducing murder to a term more appropriate to property destruction, to make it more palatable for a public that likes its blood at the Cineplex.

Nate's mom looked as if she'd run all the way from Rancho Mirage. She was flushed and sweaty, in danger of needing medical attention herself.

I heard her ask the head nurse for her son—*Nathaniel Cohen*—barely managing to get his name out between gasps.

"Mrs. Cohen," I walked up to her. "I'm Tom Valle— from the paper. I'm terribly sorry about this."

She must've taken my apology to be the concerned empathy of a coworker and not the guilty plea of the person who'd put her son directly in someone's crosshairs.

240

When I saw the pickup circling like that—why hadn't I gone back inside?

She moved toward me in a kind of slow motion, then half collapsed in my arms, and I awkwardly held on to her, somewhere between an actual hug and something to lean on. That odd inclination of the bereaved to seek physical comfort from total strangers.

She finally pulled away, gathering herself together as if she were picking her spilled emotions off the floor and storing them back where they belonged.

"I'm sorry . . ." she said, "it's just so . . . God . . ."

"Don't be silly," I said, cognizant of the uncomfortable wet spot she'd left in the center of my chest. "It's got to be awful to hear something like this. Over the phone, too. The good news is, Dr. Plith says . . ."

"Dr. *Plith*?" she repeated his name as if she hadn't heard it correctly. "What kind of name is Plith? Is he a good doctor? I mean I don't know *anything* about *anyone* here."

"He's Indian, I think. He seems very competent."

"Okay. Right." She brought her hands to her face and momentarily kept them there, as if she were murmuring a prayer.

"The doctor says Nate's going to be fine. He was very lucky. The bullet went right through his rib cage—it missed his major arteries."

She kept nodding up and down, up and down, drinking in the news in big thirsty gulps.

"Can I see him?"

"I don't know. I think he's still out of it. You'd have to ask the doctor. Of course—since you're family, maybe they . . ."

She didn't wait for me to finish, went scurrying off after

241

the first flash of hospital green, an ER nurse wheeling another patient into ICU.

I waited.

There were some magazines laid out on a small wooden table. A recent issue of *Time*, an ancient *People* missing half its cover—a newly married Brad Pitt and Jennifer Aniston ripped completely in half, leaving only Aniston with her left arm reaching oddly out into space. Someone must've wanted to set the record straight. I leafed through it without actually reading it.

I was doing something else.

Pushing an imaginary pencil from dot to dot to dot.

I'd say our deceased was black.

It was just a little odd—the timing. . . . Someone called one of my deputies. . . .

The car was already on fire. He said it was empty.

Willing to act in nontraditional formats.

I got ten hits. Ten fucking hits.

There's the outline. Now look at it and say what it is.

Say it.

What are you drawing? she asked me, the pretty waitress who always seemed to give me and Jimmy an extra helping of flapjacks. Who sometimes tousled our hair and leaned over the table on both elbows so that we could smell her perfume—like the crushed flowers my mom put between the pages of books.

A whale, I said. *An octopus. An elephant.*

She laughed. *An elephant here in the diner—whoops, I better call the zoo.*

I smiled and laughed too, feeling my cheeks flush. Complicit in the whole thing, even though I wasn't.

242

It's hard to say what a kid knows or doesn't—isn't that what Bailey Kindlon found out?

Was it my first lie?

That she was just a waitress who'd picked us, out of all the kids in the diner, to bestow her special smiles on?

Why did my mom never come to breakfast at the Acropolis Diner?

Or did she—just once?

If I tried hard enough, I could remember.

The four of us sitting in a red booth—one unhappy family—only we weren't that unhappy, not like we were going to be. Not yet. But wasn't there a coolness as my mom handed her menu back to the waitress who'd taken our order—the waitress who asked me what I was drawing, what fabulous animal I was conjuring up this time? And me not understanding why my mom wasn't smiling back at her, worshiping at the altar of her radiance like we did—Jimmy, Dad, and me?

I could remember something else, too.

My mom brusquely calling her over, this waitress—*Lillian*, her name tag said, like the flower, like a *lily*—after my pancakes had already arrived and I'd poured half a bottle of maple syrup over them. My mom suddenly pulling my plate away, just yanking it right from under me, and calling her over.

These pancakes are cold! How can you serve your customers cold food? It's disgraceful—do you hear me! Disgraceful! You are a disgrace!

Doing what moms aren't supposed to do, except when they get flowers, maybe, or are watching something sad on TV.

243

Crying.

Fat tears rolling down her cheeks as the diner went very quiet as if all the jukeboxes had suddenly shut off, and I learned that you couldn't actually die of embarrassment.

After that morning, it was just Jimmy, Dad, and me.

Every Sunday, just the three of us.

Until he left.

And if I knew it wasn't just the three of us—knew that it was the three of us plus one—I never whispered it out loud.

Not even when it became just the *two* of us.

I heard the sound of the ICU swing open, sniffed the faint odor of blood and alcohol.

A surgeon came striding out with the purposeful walk of the almighty who's still got miracles to accomplish. He pulled off his mask, using it to wipe off the sheen of sweat that covered his brow.

It reminded me of something.

That other thing that needed to be checked out—the thing sitting out there on the ledge I needed to coax back in. The thing I was trying to remember when Nate tapped me on the shoulder and said: *those science awards? I know why.*

Sure.

THIRTY-FIVE

"*Here's my notes,*" I said to him. "*What seems to be the problem?*"

I was in the office that had a stenciled Editorial on the door. He was crouched over his desk, looking as if he was half sleeping on it. He didn't have bags under his eyes as much as fully packed valises.

"*The abortion-clinic–bombing doctor?*" he said. "*You said he took his residency in pediatrics at St. Alban's, a hospital in Mizzolou, Missouri. That's what it said in your article.*"

"*Yes?*" Look calm, I coached myself, even a little affronted.

"*A spokesman from St. Alban's just called. Notwithstanding their obvious desire to separate themselves from a religious zealot and possible murderer, he swore on a stack of good Presbyterian Bibles they don't offer residencies in pediatrics—certainly not in the years you mentioned. So we have an obvious problem here.*"

"*I don't think I mentioned what years he served his residency.*"

Good, just a touch of annoyance, as if he was keeping me from doing my real work, which was scratching out my next article and not answering for a minor inconsistency.

"*No, I know you didn't, Tom. But you mention his age—43.*"

Which would pretty much tell you when he served his residency—give or take a year."

"Okay. Well, maybe he took a little longer to become a doctor. I'm sorry—he didn't tell me when he served his residency. I was kind of delighted he told me where. I mean, I think he tripped up a little telling me that—since the deal was anonymity or nothing."

He had an unraveled paper clip clenched between his teeth. It was nearly bitten in half.

"Of course, now that you mention it," I said, "he might've told me he served his residency at St. Alban's to throw me off the scent. I probably should've left it out of the article."

"You have your notes, Tom?"

"Right here."

"Good."

I leaned over and placed them on the desk, flipping the memo pad to the second page. "There," I said, pointing to the name of the hospital. "See—that's what he told me. St. Alban's. Residency served. I probably should have pushed him on it—but, you know, I was kind of holding my breath that he'd told me even that much."

He stared at my notes, running his finger across the ink like a blind man reading Braille.

"When did you interview him, Tom?"

"Oh . . . let's see . . . uh-huh, March 5," pointing to the date at the top of the page, the one I'd scrawled last night right after I'd interviewed the imaginary doctor in my head—Tom Valle, meet Dr. Anonymous—devolving my article into scrupulously ordered notes able to pass safely through the treacherous shoals of fact checkers, legal eagles, and increasingly suspicious editors.

"That's odd, Tom."

"Why?"

"March 5. You were in Florida on March 5. I remember

because I turned 55 the day before, and you called to wish me happy birthday. You were in Boca Raton doing that piece on retirement communities. That was March 5, Tom—I'm positive. Didn't you say you interviewed the doctor in Michigan?"

"Hey . . . what . . . what you're asking me?"

"I'm asking you when you interviewed the doctor. We have a spokesman from St. Alban's screaming about lawsuits and I need to know the facts. So again . . . when did you interview the doctor?"

"Well . . . lemme see . . . you know, it was more than once, of course. I talked to him on the phone, and then I met him in person in Michigan."

"You said you met the doctor in a deserted field, the ruins of some frontier town that burned down. You drove out there and he showed up in a separate car—right?"

"Yes—that's right. It might be . . . yeah, it might be that these notes were from my phone call to him. Yeah, now that you mention it, that sounds right. I probably called him from Florida."

"Okay, Tom. You used your cell, I guess."

"My cell?"

"Your cell phone, Tom. I assume you would use your cell phone to call Michigan? If need be, we can get the phone records and show that you called Michigan on March 5 from Florida."

"Show who?"

"If we end up in court, Tom, we might have to walk everyone through the process."

"Okay. The doctor obviously gave me the wrong hospital. Remember that the deal was anonymity—he didn't even give me the name of his home or birthplace. Just anagrams, remember? My antenna should've gone up. He fed me the wrong hospital and hoped I'd put it in the article, and like a stupid idiot, I did. He used me—I'll be more careful next time."

"I'm not talking about getting the wrong hospital, Tom. I asked you when you interviewed the doctor and you said March 5; only you were in Florida on March 5 and now you say you called him from there and conducted the interview by phone."

"I met him in person—I sat right across from him. As close as we are now. I told you. I just forgot I talked to him on the phone first. It was over several conversations—the interview."

"Fine. Understood. When you called the doctor on March 5 from Boca Raton and conducted your first of many interviews, did you call him on your cell phone? It was long-distance. You were in Florida—I assume you would use your cell so you wouldn't run up larcenous charges from the hotel? I'm just trying to get the facts straight, Tom."

"Well, let me think a minute, okay. Let me . . . you know, I think I called him from a pay phone."

He took the paper clip out of his mouth and carefully laid it down in front of him.

"You called him from a pay phone?"

"Yes."

"Why would you do that? Why would you call him from a pay phone?"

"That's the way he wanted it. I'd forgotten about that. He was very secretive, obviously. The whole anagram thing, meeting me where no one could see us. He didn't know whether he could trust me yet. He didn't want me to be able to see what number he was calling from."

"I thought you called him. You just said you called him from a pay phone."

"I'm sorry, I got my syntax wrong."

"Your syntax? Either you called him, or he called you. Which is it?"

"I told you. He called me."

"How would he know the number of a pay phone in Florida?"

"I e-mailed him the number. And then I was supposed to wait at the pay phone at a certain time for him to call."

"You e-mailed him the number?"

"Look, I don't remember everything exactly the way it happened. I mean, I was doing two stories at once—you said so yourself—I was down there doing the retirement home story, and so you can understand why I forgot about the pay phone. I forgot about it—that's all. That's why I have my notes."

"Yes, Tom," he said. "You always have your notes."

I'D LEFT THEM AT THE OFFICE.

My notes from my trip to Littleton Flats.

I stared at them—my interview with the army doctor.

You met the doctor in a deserted field, the ruins of some frontier town that burned down.

I'd met the army doctor in the ruins of another destroyed town. This one destroyed by flood, not fire, even if both were weapons of biblical retribution.

Uncanny.

How the echoes of my deceitful past kept bouncing back to me.

Sam Savage, suddenly bringing a long-ago story to life, a trippy little piece about out-of-work actors pulling cons for cash.

Another *exclusive* in the Valle retrospective, available online for anyone who likes their news unfit to print.

And more—something I hadn't put together before because it had been an orphan, without context. The night when I chased the plumber's pickup and suddenly became the chased.

When he'd tapped my bumper again and again, as if he were playing, well . . . *tag*.

If you looked under *D* for *dangerous fads*, you'd find another Valle scoop about a previously unreported phenomenon sweeping the nation's interstates: Auto Tag, cars tapping each other back and forth until the loser flames out like James Dean. Sprung whole from the inner recesses of my fervid and increasingly panicked imagination.

And what do you say when you tag someone? What do you whisper?

You're it.

That's what.

What was going on?

Okay, be a reporter. A real one who harbors a respect for the truth and has the facility to find it. Arrange the facts, link them end to end, make a conclusion. Figure it out.

What was real and what wasn't?

Sam Savage was real. He'd cried real tears over a real ginger ale as his real girlfriend—or ex-girlfriend, who knows by now—had shot real daggers at him across the table.

And so was *Herman Wentworth*.

Real.

Later I'd dreamt about the town—the men strolling down Main Street in old-fashioned fedoras, the odor of syrup and blueberry pancakes drifting over from the Littleton Flats Café. I'd conjured up the town, but not him.

He'd appeared out of the desert that day in his blue sports jacket and gleaming black shoes and he'd told me a story about passing through a small town fifty years ago on the way to San Diego.

250

He was an army doctor who'd been all over the world.

But he'd started out in Japan. A raw recruit just off the boat, who could've recited the freshly memorized Hippocratic oath by heart.

The newest member of the 499th medical battalion.

That was real, too.

Another thing out there on the ledge that had needed to be coaxed back in.

I'd heard of that battalion before.

THIRTY-SIX

The sheriff called in the morning and asked me if I wouldn't mind coming to the station.

I was still lying in bed, even though I should've already been showered, shaved, and on my way out. I had an excuse. I'd been up staring at the computer screen till 3 in the morning. Dredging up the past, reading through selected Freedom of Information Act reports—specifically, the ones that came out in 1994 and caused the head of the Department of Energy under Clinton to publicly apologize for atrocities that had happened over four decades ago.

"Don't you guys always say *we want you to come downtown*?" I asked him.

"Technically, it's uptown."

"Okay. Why do you want me to come uptown?"

"How about this. When you get here, I'll tell you."

WHEN I ENTERED THE SHERIFF'S OFFICE, I NEARLY KNOCKED OVER a female deputy carrying three cups of Starbucks coffee precariously balanced one on top of the other.

When I apologized, she said, "You spill it, you buy it."

Sheriff Swenson was in his customary position, leaning back in his chair with his legs up on his desk. The person not in his customary position was sitting across from him. Hinch.

Hinch was there.

I didn't tell the sheriff about the dried excrement stuck to his left boot sole. Maybe that's what accounted for the look of vague distaste on his face as I sat down.

"Hello, Lucas."

Maybe not.

"Hello," I said, then turned and said hi to Hinch.

He acknowledged me with a slight shake of his head. He seemed smaller these days—as if grief were shriveling him up.

"I thought Hinch should be here," Sheriff Swenson said. "Given the seriousness of the situation."

"The seriousness of what situation? You mean, Nate getting shot?"

"Yeah, I think getting shot is serious business. Don't you?"

"Of course."

"Great. We agree."

"So, what's going on?"

"Maybe you can tell me, Lucas."

I looked over at Hinch—for support, acknowledgment, a clue—but he seemed both there and not there. I turned back to the sheriff.

"I don't understand. I told you everything I know."

"Everything you know, huh?" He didn't sound very convinced. He sounded pretty much the way he did the day I met him, when he rolled down his side window and said: *liar, liar, pants on fire.*

253

"What exactly do you want to know that you think I haven't told you?"

"Well, now that you mention it. We don't have the actual lab report on the bullet. Not yet, of course—but our resident ballistics expert is pretty sure he knows the gun it was fired from."

"Great. Who's your resident ballistics expert?"

"That would be me. It's a small town, Lucas. We've got to multitask. If I had to guess—I'd say it was a Smith & Wesson. A .38."

It took me a second to understand why that sounded terribly familiar and to understand that Sheriff Swenson knew it would.

"I went to Teddy's," he continued. "I asked him if he'd sold any .38s lately, and guess what? He said no. At first. Then he changed his story. It turns out he *did* sell a .38. Only the person he sold it to wasn't legally able to own one. He'd served probation. But you know how Teddy is with federal gun laws."

I felt Hinch turning to stare at me.

"Yeah, okay. I bought a gun. I was worried someone was following me. Apparently for good reason."

"Uh-huh. I might want to ask to see that gun. I might want to ask if you'd mind if I drove home with you and got it. Of course, you could say no."

"What are you suggesting, sheriff? That I shot at *myself*? That I nearly killed my intern?"

"Now that would sound like one of your stories. That would be pretty unbelievable. All the same, I'd like to take a look at the gun. If you wouldn't mind."

I was going to expound on my rights as a citizen.

Go get a warrant, I was going to say.

"I think we should let the sheriff have the gun." Hinch, finally making his presence felt.

He'd used a reassuring *we*: reporter and editor in it together, side by side, thick and thin, shoulders against the wheel of official meddling. Only he'd sided with the official.

"Sure," I said, blushing. "Fine. No problem."

"Thanks, Lucas," Swenson said. "One other thing. I called that number you gave me. For *Sam Savage*. It's no longer in service. The play you mentioned has closed. And the girlfriend—*Trudy*? She says she has no idea who I'm talking about."

Okay, it felt all too familiar. I was back in New York. I was frantically shoveling manure as they wrinkled their noses at the smell. Only this time I was bona fide; I was legit.

Legitimacy isn't about being, *Tom. You either are or you're aren't.*

"Look, I told Sam that the person who'd hired him might not like the fact he's walking around anymore. He's hiding somewhere. His girlfriend's protecting him. I'd do the same thing."

"You would, huh?"

"I'm not a perp, Sheriff. I'm a reporter. I went out to cover that accident on 45. Me. Remember? You were there. Both people involved in that crash were someone else. Isn't *that* funny." I half-turned to Hinch so that I was speaking to both of them—letting Hinch in on what I'd been up to, something, okay, I should've done before. "Ed Crannell's fiction—he's a fucking actor. Dennis Flaherty's alive and well and doing antipsychotics in Iowa."

255

"So you say," Swenson said.

"Go ahead, find an Ed Crannell in Cleveland. Good luck; I tried. Then get hold of a playbill for that show. *The Pier*. Sam Savage—second lead—you'll see his picture there. And then tell me how I shot at myself."

"I told you. I don't think you shot at yourself. You weren't holding the gun, were you? Of course you could've given it to someone *else* to shoot at you. Maybe he fucked up and hit the kid."

"Why on earth would I do something like that? Why would I want someone to shoot *me*? That's fucking crazy."

"Yeah. Like making up fifty-six stories in the newspaper. What did your shrink think about that?"

I was waiting for Hinch to jump in and support this reporter the way an editor's supposed to, to tell the sheriff that he wouldn't stand for this interrogation. That he'd refuse to sit idly by while one of his reporters was being accused of laughable things and that we were both going to stand up and walk out of there.

There was deafening silence from his side of the room.

"The guy jumped me," I said. "In my own basement. Remember? I came in here to make a report and you said he was breaking into homes with a plumber's kit. So it wasn't just me getting burglarized, was it?"

"Breaking and entering's one thing," the sheriff said. "This other stuff . . . faking an accident . . . hiring *actors* . . . and I'm not even going to get into all that other stuff. . . ."

I gave it a shot. I looked directly at Hinch.

"I should've told you about some of this, Hinch, but I wanted to put it together first. I know it sounds a little out there, so I wanted to make sure I had it right—"

"Let's go get the gun, Tom," he said softly. "Let's all ride together to your house and get the sheriff the gun, okay?"

Okay.

I'll admit right now that neither of them looked very surprised when after we all drove back to my rented house—Hinch and I in one car, the sheriff behind us in another—after the sheriff followed me upstairs and watched as I opened my bed-table drawer and stared dumbly at the spot where my gun *should've* been, after I ransacked that drawer and then the one below it, then rifled through my dresser, every one of my kitchen cabinets, my bathroom, my entire basement and every inch of my office, that the gun wasn't there.

It was gone.

HINCH TOLD ME IT MIGHT BE A GOOD IDEA IF I TOOK SOME TIME off.

He assured me that this wasn't in any way, shape, or form a suspension.

No.

It's just that with the Nate shooting investigation pending and the sheriff's suspicions about me—unfounded as they might be, though it would be kind of nice to know where the gun was—and with Mary-Beth willing to take up the slack, it made sense. *Look at it this way*, he told me. *If you're right, you got a crazy shooter looking for you. Probably a good idea to keep him away from the office.*

Of course it was a suspension. I knew a suspension when I saw one.

I didn't know what Hinch believed, but I knew whom he didn't.

It was the gun.

The plumber must've stolen it, I told them—it was obvious. He'd broken into my house the day I'd caught him red-handed. Then I'd caught him trying to do it *again*. He must've gone back a third time.

No one looked convinced.

I started to tell Hinch the rest.

Halfway through the first sentence, I stopped. I had to. He had the same expression as the sheriff. The same expression as the editor I'd hung out to dry. There were too many echoes of stories past. It sounded only slightly less fantastic than it did before. The actors, the bomb-throwing MD feeding me anagrams in a ruined town, even that American soldier of fortune spraying his AK-47 all over Afghanistan.

Ask yourself. What did I have? Really?

I needed to do it by the book. Buttoned up, double-sourced, fact checked, and stamped with the Good Reporting Seal of Approval.

I was running out of time.

It's like a coming thunderstorm. You can smell it. Dead leaves begin fluttering like fans in the hands of nervous southern girls, the air turns moist, a smoky haze drifts across the sun.

A deluge was coming.

THIRTY-SEVEN

There's something spooky about driving straight through the night and out the other side.

You join a kind of spirit world that exists only while the real world sleeps—populated by meth-fueled truckers, fleeing spouses, lonely salespeople, drunken frat kids, all trying to get somewhere before daybreak.

I wondered which category I fit into.

I'd left in the middle of the night, pasted a note on the refrigerator in case someone started to worry about me. I couldn't imagine who that someone might be. When I got there, I would call Norma. It was going to take awhile, because I was going where I should've gone all along.

It had taken me some time to understand the story was there.

Follow the money, the twin deities of investigative journalism once proclaimed.

I was.

I was following the wallet.

I couldn't help picturing a dazed and doped-up Dennis Flaherty walking out of a cornfield and asking if this were heaven.

No, Dennis.
It's Iowa.

SOMEWHERE IN THE NEVADA DESERT I PULLED OVER AT A TWENTY-four-hour Stop 'n' Shop.

It was too easy to give in to the monotonous rhythm of uninterrupted motion. My mind was beginning to ramble, lapsing into autopilot for miles at a time.

I was in dire need of a sugar fix.

I bought a pack of pink Sno Balls, ripped into them with the wrapper still half-attached.

I munched away while I leafed through a rack of retro-style postcards, all with that Technicolor look that made them seem half-painted.

Hoover Dam.

The Las Vegas Strip.

A shot of Sammy, Frank, Dino, and Lawford at the Sands.

Then a different kind of sands, in another part of Nevada.

And I suddenly remembered why I was going back to Iowa and what I'd spent the entire previous night doing. Dredging up the noxious past, the kind of thing you have to do with your nose covered and eyes half averted.

It doesn't really help.

You can still smell the sick beds. You can still see the dying. What's the universal sign for the noble practice of medicine? Two serpents coiled around a winged staff.

Only they were strangling it to death.

They were devouring their own.

I wouldn't stay too long out here, Herman Wentworth said. *Remember, I am a doctor.*

IOWA DIDN'T LOOK LIKE HEAVEN.

It looked flat and brown. The air felt oppressively humid, as if it were responsible for flattening the landscape from its sheer numbing weight. Black funnel clouds blew across the horizon like tumbleweeds.

The sameness put me to sleep. You couldn't really delineate one section of Iowa from another. Only the cities broke the stultifying monotony—they flew by in minutes. Then back to amber waves of grain without a hint of purple mountains' majesty.

I pulled over at a rest stop to nap, and when I woke up, a boy was making faces at me outside the window.

I stared back at him until his father appeared and gave him a vicious swat across the back of his head. The boy seemed used to it; he walked back to the family car without a sound.

It took me a while to get going.

I felt disoriented and sluggish, as if I were moving in slow motion, the way I turned the steering wheel, stepped on the gas.

According to the map, I still had at least an hour to go.

I cranked the window wide open, letting the air slap me awake.

When I saw the sign for Ketchum City, I felt neither happiness or relief.

Just dread.

MRS. FLAHERTY MUST'VE THOUGHT I WAS SELLING SOMETHING.

She took awhile to answer the door, and when she did she was already telling me she wasn't interested.

I could see why.

261

She had the worst trailer in a tumbledown trailer park—a salesman would've been sheer out of luck.

When I interrupted her to inform her who it was that was standing there, her demeanor changed from wary annoyance to genuine warmth.

"Tom," she said, like someone who'd known me for a long time. "What are you doing here?"

"I want to talk to Dennis," I said.

"Why didn't you call? You came all the way from *California*," she said, as if that were a second miracle—first getting her son back, now this.

She didn't invite me inside. I could see she wanted to, that she knew that's what you do when someone arrives at your front door—especially someone who's just driven twenty-nine consecutive hours. She was embarrassed about where she lived.

"I wanted to talk to him in person, Mrs. Flaherty."

"Why?"

She was wearing a shapeless and washed-out shift. Her legs were threaded with spider webs of inky varicose veins.

"I'm trying to find out how someone ended up in that car with Dennis's wallet."

"Well, it doesn't matter now, does it?" she said, affecting an almost coquettish tone.

"Somebody died. I'd like to know who it was."

"Well, how's Dennis going to know *that*?"

"I don't know. Maybe he doesn't. Maybe he can help me find out."

I heard someone calling her from inside the trailer.

"Is that him?" I asked her.

She nodded.

"Dennis," she said. "Come on out. Tom Valle's here."

He stepped out in the doorway, tired and bleary-eyed, dressed in boxers and what used to be referred to as a wifebeater before political correctness ruined all the fun. His mother gazed at him as if he were standing there in top hat and tails.

"Who's *Tom Valle*?" he asked, as if I wasn't right there in front of him.

"I talked to you on the phone," I said. "Remember, Dennis? I'm a reporter."

"Huh?"

"I called to ask you about your wallet."

"Huh?"

"He's still a little groggy," Mrs. Flaherty said. "*Aren't* you, Dennis?"

"Uh-huh," he said. "What's your name again?"

"Tom. Tom Valle. I'd like to ask you a few questions."

"About what?"

"About where you might've lost your wallet. About who might've taken it?"

"My *wallet*?"

"The wallet that was stolen. That turned up in a car with a dead body."

Dennis was still rubbing his eyes; he appeared to be listing left, like someone on a sinking ship.

"There was an accident, Dennis. A car was set on fire— someone was in it. He had your wallet on him. They thought you were dead—your mom thought you were dead. Remember?"

Mrs. Flaherty reached over and rubbed Dennis's arm, as

if making sure he was actually there and not six feet under-ground.

"My wallet, huh?"

It was like talking to the elderly—to Anna's father, maybe. Someone who's misplaced their mind.

"If you give me a minute, I'll invite you in," Mrs. Flaherty said.

She retreated into the trailer and I heard the clatter of things being moved from one place to another. Dennis remained in the doorway, staring down at me with a slightly puzzled expression. A man walked out of the next trailer, nodded in Dennis's direction, then leaned against a garbage can and lit up a joint.

"You said you didn't have your wallet in the hospital. Are you sure?"

"The hospital?"

"The VA hospital."

"I let myself out, man."

"They didn't officially discharge you?"

"I let myself out."

"Okay, Dennis."

Mrs. Flaherty reappeared in the doorway. She'd changed into a skirt that looked twenty years too young for her.

"Come on in, Tom," she said.

When I walked inside, I was immediately assaulted by the astringent smell of household cleaner—the cheap kind they use in hospitals. She'd attempted a quick makeover to impress me.

She needn't have bothered. Ty Pennington wouldn't have been able to do much with the place.

It looked like a FEMA shelter. Yellow water stains trailed

down the walls. A relic of a fridge emitted a constant hum. The screen door meant to separate the kitchen from the bedrooms hung half off its metal track. There was a kitchen table of sorts, but its linoleum top had mostly disappeared.

"Sit down, Tom," she said.

"That's all right," I said. It was unbearably hot—not even a fan to move the fetid air from one part of the trailer to another.

Dennis had remained pretty much where he was, simply turning his body so he could keep staring at me as if I were an alien who'd shown up for breakfast.

"Would you like something to eat?" Mrs. Flaherty asked me, as if she were thinking the same thing. "You must be hungry driving all that way."

"No, thank you. I had something on the road." I could still taste the rancid sweetness that even hours later stubbornly stuck to my tongue. I turned back to Dennis.

"Before you went into the hospital, you said, you were living on the streets. Which ones?"

"Dunno."

"You must know what city you were in?"

"Ummm . . . Detroit. I think."

"Detroit. Great. What part?"

"By the park."

"What park?"

"The ballpark."

"Comerica Park? Where the Tigers play?"

"Uh-huh."

"Okay. How long were you there?"

"Dunno."

"Well, was it a year? Two years? Three?"

"Not sure."

"How'd you survive—how'd you eat?"

"At the Marriott."

"You ate in a *hotel*?"

"Behind the Marriott. Where they threw out the garbage."

Mrs. Flaherty put her hand to her mouth to keep something from coming out. She probably hadn't asked Dennis what life was like on the streets—she wouldn't have wanted to know about that.

"Okay, Dennis. Did you have your wallet there? In Detroit?"

"Think so. Time for my pill, Mom."

"You already had your pill, Dennis."

"No, I didn't."

"Yes, son. You did."

"What's he taking?" I asked her. "Lithium?"

She shrugged.

"Okay, Dennis. You think you had your wallet when you were in Detroit? When you were living by Comerica Park."

Another blank stare.

"Let's say you did."

"Okay."

"Where'd you go after Detroit? Take your time. Think about it."

"Seattle, maybe. I think."

"How long were you in Seattle?"

"It rained a lot."

"Yeah. How long were you there, Dennis?"

"Dunno. It rained a lot."

"Did you still have your wallet? In Seattle?"

"Yeah."

"How do you know?"

"I showed it at the VA."

"You remember that. You're sure? You showed your wallet at the VA office in Seattle?"

"Mom, I need my pill."

"No, Dennis. You had your pill. I gave you one this morning."

"Okay."

"Dennis," I said. "Why did you show your wallet at the VA?"

"I showed them my VA card. I needed help."

"So they put you in the hospital there? In Seattle?"

"Nope."

"You went to a VA hospital, Dennis."

"Yeah."

"In Seattle."

"Nope. I need my pill, Mom. It's time for my pill."

"Dennis, listen. Your mom says she gave you your pill already, okay?"

"Okay."

"Where was the VA hospital, Dennis? The one you went into?"

"Dunno."

"It wasn't in *Seattle*? You went to the VA office in Seattle. That's what you just told me. You needed help, isn't that what you just said?"

"Yeah."

"What happened?"

"The computers were down. It was raining."

"They didn't help you in Seattle?"

"Nope."

"Okay. Where was the hospital, Dennis? We're making progress here—we know you had your wallet in Seattle. You took it out and showed your VA card. You remember doing that. Where was the hospital? Where'd you go after Seattle?"

Dennis was slumping, swaying with his eyes half-closed, like a music lover lost in his favorite symphony.

"He needs to take a nap," Mrs. Flaherty said. "It's the pills."

"Can you stay awake a little longer, Dennis?"

"I'm tired."

"I know you're tired. Maybe you can stay awake a few more minutes. I need to know the name of that hospital."

"I'm tired. I'm taking a nap, Mom."

"Okay, Dennis." She brushed past me and took him by the arm, leading him into the recesses of the trailer as if he were blind. As if he were still two years old and she still told him bedtime stories in the middle of the afternoon. Maybe the whole thing wasn't as sad as it looked. She'd been deserted, by death or divorce; her son had come back to her; and now she got to be a mother again. Maybe a better one than she'd been before.

"Maybe you should go," Mrs. Flaherty said when she reappeared.

"How long does he usually nap for?" I asked.

"All those questions tired him out. He's not used to that. I think you should go. Okay?"

"I need him to tell me what hospital he broke out of. Maybe I'll wait till he wakes up."

"What difference does it make? Who cares what hospital?"

She sat down at the kitchen table. She looked out the screened-in window, which was letting in the pungent smell of homegrown weed.

"Would you like some coffee?" she asked. "It's instant—but it's okay."

When Dennis woke up, we took a walk around the trailer park.

It was murderously hot inside the trailer and only a little less brutal outside. The air felt like a wet towel.

Dennis said he'd been in Desert Storm and that the petrochemicals in the air had poisoned him.

"Saddam's killed me, man."

"Did they check you out for that?"

"Huh?"

"For chemical poisoning?"

"Don't think so. They have no clue."

Dennis seemed a little more coherent after his nap. Mrs. Flaherty said he had moments like this, where lucidity flooded back and Dennis seemed more or less like his old self.

"Can we talk about the hospital, Dennis?"

"I don't know."

"I think you lost your wallet there. Somebody stole it, maybe."

"Could be. That marine fucker, maybe."

"Who was that?"

"He was nuts," Dennis said, as if he himself were perfectly sane. "Those marines are fucking crazy."

"Why do you think it was him?"

"I don't know. His wife went commando on him. When he was overseas, man. Eighty-sixed his kids."

"She killed his children?"

"That's right. Buried them somewhere along Route 80. Then shot herself in the fucking head. He went AWOL looking for their bodies for like a year. Couldn't find them."

"Why do you think he stole your wallet?"

"Dunno."

"Well, why'd you say it was *him*?"

"I showed him my son—in my wallet."

"So you *did* have your wallet there. See, Dennis—we know you had it with you in the VA hospital."

"Uh-huh."

"You showed him a picture of your kid. How old is your son, Dennis?"

"Dunno. She won't let me see him. Fucking bitch."

He was obviously referring to the other Mrs. Flaherty, the one his mother couldn't say enough bad things about.

"What happened when you showed the marine the picture in your wallet?"

"Nothing."

"Okay. So why do you think he stole it?"

"Dunno. Maybe he wanted the picture."

"What would he want a picture of someone else's kid?"

"He's a crazy fucker—I told you."

"Well, was he still there when you left?"

"Sure. He's crazy."

"So it wasn't him, Dennis. Your wallet ended up with someone in California."

"No kidding."

"Was the marine black?"

"No."

"Okay. Forget about the marine. Think about it. You had your wallet and then you didn't. What happened?"

He shrugged.

"Did they discharge you, Dennis?"

"I let myself out."

"You took off."

"I let myself out."

"How'd you get the pills?"

"Huh?"

"The medication. They gave you your dose every day, right?"

"Affirmative."

"So how'd you get the pills? The ones you have with you?"

"Oh, that."

"Oh that what?"

"I requisitioned them."

"You stole them."

"I *need* them, man."

"What are you going to do when you run out?"

"Huh?"

"When you run out of your pills, where are you going to get more?"

"We have a problem, Houston."

"Where was the hospital, Dennis?"

"Hard to say."

"You remember the marine."

"Affirmative."

271

"You remember showing him a picture of your son in your wallet."

"Affirmative."

"Where's the hospital, Dennis?"

"Dunno."

His mind played hide-and-seek with him. Maybe it was the drugs, or maybe it was the petrochemicals from Iraq, or maybe he was just as crazy as the marine—searching the labyrinthine pathways of his cerebrum for memories, the way the marine searched Route 80 for his dead children.

"Well, we know it wasn't Seattle."

I thought about calling every VA hospital in America, but federal psych patients were protected by privacy and I didn't hold out much hope they'd tell me anything. In most mental hospitals, patients weren't even listed in the registry.

"Remember which direction you went in when you left Seattle? How did you travel, anyway?"

"My thumb, man."

"You hitched."

"Affirmative."

"Remember who picked you up?"

"A man."

"Yeah, I don't think a woman would've stopped for you."

We'd come to a playground. It wasn't much—just two swings and a see-saw—but there were several small kids there, enough of them to make some of them have to wait their turn. A few mothers, chain-smoking cigarettes and looking old beyond their years, were standing off to the side watching them with little interest.

272

"South," Dennis said.

"What?"

"The direction I went in. I went south. There's not a lot of north left when you're in Seattle."

THIRTY-EIGHT

Dennis liked to read the passing road signs out loud.

"Dawsville. Exit 42. One mile."

"Boise. Exit 59. Quarter mile."

"Roadwork ahead. Next ten miles."

I became used to it and eventually stopped looking at the signs altogether since I had my own human OnStar satellite system sitting right next to me.

When the distance between signs stretched for miles, Dennis would switch to reading passing license plates.

"A6572G4."

"M87GT2."

As traveling companions go, he wasn't bad. Except for the near-constant drone, he remained affably calm and even drifted off on occasion—though he nearly always awoke in time for the next road alert.

When I put on some music, he told me he used to play guitar in a Metallica knockoff band, and even sang two lines from "St. Anger" in fair facsimile of James Hetfield.

There were five VA hospitals south of Seattle.

If need be, we were going to visit each and every one of

them.

Dennis was my guide. It might've been the blind leading the blinder, but he was all I had.

It had taken some doing to get him into the car.

He'd just broken *out* of a VA hospital; he didn't particularly feel like going back. Mrs. Flaherty had looked at me as if I'd turned as crazy as her son when I told her what I had in mind.

Dennis was running out of meds, I told her. That was a fact.

He was still clearly disturbed—that was also a fact.

It might not have been the smartest thing in the world for Dennis to have escaped from a federal psych ward, either. I didn't know if having voluntarily committed himself absolved him from anything—but if it didn't, I wasn't going to bring it up.

I needed him.

It was the meds that convinced the both of them. She had no money for psychiatrists. She was one of the 40 million or so Americans without health insurance. Dennis needed the U.S. Army if he was going to stay on his regimen of antipsychotics.

The hospital was the best place for him—sad but true.

I would take him back there.

If we could find it.

I called Norma from North Dakota.

I'd dipped into my dwindling ATM resources again and paid for two rooms at the Sioux Nation Motel, which sported a mini-casino in the check-in area.

"I have bad news for you, Tom," she said. "Laura passed away last night."

Hinch's wife.

That was bad news, but in the scheme of things not the worst thing I'd heard recently. There was that gunshot from the speeding blue pickup, for example.

"How's Hinch taking it?" I asked.

My suspension notwithstanding, Hinch had always been good to me. He'd given me a chance when no one else on earth would've even considered it.

"About the way you'd expect. You know Hinch—God knows what he's really thinking half the time. He keeps it bottled up real tight. He was pretty devoted to her."

"Yeah. How's Nate doing?"

"Okay. He had a little infection yesterday so they put him on stronger antibiotics. His mom's here."

"Yeah, I know. I saw her at the hospital."

"No, I mean she's here. In my *house*. I'm putting her up."

"That's nice of you, Norma."

"The least I can do for the poor woman. Where are you, Tom? You sound far away."

"North Dakota."

"What in God's name are you doing in North Dakota?"

"We're looking for something."

"Who's *we're*?"

"Me and my traveling companion."

"Who would that be, Tom?"

"That would be the deceased from the car accident on Highway 45."

"You're scaring me, Tom, you know that?"

"Okay. He's not actually dead. Though sometimes he appears that way."

There was a small silence—the only sound coming from The 100 Best Songs from the '80s on the motel TV. They were up to number 22: "Girls Just Want to Have Fun."

"Tom?"

"Yes, Norma?"

"All this stuff you're talking about—I heard about some of it from Mary-Beth, who heard it from I don't know who—you aren't making it up, are you?"

"No, Norma."

"I've never asked you about, you know . . . New York and all that."

She hadn't. For a long time, I'd wondered if she even knew. It wasn't like she read the national papers—as far as I could tell, I'd never made *Us* magazine.

"I know."

"I figured if you wanted to talk about it, you would."

"Right."

"So, you want to talk about it?"

"Not really."

"Okay, Tom. You didn't give someone your gun to shoot at you, did you?"

"No, Norma."

"Yeah, I thought that sounded kind of nuts. That's what they're saying, though."

"Are they saying why I would do something like that?"

"To give you . . . *credibility*. Is that the right word? Make you the center of attention."

"I guess it worked, then."

"Huh? Didn't you just say they're wrong?"

"Someone *stole* my gun. I was trying to be funny."

"Ha, ha."

"Can you call Sam Weitz and tell him I'm out of town? That I'll be back in a week or so? He'll want to know why I'm not at bowling."

"Sure." Silence. "*Tom*?"

"Yes?"

"What *are* you looking for?"

"Credibility, Norma. Just like you said."

DENNIS WAS RIGHT ABOUT SEATTLE.

It was raining when we got there, a soft, steady downpour that caused clouds of steam to drift off the asphalt.

We drove through the downtown area because Dennis wanted to see Safeco Field where the Mariners played. Once upon a time Dennis used to be a baseball fan, but that was before reading the box scores began hurting his head. He used to be able to recite every player's statistics by heart. Maybe that's why he'd bunked out in the shadow of Detroit's baseball park after he'd ended up on the streets. To feel the nurturing presence of America's pastime.

We drove past the fish markets and restaurants that flanked the water and Safeco before we hit the highway going south.

The first VA hospital on our itinerary was on the border between Washington and Oregon—in the city of Tellings, population 159,000. At least that's what Dennis read off the map.

"Sound familiar?" I asked him.

"Huh?"

"The city name. *Tellings*? Does it ring a bell?"

"Population 159,000," he said.

278

"Right. I'm asking if you recognize the name—if maybe you were there?"

"Dunno."

Dennis had begun swatting his face even though there were no actual bugs there. He sometimes whispered things to himself, but when I asked him what he said, he'd ask me what I was talking about.

I tried to imagine what we might look like to passing motorists.

A broken-down Miata sporting another car's front bumper and a man in the passenger seat mumbling to himself when he wasn't killing phantom flies.

Then I knew exactly what we looked like.

At least to one motorist.

THIRTY-NINE

It had gotten dark almost without me knowing it.

One minute it was light enough to easily make out passing license plates—Dennis had begun reading them off again in lieu of road signs—then it wasn't.

He had to lean forward and squint, each license suddenly immersed in individual pools of sickly yellow light.

"Speed up," he said. "Can't see the last number."

I told Dennis he might want to give it a rest—eventually it grated on you, being assaulted by the constant drone of numbers and letters, the only relief provided by vanity plates like IAMGR8T and LUV2BWL.

Dennis was oblivious to my entreaties; I didn't press the matter since it gave him something to do, at least.

M65LK1 . . .

RLN895 . . .

I'm not exactly sure when it occurred to me.

L983HT4 . . .

K61MN0 . . .

Have you ever had the car radio on and begun listening to a certain song only when the next one's already playing?

Your mind meandering down its own roads, and the music far away as if it's coming from a half-open window?

VML254 . . .

HG54MT . . .

Dennis's litany of licenses was a kind of music—steady, low, and rhythmic. A tune I mostly tuned out, but half didn't.

QR327N9 . . .

KL61WT . . .

At some point, I began to actually hear it, at least become cognizant of a certain repeat phrase.

MH92TV . . .

Something about those letters and numbers. They seemed, okay, familiar. As if he'd mumbled them before, and before that, too.

MH92TV.

Twenty minutes ago, maybe, then sometime later, and then now.

MH92TV.

So what? There were hundreds of cars on this highway going in exactly the same direction we were—even all the way to Tellings. Even as I attempted to placate a bad case of the jitters, I knew that I'd heard those numbers before twenty minutes ago.

Dennis had been reading license plates since Iowa.

"Dennis . . . that license plate—which car?"

"Huh?"

"MH92TV? *Which* car?"

He seemed pleasantly surprised that something I'd previously expressed annoyance at had suddenly captivated my attention. Cool.

"Over there," he said.

"Over *where*?"

"There." He motioned to his immediate left, but when I slowed to let the red Mitsubishi to our left inch forward, its license plate said GAYSROK.

"That's not it, Dennis."

He shrugged. "No, not that one. Behind us, I think."

"Where behind us?" I scanned the side- and rearview mirrors, but it was pitch-black and all I saw were vague shapes obliterated by crossing high beams.

"Dunno, man. Maybe it's in front of us."

"Okay. What kind of car is it?"

I knew what his answer would be before he said it.

I was *Karnak the Magnificent*, the answer already pressed against my forehead, even though I was praying for something else, any other car on earth, really. A Honda Accord, a Saturn or Caddy, a sensible Dodge minivan or VW bus or Volvo.

No such luck.

"Pickup," he said.

My hands gripped the steering wheel so tight that my knuckles went white.

"You're sure?"

"Uh-huh. He's been following us since we left, man."

"Since *Iowa*? Why didn't you say something?"

"Well, you know. Maybe I wasn't seeing what I was seeing."

"Okay. What *color*? What color pickup has been following us since Iowa?"

"You're getting kind of specific, man."

I threw out pretty much every possibility I could think of, every color in the rainbow—Dennis shaking his head at

282

each one, *uh-uh*, *nope*, *don't think so*—until the inevitable process of elimination led me to the last color I wanted to hear.

"*Blue*? Was it blue, Dennis?"

"Uh-huh," Dennis said. "That's right, sure. Blue."

You're it.

Standing at the bottom of the stairs with a metal tool in his hands.

Playing Auto Tag with me on a desert highway.

Trolling down Third Street while he sighted a .38 Smith & Wesson through the window. My Smith & Wesson.

Bang.

I checked the rearview mirror.

Then the sides. Right, then left.

My heart was jackhammering. It was going to do an *Alien* and burst right out of my chest. I veered into the next lane, nearly got obliterated by an eighteen-wheeler hauling toilet fixtures, swerved back, slowed down, worked my way to the exit lane.

"Hey . . . what are you doing? We stopping?"

The next exit was coming up. Dennis had dutifully read it out loud two miles back.

Wohop Road.

"I need to pee," Dennis said.

Back to my left side mirror. I wanted to see if someone crossed lanes. There were several cars in the next lane—two separate and distinct pairs of headlights. Then, suddenly, there was one.

I squinted into the mirror. *What happened?*

"I need to pee like a motherfucker, Tom."

He'd turned off his lights.

There were two pairs of headlights and now there was one.

He'd turned off his lights.

I floored the gas. Passed eighty and kept going.

"I don't need to pee that bad," Dennis said. "I won't do it in the car."

Eighty-five . . . ninety . . . ninety-five . . .

"Maybe I will."

When the turnoff for Wohop Road appeared, Dennis didn't bother reading it. He couldn't. He was crouching down with his hands up over his eyes—the crash position familiar to any airline passenger.

Wait . . . wait . . .

Now.

I yanked the steering wheel hard to the right.

I'd almost passed the exit—on my way to the next one for sure. I took the turn on two wheels—my first wheelie since fourth grade—barely held the curve, then flipped back on all fours and rolled onto a mercifully empty service road where I kept right on going.

Listen.

Nothing.

How was it possible?

How could he know I was *here*?

At the trailer park in Iowa?

On the road to *Tellings*?

How?

Think.

Okay. There was *one* way. Sure there was. Assuming he hadn't followed me all the way from Littleton—one way.

My ATM withdrawals.

284

My credit card.

The one I'd used at gas stations, at the Nevada Stop 'n' Shop and the Sioux Nation Motel in North Dakota.

Like big, fat crumbs any good bird dog could follow with his eyes closed.

All the way from Iowa to Seattle to here.

Only . . .

You would need a special kind of access.

To get that kind of information—private bank records, credit card receipts, the kind of stuff they're supposed to guard with their lives—you would need a special sort of access for that.

"Uh, I really got to pee, man."

"A few minutes, Dennis."

I was getting there—I was close. I'd sat down on a stool at Muhammed Alley and begun drawing something, and now it was beginning to emerge. If I peered really hard at it, maybe I could even whisper what it was.

I had to move faster. I had to Texas two-step.

As far as I could tell, the plumber hadn't made the turnoff.

I'd shaken him.

I drove another twenty miles before I gave in to Dennis's increasingly pitiful demands—*I have to goooo, man*—and turned in to a twenty-four-hour Exxon station.

FORTY

You never want to end up in a hospital.

Not if you can help it.

You most definitely don't want to end up in a VA hospital.

The army and navy and air force and marines pour most of their funds into trying to kill people, not heal them.

VA hospitals stink of neglect.

The one in Tellings was no exception.

There was a man in a wheelchair yelling in the visitors' lobby. His waste bag had broken and no one was fixing it. He'd been yelling for two hours, he said.

The admitting nurse seemed oblivious to his ranting, as if she were hooked up to an invisible iPod and grooving on R&B.

She was only half-oblivious to us.

"Yeah?" she asked, a few minutes after we presented ourselves at the front desk.

We'd already skirted the grounds, walked the pathway circling the three innocuous-looking buildings that made up the complex. I asked Dennis if he remembered the place.

"Was this it, Dennis? Was this where you were?"

He didn't have a good answer. He looked like a tourist contemplating something he'd read about in guidebooks— things half-familiar and half not.

There was an easy way to find out.

"Have you worked here a long time?" I asked the admitting nurse.

"*What?*"

"Have you worked here for more than a week?"

"What's that supposed to mean?" she asked. "You making some kind of comment on my abilities?"

"Have you seen either one of us before?"

"What *exactly* do you gentlemen want?" she said, in a tone of voice that said she'd seen enough of Dennis to know he wasn't gentleman material. Me either. Spend enough time in a car and you start looking as if you live in one.

"We have a prescription," I said. "Any chance you could fill it?"

"You see the word *pharmacy* written anywhere?"

"No."

"Then why you asking me to fill a script?"

"Okay, fine."

"Is he a vet?" she asked, motioning toward Dennis. She could've asked Dennis directly, of course, but she'd obviously been around enough psych patients to know one when she saw one.

"Saddam's pumped me full of petros," Dennis answered her anyway.

"That so?"

"I've got petroleum in my veins. I need a lube job."

"Are you in charge of him or something?" she asked me.

"Or something."

"You here to commit him?"

"No. Just looking for a refill."

"You might want to rethink that. He doesn't seem so good."

"No, he's okay. He just needs his meds."

"Well, then. I've got a hospital to take care of."

"Okay, sure. And you've never seen him before—right?"

"Right."

We walked back outside, where a *Support Our Troops* sign was hanging off the front archway.

I did what I always did when we walked outside now—when we walked anywhere. I looked for a blue pickup truck.

"How many pills I got left?" Dennis asked.

"Not that many. By the way, you know they're all different colors?" Dennis's mom had anointed me keeper of the meds—put them in an old Band-Aid box and stuffed them in my pocket. I couldn't help thinking there was something metaphoric about that—futilely sticking Band-Aids on a terminal wound.

"I'm hungry," Dennis said.

"Okay, we'll get something on the road."

I'd been trying to conserve my cash because I was loath to hit the ATM again. Not that it mattered—I'd already filled the tank just before we hit the hospital, slipping my credit card into the reader like the notes UPS delivery personnel slip through the mail slot of your front door:

I was here.

*

THE NEXT HOSPITAL WAS A HUNDRED MILES AWAY IN OREGON.

Eisenhower Memorial.

Up till recently, I'd never been close to Oregon in my life. Now twice in two weeks.

"Dennis, if you see that license plate again, you'll tell me, okay?"

"Sure," he nodded. "What license plate?"

"MH92TV."

"Oh, right."

It was almost midnight. I'd decided there was safety in motion—no roadside motels where I'd need a credit card or cash withdrawal. Where someone in a blue pickup truck might creep up on us in the dark.

We reached Eisenhower Memorial at about 1 a.m.

It looked a bit like the elementary school I went to as a kid—only triple the size. A squat, red brick building with the requisite flagpole out front, the Stars and Stripes dishrag-limp in the sticky summer heat.

"What's this?" Dennis asked when I pulled into the parking lot. "Where are we?"

That didn't bode well.

When we walked up to the front desk, we suffered through a repeat of Tellings. This time the admitting nurse was a pale, owlish-looking man who asked us what we wanted, claimed to have never seen Dennis before in his life, then inquired about Dennis's sanity when he swatted a bug that wasn't there.

We took a little walk around the place anyway, just as we had in Tellings. It was a washout; Dennis had never been there.

We went back to the car, drove through the front gates.

I steeled myself for a long ride; the next VA hospital was more than three hundred miles away.

Dennis was acting fidgety.

I put him on license-plate duty. It gave him something to do. It gave me a semireliable sentry—scouring the passing jumble of numbers and letters for the ones we needed to fear.

Somewhere around 3 in the morning, I felt the kind of tiredness you just can't shake. Dennis had already fallen asleep on the job and was snoozing noisily against the side window. I was perilously close to following him, the highway's broken yellow lines like individual Sleep-ezes I was ingesting one at a time on the way to bed.

When I realized I'd drifted into the next lane—had *literally* been sleeping at the wheel—I searched for the next exit. Three miles later, I turned off the highway, looking for someplace we could grab a few hours' rest.

I found a twenty-four-hour gas station.

I pulled in—past the lit window where I could see the Indian proprietor, all the way to the back so we couldn't be seen from the road. I turned off the engine and promptly fell asleep.

Dennis woke me when there was just the faintest pink corona on the horizon.

I looked down at my watch: 5:30.

We were surrounded by low brush just beginning to emerge out of the morning gloom. I could hear the crackling of two massive power lines strung right over the station, the occasional ghostly *whoosh* of a passing car.

"I gotta make," Dennis said. "My stomach hurts."

"Okay, Dennis. Over there," pointing out the restroom door at the back of the station.

Dennis opened the car door and sat there for a moment, rubbing the sleep out of his eyes. Then he pulled himself out in sections, first his feet, then both arms, finally the rest of his body. He stumbled off to the bathroom and went inside.

I was dead tired; I must've gone back to sleep. When I woke up again, I wasn't sure if it hadn't been a dream—Dennis waking me to go the bathroom. My ex-wife had been like that—holding conversations with me at 2 in the morning, then accusing me of making it up.

But Dennis wasn't in the car. The pink light had morphed into pale yellow.

It was 5:40.

I got out, walked to the bathroom door, and knocked.

"Dennis, you okay in there?"

I heard an answering grunt.

I walked around to the front of the station in search of food.

When I entered bleary-eyed through the front door, the Indian—he was probably a Sikh since he wore one of those red turbans—didn't even acknowledge me. He was hunched across the front desk, reading a newspaper.

I walked down the aisle looking for something to eat. Gas stations were evidently oblivious to the latest nutritional guidelines. This one was pretty much restricted to the food group ending in -os.

Cheetos. Doritos. Tostitos. Rolos.

It was quiet enough that when I pulled two bags of Doritos off the shelf, the resultant crackle seemed as jarring as a gunshot.

Not to the Sikh—he remained buried in the newspaper.

"Do you have any *salsa*?" I called out to him.

He ignored me.

"Salsa," I said. "Where is it?"

No answer.

"Hey!" I said.

The air conditioner began rattling. A car drove by.

An alley cat screeched outside the window.

The power lines snapped and crackled.

Sometimes bits of knowledge come all at once—several distinct and awful realizations flooding your brain at the same moment in time, and suddenly, just like that, you can't breathe.

You're drowning.

I raced out of the store; the Doritos fell to the floor.

I screamed his name out loud.

"*Dennis!*" Flinging open the bathroom door and saying, "Oh my God, oh my God, Dennis, oh my God, Dennis . . ."

Me, who generally avoided God's name since he'd never done all that much for me, invoking it three times, like some sacred cant. Like the proscribed penance for committing a sin.

I had committed a sin.

I'd fallen asleep.

FORTY-ONE

We raced down the highway.

Away from the station, where the Indian clerk lay face down in his newspaper—Indian, *not* Sikh, since his turban wasn't really red after all, no, not until fifteen minutes ago, when someone had put a bullet into his head.

It was different in the bathroom. There was nothing there to soak up the blood. It had covered the entire floor and part of the shattered bathroom mirror. A broken shard had still been lying there on the floor.

The one the plumber must've used to slice out Dennis's tongue.

IT ROSE UP ON OUR LEFT, JUST TWO MILES FROM THE STATION—AS if God said, you acknowledge me, I'll acknowledge you.

VA Hospital 138.

Just like that.

It looked ancient, more like an armory—all stone and turrets. But it was a hospital with doctors and nurses and medicine and Dennis was bleeding to death.

On the way through the gate, I noticed the barred windows on the top floor.

I drove the car up the front door and pulled Dennis out of the car and half carried him in. Which is when the admitting nurse took one look at him and said:

"Mr. Flaherty, where the hell have you been?"

Okay.

We'd found our hospital.

"ALL RIGHT," THE SURGEON, A BRISTLE-HAIRED MAJOR DeCOLA, said, after they'd finally stopped the bleeding—of all the appendages in the human body, it's the tongue that bleeds the most. "What the hell happened to him?"

"Someone attacked him," I said.

We were sitting in the lounge: tables, bridge chairs, two mostly empty snack machines.

"No shit, Sherlock," DeCola said. "Who?"

"I don't know. He was in a gas-station bathroom about ten miles down the road, and someone went in there and got him."

I left out the part about the gas-station owner being dead.

Why?

Because he'd been shot with my gun.

They would find a .38 bullet in his head.

I knew it.

Not that the murder would remain a secret much longer—odds were that someone had already entered the station for a pack of smokes and found a body in rigor mortis instead.

I would tell the police—I silently practiced this—that I'd been sleeping in the back. That I'd heard Dennis cry out. That I'd found him with his tongue cut out. That's all.

I got my chance a half hour later. Two detectives and a patrolman came and found me in the lounge.

Major DeCola had called them, they explained.

They knew all about the dead Indian.

The patrolman was half the squad car that answered the call from a hysterical and nearly incoherent woman motorist who'd gone to the station for a fill-up and ended up running down the road in one high heel.

I related my edited version of events.

"You were sleeping in your *car*?" Detective Wolfe said. He had a certain tone to his voice. Maybe because people who slept in cars were usually the kind of people who committed crimes, as opposed to being victimized by them.

"That's right," I said.

When I told him I was a journalist, he looked even more perplexed.

"What were you doing with Mr. Flaherty?" he asked. He had the kind of clean-cut all-American looks you saw on TV shows about the military—*JAG*, maybe. "Flaherty was a patient in the psych ward here, correct? He was MIA."

"Yeah. I was bringing him back."

"Why's that?"

"*Why*?"

"Why you, Mr. Valle? What's your relation to him?"

"I was interviewing him about a story."

"Really? What kind of story?"

"About war veterans," I said. "About the tough adjustment they face back home and the raw deal a lot of them have been getting." I'm not sure why I said that instead of something else. Maybe because that's the story Wren had

295

done once upon a time. The story I now felt had led him straight to an even bigger one. I was connecting the dots. Or maybe because the plumber who'd cut out Dennis's tongue had official access to my credit card receipts, and these were three more officials.

"Okay. And both of you were sleeping in your car?"

"That's right. Dennis didn't remember what hospital he'd been in. We were working our way south, checking them all."

"He can't *remember*?"

"He goes in and out, pretty much," I said.

"Uh-huh." Detective Wolfe glanced at his partner, who was trying to get the lone remaining bag of chips out of a snack machine, smacking the side of it with his hand as if it were an unresponsive suspect.

"So you say you heard Mr. Flaherty cry out," Wolfe turned back, "and you ran to the bathroom and found him like that?"

"That's right. Then I drove here."

"You never went into the store?"

"No."

"You never heard a gunshot?"

"No," I said. "But who knows, maybe that's what woke me up."

"*Who* knows? You know."

"I don't remember hearing anything; I just woke up."

"And you didn't see anyone—exiting the bathroom, out in front, anywhere?"

"No. I was sound asleep."

"And you never went into the store?"

"No." He'd asked me that already.

"There were two bags of—what were they, John?" he asked his partner.

"Doritos," John said, in a tone of voice intimating that he could use some right now. The snack machine had stubbornly refused to yield its bag.

"Right," Wolfe said. "Two bags of Doritos were lying on the floor. Someone must've dropped them as they were running out of the store—like they were in a panic. We were wondering who that was? Since you didn't go into the store."

"The person who shot the gas-station owner?" I volunteered.

"Mr. Patjy was just the night clerk," he corrected me. "You think the shooter picked up two Doritos bags on the way out, and then said what the hell am I doing with these Doritos, and dropped them?"

"Maybe he picked them up first," I said.

"You mean he went there to buy some Doritos and then decided to shoot Mr. Patjy instead. And cut out your friend's tongue."

"I don't know," I said.

"Yeah. I don't know, either."

"What about the woman? Maybe she dropped them?"

"Yeah, that would make sense. Only we asked her and she said no. So it's kind of a mystery."

Silence.

"I wonder why they cut out his *tongue*," Detective Wolfe said.

As a warning . . . don't talk. Don't . . .

"I guess we're going to have to wait for him to tell us," Wolfe said. "Of course, he's not going to be able to talk much, is he?"

297

"I don't know; is he?"

"The doctor says no. And he goes in and out, that's what you said. So it might not do us much good."

"He was in Desert Storm," I said. "He's convinced he was poisoned—by the oil fields they lit on fire."

"He probably was," Detective Wolfe said. "It was a fucking disaster over there."

"You were there?"

"That's right."

"Army?" I asked.

"Jarhead. How come you didn't go into the store?"

"What?"

"Well, you found Mr. Flaherty covered in blood. His tongue had been cut out. Why wouldn't you run into the store for help? Or use the phone to call an ambulance? You have a cell?"

"It wasn't charged," I lied.

"Uh-huh. So why didn't you use the store phone? Why didn't you run in there to get someone?"

"I don't know. I panicked, I guess. I just wanted to get out of there."

"Uh-huh. Well, maybe the security camera will tell us what happened to him," he said, staring at me with an unwavering directness.

Then he said, "Oh, I forgot. The fucking thing's broken."

THEY PUT DENNIS IN RECOVERY, NEXT TO A SOLDIER COVERED IN shrapnel scars.

"He get that in Iraq?" the soldier asked me about Dennis.

I was sitting in a bridge chair by Dennis's side. It was

evening; the fluorescent lighting over his bed kept erupting in crackling bursts of blue and white that reminded me of distant rocket fire.

I was thinking that there was something about this hospital.

VA Hospital 138 in Oregon.

"No," I said. "Right here at home."

"Shit. His *tongue*, huh?"

I nodded.

"Tough. His old lady's not going to like that. She can sue the army for loss of marital services. If you know what I mean." He stuck his tongue out and wiggled it back and forth.

"I don't think you're allowed to sue the army," I said.

"*You're not*? Fucking bullshit lawyer of mine."

When I didn't answer him, he said, "I'm just jerking your chain."

Dennis came to about an hour later.

I must have been dozing; I woke to a plaintive mewling—like a stray cat trying to cry its way into a house.

It was Dennis.

He couldn't form actual words.

What was left of his tongue was covered in stitches.

He had thick cotton wadding stuck into both cheeks.

"Don't try to talk, Dennis. I'm going to give you some bad news. But it could've been worse. Okay?"

Dennis's eyes widened; they were bloodshot and swollen. He looked Chinese.

"Are you in pain? Nod your head if you're in pain, Dennis. If you're hurting, you can push that little button on your IV and pump some more morphine into you."

He continued to stare at me.

He continued trying to speak.

"Whoever attacked you cut out your tongue, Dennis. Not all of it. But a lot of it. I'm not sure what that means as far as . . . well, talking. I don't know. You understand what I'm telling you?"

He didn't respond yes or no.

Instead he turned his head, as if suddenly searching his surroundings.

"Do you remember what happened, Dennis? Do you remember who attacked you?"

He was searching for something else now—his tongue—rapidly swallowing in an effort to find it, then placing two shaking fingers into his open mouth trying to feel what wasn't there anymore.

He was crying.

"Keep your fingers out of there, Dennis. You're all stitched up."

He closed his eyes, moaned, banged his head against the pillow.

I looked away, at the grimy hospital window. A tree branch was tapping against the outside of the glass as if trying to get in. I waited till Dennis calmed down, till he stopped banging his head against the bed.

"If I ask you some questions, can you write down the answers?"

He stared straight up at the ceiling.

"Just a few questions Dennis."

There was a tooth-bitten pencil on his bedside table. I picked it up and placed it in his hand—he didn't exactly grip it, but he didn't drop it either. I found a discarded *Oregonian*

300

lying out in the hall. I ripped out the full-page ad for Oregon's best used-car dealership and put it in his other hand.

He stared at it with a blank expression. Then he wrote something down in an uneven, childish scrawl.

Why?

"I don't know, Dennis."

Why? he wrote again.

Why . . . why . . . why . . . over and over, like a kid who won't listen till he gets his answer—why's the sky blue. . . . Why do birds fly. . . . Why did someone cut out my fucking tongue?

"The person who did this to you—what did he look like?"

He shook his head. He pushed the magic button on his morphine drip.

"Was he strange-looking? No features, kind of?"

His eyes fluttered, half closed.

Sleepy, he scrawled.

"Did he look like that, Dennis?"

Sleepy.

"Right, it's the morphine."

I asked him again, but this time he didn't bother to answer.

He was drifting; I watched him fall asleep.

Except he couldn't.

His eyes would slowly shut, then suddenly fly open as if spring-loaded, as if he'd seen something in there that had scared him half to death. The bathroom. The plumber coming at him with a shard of broken mirror.

After a while, he picked up the pencil again.

Tell me a story, he wrote.

"A story?"

301

Bedtime story.

"I don't know any bedtime stories, Dennis."

Sleepy.

"Okay. Then go to sleep."

I'm scared. A story.

"Look, Dennis . . ."

Mom.

"Your mom's back in Iowa. I'm Tom. You're in the hospital."

A story.

"I don't know any stories, Dennis."

"Come on, man. He wants a story." The soldier had woken up and joined the chorus. "Poor guy's got no tongue. Don't you know any bedtime stories?"

"No."

"What about 'Goldilocks and the Three Bears'? Shit, everyone knows that one."

Dennis's eyes fluttered open, fixed on my face.

"Okay," I said. "Sure. I know a story. A true story."

"Shoot," the soldier said.

"It's a ghost story."

"I thought you said it was a true story?"

"It is."

"Hear that, Dennis? A true ghost story."

"There were these men," I began. "These doctors—"

"When?" the soldier interjected. "When are we talking about? *Now?*"

"No," I said. "Not now. 1945."

302

FORTY-TWO

The first day they arrived, they gathered at the Gokoku Shrine.

Partly because it had already become the stuff of legend. That wasn't surprising to them; a kind of witchcraft had been unleashed upon the world. It needed its totems and idols.

They stared at the granite tombstones, and sure enough, there were shadows seared into the stone. And yes, okay, if you squinted and stared at it long enough, they could, in the right light, appear to be the shadows of people.

Of ghosts.

There were other shadows. On the roof of the Chamber of Commerce building, imprinted onto the tower of the Chugoku Electric Power building, and two of them on the only wall of the temple left standing. But it was the shadows on these tombstones that had captured the popular imagination. Why not? That imagination had been geometrically altered, expanded beyond all previous comprehension.

One month ago this had been a city of 300,000, a military industrial hive.

Now there were six buildings left standing.

What the initial shockwaves hadn't obliterated, the resultant

303

fires had. The population had been cut by two-thirds—not neatly, but in excruciating and distinct stages that were only now making themselves known, if not actually understood.

They stood on the verge of a voodoo science, although it was more of a precipice, since there was nothing but a massive void of knowledge.

They were here to fill it.

Some of them had been in New Mexico, keeping a wary eye on the technicians and scientists and plain laborers who worked directly with the stuff they'd dubbed Kryptonite, in a not altogether playful allusion to the element that could bring even Superman to his knees. Everyone knew it was insidious stuff—it was a matter of degrees.

How much, how long, how often?

They considered themselves snake charmers trying to lull the cobra that Oppenheimer and others had coaxed out of the bottle. You danced around the danger and hoped you wouldn't get bit.

Or maybe cobra didn't do it justice—more like a dragon. That's what the techies called it when they put together the fissionable material by hand—tickling the dragon. Hoping you didn't get burned. One did—a physicist named Louis Fruton, cooked to death in 1945 by a sudden radioactive burst.

When they'd dropped Trinity at ground zero, a miniature sun had lit up the early morning sky—two thousand times hotter than the one the earth actually circles. The seven-ton drop tower had incinerated into air. Grains of sand had fused into glass. The first mushroom cloud in history had spiraled up to the heavens and sent a soft shower of white snow fluttering down on the army ants below.

The second mushroom cloud in history came three weeks later over the military industrial city of Hiroshima.

The snake was out of the bottle; its poison was in the blood.

They'd first gathered on Okinawa—the army doctors from Los Alamos and Walter Reed and Rochester, and even a few from the Mayo Clinic.

They compared notes and rifled through the existing literature. There wasn't much, and what did exist was laughably ill informed. They waited around a lot.

The war ended on August 13, but they weren't allowed into Japan until late September.

There was a seventeen-square-mile laboratory waiting for them inside Japan—160,000 living corpses that needed to be poked, prodded, X-rayed, documented, and autopsied. Mostly watched.

They were biologists studying a heretofore unknown species.

The world's first survivors.

As doctors, they'd seen the human body attacked with all sorts of things—bullets, knives, shrapnel, gases, poisons. This was something else—bodies bombarded with neutrons, beta particles, and gamma rays.

There seemed to be three distinct stages.

First, the people who died in the first few hours or days.

For these cases, they had to rely on the observations of the mostly bewildered Japanese doctors. Seemingly uninjured people had mysteriously succumbed, dropping dead on street corners, in their beds, while riding their bicycles. The doctors guessed that gamma rays had degenerated their very nuclei—literally broken down their cell walls.

The second stage seemed to announce itself about two weeks after exposure.

The victims' hair fell out. They were wracked with severe diarrhea, uncontrollable shaking, and spiraling temperatures of up to 106 degrees. Their white-blood-cell counts plummeted; their gums became bleeding sores; their open wounds festered and refused to heal. Most who exhibited this latter stage of radiation sickness died.

Those that didn't awaited a third stage, where the body over-compensated, white-cell counts soaring to make up for the internal devastation. Infections set in—generally of the lung cavity—that came and went, lingered and regressed, spared some and took others.

There was a fourth stage, of course.

This was the stage they debated back and forth, whispered about, ruminated on, fueled by thimblefuls of warm sake—not bad, this Japanese hooch—the stage they could only venture guesses about since they wouldn't, couldn't know for years.

What would happen after?

After they rebuilt the city, after the shadows faded on the tomb-stones and the temple wall, after they all went home. What then?

They could guess.

The first glimmers of genetic mutation were beginning to emerge. Radiation not only lingered in the air; it lingered in the blood.

They watched and observed as some of the survivors gave birth.

As babies emerged with stunted arms and missing fingers and cleft tongues, or with mongolism—though frankly it was hard to tell with Jap babies, being that they already looked half-Mongoloid. Then there were the cases of leukemia, of puzzling and lethal blood disorders.

An unofficial ad hoc quarantine began.

The Japanese themselves began to shun the survivors, as if they were a painful reminder of their national shame. As if these burned and scarred and disfigured people were walking metaphors of their own disfigured country. Hiroshima and Nagasaki reduced to rubble and whole sections of Tokyo scorched from the incendiary bombs of the B-52s.

They weren't employable, these habakusha—radiation survivors. They were always getting sick and missing work. They were dying in droves. They were unpleasant to look at.

No one complained when the army doctors shut some of the survivors away. Not even the survivors. They were tainted, poisoned, a new kind of untouchable. Better for us, and better for them, the doctors figured.

They could more closely monitor the survivors, have a better chance to keep them alive—those they could. They took their blood, X-rayed their bones, checked their stools. They gathered greedily around the autopsy tables to see what they could find.

Slowly, here and there, they began to experiment.

At first, only on the ones barely clinging to life. The ones at death's door. Feeding them certain diets or withholding food entirely. Bombarding them with X-rays to see if you could fight fire with fire.

They would need this knowledge, they knew.

The war might be over, but they'd simply traded one enemy for another. Japan was buckling under just fine—already pouring that nationalist zeal into economy building. Their onetime ally was a different story. The Russian Bear was in full growl, swallowing up all of Eastern Europe and poised to take the rest of it if given half a chance.

No one was under any illusions.

Hiroshima and Nagasaki were just the first two volleys in a new kind of shooting war.

It might be cold now, but it could get hot at any minute.

They needed to know what to do when the smoke cleared and all those millions of victims—because it would be millions—were cleared from the urban rubble.

307

They needed answers.

Most of them grew emotional calluses. It wasn't that hard, considering they were dealing with the people who'd sucker-punched our naval fleet at Pearl Harbor. Who'd littered the Bataan Peninsula with American corpses.

If they were a little cold and calculating about how they dealt with them, these survivors—if they began to treat them like squealing, screeching guinea pigs and not still-living, breathing human beings—it was understandable. It was for the national good. It was for the furthering of science.

The experimenting might look un-American to some.

But not when you looked at the big picture. Not then.

They deserved medals.

From their research would come the blueprint, the textbook on postnuclear survival.

Even when the doctors finally came home, even when the Hiroshima program officially ended, the experiments didn't.

They continued.

Special orders went through special channels to special places.

This time the guinea pigs weren't Jap survivors of a far-off blast.

No.

This time they were closer to home.

Emotionally disturbed boys at a children's home in Rochester, for example.

The doctors formed a boys' "science club" there.

All the boys wanted in.

After all, there was nothing much to do in that place but sit around and make baskets. And some of the boys weren't really emotionally disturbed. No. They'd been dumped there by parents who couldn't afford to take care of them. In the science club, they got to go to baseball games. They were given real hardballs and leather gloves and baseball caps.

They were given something else.

Oatmeal laced with radioactive isotopes.

Every morning for breakfast.

Every boy had to finish his oatmeal if he wanted to stay in the club. No exceptions.

And there were the pregnant women at Vanderbilt University Hospital.

The ones urged to take a special "cocktail."

What's in it? the women would ask, women in their first, fifth, ninth months of pregnancy.

Vitamins, they were told. Vitamins to make you and your baby stronger.

There weren't any vitamins in the cocktails.

There was radioactivity. Headed straight for their uteruses.

Drink up.

And then there was a certain hospital out west.

Marymount Central.

Where pure plutonium was pumped into the veins of 320 selected patients.

Some of them had cancer.

Some of them didn't.

Some of them were terminal.

Most of them weren't.

It didn't matter.

In the end, they were all doomed.

By then, the army doctors had been subsumed into the fledgling Atomic Energy Commission, later itself subsumed into the Department of Energy. The DOE whose director would years later publicly apologize for these "sick acts." But the doctors would keep the moniker they were given during the war as a secret badge of honor. Even fifty years later, it would be how they defined themselves. By three numbers.

The 499th they'd answer, when asked in what regiment they'd served.

The 499th medical battalion.

FORTY-THREE

I took an elevator to the top floor.

The one with bars on the windows.

As soon as the elevator door opened, I could feel them. There was an air of palpable constriction. It suddenly felt harder to breathe; I was walking with ankle weights attached to me.

Maybe it was the thick metal door off the lobby—though *lobby* was overdoing it, since the room seemed to serve no discernable purpose. There were no chairs and no reception desk, just an empty space between the elevator and locked door. There was an intercom on the wall.

I buzzed it.

A face materialized through the metal grill in the door.

I know. It reads like a half-remembered dream. It felt that way. It was after midnight; I'd left Dennis in a morphine-induced sleep floors below.

There was that incessant murmuring, a whispery tower of babble seeping through the locked door—everyone speaking separate languages that were decipherable only to themselves.

"Yeah?"

The voice belonged to the black man staring at me through the meshed grill. Mostly I could see the whites of his eyes.

"I'm Detective Wolfe," I said, flashing my wallet at the door and hoping the mesh screen would make it as indecipherable as his face.

"Okay?"

"An ex-patient was brought in today. He was attacked at a gas station down the road—you probably heard about it?"

"Nope."

"He was a patient on the psych ward. Dennis Flaherty?"

"Oh, yeah. Dennis. I heard something 'bout that. Cut his eyes out, huh?"

"His tongue."

"Okay."

"He's in pretty bad shape. Whoever did it killed the gas-station clerk, too."

"Uh-huh. Yeah."

"I'd like to take a look around if that's okay."

"*Here*?"

"That's right."

"What for?"

"Major DeCola said it'd be okay."

"Major *who*?"

"DeCola."

"He's a doc down on . . . ?"

"Surgeon."

"Right. He ain't a *psych*. So—"

"He said it'd be okay."

"Yeah. Well. I'm just sayin' . . ."

"He's a major," I said.

"Shit. Okay."

The magic words.

The door opened electronically—at least, it was supposed to. The black man, who introduced himself as *Rainey*, had to push it open himself.

"Everything's fucking falling apart here," Rainey said.

Maybe it hadn't been that hard for Dennis to run away, I thought. Maybe all he'd had to do was push open the door and scram.

There was a small desk on this side of the door. Rainey's, I guessed. A Styrofoam cup sat on an open newspaper as neatly arranged as a place mat. A metal bridge chair sat on the other side of the desk.

The room itself was about the size of a two-stall bathroom. It smelled like one. There was the odor of stale urine and male sweat. Of confinement.

"You knew Dennis?" I asked him.

"You don't *know* anybody here, man. You don't want to know anybody. Most of them don't know which way is up."

"He knew which way was out, though, didn't he?"

Rainey chuckled. "Sure. Okay. Dennis flew the coop."

"He stuffed a lot of meds in his pocket before he left, too. What floor's the dispensary on?"

"Not this one."

There was a door opposite the door I'd walked through. The door to the actual wards, I guessed. The looney bin.

"Can I see Dennis's room?"

"It's just a bed, man."

"Right. Show me anyway."

He shrugged, scratched his head, said: "You're the boss."

He fumbled for a key and fitted it into the lock; the door swung open.

I'd expected something worse.

It looked like a dormitory. A dormitory in an old boys' school—okay, an old, *old* boys' school. But still. A regular-looking hallway led to regular doors that opened onto regular rooms with regular rows of cots.

We stood in the doorway of Dennis's old room and Rainey put his finger to his lips.

Don't make any noise.

I doubt we would've disturbed anyone. The patients were tossing, turning, mumbling in their sleep. Some of them appeared to be sleeping with their eyes open.

"Which bed was Dennis's?" I asked.

"Let's see . . ." Rainy whispered. "Over there." He pointed to the far end of the room. "He liked the window. Liked seeing the sky. He was used to living on the streets, maybe."

"Maybe."

"See, just an empty bed. Told you."

"I want to take a look at it."

"You are looking at it."

"I'd like to take a closer look."

Rainey shrugged.

We walked down the center aisle, past the murmuring, shifting bodies flanking both sides of the room. The smell was worse here—sour and medicinal.

Thin beams of platinum moonlight spilled across the wooden floor. I nearly tripped over someone's shoe.

"This one?" I said. It was the last bed, directly under the window. The mesh screen sliced the moonlight into neat little squares.

"Uh-huh."

The bed was made up in military style, the gray blanket pulled tight in impeccably neat corners. You could probably bounce a quarter off it. A wooden shelf hung over the bed, but there was nothing on it.

I sat down, tried to imagine what it was like to live here—among other disturbed people who once carried guns.

"What about that one?" I asked.

The bed directly across from Dennis. It was the only other empty bed in the room.

"That one?" Rainey said. "Oh, that was Benjy's."

FORTY-FOUR

Benjamin's shelf was still filled with stuff.

Old books, mostly—primers, textbooks, comics, the kind of things that parents usually lock away in an attic chest for safekeeping. Only there weren't any chests in a VA hospital, certainly no attics, and no parents to lovingly store the mementos of childhood.

"He was black," I said. "Benjamin was black."

"Black as me," Rainey said. "What you interested in him for?"

"He flew the coop too, didn't he? Dennis wasn't the only one who knew the way out."

Rainey nodded.

"I think he took something of Dennis's with him," I said.

"Okay."

"How long was Benjy here? In this hospital?"

Rainey smiled. "Shit, who knows? He was a lifer, man."

"A lifer, sure. But Benjy wasn't a *vet*, was he?"

"It's a vet hospital, ain't it?"

"Yes. But maybe it wasn't always a vet hospital?"

"Can't help you. Before my time. Just knew the poor fool was here forever."

"Was he a fool?"

"Shit, he was *here*, wasn't he? Of course he was a fool."

"You ever talk to him, Rainey?"

"About what?"

"About anything? The weather. The World Series. The price of gas?"

"Hey, I told you. You don't want to know the people in here. They come here, they got no minds. They're as nuts as Dennis. Benjy talked to himself."

"Was he on drugs? Like Dennis?"

"Every color in the rainbow, man."

"Right. Maybe that's why he talked to himself."

Rainey shrugged.

"I don't think Benjy was a poor fool," I said. "I think he was a poor *something*, though. When did he break out of here?"

"I don't know—a while ago. Before Dennis."

"Sure, before Dennis. Were they friends, Dennis and Benjy? Did they hang out together?"

Rainey shook his head. "Told you, Benjy was a lifer. Lifers stick to themselves. Dennis was fresh off the streets."

"Do you let patients keep their wallets, Rainey?"

"Sometimes. We let them keep a little money—you know, for snacks and things. Some of them have pictures in their wallets—you know, of their wives or kids. So why not?"

"They ever get their hands on more than a little money?"

"Well, they're not supposed to."

317

"Yeah, but *do* they?"

"Sure. I guess. People visit. They get sent stuff. They play poker—supposed to be for matchsticks, but you know?"

"Yeah, I know. So maybe now and then, those wallets have more than just snack change and pictures."

"Okay, sure."

"Did Dennis ever play poker?"

"I guess. Why?"

"Benjy ended up with Dennis's wallet. I was wondering if it had a lot of money in it. Poor fool that he was, he knew enough to know he'd need some cash to get from here to there."

"Where's *there*?"

"California. To see his mom."

"Oh yeah? How you know that?"

"Right after he saw her, he got into an accident."

"A car accident?"

"No. I don't think so."

"What kind of accident?"

"A fatal one."

"Yeah? Too bad."

We were whispering, but I could see one or two heads rising from beneath white sheets like ghosts.

"Where would Benjamin's medical file be?"

"Down in *Records*, I guess."

"Where's that?"

"On four. He broke outta here just to see his mom, huh?"

"Well . . . he hadn't seen her in fifty years."

"*Huh*? Why's that?"

318

"He didn't know she was alive."

"For *fifty years*? How's something like that happen?"

"Easy. They told him she was dead."

"Well, why didn't she come see him?"

"Because they told her *he* was dead."

"Who's *they*?"

"Is there a TV here in the ward, Rainey?"

"Uh-huh. They like watching the soaps—and those three motorcycle rednecks on Discovery."

"What else do they like?"

"Golf. All that whispering soothes 'em."

"What about the morning show on NBC? They ever watch that?"

"Sometimes, sure."

I began collecting the dusty books from Benjy's old shelf.

"Don't worry; I'll return them," I said, even though it looked like Rainey didn't really care.

"Hey," Rainey said, "if he thought his mom was dead, how'd he know she wasn't?"

"Somebody told him."

Belinda was our homegrown celebrity, Mr. Birdwell said. *You know that weatherguy on NBC—Willard, what's his name, Scott—who wishes happy birthday to 100-year-olds around the country? He put Belinda's picture on a few weeks ago.*

"He got to see her before he died, huh?" Rainey said, letting just a hint of tenderness seep into his voice.

"Yes. Before *she* died, too."

"That's nice."

I sat down on Benjamin Washington's cot. I tried to imagine that particular morning. Starting the day on OJ,

319

Zyprexa, Haldol, and Seroquel, the breakfast of champions, then shuffling off in a half stupor to the TV room for a little Katie Couric and friends. And then that roly-poly weatherman with the bad toupee comes on and says: *Let's wish a big happy birthday to Belinda Washington from Littleton, California—she'll be 100 years old. Happy birthday, Belinda.*

Mwah.

"You know he was castrated?" I whispered to Rainey.

"Uh-huh, sure. I seen him in the shower."

"You know why?"

Rainey shrugged. "Thought it was a war wound. Lots of people missing lots of stuff in here—not just their minds."

"Benjamin Washington was a civilian."

"Benjamin *who*?"

"Washington."

"Nuh-uh. *Briscoe*. His name was Benjamin Lee Briscoe."

"You sure?"

"Nah—I'm making it up. *Course* I'm sure. Maybe you talking about the wrong guy, huh?"

Okay, something was wrong. But I wasn't talking about the wrong guy. I wasn't. Yet something seemed oddly familiar about that name.

Briscoe.

I leafed through Benjamin's childhood primer. A journey through the alphabet. At some point, someone had tried to teach him something. He'd scrawled his first name across the cover: *Benjamin: age 9.*

"How'd he get out of here, Rainey? You said he was all doped up."

"Nah—I said he talked to himself. You said it's the meds."

"I bet he would've stopped taking them. Pretended to swallow them maybe, but spit them out instead. He would've wanted a clear head."

"If you say so. That what Dennis did?"

"No."

I WOKE DENNIS UP.

His eyes were dreamy-looking, peaceful, as if he'd been somewhere where he still had his tongue and could read license plates and road signs to his heart's content.

"Dennis," I said. "Just listen and nod your head, okay? Either yes or no, okay, Dennis?"

He nodded yes.

"You made a trade. That's how your wallet ended up with someone else."

He stared at me.

"His name was Benjamin. He was going to break out of here—he was going to run. Remember?"

No response.

"Maybe that gave you the same idea. Benjamin didn't want his meds anymore—he didn't need them. But you did—you needed them. You had a little money in your wallet; you had some ID in there too, maybe. Benjamin needed both. He was a *ghost*. He had no identity—none. And he was finally going out into the world."

Dennis stared at me.

"You traded him your wallet for his meds. Every color in the rainbow. That's how a black man who burned up in a car in California ended up with your wallet in his pocket."

Dennis blinked.

"I know you can't remember stuff. I know it's all a

fucking haze. Try to remember this. Just try. Yes or no?"
   He nodded.
   Yes.

FORTY-FIVE

I brought the detritus of Benjamin's sad life to the dark and deserted lounge.

I bought a cup of mud-colored coffee from a machine and sat down at the table.

I opened the primer. *Benjamin: age 9.*

Every page contained a letter—first page letter *A*, second page letter *B*, third page *C*, and so on.

Benjamin had written each letter ten times, both in caps and lowercase. Then a word using that letter.

The *A* word was *apple*.

Then a picture of the word—a red apple in crudely drawn crayon.

Then *apple* was used in a simple sentence.

I eat apple, Benjamin wrote, in a 9-year-old's syntax that he would never outgrow.

Happy hundred birthday.

I wish you hundred hugs.

It would've been hard to outgrow anything while being weaned on various mind-benders.

The *B* word was *bed*.

The bed he'd drawn looked pretty much like the one I'd just left in the ward. A child's vision of it. Same color blanket. A small black scarecrow with crooked little Zs shooting out of his mouth.

I sleep bed.

For fifty years that's what he'd done, until one day he saw his mom on TV, the one they'd told him had died in the flood with all the others. Then he woke up.

I went through each page.

Car.

Dog.

Elefant.

Fire.

Goat.

House.

Ice creem.

Jump.

Then the *K* page.

I stared at this word, because it wasn't a kid's word at all.

No.

I'd seen this particular word before.

When a folded letter fell out of a cracked picture frame and whispered *come follow me*.

See, I wasn't talking about the wrong guy, Rainey.

The picture was a street filled with little stick figures raining tears. Their little stick arms were raised in childish terror. Of what? A blue giant. He was looming over them with a scythelike knife dripping thick, red drops of blood.

I stared at the sentence.

I live Kara Bolka.

K for Kara Bolka.

That's why I was never able to find it. Why I could've scoured the phone directories from now till doomsday and still come up empty.

Greetings from Kara Bolka.

Kara Bolka wasn't a person.

It was a place.

FORTY-SIX

"Ten-hut."

That's the way the soldier covered with shrapnel scars informed me I should probably wake up. That I had visitors.

Only I'd been visiting a place where little children cowered in terror before blue giants with bloody knives. I had trouble opening my eyes and focusing.

Detective Wolfe. He was standing there with a new partner who didn't look much like a policeman. There was a palpable menace in the room.

"Good morning," I said.

"Maybe not," Wolfe said. "You said you're a reporter but you're not just *a* reporter, Mr. Valle."

Dennis was up, too. Dried blood had formed around the corners of his lips.

"You're famous," Detective Wolfe continued. "You didn't tell me you were famous."

The other man had pulled up a chair and placed one foot on it, resting his arms across his knee. Detective Wolfe might've been asking the questions, but his new partner seemed to be the one listening.

"For fifteen minutes," I said.

"You're being modest," Wolfe said.

"No. Not really."

"Come on, Tom. *Fifty-six* stories? That's quite a fucking accomplishment. Maybe you should've let me in on it."

"Why? It didn't have anything to do with Dennis being attacked in the gas station."

"No? You might, I'm just saying here, fall under the heading of *unreliable witness*. Given your habit of lying through your fucking teeth."

"Old habit. I've been working at a newspaper for more than a year."

"You're on *leave* from a newspaper—you were sent to the corner for being bad. Something to do with someone getting shot."

"That someone was supposed to be me. He missed."

"He *who*?"

"The shooter."

"Right. There's a suspicion the shooter had your gun."

"He stole it."

"Yeah, that's what you told everybody."

"That's what happened. Why would I want someone to shoot me?"

"Maybe you didn't. After all, you didn't get *shot*, did you? Someone else did."

The other man occasionally closed his eyes and nodded at something or other.

"Here's the thing," the detective continued. "Mr. Patjy was shot too. The shooter was nice enough to leave an empty cartridge outside. He was shot with a Smith & Wesson .38. Just like the kid in Littleton. Just like the gun

327

you purchased—illegally, apparently, from Ted's Guns & Ammo."

Okay, it had just been a matter of time.

Time's up.

"I told you. I was asleep in the car. I woke up and found Dennis in the bathroom."

"Right. You like Doritos, Tom?"

"Not especially."

"Somebody did. Their prints are all over the bags. The ones they dropped on their way out."

I didn't answer him.

"Back in New York, after you were *arrested* for—what was it, breaking and entering, malicious destruction of property, lying your ass off—after that, you were court-ordered into therapy. It was your get-out-of-jail-free card, wasn't it?"

"I wasn't going to jail. Not for a first-time offense."

The other man squinted, furrowed his brow in thought.

"I'm asking if the court recognized you as having mental problems."

"I had problems. I don't think I would define them as mental."

"How would you define them?"

"I was trying to get ahead. I made things up. That was a problem."

"Now it's my problem."

"Why?"

"Don't act stupid. I've just told you why."

"I don't see it that way. I didn't shoot *anybody*. I didn't cut out Dennis's tongue. And here's the wonderful thing— you can ask him. He's right here. Give him a pencil. Ask him who attacked him in that bathroom. It's the same person who killed Mr. Patjy. And yeah, I'm 99 percent sure it's the same person who shot my intern in Littleton. He's been following us."

"Thanks for telling me. Maybe you forgot that withholding information in a homicide is a crime. Anyway, we still have a little problem."

"What's that?"

"*What's that?* Your friend here—no offense—is a *fucking mental case*. Which means whatever he says means 100 percent *shit*. He goes in and out—your words, not mine. Swats bugs that aren't there. Which makes him just a little, only a *tiny* bit, less reliable than you are."

That seemed to jar the other man out of his reverie. He trained both eyes on me.

"Aren't you in the wrong ward, doctor?" I asked him.

He smiled. "Was my Freudian slip showing?"

"Kind of."

I turned to the detective.

"You know, if you wanted to have me psychoanalyzed, you should've asked."

"Really? What if I wanted to put my fist down your throat? Should I ask you that too?"

"Okay," the doctor said, looking slightly alarmed. "We're just talking here."

"You're just talking, doctor," Wolfe said. "I've got a dead body and a vet who can't speak anymore. You're not a vet, are you, Tom?"

"Not unless ROTC counts."

"Didn't think so. I fucking hate it when I have to take in a vet."

"Are you taking me in?"

"I don't know. Should I?"

"I wouldn't recommend it. I didn't do anything."

"Right. But you speak with *forked tongue*. Maybe you're just off your rocker. Is he off his rocker, doctor?"

"I'm not familiar with that diagnostic term," the doctor said.

"Okay, use another term. Is he sociopathic, schizoid, delusional, paranoid? *Doctor, doctor, give me the news.*"

"I've listened to him for less than five minutes—I wouldn't know. Sorry for talking about you as if you aren't in the room, Mr. Valle."

"For crying out loud—how long does a diagnosis *take*, doctor? Haven't you ever watched an expert psych on the stand? Two minutes with the defendant and they just *know* he wasn't responsible for his actions."

"I'm afraid expert testimony isn't my forte."

"You've got to have a forte, doctor. You don't go anywhere without a forte these days. Take mine, for instance."

"Which is?" the doctor asked.

"Closing cases. It's the marine in me. Don't leave anybody on the ground. Nobody. Not ever. I've got one on the ground and one in a hospital. And I've got *this* world famous bullshit artist over here telling me he didn't do anything."

"You want my opinion?" the doctor said.

"Sure."

"He didn't do anything."

"What happened to 'I've listened to him for less than five minutes'?"

"Call it a first impression."

It was decidedly odd being talked about as if I weren't

there. I was back in the New York City courtroom—my lawyer against theirs, debating my fate as I sat there and mostly kept my mouth shut.

"*He was in that store, doctor*. I'll bet you one hundred dollars his prints are all over the Doritos," Detective Wolfe said. "Otherwise he would've gone in and told the Indian to call an ambulance after he found Mr. Flaherty with his tongue cut out. But he didn't go in. So either he was in that store first and saw the dead Indian, or he was in the store first and he killed the Indian."

"And then cut out Mr. Flaherty's tongue? The man he was escorting back to a hospital for treatment?" the psychiatrist asked. "Forgive me, but I think both events are twinned. He did both or he did neither."

"Okay, fine, he did both."

Major DeCola walked in and said that he needed to examine Dennis and would we please clear the room.

Now.

Court recessed.

FORTY-SEVEN

I've forgotten to mention something.

I told you right at the start. I'm a little shaky on the time line—on specificity. What happened when. When what became known or just suspected.

I called that laboratory—Dearborne Labs. In Flint, Michigan.

Remember?

That letter from Dearborne Labs in Wren's cabin. *To Mr. Wren: Preliminary results of your specimens have confirmed your concerns. Please see attached lab workup.*

But the attached workup wasn't attached.

So I called them.

I wanted to know if Wren's medical problem had anything to do with him fleeing town.

"Hello," said a young-sounding woman's voice.

"Hello," I said. "Hello, this is John Wren. I sent you some specimens a while ago and I never got the results back. Naturally I'm concerned about my health and would like to get an answer one way or another."

"Your health?"

"Yes. You tested some specimens and I'm waiting for the results."

"Right. You mentioned your *health*?"

"That's right."

Silence.

"We test *soil* specimens here, Mr. Wren."

"Soil specimens." I echoed stupidly. "Right. That's why I'm concerned. Because I haven't been feeling good and I thought there might be something in the soil."

She asked my name again; she told me to hold. Then she came back on the phone and told me the results had been sent to me more than *three years* ago. Why was I calling now?

"I forgot," I said.

As it turned out, there *was* something in the soil.

"You were right," she said.

"Okay. Great. Remind me what I was right about."

"It's hot."

"*Hot*? What do you mean?"

"You might want to get yourself a Geiger counter, Mr. Wren. The soil you sent us—it's *radioactive*. Can I ask where you got it from?"

She could ask, but I didn't have to answer.

I hung up.

I was still concerned about Wren's *health*.

Back in Wren's cabin, when he'd called me from Fishbein.

When I attempted to take the edge off and chat about fishing *rods*.

I told you. I'd done a story on a professional fishing contest up in Vermont. I'd sat around with men whose arms resembled twisted cord, who liked kicking back at night sucking on filterless Camels and swapping fish stories.

I fit right in.

I took notes for the article. I picked things up.

That's what journalists do. We learn a little about everything, just enough to be wrong.

The men talked about their rods as if they were old girlfriends. Debating the merits of one over another with a nostalgic and loving eye.

I asked Wren about the rods leaning up against his wall. What kind they were.

He'd hesitated and said: *trout rods*.

There are all kinds of fishing rods.

Freshwater and saltwater, fiberglass and graphite, casting and fly.

There are twelve-foot rods, four-foot rods, and every size in between.

There aren't any trout rods. Or flounder, tuna, or swordfish rods, either. That's not how fishing rods are categorized—by the fish. Anyone who took fishing seriously, who'd retired to a deserted fishing camp to spend his days pulling lake trout of the water, would've known that.

One other thing.

Everyone has cleared out. I used to see them in the parking lot when I peered out the windows. Salesmen, RVers, families caught between point A and point B, even the semipermanent residents like myself who took their motel rooms by the week.

No more.

The motel's deserted. It's down to me.
It's what you do before a siege.
You clear the area.
You isolate the target before you go in.

FORTY-EIGHT

I was still a free man.

I still had time.

Until they matched my prints; as someone who'd been on probation, they were on file. Until Detective Wolfe convinced some assistant-assistant DA that you didn't really need all that much evidence when you were dealing with a convicted liar.

Maybe you didn't.

Even though someone once calculated we lie a hundred times a day. To our bosses, employees, clients, spouses, kids, citizens, policemen, bill collectors, relatives, friends. To caseworkers from Children's Protective Services. And to ourselves. And after we lie to ourselves that there's a God, we go and lie to him, too.

Some lies are bigger than others.

The lie they'd told Benjamin. The lie they'd told Belinda.

The lie they made Lloyd Steiner tell.

I knew all about big lies.

Benjamin's records were down on four just like Rainey

said. The nurse down there was kind enough to hand them over to me after I trotted out my Detective Wolfe imitation again and requested them.

There was a problem with Benjamin Washington's records, of course.

They didn't say *Benjamin Washington*.

Rainey was right about that. They said *Benjamin Lee Briscoe*.

Born 1948. Vietnam vet. Charlie Company. Served in the Mekong delta from 1966 to 1968.

Something was whispering to me.

I sat down on a hard plastic chair and stared at the wall. The nurses used it as a kind of bulletin board. There were notices for apartment rentals, cake sales, dogs up for adoption, babysitters, even birth notices.

Birth notices.

The opposite of which are what? Death notices. Obituaries.

I reached into my back pocket. I pulled out my wallet and searched through the back fold where I'd slipped John Wren's phone number a few weeks ago.

I'd scrawled it on the back of something.

A picture of the Vietnam memorial.

Black polished granite with an endless river of names frozen in stone.

I had to squint before I finally saw his name. *Eddie Bronson* wasn't the only name on that wall.

A little further down, stuck between *Joseph Britt* and *James Bribly*.

Hello.

Benjamin Lee Briscoe.

That's why the name had seemed familiar.

When I'd found Eddie Bronson's name that day in the *Littleton Journal*, it was surrounded by other names. I'd stared at the picture one night in drunken reverence, a onetime obit writer contemplating the saddest obit of them all.

Benjamin Washington had died fifty years ago in a flood.

But he'd been reborn.

Just like the disoriented vet who'd wandered into the town gazebo that day.

He'd been reborn, too.

"Who's Eddie Bronson?" Wren had titled his article.

Then Wren had gone to Washington and found out.

Eddie Bronson was MIA, was fertilizer in some Vietnamese rice paddy. The crazy vet who'd set up shop in the town gazebo had taken his name. He must've been suffering *survivor's guilt*. That's all. Not uncommon to take the name of a dead buddy when for some reason you're still breathing, when your life has turned to shit. When the fog of war has followed you around like some black cloud.

Except . . .

He might've had survivor's guilt, but it wasn't Vietnam that he'd survived. Something worse.

They'd hustled him off to an *institution*.

When I handed the records back to the nurse, I asked her about this one.

This institution.

Did the hospital *always* belong to the VA? Or was it something else before that?

How'd you know? she asked. Yeah, it used to be a

338

research hospital. Back in the forties and fifties. *Run by the medical division of the DOE.* It had a children's wing specializing in rare cancers.

Did she remember what was it called?

Marymount, she said.

Marymount Central.

Thank you, I said.

I went to say good-bye to Dennis.

He wasn't there.

"He threw a fit," the soldier said. "They took him back up to the cuckoo ward." He was obviously happy to have the room to himself again. "He went nuts. Check that—he's *already* nuts."

"Someone cut out his tongue," I said. "That can kind of upset you."

I should've taken off right then. I was armed and dangerous, loaded with combustible knowledge, and I should've run.

But Dennis was lying in a hospital unable to form words anymore, and just like with Nate the Skate, it was my fault.

I'd put him in harm's way.

So I went back upstairs, took the elevator to the penthouse, and buzzed the intercom.

When Rainey saw me, he smiled.

Which should've been my first clue.

Maybe I was disoriented—I hadn't slept much lately—and when I did, I spent most of the time being chased around by blue giants and 80-year-old doctors. In my dreams and waking nightmares, I knew they were the same person now.

"Why, hello there, Detective Wolfe," Rainey said.

I didn't pick up on the tone. That mocking singsong quality.

"I understand they've brought Dennis back up here," I said.

"That's right."

"I need to see him," I said.

"Sure thing. No problem."

He opened the door.

"I'll stick you in a room somewhere while I go get him. That sound all right to you, detective?"

It sounded fine. I was going to say good-bye to Dennis. I was going to go to one last place and wrap this thing up and go win a Pulitzer Prize.

"Hope you don't mind the decor," he said, after assuring me he'd be back with Dennis in a jiffy.

I didn't mind the decor. I didn't notice it.

I was admiring my connect-the-dots drawing.

Look, everybody.

I was holding it up for the whole diner to *ooh* and *ahh* over, my dad and my mom and my editor and my PO and Dr. Payne and the reporter who'd knifed *I lie, therefore I am* into my desk. Benjy and Belinda and Nate the Skate and Norma and Hinch. Them too. I was emerging from a dark cave and bathing in the glow of the resurrection.

It wasn't completely filled in.

Enough of it was.

Let me take you from dot to dot.

John Wren had found a disoriented and traumatized Vietnam vet sleeping in the town gazebo. *Eddie Bronson*— that's what he said his name was.

Dot one.

At some point Wren had gone to Washington and discovered something puzzling. Eddie Bronson was a Vietnam corpse. MIA. He was up there on that wall. People were incapable of dying twice.

Dot two.

So who was this Eddie Bronson? Obviously a vet suffering from some kind of survivor's guilt. Someone disoriented enough to take someone else's name and forget his own. Forget his family, his past. But not the way home.

No.

Of all the town gazebos in America, he'd bedded down in that one. He'd called it home.

Why?

Because it felt that way.

Close enough, at least.

Once upon a time, he'd lived just twenty-three miles down the road in a town that no longer existed.

In Littleton Flats. Wren would've found that out.

Dot three.

But everyone in Littleton Flats that day had *died*.

Everyone.

Including Benjamin Washington.

Unless they hadn't.

Wren had begun his exposé on the Aurora Dam Flood.

Discovered things.

Gotten all excited. Then gone off the deep end— *Littleton loco*. That's what they said. Locked himself in the offices of the *Littleton Journal* one night and wouldn't come out.

Why?

What was he doing there that night?

He'd been evicted from the premises, then gone and *holed himself up somewhere to work* on the story.

What *was* the story?

I think I knew.

It was a story about MIAs helping one another out.

Purely for bureaucratic purposes.

Those MIAs up on that granite wall—their records remain open in the VA system as long as their bodies remain *missing*. They'd helped out a few MIAs from a different kind of a national disaster. Unknowingly, of course. They'd given them their *names*. The disappeared from Littleton Flats—where it wasn't a dam that blew sky-high that Sunday morning.

No.

You might want to get yourself a Geiger counter, Mr. Wren.

I still hadn't really looked at where I was.

If I *had*, I would've noted that it resembled a padded cell minus the padding. I would've been aware that Rainey *hadn't* come back in a jiffy, that one minute had become two, then three, and four and five.

Time needed to register.

Tick-tock-tick-tock-tick and suddenly it was *fifteen* minutes after Rainey left. Suddenly I was sitting on the hard metal bench, which folded down from the wall. I was in a room you didn't want to spend too much time in.

I wasn't collecting accolades as I showed off for the crowd.

I was staring at my surroundings. I was reading what various incarcerated people had knifed into the wall.

I am a man of constant sorrow, someone had scrawled.

Call God collect.

I am MIA from the world.

And this:

Greetings from Kara Bolka.

Even as I stood up and walked the four feet to the door—it had a small grill in it like the door outside the elevator—even before I turned the knob, I began to sense that it might not open. That doors can open and doors can close and sometimes open doors can become closed ones.

I grasped the knob and turned.

Locked tight.

I put some wrist into it. Nothing.

I pushed against the door as if making sure that it was really, truly locked. I tapped on it, politely at first, as if it might be a misunderstanding, just a technical glitch, and Rainey would come running over in one minute to open it up and apologize.

After a while, I started pounding on it.

"*Hey*! Hey, *Rainey*! What's going on here?"

Sometimes when you shout a question out loud, you already know the answer. It's mere formality. *What are you doing?* you yell when someone pulls a gun on you in a dark and scuzzy part of town. You *know* what they're doing. They're preparing to shoot you.

"Hey, c'mon! Open the damn door. What *is* this?" I shouted, with the rising panic of someone trapped between floors.

It took ten minutes for Rainey to show up.

Long enough to have bloodied my knuckles and to be dripping in sweat. To have put numerous scuff marks on the bottom of the door where I'd tried to kick it open.

343

Rainey wasn't smiling anymore. He wasn't letting me out, either.

"Shut the fuck up," he said.

"You know what you're doing? I'm a cop."

"Yeah, I'm a cop too. I'm the fucking chief of police."

Okay, charade up.

"Okay, fine. I'm a *journalist*."

"You don't say?"

"My name is Tom Valle. I'm from the *Littleton Journal*. Sometimes reporters have to lie a little to get the story. You can't lock us up for that. Otherwise we'd *all* be in jail. Look, just let me out, and we'll forget about this. . . ."

"Lie a *little*? That's a lie right there. That's a whopper."

Someone had been talking to him.

"*Look*, you're breaking the law here. You're aiding and abetting the wrong people. Right here—right in this fucking hospital." Sometimes the first time you know you're really scared is when you hear it in your own voice. Up till then, you think you're doing okay—you're in control, you're going to get out of this.

"Wrong people, right. That's good. That's funny. Why don't you just be cool, okay? Why don't you sit back down?"

"Rainey, let me out of here. I'm a *reporter*, for god's sake. There's something criminal going on here."

"Yeah. You're right about that."

"I'm not the criminal."

"Yeah, you're the cop. You're Detective Wolfe."

"You wouldn't have let me in if I told you I was a reporter."

"Well, now that you put it that way . . ."

"You're going to let me out?"

"No."

He was taking orders. This was a military hospital and he was taking orders.

"Look, you can't just lock me up. This is fucking nuts. I have *rights*. . . ." It was a tired refrain, something he probably heard a hundred times a day. It was like every prison on earth. No one's guilty. No one belongs there. It's all a mistake.

"Rights, huh," Rainey said. "I got the right to some peace and fucking quiet. So sit down, and shut the fuck up."

I screamed something. I'm not sure what it was—something with lots of four-letter words in it.

I managed to stop screaming just long enough to hear someone whispering.

Out there—out where Rainey was.

He'd ducked away to the left of the grill—I could hear a conversation going on. I couldn't make out the words.

"Hey! *Hey*! Who's that? Who you talking to, Rainey? *Hey*!"

More footsteps. The sound of cart wheels rolling on tile.

The doorknob jiggled, turned.

I instinctively backed away, edged closer to the wall.

Rainey and two orderlies in blue scrubs. They'd obviously been picked for their size and not their bedside manners. One of them had a syringe in his left hand.

"What's that?" I said.

"What's it look like?" Rainey said.

"I'm not taking a shot."

"Okay. Whatever you say."

"You're committing a crime, don't you get it? You're going to jail."

"Nah, I'm going home. After we put you to bed."

"I'm not taking a shot."

"You're agitated, dude. Agitated people make me agitated."

The orderly with the syringe in his hand looked Samoan, like one of those NFL fullbacks with a last name you can't pronounce. He smiled and said, "Come here."

"No thanks. I'm fine right here. Thanks anyway."

"Look, man," he said with weary exasperation. "We can do it hard or easy."

"Okay—easy. Let me out of here, and I'll go *easy* on you. Promise. On all of you. I understand. You're taking orders. I get it. You're orderlies; orderlies take orders. *I'm not a patient*. I'm a reporter. I'm doing a story."

"Better spell my name right, bro," the Samoan said. "It's got eleven letters."

"*Name*? Hey, I won't *mention* your name. Just let me walk out of here and it's all copacetic. It's all cool."

"You really want this?" Rainey said. "You want to be hog-tied, straitjacketed, fucked up? You want the whole shit storm?"

"Okay, fine, you win," I said.

There was a slight space between the Samoan and the door, a crack of daylight a good running back might blow through like a category 4 hurricane.

"Can I roll up my own sleeve?" I said.

I hadn't played football since childhood—three-on-three street ball where you had to keep one eye open for darting cars. I'd been considered *shifty* back then, a good thing on 167th Street even if it was a not-so-good thing later on in the newsroom.

I tried to look relaxed, resigned to my fate.

It's hard to do with every muscle in your body quivering in alarm.

Agitated people made them agitated. Relaxed people made them relaxed. See. Rainey was already leaning back against the wall. The other orderly was leaving, no longer needed—*gone*. The Samoan folded his arms, like a patient husband waiting for his wife to vacate the dressing room so he can go home and watch the game.

"Which arm you guys want?" I asked.

"Your choice, bro," the Samoan said.

"I'll go left," I said, "since I'm a righty," starting to methodically roll up my sleeve.

One, two, three.

One, two, three.

Get off my old man's apple tree. . . .

Straight from 167th Street, Queens.

I ran to daylight.

Surprising them just enough to slip past the Samoan's attempt at an arm tackle.

Fast enough to burst through the open door and into the hallway.

Cool enough to blow past a doctor/orderly/patient without stopping to register which.

Run, Forrest, run. . . .

I might've made it. Really.

All the way to the elevator and down to the ground floor where I could've made a scene, could've said *can you believe what these guys are trying to do to me, can you*, where Major

347

DeCola would've sent them scurrying back up the psych ward.

I might've, but I ran into a brick wall.

It was human.

THE SAMOAN MUST'VE GIVEN ME THE SHOT AFTER ALL.

When I woke, coughed, sputtered, opened my eyes, and *looked*, I was staring into a mirror. A funhouse mirror, where your reflection blurs like a rained-on watercolor, distorted enough to make you feel uncomfortably queasy.

My reflection was smiling at me, even though I was pretty certain I wasn't smiling back.

That made me even queasier.

"Hello," I said, my voice sounding as if it were coming through a bad cell phone connection. "Hello. Who are you?"

"You asked me that already," the reflection said. "I'm a plumber, remember? I'm doing routine maintenance." The same whistling falsetto I'd heard in my basement that day. *Like a girl*, Sam said.

He was still smiling at me.

You can't touch me, that smile said. *Can't . . . can't . . . can't . . .*

I couldn't touch him.

I was lying down. My legs and arms were strapped tight.

"You followed us to that gas station," I said, still in that strange, faraway voice. "You tracked my credit card receipts and you followed us."

He laughed. "*Credit card*?" He shook his head. "Now that wouldn't have been very efficient," he said.

"You knew where we were? How?"

348

"You're an *investigative* reporter. Figure it out."

Like a dream.

"Why am I tied down?" I said.

"Oh, that," he said. "You were resisting treatment."

A birth defect, I thought, looking at his face. I'd imagined it was an accident—a horrible smashup where they couldn't put Humpty Dumpty back together again. It wasn't. He had no scars. It was a malfunction in the manufacturing process. He'd come out this way.

"You were there at the gas station. I can't figure it out," I said.

"No?"

He put his hand by his ear and pantomimed something. We were playing charades.

Okay. Of course.

"My cell," I said. "You used my cell phone."

"I can't comment. I mean, is this off the record? I wouldn't want to be quoted or anything."

"You triangulated my signal."

They could do that now—satellites able to pinpoint your location to within six inches. You don't have to be using your phone, either—it just has to be on. That's how he was able to be *right* there. To follow us on the highway, then creep up to the gas station where we'd fallen asleep.

"You killed the clerk," I said. "You cut out Dennis's tongue."

"Wow. When you put it like that, it sounds kind of mean."

"Why? I was asleep. Why didn't you just kill *me*?"

He giggled, said nothing.

"What do you want? What are you going to do with me?"

"I'm a plumber. Not a psych."

"I'm not crazy."

"Of course not."

"I know about Kara Bolka. I know about the 499th medical battalion. I know what happened to Littleton Flats."

"Hell of a story, ain't it?"

"If I know, if I figured it out, someone else will. Don't you people get that? It won't be just me. You can't put the water back in the bottle. It's *spilled*. It's all over the fucking floor."

"That's what plumbers do. We fix leaks."

"I'm the leak," I said. Needles and pins. There were needles and pins in my legs. "You're fixing me."

"Don't worry. No bill for my services," he said.

"What happened to your face?" I asked.

"My *face*? Why? What's wrong with my face?"

"It isn't there."

"Oh, that. Took too many left hooks."

"That's not from boxing."

"Okay, you got me. That's what I tell women in bars."

"Do they believe you?"

"Never."

"What happened to your face?"

"I was in an accident."

"There aren't any scars."

"It was an accident of birth."

"Where? Where did the accident take place?"

"In a hospital."

"Which hospital?" I asked, knowing what the answer would be even with my brain swimming in drugs, knowing the answer.

350

"This one. It wasn't always a VA hospital."

"No. It was a *research* hospital," I said. "For the DOE. I know what kind of research, too. You were here. Another resident of Kara Bolka."

"Kara Bolka," he repeated. "Ahhh. That was just their nickname for it. The docs. A kind of a joke, really. We weren't *residents* of Kara Bolka. We were its refugees. We lived like rats in its shadow. It was our bogey-place. It's the story they told us to keep us scared."

"Yes. But who was the bogeyman? Bogey-places have bogeymen."

He smiled. "I think you met him."

"Yeah. Someone else did too. Only she didn't know it at the time. She was 3."

"The little girl," he whispered. "Bailey."

Believe in fairy tales? Ever read one as an adult? Maybe you should. Even when you stop believing in goblins, they can scare the shit out of you.

Fairy tales can be read two ways.

"Bailey saw things the way a little girl would," I said.

My voice sounded like radio static.

"Rescue workers in white hazard suits looked like something else. They looked like robots with no faces. The noise their radiation detectors made sounded like a language— clicking away at one another like dolphins. Doctors with surgical masks became aliens without mouths. Their MASH unit looked like a spaceship. She remembered a bright blue light—he had the bluest eyes I've ever seen."

"Thank God for the *we are not alone* crowd, huh?"

"Why?"

"*Why?* Why what?"

351

"Why didn't Bailey become another refugee? Why wasn't she carted off like the others—like Benjy? Why wasn't she locked away in Kara Bolka?"

"I wouldn't know. I wasn't born yet."

"You were born after it happened. Here."

"Uh-huh."

"Your mother—what happened to her?"

"What do you think happened to her?" he said. "Neutrons and gamma rays happened to her. She was microwaved. I'm what came out of the oven." He laughed again, but this time, it sounded thin and bitter.

"But you . . . ?"

"What?"

"You're doing their dirty work."

"I *am* their dirty work. Besides, my job opportunities were kind of *limited*. Call me an honorary trustee who graduated to bigger and better things. And listen, you can't beat government pensions."

"Which part of the government? The DOE?"

"Let's just say a part that doesn't appear in their directory."

"You became their hired killer. Their *plumber*. Even after what they did?"

"Learn your history. You know who the worst guards in the Nazi camps were? The most brutal? Not the Nazis. The *kapos*—the Jews given their very own rubber truncheons."

"You weren't being threatened with the gas chamber."

"No, just with the top floor of this hospital. That was enough. Besides, *they* didn't destroy Littleton Flats. The ghost in the machine did."

"I'm not talking about Littleton Flats. I'm talking about what they did to Benjamin. What they did to you."

That eerie falsetto. The Italians called it something else, of course.

Castrato.

"They mutilated you. When you were a baby. Just like they did to Benjamin. They castrated both of you."

That smile again—you could see it for what it was now. Sneer first, and it won't hurt as much when they sneer back.

"See *this*?" He pointed to his face. "Sure you do. Take a good look at it. They thought one of these was enough. They were protecting the gene pool. Hard to blame them."

I thought his expression was saying something else. Look what they did to me. Look.

"How many survived?" I asked him. "Benjamin, your mom. How many made it out that day?"

"Sorry. I told you. I wasn't born yet."

"When the hospital turned VA, they gave them legends," I said. "The children that survived. The names of MIA vets around the same age. They *needed* to account for them being wards of the VA—to absorb them into the system. Benjamin Washington became Benjamin *Briscoe*. He was lucky—he got to keep his first name. And there was one other survivor, wasn't there? At *least* one. The one who wandered into Littleton three years ago and went to sleep in the town gazebo. That's what Wren found out when he went to Washington—why he came back and began to ask questions about the flood."

"That's on a need-to-know basis," he said. "Let me check the list and see if you're on it. I'll get back to you."

"I made copies of everything I have. Everything I know. It's with the right people."

"Uh-huh," he said, looking almost bored. "I don't think the right people answer your calls."

"A story's a story."

"And you're a real storyteller. Only your stories aren't real. They come with grain of salt included. Pound of salt, if we're being honest. Of course, we're not. Being honest, I mean. You didn't make copies of anything. The *right people*? Even the *National Enquirer* won't take your calls."

"You're right," I said. "I didn't make copies of anything. No one will believe me. So you can let me go."

He didn't bother answering me.

"My legs are going numb. Can you loosen the straps?"

"You have a note from your doctor?"

"Please."

"Practicing medicine without a license is a crime."

My dentist once went a little overboard with the gas. Not that pleasant floating sensation—more like I was floating right out of the stratosphere, where the air's too thin to breathe. It felt like that. The plumber would say something, but it took a while for the words to actually appear. They needed to travel all the way to Mars.

They'd pumped Benjy with the same stuff.

All that mumbling around the psych ward. Maybe he'd mumbled about explosions and floods and doctors wielding scalpels. About his real last name being *Washington* and him never setting *foot* in Vietnam. It didn't matter. It was all sound and fury, a tale told by an idiot.

Get used to it.

When I tried to ask the plumber what was going to happen now—would I live or die or maybe live a kind of walking death like Benjy—I couldn't form the words. They came out garbled. I felt like giggling.

I was in the same room I'd been in before. I noticed that now.

There was a place on the wall reserved for me. I could post my own letter from Kara Bolka. *I am MIA from the world. Call God collect.*

This was the worst part of the psych ward.

The place they put the hopeless ones, the ones who don't even get *plastic* spoons.

Don't listen to anything he says—that's what they'd tell the orderlies. He lies. He'll say anything. He'll tell you he's a reporter; he'll babble about nuclear reactors and eight hundred dead and horrible coverups and Kara Bolka. *What's Kara Bolka*, you say? Who knows? The ravings of a paranoid schizophrenic with homicidal tendencies. They say he killed a gas-station clerk. That he *shot* a 19-year-old kid in Littleton, California. He cut out poor Dennis's tongue.

It sounded like a good story. If someone told me a story like that, I would pitch it to Hinch. I'd write it up.

I would.

FORTY-NINE

An isolation cell.

That's where I was.

No comingling. At least, not yet.

They came in twice a day to give me shots. To dumb me down, send me floating back up to Mars where little blue men can strap you down and put weird thoughts into your head.

There was no window. I stared at the wall a lot. The ceiling had water stains on it that began to resemble things if I looked at them long enough. Like clouds in a dishwater sky. One stain looked like a barber pole with those funny alternating swirls. There was a profile of George Washington up there. Scout's honor. A '58 Chevy with cool back fins.

This is what you do when you are locked up and shut away.

When your brain is being slow-cooked.

They were using first-rate narcotics, too; psychotropics must've come a long way over the years. Every day, they performed a frontal lobotomy on me. No ice pick needed.

Still.

I learned to concentrate, even though it was like peering through fog. I learned to squint, mentally speaking. To herd those little neurons together and say *come on guys, one, two, three. . . .*

I chiseled things into the wall to see if it was actual English. If it was remotely intelligible.

If it made sense, then I did. If it was crazy, then I was. It was a test.

I wrote down names. A kind of mental exercise.

My bowling team. My coworkers. Sam, Seth, Marv, Nate, and Hinch. A folk band, a law firm of disreputable ambulance-chasers.

I spelled them backward and forward and inside out.

I connected them like train cars and took them out for a spin.

I made Belinda and Benjamin the passengers.

I took the train apart, added the names of everyone I knew, mixed the cars up, sent it back down the line. I smashed it to smithereens.

I alphabetized the wreckage.

A before B, which precedes C, which rhymes with D, which sounds suspiciously like E.

I started with Anna.

Okay, you're probably way ahead of me.

You figured it all out when she first told me her name in the bowling alley parking lot. When she leaned over the fuselage and showed me what a real chassis looks like.

You've been trying to scream it at me ever since.

You've been wondering when it would penetrate this thick skull, dawn on me with one big resounding *duh*.

357

Maybe I just needed a Haldol cocktail and four soft walls to write on.

And time on my hands.

I needed to be relieved of reporting on the latest mall opening and the price of two-headed alpacas. I needed time to muse.

I scratched her name into the plaster, number one on Tom's Alphabetized List of People who didn't know I was here and wouldn't have cared less anyway.

Anna Graham.

I had to stare at it long enough for the letters to blur, for two words to merge and become one.

AnnaGraham.

I had to sound it out like that.

AnnaGraham . . . AnnaGraham . . . AnnaGraham . . . whispering it out loud before I finally understand that I was whispering something else.

Anagram.

Anagram.

Anagram.

I stopped whispering.

I was struck dumb by what I'd refused to see.

Anagrams.

I knew all about anagrams, didn't I?

My bomb-throwing anti-abortion pediatrician—or was it *obstetrician*, I forget—had fed me *plenty* of anagrams in his pathetic attempt to throw me off the scent.

They weren't any match for this intrepid reporter.

I'd cracked them all.

Except, oh yeah, he wasn't actually real.

After certain inconsistencies were discovered in a recent story this paper ran about a pediatrician and anti-abortion terrorist, we conducted an exhaustive investigation. We must regretfully inform our readers that Mr. Valle, the author of this story and a reporter for this newspaper for a period of more than five years, was found to have fabricated significant particulars of this article. In addition, he is now suspected to have fabricated all or parts of fifty-five other stories. When this became known to us, Mr. Valle was immediately terminated, subject to future penalties and possible prosecution. We have also announced the resignation of our long-time senior editor, and have instituted some significant changes within our system that we hope will prevent this kind of journalistic fraud from ever happening again. We apologize to all of our readers who put so much faith in our integrity.

Fifty-six stories.

Including one about a group of struggling actors in L.A. who rented themselves out for con jobs.

And one about a crazy fad called Auto Tag.

And one about a doctor I met in the ruins of a destroyed town.

Where the doctor fed me anagrams.

Okay, Anna.

I'll go where you want me to go.

Anna Graham.

Hamnaagran.

Gramahanna.

Man. Gram. Ana. H.

I furiously worked at it. It consumed the entire afternoon—or was it the morning? It was hard to tell without a window.

I couldn't unravel it. The letters stuck together, clammed up, and refused to speak to me.

Then.

Anna had *two* names.

Of course.

It took me less than ten minutes to take that second name apart and put it back together again. In psychotropic time, the blink of an eye.

AOL: Kkraab.

The anagram that Anna had wanted me to see.

Rearrange the letters of *AOL: Kkraab* and you suddenly have it right there in front of you.

I'd already gotten there first. When I'd found Benjy's primer. It was in case I didn't get there first.

Karabolka.

That night I'd went and found a computer in the nurse's station.

I'd tooled around the Net. I'd found all the appropriate sites.

Half of them were in Russian.

Karabolka, after all, was a Russian name.

It's time you heard the story.

Why not?

It's past due.

The story Benjy must've heard.

And the plumber.

And the man who'd wandered dazed and disoriented into Littleton three years ago, and whoever else had popped to the surface that day, rescued from one kind of oblivion only to be thrust into another.

Not exactly a bedtime story, not unless you want to

scare someone half to death.

The kind you tell only over campfires in a pitch-black wood.

A true Brothers *Grim*.

The epilogue the 499th had been waiting for.

Hiroshima Redux.

Except no one knew.

No one.

It was a big, fat secret.

Shhhhhh. . . .

FIFTY

First off, it was *Karabolka*.

Just one word—Benjy had no talent for syntax. It must've sounded like someone's name to him.

The name for hell on earth. For purgatory. For *whoops*.

The name of a Russian town.

A Russian town situated just upwind from a Russian city that had no name.

A city that never appeared on any map.

Never.

Not one.

You could search and search and you would never, ever find it. It was invisible to the mapmakers of the world. McMillans would've never heard of it.

No one dared breathe a word.

It was built in the Ural Mountains by walking skeletons from the gulag. They were its very first casualties, thrown into open pits after they died from malnutrition and TB and general beatings, then sprinkled over with lime. Just like the Nazi *Einz gruppen* had done to the Russians at Babi Yar and Stalingrad and Minsk in the Great Patriotic War.

This nameless city would serve one purpose and serve one god.

The great God of Plutonium.

That's it.

It was one note, one track—a one-trick pony ridden into oblivion.

Mother Russia's illegitimate child.

It had no name; it was *Secret* with a capital *S*.

Its secret nuclear lab churned out secret plutonium.

Its secret nuclear workforce dumped secret radioactive waste into secret storage tanks.

Its secret police watched over 80,000 secret citizens.

What was the very first whisper of this secret?

The smoke.

Lots and lots of it.

Long, thick, twisting plumes of it, like braids of a babushka's hair.

That's what it looked like to the people in the town of Karabolka.

Tartars, most of them, part of the ethnic soup Stalin liked to stir to a slow boil, occasionally skimming the fat off and dumping it somewhere in Siberia.

The Tartars came out of their houses and stared at the smoke billowing out from the tree line downwind from them.

Forest fire, they thought.

A huge, hellacious inferno of a forest fire.

But a forest fire.

They didn't know what it really was because the secret city was so secret that they had no idea it was there.

None.

They had no clue there was a massive atomic city sitting just twenty-two miles away from them in a deep dark wood.

That the forest fire wasn't a forest fire.

They couldn't know that the cooling system of the secret nuclear reactor in the city with no name had unaccountably shut down.

That the heat had ballooned in a storage tank filled with toxic radioactive sludge.

That it had finally and irrevocably blown sky-high.

That it had exploded with the power of seventy tons of TNT.

Of four Chernobyls.

Of ten Hiroshimas.

That it had torn the roof off the storage building and sent radioactive debris hurtling miles into the atmosphere.

They only knew what their eyes told them.

By the next morning, thick orange-black soot covered everything in Karabolka.

Every single thing.

That's when a squad of Red Army soldiers showed up and sealed off half the town.

The Tartar half.

No one in. No one out.

Because there were really two Karabolkas. The *Tartar* Karabolka and the native *Russian* one.

The native Russians were told the truth. They were immediately evacuated in long black lorries. They never came back.

The Tartars were told a lie.

They remained.

Once there were two villages. One village where they always told the truth. Another village where they always lied.

Crude oil had seeped into the groundwater. This was the lie the Tartars were told.

That's why their cows and sheep and pigs and horses were all dead or dying.

That's why their well water tasted like metal.

That's why orange-black soot covered everything.

That's why the Red Army was there.

Crude oil.

Someone had to clean it up.

They'd been elected.

The Red Army soldiers marched them out to the fields, where they ripped potatoes and carrots and yams out of the ground with their bare hands and buried them in long pits.

They were led single file into the now-deserted Russian half of Karabolka, where they scrubbed the soot off bricks and tore down the single-room clapboard houses.

They were taken into eerily silent barns, where dead livestock was pulled out by the tails and thrown into pits of noxious lime.

Most of the workers were children—8, 9, 10, 11.

Boys and girls.

Making daily class excursions into the hot zone.

Their hands began to bleed.

Lesions soon covered their bodies like mosquito bites.

They vomited green bile.

No problem, said the soldiers.

It's the oil. Clean up the town and everyone will feel better. All the sickness will go away.

All the headaches and the nausea. All that rectal bleeding and green vomit. All those open sores and bald scalps. Gone.

The cleanup continued for an entire year.

When winter came, snow refused to stick to the ground.

The well water remained brackish, foul. It tasted like tin.

A kind of sleeping sickness took over the town.

It didn't matter.

They stayed put.

The children kept going into the fields, into the dead barns and deserted houses.

Later on, they'd be referred to as the *young liquidators*—much later, when things became known.

The children with radioactive hands. The children of the damned.

An entire generation that simply dropped dead.

Five thousand Tartar children eventually dwindling to under a hundred.

Including the newborns.

The ones born weeks, months, even years later.

Children unlike any other children on earth. Children that belonged in a traveling carnival or suspended in specimen jars.

Which is where some of them ended up. You can go to the Chelyabinsk Museum of Embryology today and see them there.

The ones torn from polluted ovaries, pickled in formalin, and arranged into rows on long wooden shelves.

Faces of fish. Legs of newts. Eyes of eels. Scaly skin, hoofed feet, and puppy-dog tails.

Like an ancient curse come calling.

As if it hadn't been radioactive sludge in that secret storage tank at all, no, but a witch's brew spewed out onto the innocents.

That was the secret.

The secret that couldn't be told. Must not be. Can't ever be.

Except . . .

Every so often, when the children were out there in the fields, digging their bare hands into soil the color of night. Every so often a noise. Up over their heads, somewhere in the heavens. Like a whisper from God. Loud enough to hear even if it was soft enough to forget.

But *there*.

The Red Army men watching over them with rifles never seemed to hear it.

But *they* did.

Maybe God whispered only to children.

To the young liquidators who were fast becoming the liquidated. Maybe it was for their ears only.

A promise.

A vow.

An acknowledgment of their suffering.

I will not forget.

I won't.

God sees everything, doesn't he?

Someone *was* watching.

It wasn't God.

It was a single glass eye.

It was a shutterbug zipping along at five hundred miles an hour.

Clicking away at fifty frames per second in a belly of

aerodynamic steel. Whooshing above the radar, like Icarus on his way to the sun.

The *U-2*.

The *secret plane*.

Take a moment to marvel at the symmetry, to bask in the ironic glow before you laugh yourself sick.

America's secret plane. On a secret flight. Over a secret Russian village. Which had just suffered the biggest secret nuclear explosion in history.

We won't tell if you won't.

We won't tell because we're not flying secret planes over Russian airspace. No.

You won't tell because you're not churning out secret plutonium that has just gone up in smoke. You're not murdering your own children. No.

Deal.

God wasn't whispering to the children.

It was the whisper of two enemies unable to scream.

Back home where the secret film was blown up and pored over and analyzed and dissected, they took what lessons they could. If something should ever happen here— not that it would, not that it could, but just supposing it did, just preparing for any contingency, no matter how preposterous, how blatantly ridiculous, but still—if it did, we'd know the drill. We'd understand how to deal with it.

We'd take the proper measures.

THEN IT DID.

FIFTY-ONE

Snapshots.

My days passed like an album being flipped quickly to the back page, little pictures that were sometimes blurry, sometimes not. Sometimes I was even able to remember them.

"How did it happen?" I asked Herman Wentworth.

Stay in a hospital long enough and eventually you get to meet the head doctor. Okay, the *retired* head doctor.

The head doc emeritus.

"Human error," Wentworth said. "A little problem with the cooling system. It was trial and error back then."

A little problem . . . trial and error. Talking about a nuclear plant blowing sky-high as if they'd been building a volcano in science lab and the teacher ended up with some black on his face.

Just a little accident.

It happens.

"That's what happened in Russia," I said. "The same thing. The cooling system malfunctioned."

"Yes."

Wentworth was injecting me with something. I was staring up at the father of our country up on the ceiling.

Hello, George.

"The Aurora Dam plant was just a cover," I said. "They needed the water to cool down the core."

"They had their secret plants," Wentworth said. "So did we. It was a different time. We lived under the shadow of nuclear Armageddon. Hard to imagine now. The pervasive fear."

"And when the plant blew, it was just a dam bursting. A *flood*. Only the water wasn't swimming with dead bodies and microbes—not *just* dead bodies. It was swimming with radioactivity. You covered it up. Took whoever survived that day and hid them away. America's own little Karabolka."

"What do you think? It was 1954. Tell the world we'd just had a twenty-two-megaton nuclear accident? Tell the Russians? Tell the American people? Like I said, it was a very different time."

"There were a lot of things you didn't tell the American people about back then. That boys' school in Rochester. The pregnant women in Vanderbilt. And this place. When it was Marymount Central. By the way, VA Hospital 138— was that an inside joke? *Uranium 138*—where mushroom clouds come from."

He didn't answer me; he was pulling out the syringe.

"You let one go," I said. "One survivor. The little girl— Bailey Kindlon. Why?"

"Ahh . . . Bailey. So scared, so little. She'd mostly stayed out of the water. Radioactively and relatively speaking, she was clean. And she was only 3—that too. She maybe wouldn't have seen things some of the older ones did—or understood them."

"When you told me you were in the 499th, I should've known right then. The good old days in Hiroshima. What's *in* that shot? It hurts."

"Something new. Think of it as sodium pentothal. Times ten."

"All those mutations in Japan. Then in Karabolka. They scared the hell out of all of you."

"They educated the hell out of us."

"Not enough. You needed more."

"Everything has its price. Lab rats will tell you only so much."

"So you used human ones. In Rochester. And here. Then Littleton Flats happened and you knew what to do. You knew where to bring them. You castrated them—no baby gargoyles to offend your sensibilities, to give birth to other mutations down the line. You drugged them into oblivion. Benjamin. And the other *vet* who got away, who wandered back to Littleton like a homing pigeon. You never forget the way home, do you?—even with your brain fried, you still know. Wren found him sleeping in the gazebo. Later he found his name there on the black wall in Washington. People can't die twice, can they?"

"Is that what you read in Wren's article? The one he wrote about the Aurora flood?"

"There was no article about the Aurora flood. Wren never finished it. It never ran."

"Of course. It never ran. But maybe it was written. Maybe he left it somewhere?"

"I don't know what you're talking about."

"We'll see."

ON TO THE NEXT PAGE.

Rainey.

I didn't know whether Rainey was in on it or not. Probably not. Just a soldier doing his job.

I asked him how I could be swallowed up. Legally. Not that anyone was playing by the rules. But just suppose they were.

"We are playing by the rules. People who are a danger to themselves or to others," he recited. "I think you qualify."

"I'm not a vet. This is a VA hospital."

"ROTC. You qualify."

"There was a psych who came to see me with the real Detective Wolfe. He thought I was perfectly sane. Maybe I can see him?"

"What's his name?"

"I don't know."

"That's a problem. But if I run into anyone who thinks you're perfectly sane, I'll let you know."

"How's Dennis doing?"

"Hard to tell. He doesn't say much."

"I didn't do that to him. I brought him in. I saved his life."

"I'll tell him to write you a thank you note."

"I'm telling the truth."

"Sure thing, Pinocchio."

A STORM.

I could hear it raging outside the walls. Thunder. Like standing too close to a bass amplifier at a small club. The

372

vibrations making my ribs rattle.

It's a hard . . . it's a hard . . . it's a hard rain . . . gonna fallll-
lll. . . .

I sang.

I was my own iPod.

I stayed with the canon of Dylan.

You better start swimming or you'll sink like a stone.

Anna's favorite quotation. Remember? Listed on AOL:
Kkraab.

Maybe it had been another clue for the clueless.

The Aurora Dam Flood.

You better start swimming.

Benjy must've swum like a motherfucker that day.

And Eddie Bronson, whoever he really was.

And the plumber's mom—her too. Swimming out of
one kind of trouble and right into another. Right into the
jaws of a shark.

Swallowed whole.

Who was Anna?

If she wasn't *Anna Graham*, then who was she? Really?

Some of what everyone tells you is true. The first rule in
the Liar's Handbook. It's what makes it believable. It's
what sells it.

I would have to ponder that one.

I really would.

THE MIDDLE OF THE NIGHT.

A faint red glow seeped through the door like blood.

I heard footsteps—more like a soft shuffling.

Stopping and starting, like a mechanical toy that moves
two steps before it stops and needs rewinding.

373

Someone was working their way down the hall. Stopping at each cell before moving on.

It wasn't Rainey, or the Samoan, or one of the other orderlies. I knew their footsteps by now. They had distinctive walks—jaunty, heavy, purposeful.

This was different.

I heard someone's breath just outside my door.

The grill was moved to the side—the red poured in, turning my cell into a darkroom.

A strange sound.

Part speech and part moaning and part something else.

I sat up and stared at a single eye peering into my room.

That sound again.

Half-human.

Or maybe the opposite.

Too human.

"*Dennis*," I whispered. "It's me, Tom."

The eye nodded.

I tiptoed to the door, put my face up against the open grill. "Look. They've locked me up, Dennis. They're gonna throw away the key. Understand?"

Dennis stared at me without answering one way or another. It was possible that *understanding* and *Dennis* were mutually exclusive now.

"Your friend Benjy. That's what they did to him. Then they killed him. There's something they don't want to get out."

I couldn't tell whether Dennis was digesting any of this. Whether I was as indecipherable to him as he was to me.

"Dennis, I need to get out of here. *Help me*."

He made that sound again. A deaf person who's never

heard human speech. Like that. He could've been saying yes. Or no. Or maybe. He could've been asking for his meds.

"Dennis, you understand what I'm saying? They're burying me."

The eye moved. The grill closed shut. I heard that soft shuffling moving off down the hall.

I WAS ALLOWED A SHOWER.

The shower stall was open so they could watch you. It had metal hand-grips attached to the wall to keep doped-up vets from falling down and killing themselves.

On the way in, I passed someone on the way out.

Sluggish, heavy-lidded, and twitchy. He had *Semper Fi* tattooed on his arm.

Maybe this was the *marine fucker* Dennis had spoken of.

The one who'd gone AWOL searching for his kids' bodies on Route 80.

I said hello.

The marine stared through me as if I wasn't there. As if I'd turned invisible. I had.

No one could see me.

I was the invisible man.

I ASKED SETH HOW HE DID ON BOWLING NIGHT.

Who'd replaced my irreplaceable 132 average?

If he'd gotten his revenge on the Judas Priest–tattooed A-hole who'd sucker-punched him in the alley?

If Sam had successfully peddled any insurance policies lately?

Seth wasn't really there, of course.

Which was kind of scary.

Seth answered me anyway.

Which was scarier.

ONE NIGHT I DREAMED I WAS BACK IN QUEENS.

The night of the blizzard.

When my mom put away an entire bottle of Jack Daniel's. When I heard her muttering to herself about the toys Jimmy had left scattered around the living room. When I herded Jimmy into the bedroom and tried to shut the door, because I knew what was coming.

So did he.

Jimmy, who was smaller than me and therefore more vulnerable and much easier to fling around like a rag doll. Who looked more like my father, the father who'd deserted us for a younger and prettier woman who always brought us extra pancakes in the Acropolis Diner. Jimmy, who always took it from her with a stoic look of what . . . *defiance* maybe, even at 6, somehow finding that grown-up emotion within him—which enraged her even more. Of course it did. Made her do things to him with scalding bathwater, the bedroom radiator, my dad's old belt buckle.

Things that eventually made Jimmy scream and wail and whimper, and me cover my ears in the false sanctuary of my bedroom, because defiance will get you only so far.

I herded him into the bedroom that night and shut the door. Thinking, this time, I will not let her in. I won't. She'll huff and puff but I will not let her blow the door down. I tried, tried as much as a 9-year-old can. Not enough. She pushed her way in and grabbed him by the arm, dragged him kicking and screaming out of the room.

And I could hear it.

I could hear all of it.

Even with my head in a vise of my own making, down on the ground, ears covered up.

The wind howling outside but an even worse howling coming from the next room. A blizzard outside and a blizzard inside, Jimmy being slammed against things. The whop of belt against skin.

That awful shrieking.

Which finally, oddly, and suddenly stopped. Just stopped.

In my dream, I do not walk out of the room, believing that it's all over, that Jimmy will be sitting there, bruised of course, even bleeding, but still *Jimmy*, still alive.

I do not walk out and see him lying there on the floor, stock-still and strangely blue.

My mother does not order me to go back into my room and write down what happened. The story of clumsy Jimmy, of a 6-year-old who just could not get out of his own way. The story I will dutifully recount to the police and the caseworker from Children's Protective Services and my own father, in all its awful and meticulous detail.

My brother Jimmy slipped on the ice and he hit his head.

He is always falling down and stuff like that.

He is really clumsy.

No.

In my dream, my father returns to save us. He comes back to his family.

I hear him shuffling up our front stoop.

Sloshing through the wet snow.

Banging on the front door.

He's going to walk in and shake the snow off his slicker, and run to Jimmy and make him wake up.

The door opens.

Dad, I say. *Dad*.

But he can't speak. The frigid cold, the swirling snow. He can't speak.

He motions me to come closer.

I run to him in my Batman PJs, but they've somehow changed color. They're drab and gray.

And my dad. Something's wrong with him. He can't speak. He's talking but nothing's coming out of his mouth.

He grabs me by my PJs and pulls me out into the snow.

But there is no snow.

Just an empty hall tinged in red.

Shhh. . . .

He can't speak, but he's still able to whisper.

Dennis motions for me to follow him.

There's a key glinting in his hand.

MAYBE I SHOULD'VE ASKED MYSELF HOW HE GOT IT.

The key.

You could drive yourself crazy with that stuff.

FIFTY-TWO

If you were the night garage attendant at VA Hospital 138, this is what you would've seen: a sleepy-looking orderly making his way across the deserted parking garage.

"Long day?" you would've asked him.

The orderly would've nodded and said, "Yeah." Then he would've searched through his pockets, looking suddenly surprised and irritated.

"Jesus," he would've said, after turning both pockets inside out. "I lost my parking ticket. It was right here this morning."

You would've nodded in sympathy.

After all, the poor guy looked half out of it. If the truth be told, he *stank* a little—as if he'd been running a marathon. As if he'd spent all day wrestling unruly patients into submission.

As if he'd plucked his stinking blue work shirt out of the dirty pile in the hospital laundry room.

"What kind of car?" you would've finally asked him, taking pity and kind of eager to get his fetid presence out of your immediate breathing space.

"A Miata," the orderly would've answered. "Silver-blue and kind of beat up."

"Okay," you would've said. "I'll go find it."

"You sure?" the orderly would've asked, not wanting to get you into any trouble. "I really appreciate it."

"No problem," you would've answered him, already walking out of your glass booth with a handful of numbered keys, on your way to the lower level, where, if memory served you correctly, you'd seen the silver-blue Miata with a lopsided bumper.

Sure enough, that's where you'd find it. Then you'd check the ticket on the dashboard, fit the right key into the door, and drive right up to the very grateful orderly who looked like he could really use a good night's sleep.

You'd watch as the orderly settled into his front seat and drove away. You'd think that car and driver suited each other. That even though neither was particularly ancient, they'd accrued a lot of mileage.

It was just a matter of time before they both broke down.

I FOLLOWED THE SAME ROADS I'D FOLLOWED BEFORE.

I was okay for gas. I had mad money—a credit card stored in my glove compartment just in case. My cell phone was in the cup holder where I'd left it. There was no need to turn it off and make it invisible to prying satellite signals. It was out of power.

The surroundings were familiar.

The thickening forests and creeping cold.

I was headed somewhere I'd been.

Back to six log cabins on the shore of Bluemount Lake.

I knew where the turn-in was this time.

I knew that I had to circle the lake two times like some-one playing Duck, Duck, Goose, roundabouting my way to that sign nailed to a tree.

I knew the car would shake, rattle, and roll its way through the woods.

I knew that when the forest spit me out on the edge of Bluemount Lake, there would be no one coming out of that porch to greet me.

I pulled up to the cabin porch and sat there for a minute, as if I might be wrong. As if Wren would open the door and invite me in for some vitriol and secondhand smoke.

Nothing.

I got out and walked up the steps. I pushed the door open and walked inside.

There was no stove going this time, but it was still early afternoon. There was enough sun to take the chill off.

No one had bothered to clean up the clutter. I saw it for what it was now—someone had ransacked the place. Just like they'd ransacked my basement before I'd moved in.

I sat there and went through everything this time.

Everything they must've gone through, too. I didn't really expect to find anything, but it was due diligence. You never knew. Back when I was starting out in journalism, we called it *gold mining*. Why? Because in your average gold mine, it takes three tons of earth to accrue a single ounce of gold. The particles so small that they're referred to as *invisible gold*.

Sometimes you have to sift through a lot of mud to find what's invisible.

There were some personal letters addressed to Wren.

An ex-flame named Dorothea—she didn't write her last

name; ex-flames don't need to—reminiscing about steamy times in the Florida Keys.

A Mr. Poonjab from Micronesia—one of Wren's acquaintances from his days as a foreign stringer, maybe. Mr. Poonjab offered best wishes from his wife and family.

Wren, himself, didn't seem to have had a family. No letters from wives. No Hallmark birthday cards from the kids. That would've made it convenient for them—Wren not having any family. That and his sudden penchant for being alone.

Mr. Poonjab said he'd be forwarding what Wren had *requested* in the next post.

It was impossible to know what that was.

What would someone want from Micronesia?

Coconuts? Palm fronds? Seashells?

Maybe something more germane. The United States had obliterated that South Seas idyll with nuclear test bombs until the 1960s—an island chain so polluted with radioactivity that it was largely uninhabitable. The United States was currently resettling the population and paying bargain-basement reparations.

Maybe Wren had needed a first-person account from the nuclear moonscape.

There were two medical journals under the couch, one of them a dry and sober treatise on the effects of radioactive fallout.

There were ten copied pages from a book on America's fledgling nuclear weapons program.

A biography of the Hiroshima Maidens—a group of disfigured nuclear survivors who'd become something of a traveling vaudeville show.

A study on Los Alamos soil samples.

Sure.

He must've driven out to Littleton Flats, just like I had. He must've scooped up some of that red dirt and sent it away in vials to Dearborne Labs. *I think it's radioactive*, he must've told them.

I think it's hot.

He was right.

There were the usual household bills—mostly from Wren's years in Littleton.

Oil and electric.

Telephone and cable.

A receipt from a roof gutter cleaner.

An estimate for a carpet cleaning.

There was a construction bill signed by Seth Bishop. Sheetrock work.

Five hundred dollars scrawled in Seth's spidery script.

There were yellowed articles with Wren's byline, posted from the exotic and mundane.

Thailand. Poland. Newark. Cleveland.

There were doctor bills. Wren appeared to have suffered from mild arrhythmia, high cholesterol, and occasional depression. I found a prescription for Xanax—a drug whose popularity around the newsroom was second only to uppers, since it was known as an anxiety soother. Reporters under murderous deadlines tended to have a lot of anxiety.

I went through everything. Then I repeated it.

I looked through Wren's desk for a flashlight.

It was still light out, but I would be trekking into the woods.

THE TREES FORMED AN ARCHING CANOPY OF ALMOST ABSOLUTE black.

The trunks were mossy and slick.

The ground was a mulch-mix of dead leaves, pungent earth, and tangled roots.

Occasional deer announced themselves with whippetlike flashes of their retreating tails.

Chipmunks darted between the dead branches.

I walked an uneven perimeter around the cabin side of the lake.

I kept sinking into the soft ground; in ten minutes I was sweating through the University of Oregon T-shirt I'd plucked from a five-dollar Kmart rack on the way.

I'd done a story on a forensic guru down in Mississippi who planted his garden with donated cadavers—mostly the nameless dead who ended up with the state. He wanted to document what time and soil and weather did to the human body, to meticulously chart the deterioration in bone and sinew and tissue.

Some of the bodies were left rotting in the air.

Others he buried at different depths, digging them up at various intervals to check for damage.

He soon discovered that he wasn't the only one doing some digging. His garden abutted a nature preserve. Black bears and wild boars were able to sniff the buried remains. They had no trouble digging through up to six feet of earth to find them.

He'd described what it looked like.

Like a table at an all-you-can-eat buffet that hasn't been bused yet.

A mixture of gnawed bones, snapped teeth, and dung.

If you buried someone out here, they wouldn't stay buried for long.

I walked through swirling clouds of gnats.

Mosquitoes dive-bombed me like fanatical kamikazes. I squashed at least ten of them on my arms; when I looked at myself in the mirror that night, I resembled a survivor of paintball.

I drifted through smoky pillars of fire—those few cracks in the overhanging tapestry where the sun managed to fight through.

I tried to keep the lake in view at all times—mostly mere glints of it, enough to keep me from wandering in circles or, worse, plunging into the primeval forest and drowning in it.

I was out there one hour, two, three, till it got dark enough to give up.

I circled back and went to sleep in the same cabin as last time.

In the morning I tried again.

This time I went directly out from Wren's cabin—a straight line into the woods.

I was out there all morning; I was hot and frustrated.

I sat down on a tree stump and stared at the dappled patterns on the leaves.

White streaks all helter-skelter, having to do with the way the sunlight poured itself through the branches. The way it splashed down.

Like staring at a Jackson Pollock and trying to find meaning in it.

The casual arrangement of things.

I was looking at one particular pattern—I was forming my own pictures out of it.

When I looked for its source, I couldn't find it.

When I searched the leafy canopy for cracks, there were none.

Not one ray of sunshine being let through.

I heard the thick drone of insects. Smelled something.

A vague scent—musky, sickly sweet.

Something that must've once been truly awful, but was now barely tolerable.

I noticed the clumps of moist black earth flung here and there. Discerned the clouds of swarming insects—horseflies, gnats, flying beetles.

Drive into the woods now and they won't find you till next year.

I had to push a thick dead vine out of the way to finally stand there.

Up close.

Where the streaks of white sunlight looked like a wrinkled Halloween costume that's been ripped off and thrown in the corner.

You know the one.

The skeleton.

I had to swat the bugs out of my eyes. I had to keep staring at it.

The white streaks of light that weren't. The bones. They were dead white.

Bitten in half so that whatever had dug them up could get to the marrow.

I wasn't a bone expert, of course. I couldn't tell a deer bone from a human one.

I didn't have to.

Deer don't wear pants.

Tan chinos, with the Gap waist snap still attached.

FIFTY-THREE

She answered her phone on the second ring, then even more surprisingly, she didn't hang up.

Maybe because I asked her if she was going to go back to her maiden name after the divorce.

Back to the name *Steiner*.

She went silent, one of those strangled pauses that say more than words can. Then she agreed to meet me on Lincoln and Ninth.

The first day I'd met her, she'd told me about her father.

My pop was a mechanic, she'd said, after I thanked her for fixing my coil wire. *He basically lived under the hood.*

Just like someone else I'd heard about.

He took auto-mechanic classes in jail—that's what he ended up doing when he got out. . . . The boy-wonder engineer, fixing cars for a living.

There was more.

At our second dinner, after she happened to mention that she'd known Wren.

That's where we'd met, she said. *At the home . . . to try to scare up some memories.*

And what was Anna doing at the home?

My pop. He's got Alzheimer's, she'd said.

And when I'd asked Wren—not really Wren, but whoever was on the phone with me that day—if Lloyd Steiner was still alive?

Barely.

Did you try to speak with him?

Uh-huh. Let's just say he's not talking.

It was possible.

Maybe even plausible.

So you think Lloyd Steiner went to jail for ten years to appease the public and kept his mouth shut all that time?

Maybe he had kept his mouth shut.

Just not forever.

I called the home. I introduced myself as a concerned relative. I asked a sympathetic-sounding attendant how Mr. Steiner was doing today. "Lloyd Steiner? Is he okay?"

"No change. We're pretty much down to force-feeding him now."

It's what you do for someone you love, she'd said. *He's my dad. I'd do anything for him.*

In the end, maybe that's what she'd needed to do.

Anything.

That picture she showed me.

Cody on the push-and-pedal. The kid pumping his legs like nobody's business—striking out on his own. Going wherever he wanted to—exploring the great wide world.

Except he wasn't.

Mom was right behind him holding on to that pole and steering him where she wanted him to go. It was an illusion.

Dirty trick, huh?

Yes, Anna, it was.

It was.

IT'S FUNNY HOW SHE STILL STIRRED SOMETHING IN ME.

Maybe it's our nature to let the body forgive what the mind can't.

Or else we'd all be at one another's throats. And we'd never let go.

"Someone paid you a visit three years ago," I said. "A creepy-looking man with a voice like a girl's."

We were standing on the corner on Lincoln. Early evening, lots of foot traffic heading toward the promenade.

She nodded.

"Your dad was in the early stage of Alzheimer's by then. It was probably his last chance to get something out. Before he vanished—the part of him that could actually communicate with the world. That could still form words."

She turned away, rubbed something out of her eye.

"This man paid you a visit. He said something like this—I'll paraphrase. Your daddy made a deal. A long time ago. He's got to honor it. Even if he's gone off the deep end of the ocean—even if he's begun muttering things to local reporters. A secret's a secret. A deal's a deal."

There was something in her eyes.

Tears.

"He'd begun talking about the past," she said softly.

I nodded. "Sure."

"That's pretty much all he talked about. It's what happens when you start going. . . . That's what the doctor said . . . Like counting backward when someone's putting you under. And then you're asleep. You're gone. Sometimes he was actually there, back in the 1950s . . ."

"1954," I said. "I bet he spent a lot of time in 1954. The year Wren was interested in hearing about. The year of the *flood*. By the way, what's your real name? I feel silly calling you Anna."

"Does it matter?" she said.

"No. Guess not. The deal your father made. Maybe it was the best deal he could get. Under the circumstances. I think they would've gotten him one way or another—he had a history. He spent ten years in jail, but he did something for his family. He got *something* out of it. You must've come later. After he got out."

She nodded. "They'd had a ten-year coitus interruptus." She forced a smile. "I guess they were making up for lost time."

"You met Wren at the home. Maybe the creepy-looking man told you to do that—your dad's blabbing about things he has no business talking about, and he's talking about them to a *reporter*—get over here and keep an eye on him. Or maybe you met Wren first—when you were visiting your dad. And he sought you out and asked if he could speak to him. About a flood. And a town. It doesn't matter. Either way, you became Wren's friend—a kind of confidante?"

"Yes."

"He *was* excited. Just like you said. He'd discovered something that happened just twenty-three miles down the road. Something awful. Something huge. Your father must've confirmed it. Did he *give* Wren something? Did he hand him more than his memories?"

"No. I don't think so. Why?"

"Because they got scared enough to do something. Because your father's memory wouldn't be considered exactly rock solid. Not anymore. Because . . ."

"Look, I can't *talk* about this."

She still looked sad—something else now. Frightened. Even here, in the middle of a breezy Santa Monica evening, scared stiff.

"What did he threaten you with?" I asked softly. "Your dad, sure—but he's half-dead already. You have a son. Your mom—she's still alive. Did he force you to make the same choice your father did? Protect your family? Or don't."

She didn't answer. She didn't have to.

"You became their spy. You kept tabs. They needed to know how much your father told Wren. What. If he'd given him something *tangible*. That was your job—be Wren's friend but their eyes and ears. Help put the water back in the bottle."

A car slowly turned the corner; she took a step back as if she were about to break into a run.

"Did you tell him? That you're meeting me here?"

She shook her head. "No."

"You're sure? You're not lying to me?"

"No."

"Good, then you can stop peeking behind your back. Your father. He talked about the past. 1954. He spilled the beans. The dam that really wasn't. The little explosion the history books don't tell us about. He didn't *give* Wren anything? Nothing?"

"No." She looked up. "Why do you keep asking me that?"

"I told you. They got spooked enough to do something."

"They weren't the only ones who got spooked."

"Wren?"

She nodded. "He knew. That he was being followed. He thought his phone was being bugged. He didn't know whom to trust anymore."

"He trusted you, though, didn't he?"

"Yes," she nodded. "He trusted me. He started to worry that something bad was going to happen to him."

"He was right," I said. "They killed him."

She turned pale, went deathly quiet like she had over the phone.

"No," she whispered. "No. He *e-mailed me*. . . ."

"Not Wren. He was buried out in the woods. I found his body."

"They said no one would be hurt if I went along. . . . I swear to God . . . you have to believe me. . . . They *promised* me . . ."

"I believe you. You were told what you needed to be told. Be Wren's pal. No one will get hurt. Ask him things. Tell us what he says. They lied."

A car rolled by, playing the latest from Eminem: *yoh . . . yoh*.

"So what *did* Wren say?" I asked her. "Aside from being worried that something was about to fall on his head?"

"He didn't tell me the details," she said. "He said it was safer that way. He was doing a story on the flood. He said they'd covered up something—the government—a big accident that happened in the fifties. The flood was the least of it. He said you can keep a secret for only so long and then you can't. He said my father helped make everything clear to him. That I should be proud of him. That he was going to break the story wide open. Even if something happened to him. Even then the story was protected."

"*Protected*? What did he mean?"

"He wouldn't tell me. He said the story was someplace they couldn't get to it. That's all. That it was protected. That sooner or later, someone would bring it into the light."

"Into the light? That's what he said?"

She nodded.

"Did he mention an army vet who'd wandered into town? Eddie Bronson?"

"No. Why?"

"Because he was the trigger. Because he set everything in motion. Because he was someone who should've died in the flood, but there he was—still alive. That's when Wren started to dig into the history of Littleton Flats. Just like I did. Three years later."

She looked genuinely perplexed. She was telling the truth; they'd told her only what they wanted her to know.

"When did they inform you that your services were needed again?" I asked her.

"The day before I ran into you."

"But you didn't just *run* into me."

"No."

I tried to calculate. My mind wasn't what it used to be. The drugs had dulled the edges, loosened the coil wires.

Benjy had flown the coop. They knew he was headed here. They got scared. He'd seen his mom—he'd called the fucking sheriff's office? Who else had he talked to?

"They gave you that stupid name. Do you know why?"

She shook her head.

"Come on, any idiot could see it. Any idiot except this one. Anna Graham. *Anagram*. They opened that AOL account for you. You really don't know why?"

"No. I really don't know why. Why did they want to make my name an anagram?"

"Because a doctor had fed me anagrams in a story two years ago. A story I made up. My reservoir of creativity might've been running a little dry at that point. I was down to borrowing the conventions of a thriller."

She shook her head. "I don't get it."

"That's two of us. I think I'm beginning to, though. I am. You loosened my coil wire. You fixed my coil wire. You went out on two dates with me. But you didn't know who I was? Tom Valle? My sordid past?"

"No."

"Life is full of surprises. Did you ever meet anyone else? Besides the man with no face?"

"No. He found me three years ago. In Santa Monica. Rang my bell and said he needed to talk to me about my dad. Okay, I said, sure, come in. I made him coffee. This was before he threatened my *kid*. My *mom*. As calmly as someone discussing the weather. When I picked myself up off the floor, I told him to get out and go screw himself. I was going to go to the police, the FBI. He held the phone out for me. 'Remember to spell my name right,' he said. You understand, he was very clear about this—that he was unofficially *official*. That I was fucked. I did what I needed to. I didn't know about Wren. Honest to God I didn't."

It was odd. Having someone beg me to believe them. If it wasn't the definition of irony, it should've been.

"I believe you," I said for the second time. "Did they tell you what to say to me? Fed you stuff to feed me? You didn't just happen to mention that you lived on Fifth, near the promenade, did you?"

"No. Why was that was important?"

"They were hoping I'd take a stroll there. That I'd *pursue* you." I felt myself blushing—the awkward 13-year-old picking someone for Seven Minutes in Heaven who didn't want to be picked. Not by me. "I did pursue you—stupid me. Have you been to the theater lately? Maybe you saw that hysterical sex comedy that takes place on the Santa Monica Pier?"

"No. Why?"

"Forget it. It doesn't matter."

The foot traffic had thinned a bit. A slight breeze was swirling, lifting the mimosa petals on the sidewalk flower-pots, fluttering the edges of her thick, lovely hair.

It would've been nice, I thought. If she had really liked me. If she hadn't been told to smile at me across the rec room of the nursing home. If she'd listened to my pathetic story and said I *understand; I forgive you. I will love you anyway.*

Now she looked up, those big brown eyes.

"I still don't get it," she said. "Why would they want me to tell you anything?"

FIFTY-FOUR

I still had a key to the *Littleton Journal* office.

I drove back into Littleton in the dead of night.

I parked in the strip mall and sat in my car until I was sure no one was around. No kids chugging beer out of paper bags, no Mr. Yang cooking up some Peking duck for tomorrow's lunch crowd.

I let myself in and headed to the back.

That's where the paper was paginated. It was all done by computer now, of course. Each page spit out as a separate unit, then brought over to the printing press on Yarrow Street where it was made whole.

The older issues were stored on microfilm, but everything from ten years ago and forward was hard-drived.

Once an issue was deemed finished—by Hinch, of course—you had to save it in a separate file, where it was organized by date. I'd done it myself; at the *Littleton Journal* we multitasked.

I logged in and scrolled back to three years ago. To the issue with the story about Eddie Bronson. The last issue Wren worked on before he disappeared.

Not to read it again; I pretty much knew it by heart.

I was looking for something.

When I found it, I'd know what it was.

I went back and forth and back—scroll, *click*, scroll, *click*. That issue, then on to the next, then back.

I skimmed the stories. "Who's Eddie Bronson?" A review of a newly released DVD, four stars. The weather forecast—*hot and dry*, followed by *hot and dry*, then more *hot and dry*. A two-for-one deal at the DQ.

Call it peripheral vision. The thing you don't really see, but it's okay, your brain does. It's paginated there for future reference.

The little number on the right-hand corner of page 1.

Every issue of the *Littleton Journal* has one—the computer automatically places it there. Every issue since its inception—an issue number. It marks time; it says we might not be a venerable paper, but we have a venerable history.

We have roots. We go back.

The issue with "Who's Eddie Bronson?" was number 7,512.

I went forward to the next one.

Then back one more time to be sure.

"Okay," I said out loud.

Got it.

I WAS BACK IN MY LITTLETON HOUSE.

I'd let myself in through the back door, just in case.

Someone had been there first.

I could've been in the cabin by the lake. The clutter was indistinguishable. One mess looks pretty much like another.

I went upstairs and stood under the shower spray for twenty solid minutes, trying to wash off the stultifying stink of incarceration. Trying to get my head straight. I wondered if craziness was catching. I'd noticed sudden tremors in my hands, fingers clenching and unclenching, as if they had something they urgently needed to pick up.

When I walked naked into my bedroom and opened up my underwear drawer, I said: "There's the gun."

Speaking it out loud, as if I were casually pointing this out to another person in the room.

He'd put it back nicely and neatly.

The gun that shot Nate the Skate. That put a bullet through Mr. Patjy's head.

Guns don't kill people. People do.

I pulled on some sweats and stuck the gun in the waist-band, like a gangbanger might.

I was in a hurry.

If they'd planted the gun, it was so someone could find it. Preferably with me holding it.

That's what I was doing as I held my breath and flicked on the downstairs light—holding the gun with my arm straight out like I'd seen in TV police procedurals, not putting it back into the waistband of my pants until I'd visually reconnoitered the room.

Empty.

I sat on the bottom step and stared, the class dullard desperately trying not to fail again. I rode herd on what little intelligence I had left. I was back in the Acropolis Diner; I was almost done. The check was due. We needed to leave.

You're it, he'd said to me. *You're it . . . you're it . . . you're it. . . .*

Yes, I know.

And now, finally, I understood why.

"HEY, MAN, WHERE THE *FUCK YOU BEEN*?"

The first words out of Seth's mouth when I rung him up, still sitting on that basement step.

He seemed personally aggrieved that I'd taken off without telling him. People had been asking his take on things. The shooting. The missing gun. The sudden notoriety these things had pulled kicking and screaming into the light of day. In Littleton, the day could be long, hot, and brutal.

He'd had to lie a little. Act like he knew more than he actually did. As if he'd been in my confidence all along. I'd robbed him of the full pleasure of basking in infamy by association.

"Working on a obituary. Like I told you."

"Yeah? You might want to start on yours while you're at it."

"Why's that, Seth?"

"The sheriff came by and interviewed me."

"Oh?"

"*Oh*? That's all you're gonna say? *Oh*? Shit, if I knew you were a desperado, I would've hung out with you more often."

"What did you tell him?"

"That you can't bowl for shit. And the next pussy you get will be your first. How's that?"

"Pretty accurate. Did the sheriff seem pleased with that?"

"I don't think he has a sense of humor."

"No."

"So, you going to tell me what's going on? Or do I have to wait to read it in the fucking *Littleton Journal*?"

"That all depends."

"Oh yeah? On what?"

"If you can help me or not."

"If I can help you do *what*?"

"Know what's going on."

"Huh? I'm a little buzzed right now, okay? You're not making it any fucking easier."

"You did some Sheetrock work for Wren a few years ago."

"Sheetrock? Nope."

"I saw the bill."

"You saw the bill. Okay. Doesn't mean I did the work."

"Where did he want the work done?"

"Where? His basement."

"Why? What was in the basement? Did he have damage down there?"

"As a matter of fact, yeah. There was a fucking hole in the wall. He wanted me to fix it."

"For five hundred dollars?"

"Hey, that was my *starting* price—I would've negotiated *down*, man. Besides, he wanted the whole fucker fortified."

"Why?"

"Why what?"

"Why did he want the basement wall fortified?"

"I don't know. He said the insulation was shitty. He said he needed protection against flooding."

"Against *flooding*? In Littleton?"

"Hey, what's with that tone? It's *my* job to tell him he's nuts? Didn't he lock himself in your office one night or something?"

"Or something. That's what he said to you. His words? 'I need protection against flooding'?"

"Yep."

"You never did the work?"

"Uh-uh."

"Why not?"

"I don't know."

"You don't *know*? What's that mean?"

"I mean I don't know. It means I forget."

"When did he ask you to do this work? Was it around the time he locked himself in the office—around then?"

"Yeah."

"So when were you supposed to start?"

Seth sighed. "He said he might be taking off. If I didn't hear from him in two weeks, I should just go ahead and do it."

"So he paid you? In advance?"

Believe it or not, it's possible to hear someone squirm over the phone.

"Uh . . . yeah."

"And you didn't hear from him for more than two weeks? You didn't hear from him again, ever?"

"No, guess not."

"But you *didn't* do the work? Why's that?"

"I must've forgot."

"Sure. You forgot. You were already spending the money—so why do the work? He was nuts; who was to know."

"Sue me. I'm human."

"Yeah."

"Hey, ever hear about throwing stones, amigo?"

IT WAS HERE ALL ALONG.

I'd stared right at it.

That day I came down here and retraced the plumber's steps.

I'd moved a book aside and seen that hole in the wall.

The book with plaster dust on its jacket.

Hiroshima.

I'd thought the plumber was the one who'd smashed the wall in. It wasn't the plumber.

It was Wren.

The night before he left. Before he headed off to the lake.

But not before he *protected* the story.

I'd peeked into that hole and saw what you usually see on the other side of Sheetrock in these parts. The same thing the plumber must've seen, then dismissed like I had.

Newspaper insulation. It's abundant and cheap, and since you don't exactly have to worry about blizzards in the middle of the California desert, it does the job.

Only this newspaper wasn't cheap. It was ridiculously expensive.

It cost Wren his life.

I moved the books aside.

I stuck my hand inside the hole and gently, slowly, carefully pulled the crinkled newspaper out of the hole.

A front page of the *Littleton Journal.*

Lots and lots of front pages. The wall was stuffed with them.

The issue number still clearly legible in the right-hand corner.

7,513.

The one missing in the files.

The issue with "Who's Eddie Bronson?" was 7,512.

The next issue, featuring a movie review of *Harry Potter and the Sorcerer's Stone* and a recap of the latest meeting of the local DAR Society, had been 7,514.

One issue number skipped.

What I'd discovered as I scrolled back and forth and back.

How does *that* happen?

Easy.

One issue went to press the night Wren locked himself in the office. One front page. This one. That's what he'd been doing in there that night. Not breaking down. Not howling at the moon. Howling at the injustice. Trying to get the story out. Before he disappeared into the void.

He hadn't had time to save it. But the computer automatically gave it an issue number, and when the next one went to press, it was one number higher than it should've been. No one would have noticed—no one was keeping count.

America's Unknown Nuclear Disaster

The headline of the issue that never ran.

Three-inch type.

All in red.

And something more. It came complete with illustrations.

A schematic drawing. A diagram.

403

A fucking *blueprint*.

Faded, crisscrossed with lines, even a layman able to discern the shape and function of the thing being built.

The core. The fuel rods. The shell.

A *real* blueprint. As opposed to fake ones they'd trotted out at Lloyd Steiner's trial.

Yes, Anna, your father did give something to Wren.

Something he must've held on to all those years. Hid away—a kind of legacy. For you, maybe. So you'd know who he really was. That he might've gone to jail, but he was never guilty. Not really. No guiltier than anyone else who'd helped build a nuclear reactor out in the desert and kept their mouth shut after it blew sky-high.

Wren's Rule Number One.

Back up your notes for protection.

He had.

Sooner or later, he'd told Anna, *someone would bring it into the light*.

Literally.

Unfortunately, he'd made one mistake.

He'd anointed Seth Bishop the protector.

Seth Bishop, who, hearing neither hide nor hair of Wren for two weeks, was supposed to rip two hundred front pages of the *Littleton Journal* out of a wall and, even with his limited intellectual curiosity, understand that someone needed to see them. That its three-inch headlines were screaming bloody murder.

Only Seth adhered to the credo of the dedicated stoner. No need to do the work if you've already got the cash—no doubt already blown on some primo Panama Red and six-packs of Coors Light.

ON MY WAY OUT OF LITTLETON, I HEARD A SIREN GOING IN THE opposite direction.

The sheriff on his way to make the climactic arrest, I supposed. Perpetrator and gun, nabbed red-handed.

He'd find an empty house with an empty drawer.

I made one stop before I pulled onto Highway 45.

Mrs. Weitz opened the door, then continued to stand there—all three hundred or so pounds of her.

"Is Sam home?" I asked her.

She appeared to be on the verge of lying to me, but then Sam yelled from the kitchen, asking her *where the damn Yodels were*, so she had no choice but to let me in.

"It's okay," I told her, as she moved aside, barely, to let me through. "I won't be staying long."

Sam was more hospitable than his wife. Though he did surreptitiously peek through both study windows before pulling the shades, wondering, I imagine, if there was about to be a major guns-drawn bust in his front yard.

"Jesus." Sam's first word to me. "You have no idea what they've been saying about you."

"Yeah, I do."

"Is any of it true?"

"Not much."

"Okay—good enough for me. Anything for a bowling team member. You need some help?"

"Just a little."

"Shoot." Then he blushed and said, "Poor choice of words." He'd noticed the gun peeking out of my waist-band.

"How long have you been trying to sell me some insurance, Sam?"

"What? Wait, come on. You mean to tell me you came all the way here for *insurance*?"

"Yeah. Exactly."

FIFTY-FIVE

I am here.

In room four of the roach motel.

Disgraced journalists check in, but they don't check out.

I am almost done. Nearly. Just about.

Have you got it all?

Have I sufficiently illuminated? Enlightened? Made clear?

Do I need to regurgitate the whole enchilada?

What don't you get?

What they did? What they constructed? What they cobbled together, like a movie assembled scene by scene, as if by screenwriter by committee?

What did *Wren* say over the phone? The *faux* Wren, of course, one of several in a crucial cast of players. If I had to guess, another actor hired from that Web site, and told what to say—a simple voice-over job this time.

It reads like a bad movie, he said.

Don't you get it? Don't you see?

It was supposed to.

That was the whole point.

It was its whole raison d'être.

Back in New York, when I was down to borrowing the conventions of a cheap thriller:

Anagrams.

Clandestine meetings in the ruins of destroyed towns.

Con men actors.

Auto Tag.

The works.

I read them. Your canon *of deceit,* he said to me.

I read them.

Of course they read them. But they did more than read them. They *studied* them. Then they *re*-borrowed them, those hackneyed conventions, wove them together into a veritable masterpiece of Valle's greatest hits.

Remember how he'd goaded me over the phone—never went five minutes without reminding me what a disgrace I'd been. How I'd dishonored an entire profession. How I'd set journalism back fifty years.

Fifty years exactly.

All the way back to 1954.

Why?

Why goad? Why needle? Why prod?

Why was he such a fount of useful information?

It was part of the script.

They told me about Lloyd Steiner.

They sent Anna Graham into Belinda's birthday party, then into the parking lot of Muhammed Alley, where she scrawled that anagram into my fuselage.

Kara Bolka, my muse, my siren.

And the plumber. When I first woke up, strapped down and shot up.

How helpful was he? What a chatterbox. What a blabbermouth.

Why?

You still don't grasp it?

They were trying to *hide* something, you say? Weren't they?

Yes.

And no.

You can't put the water back in the bottle. It's spilled, I told the plumber that day.

He hadn't disagreed with me.

He couldn't.

Plumbers fix leaks, sure.

But sometimes, they do exactly the opposite. They *flush* those old and leaky pipes; they send all that rotten water shooting out at a hundred miles an hour. They cleanse the system.

You can only keep a secret so long, Wren had told Anna, *and then you can't.*

It's a fact.

Two people can keep a secret, someone once said, if one of them is dead.

One of them was. Wren. He was dead. And Eddie Bronson—him too, I imagined. Not to mention that poor gas-station clerk, who was simply caught in the crossfire, metaphorically speaking.

And Benjy Washington.

Who'd flown the coop and headed back to Littleton.

Which must've sent them all into a dither.

He'd made it into the nursing home. He'd seen his mom. He'd called the sheriff's office. Who else had he talked to? Who else had he sat down with and told the story to?

First Bronson flies the coop. Now him.

Where would it end?

After all, Wren might be as dead as a doornail, but they were still *scared* stiff of him. Scared of a corpse.

Why?

Because he'd told Anna, plain as day:

The story was protected.

The story. The secret.

Protected.

The story was someplace they couldn't get to it.

But somewhere someone else could. The story would be brought *into the light*.

What did he mean?

They'd ripped his house apart to find out. They'd ripped his cabin apart.

They'd sent the plumber back into my house three times after Benjy made it back to Littleton.

Here's the irony.

If they'd *really* ripped his house apart, taken that Sheetrock by the hands and pulled the walls down, they would've found exactly what they were looking for.

Nestled there behind the Sheetrock. The story Wren had painstakingly pursued and put together and paginated in the dead of night, too paranoid by then to share it with someone like Hinch. *He didn't know whom to trust anymore.* Littleton loco, and for good reason.

Only they didn't rip his house apart.

410

The sword of Damocles was still hanging over their heads.

Wren had put it there.

What's a plumber to do?

Easy.

You set up a Web site for desperate actors who, if they aren't willing to kill for a part, won't care if you do.

You send the biggest liar in the universe out to Highway 45 to cover an *accident*.

You play Auto Tag with him on a desert road.

You send a doctor on a house call to a dead town.

You make sure a dreamy-looking girl named *anagram* bats her eyes at him in the parking lot of Muhammed Alley.

You direct him to Fifth Street, just off the promenade.

You goad.

You needle.

You prod.

You steal his gun and shoot someone with it.

You lock him in a mental ward and throw away the key.

But just for a while—just long enough to blacken his veracity that much more.

Then you put that key in poor Dennis's hands and you set him free.

Now do you understand?

Now do you see?

Sometimes it doesn't matter if a secret comes out.

It does not matter.

As long as you control how.

FIFTY-SIX

I turned my cell phone back on two weeks ago.

Emitted its signal to those tireless satellites spinning slowly in space that would've bounced it back to earth, where some exhausted tech in the NSA or the FBI or maybe just the DOE would've triangulated, diagrammed, and computed it, then sent it on up to the interested parties.

Two weeks ago, when I first arrived in room four.

What did people do before Microsoft Word?

Before laptops, cursors, delete keys, desktops—before backing up, dragging things in, and dragging things out?

Before you could make one document two. Drag it onto the desktop and rearrange it, pare it down, edit it just so.

This is *Document One*.

Which either will or won't make it to where it needs to go.

I have no such fears about *Document Two*, which is the only one left on my computer.

It reads remarkably like this one—minus a few things. Minus the insights, conclusions, and connective tissue. To go back to what must by now be a tiresome and overused analogy—think of it as a connect-the-dots drawing minus the connections.

The dots are there.

The entire cast of characters.

Miss *Anagram* and *Sam Savage* and Doctor Death himself.

Benjy and Bronson and Bailey et al.

It is the story the way they wanted it written.

Why they kept leading me on and putting a cork in me at the same time. Letting the leash out, then jerking it back. Why they tainted me, incarcerated me, and then set me free.

For this.

Another saying comes to mind—courtesy of Stalin or one of his minions, orchestrators of the first Karabolka.

Forgive me it if I get it wrong. Something about history. *It's not what happens in history that matters*, he said.

It's who writes it.

Me.

That's who's writing it.

Tom Valle.

I was meant to tell the story that was never meant to be told.

Before someone else told it.

Because once a story's been discredited—once it's been ridiculed, ripped apart, and indicted—it forever loses its claim to legitimacy. It passes into urban legend, to the canon of conspiracy theorists, onto the refuse pile of hack history. Remember that story about a certain president's discharge from the National Guard? By the time handwriting experts had discredited the documents, by the time a national anchor had resigned and a nationally respected producer was fired—by then, it didn't matter if the basic truth of the story remained unchallenged. It was trash. It was a tissue of lies. It was garbage.

The very fate awaiting *Document Two*.

It will be dissected for the amusement of the public—those who give a crap. It will be snickered at, railed at, and ultimately reviled. It will be held up in journalism classes at serious-minded universities across the country as an example of what not to do, a cautionary tale for every cub reporter about to enter the fray.

It will belong to the LBJ-killed-Kennedy crowd, to the Area 51 cabal, to the Bailey Kindlons of the world.

Because even if you bought the *anagrams*, the *hired actors*—even if you did, you would have to consider the source.

Enough said.

That's what they wanted.

That's what I'll give them.

I've left it here on my computer—right at page 1.

I am writing this as fast as I can.

I, myself, am going for a stroll now.

I've already called the front desk and asked them to send Luiza in to clean the room again. I told the manager that I'll be taking a walk to get out of her hair. Behind the motel, maybe, where I've seen a path leading out to the dusty flats.

When I hear her knock at my door, I'm already up and on my way.

Half an hour maybe, I think.

At least that.

Enough time for them to come in, put that Evelyn Wood speed-reading course to good use, and get the gist of it.

I'm leaving an offering at the altar and hoping to mollify the gods. Vengeance might be theirs, but if you proffer the proper sacrifice, might you still be spared?

Luiza wordlessly passes me on her way into the room, and suddenly I'm standing on the deck in the full glare of afternoon. The deserted parking lot. The dead air.

I descend the stairs one rickety wooden step at a time.

I look neither right nor left. Certainly not behind. I've been there, done that. It's eyes forward now.

I lope across the parking lot, dead man walking.

Because that's what I am.

One way or another.

I said this is my last will and testament, and it is. I've said you are its executor, and you are.

It sits in my pocket, this story, on a shiny CD.

It is next to a forged license, courtesy of Luiza, who slipped it under my door some time ago, after our conversation about illegal documentation. After I slipped her five hundred dollars.

It's only a license, but it's a start.

Tom Valle will be dead.

One way or another.

Dead.

In my other pocket is the Smith & Wesson.

In case the sacrifice isn't enough. In case it's better to have the author dead than alive. The crazy reporter who must've shot himself out in the desert behind a ratty motel. The last refuge of a liar.

I don't know.

I'm not a mind reader.

I will walk and walk and I will not come back, and I will not turn around until I hear the sound of their boots, and then I'll know.

It's hot out here behind the motel, where the desert stretches all the way to Nevada. But it seems like I've been enveloped in chill for years. I am warm for the first time in forever.

This story's in my pocket. On a shiny CD.

I will take it with me and we'll see.

I walk and walk and walk.

I'm aware of the time passing, but it's all time. It's not minutes; it's years. It's then to now. It's the Acropolis Diner and Queens, New York, and the night of the blizzard and *what happened, Tommy* and someone standing behind my right shoulder to read my faltering copy. It's bratwurst sandwiches and walks in Bryant Park and that terrible day when I didn't have the guts to go into his office and say something. Anything. Like another day when the truth refused to come out of me.

When I finally hear them, it's not their boots.

It's their tires.

Their engines.

Two Jeeps, I think.

Don't worry.

I have one last secret.

One.

I have appointed another executor.

I have heeded the rules of Wren and protected the story.

My editor. He is shuttered away in his mountain house

in Putnam County, New York. Faded, sure, but still faintly glowing, still a beacon for those who believe that we can do good and necessary things in this world. There's a reputation in tatters there that can still, even now, be mended. There's an injustice there that can still be rectified. There's a fearsome debt that can still be repaid.

By now, Sam would've sent it to him.

He would've answered the knock at his front door and signed for the package, then sliced it open with the penknife he'd begrudgingly accepted on one of his unacknowledged birthdays.

He would've pushed his bifocals down on his nose and read what looked like the front page of a small-town California newspaper. The *Littleton Journal*. Where had he heard that name before?

He would've read it more than once. He would've seen the note I sent along with it. The one that explained how this particular front page had never seen the light of day. Till now. But that it wasn't too late. It's never too late. There's no statute of limitations on a story—something he used to say.

He would've dismissed it, of course.

At first.

Recalled my phone call and been ready to airmail it into the waste basket. But there was that *blueprint*. He would've been forced to study it—how could you not? The date and location and name clearly written there in official-looking type. He would've gone online. He would've looked up Littleton Flats. The flood. The dam. Lloyd Steiner. VA Hospital 138. He's a journalist. He would've done what a journalist does. He would've investigated.

417

He wouldn't stop investigating until he found out. One way or another.

He will get the story out.

Not under the byline of a disgraced *fabulist*—the polite term for me. For pathological liar. No. It will come out under the byline of a much-respected editor whose only crime was having had me as a reporter.

The engines grow louder.

I still haven't turned around.

I will wait until they're right *there*.

I grip the gun in my left pocket. Mano a mano. Duel in the desert. Every gunfight I'd ever seen on my living room TV back in Queens.

Maybe I'll make it. You never know.

Either way, Tom Valle will be dead. Gone. Forgotten.

If not in a blaze of glory, in the pale hue of redemption. I have taken the liar out to the woodshed and I have finally set him right.

I grip the gun. I turn.

The words of something flit through my mind. Something they read at Jimmy's funeral—I'd never forgotten it; years later I looked it up and memorized each word. An appropriate sendoff for Jimmy, and Benjy, and Eddie Bronson, for all the doomed children in this world, those who grow up and those who don't. For everyone we can't help mourning for.

Even me.

I am standing upon that shore. A ship at my side spreads its white sails to the morning breeze and starts for the blue ocean. Soon she hangs like a speck of a white cloud just

where the sea and sky mingle. And just at the moment when
someone at my side says "There! She's gone!" I know there
are other eyes watching the ship coming, and other voices
ready to take up the glad shout, "Here she comes!"
And that is dying.

I hope it's true.
I hope it's true.

DETOUR

James Siegel

'As original a crime novel as one is likely to come across . . .'
Irish Times

Central Park, New York. It was the small girl chasing a pink balloon that had given Paul and Joanna the idea; to end five years of failing to conceive, and to adopt. Which is why they are travelling to the Santa Regina orphanage in Colombia to meet their new daughter.

It is meant to be a new beginning in their lives. But it is not the new beginning they were expecting.

Colombia is a dangerous place, particularly for a foreigner with a wife and daughter to protect. Paul would do anything for Joanna, and now he is going to have to. He's got eighteen hours to get a deadly consignment to an address in New York. He dare not be late. He dare not dial 911. Because if the delivery doesn't arrive, he'll never see his newly created family ever again . . .

'First-rate entertainment . . . an exhilarating ride'
Publishers Weekly

Crime Fiction

978-0-7515-3613-3

DERAILED

James Siegel

Now a major motion picture

'*Derailed* is high quality entertainment' Nelson DeMille

Advertising director Charles Schine is just another New York commuter, regularly catching the 8.43 to work. But the day he misses his train is the day that changes his life. Catching the 9.05 instead, he can't help but be drawn by the sight of the person opposite.

Charles has never cheated on his wife in eighteen years of marriage. But then Charles has never met anyone like Lucinda Harris before. And though Lucinda is married too, it is immediately apparent that the feeling is mutual. Their journeys into work become lunch dates, which become cocktails and eventually lead to a rented room in a seedy hotel.

They both know the risks they are taking, but not in their worst nightmares could they foresee what is to follow. Suddenly their temptation turns horrifically sour, and their illicit liaison becomes caught up in something bigger, more dangerous, more brutally violent. Unable to talk to his partner or the police, Charles finds himself trapped in a world of dark conspiracy and psychological games. Somehow he's got to find a way to fight back, or his entire life will be spectacularly derailed for good . . .

'With its clean prose, high-velocity plotting and sharply drawn characters, this novel is the bomb' – *Publishers Weekly*

Crime Fiction

978-0-7515-3463-4

I SEE YOU

Gregg Hurwitz

'Crime fans looking for something different
will love this one' *Booklist*

When bestselling thriller writer Andrew Danner wakes up in a
hospital bed with no idea how he got there, he is horrified to be told
that he is responsible for the murder of his ex-fiancée.

In the resulting celebrity trial, Drew is exonerated on the grounds of
temporary insanity caused by a recent brain tumour. But he still has
no idea if he did kill Genevieve, and is desperate to find out.
Haunted by what appear to be his bizarre night-time actions – did
he really cut his own foot with a knife? – Drew is shocked when
another woman is discovered dead, murdered in the same way as
Genevieve.

Trying to clear his name and understand what's happening to him,
Drew enlists the help of a tame forensic scientist, a sympathetic
detective, his staunch friend Chic who has helpful underworld
connections, and an over-confident teenager. Can Drew discover
what really happened that night and unmask the real killer?

'Pure nail-biting, stay-up-all-night suspense.
Gregg Hurwitz rocks' – Harlan Coben

Crime Fiction

978-0-7515-3977-6

FEAR

Jeff Abbott

'I killed my best friend. I didn't mean to, but I did.
This is my story.'

Miles Kendrick is in a witness protection program, hiding from the mob and constantly haunted by his best friend's death. With the aid of psychiatrist Allison Vance, Miles is trying to hold onto his sanity and to recall the events of that tragic night. But when Allison is blown to pieces by a bomb planted in her office, Miles becomes caught up in a deadly conspiracy way beyond his worst nightmares. Pursued by an ex-FBI detective turned hitman and helped by a mentally broken ex-soldier and a reclusive woman whose life has been destroyed by violence, Miles is in a battle to get his life back – or just stay alive.

A gripping, breakneck-paced thriller, *Fear* will not let you go until the last bullet flies.

'From *Panic* to *Fear*, Abbott has more than raised his game'
Mirror

Crime Fiction

978-0-7515-3832-8

Other bestselling titles available by mail:

☐ Detour	James Siegel	£6.99
☐ Derailed	James Siegel	£6.99
☐ I See You	Gregg Hurwitz	£6.99
☐ Fear	Jeff Abbott	£6.99

The prices shown above are correct at time of going to press. However, the publishers reserve the right to increase prices on covers from those previously advertised without prior notice.

———————————— sphere ————————————

SPHERE
PO Box 121, Kettering, Northants NN14 4ZQ
Tel: 01832 737525, Fax: 01832 733076
Email: aspenhouse@FSBDial.co.uk

POST AND PACKING:
Payments can be made as follows: cheque, postal order (payable to Sphere), credit card or Maestro Card. Do not send cash or currency.

All UK Orders	**FREE OF CHARGE**
EC & Overseas	25% of order value

Name (BLOCK LETTERS) . . . .

Address . . . .

. . . .

Post/zip code: . . . .

☐ Please keep me in touch with future Sphere publications

☐ I enclose my remittance £ . . . .

☐ I wish to pay by Visa/Delta/Maestro

Card Expiry Date ☐☐☐☐   Maestro Issue No. ☐☐